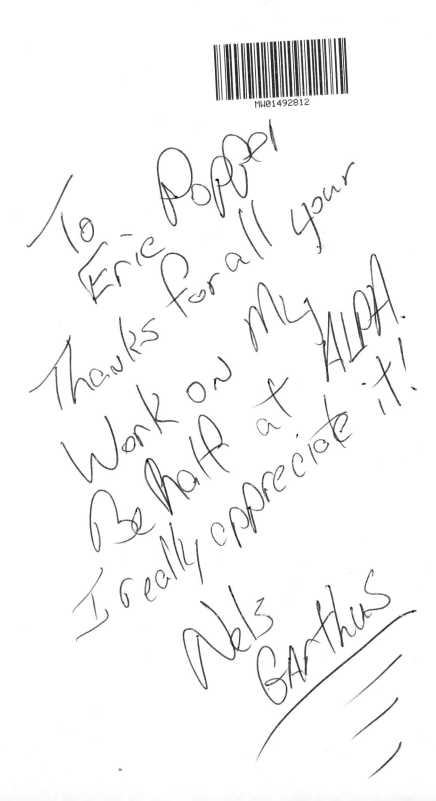

To Eric Popper
Thanks for all your
Work on my
Behalf at ALPA.
I really appreciate it!

Nels
Barthus

Absence Makes the Heart Ponder

Nels Garthus

Orange Hat Publishing
www.orangehatpublishing.com - Waukesha, WI

Published by Orange Hat Publishing 2013

ISBN 978-1-937165-51-2

Printed in the United States of America

www.orangehatpublishing.com

This book is dedicated to my wife and two miracle children. You all amaze me in some new way every day, and I consider myself blessed by your love.

For C.G., A.G., and T.G., who showed me the way. I love you.

Special thanks to Colette, Julie, and Julie, My sounding boards and insightful early readers/editors.

And to H. Moe, a distant hero and early mentor in my life, Thanks for your unfailing inspiration throughout the years.

Foreword

Henry David Thoreau, in his 1854 book *Walden*, wrote: "The mass of men lead lives of quiet desperation." As a man approaching middle age, I can assure you he was correct—with "quiet" being the key word worth noting. This book, in simplest terms, is a fictional autobiography of three men as they approach middle age. Beginning briefly in 2011, it rapidly retreats to 2001 just after the tragedy of 9/11 and then proceeds chronologically toward present day.

From early childhood, boys (at least in my experience) are taught either through nurture or nature to tough it out, suck it up, and soldier on. Later in life these coping techniques manifest themselves with men in the typical fashion: Parents and spouses often find their sons or significant others emotionally distant and unwilling to communicate. Many men I work with or know through my kids' school have a hard time sharing their thoughts and concerns with anyone, let alone those closest to them. Women, by contrast (at least in my wife's many circles), seem to make friendships much more readily and communicate their concerns more easily. So when a guy (and I speak from experience) can finally connect and communicate with another guy and form a lasting friendship, it is a rare and wonderful thing indeed. That's what this book is about.

Absence Makes the Heart Ponder is a story about three men: Jon Foster, Sebastian Everest Koh, and Peter Steglin, as they juggle their personal, professional, and private lives in an effort to create a legacy for themselves and prosperity for their families.

They meet in their early thirties just as their high

school and frat brother friends are leaving Milwaukee, Wisconsin, for other locales. Jon, Sebby, and Peter, like so many other men, look to their significant others to fulfill all their needs, when in truth, the easy banter, self-deprecating humor, and nuanced ridicule of their male friends is something the women in their lives cannot possibly emulate. It's a guy thing, just as it is female thing. But where the story of female friendships and relationships is so often written about, male camaraderie is not.

Absence Makes the Heart Ponder comically follows the three thirty-something men as they approach middle age and shines a little light on their quiet desperation. Through the bonds they form with each other and strengthen within their families, they slowly come to accept their true individual nature and fate. In the end, and with the help of an old sailboat, they face middle age together head on.

For the male reader, I hope this book is not only a fun adventure and humorous look at what only we as men share, but also an invitation to at least consider opening up more to those around them. I think they might be surprised to find they are not alone.

For the female reader, I hope this book provides some insight into the thoughts and concerns the men in their lives are probably having as they approach middle age, as well as a secret courtside seat to listen in on our hopes, fears, and concerns. There is more going on in our heads than many might realize.

Overall I hope everyone enjoys reading this lighthearted bit of fictional adventure, disaster, and romance as much as I did writing it.

If you came of age during the eighties and enjoyed movies like *She's Having a Baby*, *The Big Chill*, and *Singles*, or if you like the movie *Castaway*, the HBO series *Sex and the City* or *Entourage*, you may notice the influence they have on my work. Those stories as well as many in my own experience are the auspice for the book.

Chapter Index

Introduction

Men in the Middle Ages
Told By Jon

"Dad!" the little girl shouted excitedly. "Dad . . . watch me!" she repeated two more times, her voice growing more agitated and impatient with each passing moment.

But he just sat there on the playground bench next to me—ambivalent or oblivious, I hadn't decided yet. All I knew was that those seconds probably seemed like an eternity to her. I guessed she was five years old or so, about the same age as my son, Ben, who I watched as he ran feverishly around the playground equipment trying to decide what to do next while we waited for his sister, Bergen, to get out of school.

"Dad, Dad, can you push me?" she asked, but it was now all too obvious she wasn't going to get the response or attention she so desperately desired. By the looks of things, I figured she would be lucky to get any attention at all, and I noticed I wasn't alone in this recognition. The little girl had already started to resign herself to being ignored.

Even then he just sat there next to me on the bench, staring at his iPhone—not typing or texting or surfing—just staring incessantly at a family picture fading in and out as he refreshed the screen over and over again, immersed in a digital morass, deaf to his own daughter's pleas for attention and the world around him.

Who is this guy? I thought to myself as I waited for him to acknowledge his daughter.

Yeah, I'm guilty of that—Judging others is an on-again-off-again hobby I indulge in, depending on how confident or messed up I'm feeling in my own life. The more confident I feel, the more I judge others, the less, well . . . the more likely I am to try and walk a mile in their shoes before I claim to understand the situation, which I never really honestly do.

Interestingly enough, my wife, Elise, has told me numerous times that with her it's quite the opposite. The more confident she feels, the less she tends to judge others, while by contrast the more impatient or downtrodden she becomes in her own life, the more she tends to critique everyone else around her.

Anyway, he just kept sitting there, disregarding his own daughter's need for attention, and it was beginning to bother me. *Is he deaf?* I wondered. Or was he just one of those parents who perpetually ignores his kids, like lost baggage at an airport: "Aahhh, excuse me . . . Does this bag (I mean, child) belong to anyone?"

He wasn't talking to or texting anyone on his PDA. He wasn't on some eBay auction that was about to close or watching "the game." ("Nope, can't be bothered. The game is on." I have heard that one before. As if somehow the act of watching the game will affect the outcome, or they won't replay any important highlights a million more times. But I digress.)

He must *be deaf,* I thought again.

"It's not polite to make fun of one's afflictions," my father always said. I could hear his voice ringing in my ears.

I wondered if he was just weird or depressed or overmedicated or something. *I need to stop judging people,* I berated myself. I tried to concentrate on Ben while we waited for Bergen to get out of school so we could take her to dance class. I was also watching for my friend Sebby to arrive so he could show Ben and me his new sailboat. It was a beautiful day for early May, a rarity in Port Washington, Wisconsin, as Lake Michigan usually plays havoc with the weather until June.

Port Washington is a quaint harbor town of ten thousand or so people that resides twenty-five miles north of Milwaukee, Wisconsin. It is not a suburb of the big city (at least not for the near future anyway) and maintains the persona of a sleepy, blue collar, seaside village. It has a great history ranging from commercial fishing to furniture manufacturing, as well as many other small industries now decimated by globalization and the recent economic downturn. But even so, every summer, "Port," as the locals call it, comes to life with an influx of boats, tourists, and those who live inland and just want to escape the heat, as it's always cooler by the lake.

A large Catholic church built out of quarried stone sits majestically on top of a hill very near the harbor facing southeast. Next to it, an old lighthouse, now completely refurbished and almost operational, peers out, scanning the horizon for ore ships and lake freighters, the local charter fishing fleet, and the myriad colorful sailboats that frequent the area for its ever-present wind.

The main street into town cascades ever downward in elevation as it meanders eastward between eclectic storefronts and coffee shops from the interstate some miles away. It then turns ninety degrees to the north and climbs up the same hill next to the church, passing small pubs, restaurants, and unique shops before splitting the residential neighborhood to the north of town and rejoining the highway that continues toward Green Bay.

A gray breakwater of cement and stone reaches out into the lake, ending at a smaller lighthouse that serves as the gateway to the lake. Waves routinely pummel it, sending spray and water high into the air in a furious display of mettle and might. Lake Michigan, after all, isn't just a lake. It is a Great Lake, an inland sea, far more vast and powerful than most give it credit for. People from either coast are always amazed to find locals surfing near the harbor. The waves are that big. It affects everything from the weather to the very lifeblood of Port Washington. Even the local McDonald's in town was built to look like a lighthouse. You have to carry a jacket with you at all times. Even in July or August, if the winds shift from west to east, the temperature can drop ten to twenty degrees in an hour. You either love it or you hate it. I still missed Maine, where my wife, Elise, and I used to live, but this at least felt like a close second. I guess I was only then, after five and a half years, beginning to appreciate my adopted hometown, but I would grow to love Port. It was the spring of 2011, and at least for the moment I felt like life was pretty good.

The school's ten-minute warning bell rang and jolted Deaf Dad from his iPhone. *So, obviously he isn't deaf,* I thought as I watched him come to.

"Jon, man what's up?" a voice called from across the playground, interrupting my thoughts. "What a great day, huh?" It was Sebastian; he strode toward me from his Land Rover Defender 110. "Hey, Benjie, dude! Do you want to go see my new sailboat? Where's Bergen? Still in class?"

Sebby always made an entrance, no matter what. If it wasn't his car or suit or truck or latest girlfriend, it was his sheer presence— six foot three inches; 180 pounds or so; big hands, bigger feet; built like a pro-beach volleyball player or an Olympic swimmer; wavy, dark hair; olive skin; and mischievous hazel eyes. He was a mix of Mediterranean Johnny Depp suave cool; Tom Seleck, Magnum PI, full on man's man; and Adrian Grenier's boyish charisma. More successful, handsome (yes, even I, a fully heterosexual male, can attest to it), and magnetic than anyone had a right to be. I have always been a tad envious, I'll admit.

As Sebby approached Ben on the curvy slide, I noticed that it probably wasn't the ten- minute warning bell that awoke Deaf Dad from his cell phone stupor but instead his seeming familiarity with Sebastian, because he abruptly got up and walked toward him, and they greeted each other with a hug. After some more pleasantries, Sebby motioned me to come over for introductions.

"Jon, this is my old friend Peter Steglin. Pete, this is my old friend Jon Foster—and I do mean OLD! Both of you, jeez, you look like hell! What's up? Do you two know each other?" Sebby asked. "What a great coincidence. I haven't seen you in forever, man," he said to Peter. "How's it going, Pete? How are Owen and Campbell?" He paused, checking the playground over. "Oh there she is . . . What a cutie! She's getting soooo big!"

Now that I had a closer look at Peter, I could see that he looked like he had been punched in the stomach. I didn't even know him, but Sebby was right—he did look like hell. Did I look that bad? Man, I needed to join the YMCA or get a life or something.

Peter summoned his voice and said simply, "It's final."

"What's final?" Sebby prodded.

Peter gave him a glance as if to say, *Duh, man . . . Don't you remember? Don't you care?*

I was standing right there, and this seemed like a private conversation, so I tried to seem distracted by Ben, just to be polite.

"Our divorce," Peter said quietly, although strangely he sounded somehow relieved. Then slowly he began to unload on Sebastian, and I quickly understood his fixation on the family photo on his phone. He wasn't a deaf dad, just a newly divorced, devastated dad. "She got the house and my truck, and I got the kids on the weekends and Wednesdays."

"The truck . . . what the fu—" Seb stopped himself, quickly realizing he was on a playground and not at the local bar. "Why did she get the truck? Why not the car? What does she need the truck for? You need your work truck!" Sebby's questions came in rapid succession, and I could tell that he truly cared for Peter's plight. "That really sucks, man!" he said. "Would you like to bring the kids down to the marina? We're headed there now to check out my new boat. I just got it back in the water. . . You're welcome to tag along."

"Nah . . . Sebby, thanks, some other time," Peter said.

"Okay, well, let's do lunch next week. When are you free?"

"Wednesday or Sunday nights, otherwise I'm at Home Depot or with my kids. It's pretty slow going out there construction-wise."

"I'll call you. We'll go sailing or something."

"Okay," Peter replied meekly.

"Count on it!" Sebby responded enthusiastically, trying to lift Peter's spirits. "Count on it," he said again, softly this time.

Just then the final school bell rang and a deluge of children engulfed the playground. We found Bergen, took her to dance class, then headed over to the Port Washington marina to gush over Sebastian's new Jeanneau Sun Odyssey 43 DS named *Noemocean*.

As we walked toward Sebby's boat near the end of one of the floating docks, I quickly came to one simple conclusion: This wasn't a boat. This was a yacht!

"Come on," Sebby insisted. "Climb aboard!" He took Ben's little hand to help him make the jump from the dock to the rail. I just stared at it as I strode slowly back and forth admiring its lines like some fashion reporter in Paris for Spring Fashion Week. Sebby's new sailboat was long, beamy, and sleek. Its dark-blue hull was only interrupted by two small lines—one crimson red, the other teal green—stretching her entire length. I fell immediately in love.

I've always wondered why most, if not all, boats are named after women and somehow take on a female persona. Have you ever seen a boat named *Bob* or *Bruce*? Nope, neither have I, but I've noticed plenty named *Jenny* or *Sweet Susan* or whatever. I'm guilty of it too. That day on the dock admiring Sebastian's new yacht, I wasn't three minutes into my perusal before I was already referring to it as "her" or "she." What is up with that? I suppose some guys refer to cars or their trucks that way. I know a lot of airplanes were named after women, especially during World War II. I can't explain it. It just feels right.

Sebastian interrupted my perusal and asked, "What are you doing this July? Do you want to do the Mac race with me?"

"Are you serious?" I asked excitedly. "You're kidding, right?"

Sebby smiled. "You in?" he finally asked after a long pause.

"Definitely!" I declared emphatically.

I felt truly honored and instantly excited to be asked. Even though I had sailed with Sebastian many times before around Milwaukee and Port Washington, this was the Chicago-Mackinac race, the granddaddy of them all for inland sailors, not just some excuse to go day sailing or another beer can regatta around some buoys. I could hardly wait. Then again, maybe it was his new sailboat floating there in front of me. She was, after all, one hot yacht.

Chapter 1

The Numbers Are All That Matter
Told By Sebastian

Jon and I met the summer of 2002 in, of all places, a urologist's waiting room. I was thirty-one, and I suspected Jon to be about the same. Nervous, fidgety, and obviously uncomfortable in his own skin, he had a sort of Tom-Brokaw-Brian-Williams-nightly-news-anchorman vibe going on. His brown hair was parted so straight, he must have used a ruler—I mean all the way down to the scalp. I could see the white line from across the room. He sat extremely upright in a chair across from me reading an old *Forbes* magazine. His bushy eyebrows furled in some form of open disgust or contempt for what he was reading; his dark eyes were transfixed on the page. He had a five o'clock shadow already forming on his neck and face, although it was barely ten a.m., the stubble hiding two rosy cheeks that were forced to share space with a rather prominent nose. I guessed he was probably five-eleven or so, maybe 170 to 180 pounds. He was dressed all preppy, like he had just stepped out of a Lands End catalog, with nothing out of place. His oxford was buttoned almost all the way up, his tan chinos were neatly pressed, and his penny loafers were all shiny; he was even wearing socks.

Who wears socks in the summer? My old, faded-blue Sperry Top-Siders were the best. Even if one was missing its tongue and neither had laces, I lived in them all summer when I wasn't working. *I bet he's a former Boy Scout,* I thought to myself as I glanced at him occasionally while I read some stupid article entitled "Six Foods for

Increased Female Libido and Nine Foods Men Should Eat" in an ancient *Men's Health* magazine. I slouched low in the leather waiting room chair, my nylon shorts sliding easily toward the front of the seat until my upper torso was nearly horizontal, then I boosted myself up again.

Even though I didn't yet know him, I could tell Mr. Chinos and Socks across from me needed a distraction; he just looked nervous, and we were the only two men in the waiting room, so I introduced myself with a sort of joke.

"Dr. Slocum . . ?" I asked out loud, looking in his direction to see if he was also seeing my physician. "Ironic name for a urologist, don't you think? Slocum," I repeated. "You can't make this stuff up."

Startled, as if he wasn't sure I was really talking to him, he nodded and then slowly smiled as my revelation only then began to dawn on him.

"Don't you think he needs some new girly magazines in the blue room?" I said openly and abruptly. "Those women are probably my age by now."

I could tell immediately that he knew what I was talking about but was too reserved to comment. "My name is Sebastian, Sebastian Everest Koh," I said in my best "Bond, James Bond" impression. "Most of my friends call me Sebby."

(Silence . . . Except for the elevator music wafting around between us.) *Man, this guy is a stiff,* I thought as I watched him searching for something to say.

Finally he caved and broke the awkward impasse. I was glad too, because I had no more material to offer up. "I'm Jon," he said very sheepishly. "Jon Foster."

He was obviously taken aback by my solicitation. Truth was, I was just bored. I shouldn't have put him on the spot like that. Maybe he was ashamed to be there at all, let alone forced to admit it publicly to a complete stranger. But I had opened my big mouth and now had to continue with the small talk or risk appearing like someone with dementia. I was instantly mad at myself for starting the conversation. Where could it possibly go? The nurse would likely be calling Jon's name any moment. It was probably his time to tee it high and let it fly, and he needed to concentrate or psych himself up or something, but it was too late.

"Hi, Jon," I replied and then thought, *Jeez, this is beginning to sound like an AA meeting or something.*

There was another long, awkward silence, and I hate long, awkward silences, so even though it was against my better judgment, I inquired, "How do you think the Brewers are going to do this year?" I was trying to strike up some form of brief conversation and then go quietly back to reading my magazine. I didn't even follow major league baseball—or any sports for that matter. It just seemed like the "guy" thing to ask.

Jon paused for a second, looked over the top of his magazine, and stared straight at me. Then he said in a supremely dry and sardonic manner, "I don't know. They seem to be sort of a first-half team this year. They never have anything left by the third period, and they don't have anyone who can shoot a three. They might make it to the ALCS, the Sweet 16, or even the AFC West championship, but they'll never make it to the Super Bowl and win the cup unless they use their second quarterback, get some defense in the post, and start skating better. But on the bright side, that Andre guy, I really like him. He can really bend those corner kicks. What do you think?"

I was shocked. Jon was either the biggest asshole ever or a stone-cold comic, both brutal and funny at the same time. He never even blinked. I chose to be an optimist and hoped for the latter. *That took some balls,* I thought as I laughed out loud. I wondered if that was a canned answer or if he just winged it. Either way, it was really impressive. "So you don't follow sports much I gather?" I was still chuckling after his rant.

"No, sorry." Jon shrugged his shoulders.

"That's okay, I really don't either."

"You're the first one to get my sense of humor, though," he added. "My wife doesn't even get my drift half of the time."

"I just wanted to break the ice. This cheesy music is slowly killing me, and I've read every magazine twice."

"Yeah, I know what you mean." Jon held up the magazine in his hands."This *Forbes* is reporting the tech bubble and crash as if it happened yesterday! It's over a year old!"

"I know, this magazine is dated August 22, 1999," I responded as I rolled my eyes.

"So you've been here before, then?" he inquired.

"Yeah, many times. . . . Are you being tested, or are you just here for their layaway program?" I knew it was abrupt and intrusive, but that's me, so be it.

Jon put down his magazine and slowly proceeded to tell me about himself and his wife and their trouble conceiving children. He had recently gone through varicocele surgery with Dr. Slocum and hoped today that his "numbers" had improved. Jon was an airline pilot; his wife, Elise, was a teacher. They lived in an apartment in Mequon, a suburb on the north side of Milwaukee.

I in turn told him about my psychotic ex-girlfriend Courtney from two years earlier, my paternity scare, and my subsequent efforts to freeze "A TON" of my stuff before going under the knife. "I never want to wait on a woman's period ever again," I told Jon openly. "And the thought of being linked to that woman for eternity scared the hell out of me! Let alone a kid!" I added. "No amount of hot sex is worth that!"

I checked Jon's face for tacit approval, but he was on the other side of the fence, hoping for big numbers, while I now just wanted to shoot zero and never have to worry about anything like that ever again.

We bonded over sailing, skiing, and investing. Jon was well traveled, obviously, but also had a fair knowledge of the markets, which really became apparent when I told him I was an analyst at Promise Wealth Management. That sparked his interest, and he began to really open up. I have a way of doing that. I should have been a therapist or bartender or something other than a stockbroker, but the money is just too damn good, and the action is better than Vegas.

"I have an old center cockpit S2 at McKinley Marina, if you're interested sometime," I offered vaguely. I had been hoping to replace one of my coworkers from his position on my pseudo-racing team for my sailboat, which was really slow. It was rather spur of the moment, I guess, in retrospect, but Jon seemed like he might make a good addition to the team.

My crew, if I could exaggerate and call them that, and I met ostensibly for the weekly beer can races near Milwaukee's inner harbor, but also (more importantly) for the mid-week excuse to party afterward. Richard, one of my contemporaries at Promise was kind of a dud and not much into real excitement. Maybe he was into virtual stuff, I don't really know. He was always on his computer, and mostly preferred to watch than to actually get in the thick of it, so I didn't think he would mind losing his spot on the boat.

Milwaukee in the summer is all hops, barley, Harleys, and babes. I loved summer, and Jon needed a distraction, I just knew it. I could see it in his eyes. I figured he must know something about headings and true versus apparent wind, being a pilot and all, which was more than I could say for Richard and some of the others on my beloved sailboat, *Slomocean.*

Jon was interested and flattered by the offer, yet he was hesitant, as if I was hitting him up for a date or something. I could tell he was into sailing and eager to pick my brain about stocks and funds and what not, but I knew he was figuring out at that very moment just how to ask his wife for permission to go sailing and the subsequent mandatory lager fest. It was obvious he was on a pretty tight leash (by the way he rubbed his neck, I knew his collar was bothering him). Jon just needed a longer lead. Surely his bride could grant him a little freedom. He just had to phrase the question properly.

I sensed his skepticism as to why I, a complete stranger, was offering this opportunity to him. How would he "put out" on this man date? What did he have to offer in this bromance? I could see all this in Jon's face and hands. In short, I could read him like an open book. I should have been a professional poker player. I was calm. I was cool. I was collected. Now securely a thirty-something man and a star stock trader and analyst (I called the tech stock bubble of '99 to '00 at Promise Wealth Management before anyone else saw it coming and saved everyone's asses as well as a few hundred million dollars in assets) with money in my pocket, my first real place in the Third Ward (the coolest and hippest part of Milwaukee, in my opinion), and my beloved sailboat, I was a player.

The next Wednesday, Jon met me at the marina. I introduced him to my coworkers and my new girlfriend, Christy. (*Kimberly, Kate, Krista—I always seemed to do well with Cs and Ks. Damn, I missed the C-K years from '98 to '02.*) How did I get so old so fast? It was the sixth or seventh beer can buoy race of the summer. A nice southwesterly breeze swept in over Milwaukee's downtown skyline, pushing every wannabe America's Cup captain and crew slowly around the markers that formed the course for the evening. We all took turns at the helm learning the boat, as well as each other's strengths and weaknesses, grinding on winches, and pulling in on the sheets. It was a ragtag operation, but it slowly began to at least resemble sailing and look less like bedlam. Jon fit right in and was a welcome addition to my crew.

The western horizon migrated the spectrum from yellow to orange to pink and finally violet as we rounded the final buoy and headed back to my slip. Those long summer evenings and, in particular, dusk on the water are perhaps some of my favorite memories of my late twenties and early thirties living in downtown Milwaukee.

By the time we tied off *Slomocean*, the lake and sky were one color, and it was Miller time, but Jon wasn't aware of our traditions yet and offered up a case of some new microbrew he liked called Spotted Cow. At first I considered this sacrilege, but then I found out that it was actually brewed right here in Wisconsin. And to top it off, it was really exceptional.

From there on out, I somehow knew I could trust Jon. He was a straight shooter and a good guy with great taste. I still thought he needed to loosen up a bit, but then I think that about most guys, especially the ones who are married. Everybody needs a project from time to time. Maybe God had made me strike up a conversation with him for reasons unbeknownst to me. I was sure Jon could teach me a lot of stuff I didn't know. Perhaps in some weird way I could return the favor.

It's odd, the things my mind chooses to file away and recall so vividly when there are so many other important things I seem to forget, but I will always remember that evening, if for no other reason than because I made a new friend. I guess as you get older, that's a rare thing!

Chapter 2

Ghosts of Boyfriends Past
Told by Peter

In 2001, shortly after the tragedy of 9/11, I, being brash and stupid, as well as arrogant and annoyed, told my boss to "fuck off!" I left his cookie-cutter construction firm building boring vinyl boxes in the southern and southeastern suburbs of Milwaukee to boldly start my own business and create a brand for myself. I wanted to try and make some real money building real homes on the north side, around Mequon, Grafton, and Cedarburg. I needed to call the shots and take some risks to get my own business venture up and running now while Heather, my wife, was still interested and secure in her job as an HR rep at a local company. I knew she wanted to have kids and stay home with them once we started that chapter in our lives, but I had to break free from being just another good hammer, show some initiative and some vision before the mortgage and bills became my sole responsibility, or it would never happen. I desperately didn't want to get stuck in a job, especially one I was growing to despise. I wanted a career. I wanted more for myself and for Heather, so having a legacy of kids would have to wait.

I spent the fall of 2001 and winter of 2002 building a website, printing business cards, and attending any home show or open house I could, trying to drum up new business, but it was very slow going. A few bathroom and basement remodels led to a kitchen project and, miraculously through some twist of fate (somebody knowing somebody who knew of someone), a meeting with a guy named Sebastian Koh in late March 2003.

"Peter Steglin . . . you come highly recommended from my new boss," he began on the phone before I could even say hello. "I would like to meet with you about some property I just bought east of Hwy 43—walk it with you and give you my ideas for a house. How does Tuesday at four sound?"

As quickly as I said, "Great," he hung up the phone.

This was a big chance. This was what I had been dreaming about and planning for. This was my big break. I could hardly believe it, and I couldn't wait for next Tuesday to arrive.

Mr. Koh and I met on his property just north of Mequon Road east of Hwy 43 at four p.m. sharp. We walked the property boundaries discussing everything from exposures to his love of Frank Lloyd Wright's architectural style, from his Polynesian ancestry to his preference for Shaker- like minimalism.

Truth be told, Sebastian did most of the talking; I just listened and took some notes on a big yellow legal pad. I figured that would make me seem more professional, like I had done this before.

Could I start immediately?

"Yes, sir!" I said.

Could he be in by Christmas?

"Yes, sir!" I repeated assuredly.

Could I please stop calling him sir? After all, we were nearly the same age. "Call me Sebby!" he insisted.

"Absolutely!"

I said yes to everything, whether I knew the answer or if I could actually do it. I was just so happy to have the opportunity to build a house, call the shots, and create something that would be original, daring, and green. I couldn't believe it: Steglin Homes, LLC was off and running. Now all I had to do was fulfill Sebastian's long list of wants, dreams, and desires for his new home and turn every detail he presented me into reality in nine months. No problem!

We met twice weekly for the first month while I worked feverishly on permitting, a construction schedule, and hiring various contractors for excavation and cement work as well as a few good hammers for my crew. It was obvious that Sebastian had done a lot of homework ahead of time and knew exactly what he wanted, which was an ICF home (a highly energy-efficient method of construction using insulated concrete forms) with all the green technology he could get his hands on. Even though I was unfamiliar with much of it, I buried myself in books, brochures, websites, and DIY chat rooms to become the expert he needed me to be. It was baptism by fire, but I loved every minute of it.

I didn't see Heather much the first month or so of the project, but I think she could tell how happy I was to be out on my own calling the shots and busy to boot. What little time we had together was on Sundays, since I was working twelve-hour days the other six days of the week, attempting vehemently to make good on the promises I had made to Sebastian. After all, a man is only as good as his word.

I told Heather about the project, the schedule, and the design. She easily followed along, asking questions only a general contractor's wife would know to ask, while reminding me to call this person or that person about things she had overheard me discussing on my cell phone. (Lately I was always on my cell phone.)

Once I filled her in, we were back to our normal routine, until one day she overheard me mention Sebastian's name. "Did you just say Sebastian Koh?" she interrupted as I tried to complete an order for some special acoustic tile he wanted for the basement.

"Oh my God, I know him!" she shrieked like a school girl. "I mean, I don't know him, know him, but he dated some girls I knew at the University of Wisconsin! What does he look like? Is he married? Are you redoing his bathrooms? Why didn't you tell me? OH . . . MY . . . GOD! Is HE the one you're building the house for?"

I just nodded, because I couldn't get a word in edgewise.

"So he lives around here?" Heather asked excitedly. She rattled off questions faster than the smart lady on *The Weakest Link*. Apparently I had some explaining to do, but why was she acting like a fifteen-year-old girl after a Backstreet Boys concert comparing notes with the lucky girl who got to go back stage?

I got her up to speed once again with all the ins and outs of Sebby's home construction project, but it all too soon became apparent to me that Heather wasn't really interested in the details of Sebby's house. She just wanted to know more about Sebby. And she didn't like me calling him "Sebby" for some weird reason. She greatly preferred Sebastian; it was really strange. In fact, she couldn't stop saying "Sebastian." It just sort of rolled off her tongue, and before I knew it, we had seemingly traveled back through time to high school again.

I had seen this look before, this act, this attitude, back in 1989 when Heather was our school's social butterfly flitting about and spreading rumors, but where I was "just a friend" to every girl who at least knew my name. Oh, don't worry, I remember it well. Heather and her posse trying on boys like clothes at the mall, comparing notes, gossiping, partying, and then occasionally getting their hearts broken and being single just long enough, their social calendars just free enough, to become bored and accept an invite from a guy like me (average Joe, five eight, 190 pounds, a chubby Jon Stewart maybe, but with acne and a horrible unibrow) out on what I thought was a date. In reality however it wasn't. I always ended up being the shoulder to cry on. The guy who wouldn't try anything. I was safe, secure, and BORING. "Peter, you're such a nice guy," or "You're such a good friend." The date invariably ended early, with me (forty dollars poorer) dropping her off at another girlfriend's house so that they could figure out which jock, bad boy, or rich kid to sex up—I mean, set up—next:

"If you date Brad, you could be the next homecoming king and queen!"

"Yeah, but Kyle has a car, and his parents are loaded!"

I could only imagine their conversations and how they must have talked back then. It wasn't the trip back down memory lane I needed right now. "I gotta go pick up some two-by-four studs and a new nailer at Home Depot," I told Heather, hoping to change the subject.

By the dreamy look on her face, I could see that she was thinking of picking up another stud and doing some nailing of her own, and she was my wife! What a blast from the past. It was like a sucker punch to my still fragile ego. *Note to self,* I vowed, *keep Heather away from the job site when Sebby—I mean, Sebastion XOXO—Koh is around.* Was that U2's "Rattle & Hum" blasting on my truck's radio? I needed to get back to the present and bring my wife with me. The last thing I wanted was to get stuck in the eighties all over again.

I guess you have to know my wife. How can I sum her up? Do you know the actress Mila Kunis, who played the part of Jackie Burkhart on *That '70s Show*? You know, daddy's little rich girl, popular, confident, a little bit of a bitch. That, in a nutshell, describes Heather, only older and curvier. Imagine Mila Kunis's character at thirty. Heather even looked like her back then—petite, dark hair, olive skin, brown eyes, beautiful. No wonder she didn't give me much more than a high-five and a hug in high school. She could (and did) get any guy she wanted in the late eighties.

Raised by her dad after her parents' divorce (or D-Day as she called it), he gave her everything materially to make her happy (still does) and to win her over in their maternal-paternal tug of war. He was a big wig at a multinational Fortune 500 company and steadily climbed his way up the ranks to vice-president before retiring. A UW alum of the highest order, his veins coursed with Badger blood, and he always wore a red tie. There was nowhere else he wanted her to attend. So after high school, it was off to Madison and the Badger cheer and dance teams as she flirted with the lofty goals of becoming a doctor, lawyer, or physical therapist.

Truth be told, my wife was never really great at academics, but she did excel at kissing ass, which didn't get her as far with fifty thousand other students and faculty on campus as it did in small town Wisconsin. She no longer stood out. At UW Madison, Heather was a small fish in a big pond, and the realization that she wasn't as special or talented or smart as she thought she was back in high school slowly sunk in.

One day it all got to be too much for her, so she tucked her tail between her legs and moved back home to Daddy, dropping out after three years of college and the equivalent of two years of general credits. Her sorority girl partying, dancing, and cheering days were over, and the only thing she had to show for it was a bunch of cardinal-red sweats and the freshman fifteen. Back in Mequon, her dad got her a job as a receptionist, and she worked her way up from there into the HR department.

Don't get me wrong, I love Heather. I am not picking on her for dropping out. Hell, I didn't even go to college. I'm not coming down on her for being rich or popular or anything. She is beautiful, voluptuous, funny, and witty. I did better by her than I ever hoped or dreamed, and I believe we were meant to be, but I would have to back up a bit to explain.

You see, I am the younger of two brothers, and I'll try to get to the point, but this is hard for me to talk about. Ryan was the first born on either side of the family. He was the golden child. By the time I was fourteen and he was sixteen that was already apparent to me. He was taller, faster, smarter, and more attractive than me, and he let me know it all the time, as did the girls who were already lining up to date him. I could handle that. After all, I looked up to him and idolized him to some extent. What burned me up were the things my parents didn't think I noticed or knew about, like the college fund they established for him but not me or the way they attended everything he did and bragged openly about him to friends and family but not about me when it was my turn to shine, which maybe in hindsight I never did. But I should have in their eyes . . . at least until that day anyway, at least until I quit trying, at least until he died.

Ryan died November 25, 1986 in a freak accident while bow hunting for deer. It's still a bit of a mystery, I guess, as to what happened. He must have slipped while climbing in or out of his tree stand or failed to tie himself in and fallen out. Either way, the tip of one of his arrows impaled him in the neck. My father found him that night, and after that, everything changed.

My mom blamed my dad for teaching him to hunt and for not being out with him that morning, but it wasn't my dad's fault. Ryan had just gotten his driver's license and was more than eager to take advantage his newfound freedom.

From there we all just drifted as a family—as far apart as we could without separating. We should have come together and supported one another, but for some unknown reason, we just didn't. My mom tormented my dad with guilt, so he took to driving truck more than ever and was gone all the time, and she just disappeared right there in front of me, becoming a pale, frail shell of her former self. She was never the same. As for me, well I just sort of gave up. I was saddled, and I couldn't carry his weight. I heard, "Your brother was this!" or "Your brother would have done that by now!" My mom rarely said Ryan's name after he died. I suppose it just hurt too much, But she spoke of him and his accomplishments all the time, even those in the future. For me it seemed like his legend only grew, and I couldn't compete.

At school it was much the same. I was "Ryan's little brother" to almost everyone. The teachers talked about him, the coaches praised him, and the girls missed him. It was like I was living with a ghost—with one exception: Heather. She was my angel even then. Heather never once referred to me as Ryan's little brother or mentioned him after the funeral. With her, I was always Peter, and even though I knew she wasn't interested in me as a boyfriend, I was already in love with her for that.

When high school finally ended, I felt like a weight had been lifted from my shoulders. I no longer had to be anyone's little brother. I could pick and choose anything I wanted to be. I no longer had to hide out in the shadows of my home to avoid showing my parents an odd comparison of what might have been with Ryan. I could just leave, and I did.

Ryan would have gone to college. That was a sure thing. I had to go down a different path or risk being saddled again, so I chose construction. Besides, it was the quickest way to a paycheck and my own place, even if I had to share it with three other guys like me. Fortunately I was good with my hands and eager enough that my boss noticed and sort of took me under his wing, giving me special projects and extra training along the way.

From the time I graduated until the summer after I turned twenty-one, I never saw Heather. I guessed she was off doing the college thing, but I thought about her often and compared the few girls I dated back then to her incessantly. It wasn't until Summerfest of that year that we bumped into each other by accident. She almost didn't recognize me. I guess three years of hard labor, lax cooking skills, and a tight budget had changed me from chubby, pudgy Peter into someone leaner and meaner—probably twenty pounds lighter and twenty times stronger than I was back then. Plus I was wearing my work boots that day, which easily made me an inch or two taller! But to tell you the truth, I hadn't really noticed these changes myself until that moment.

"Peter? . . . Peter, is that you?" Heather stopped dead in her tracks and almost dropped the beer she was carrying.

"Heather, wow . . . long time." I didn't know what to say, but it came off as casual. Frankly I was surprised I got that much out. She looked great.

We talked for a while until she had to run to get into one of the concerts with her friends, but then I noticed something I will never forget. When she turned to leave, she looked back, not once, but twice, and even commented something to one of her girlfriends as she smiled. Her eyes gave it away. I had never seen that look before from a woman. I normally never pick up on stuff like that, but that day for some reason, I did. And you know what? It gave me hope—no, more than that. That look of approval from over Heather's shoulder gave me confidence—maybe even a little swagger—I never had before that day, and I used it to my advantage. So, long story short, we soon started dating and the rest is history. Sometimes I guess you do get a second chance to make a first impression.

The neat part was that the new me kind of stuck around for a while. Heather was a huge boost to my ego. I mean, people not in the know were shocked when we showed up at our ten-year high school reunion together. At the age of twenty-eight, I had finally made it "in" (via marriage) with the popular kids.

I guess she loved me for my integrity, security, stability, and undying devotion to her, I don't really know. I never asked her out of fear she really didn't love me but married me anyway. I am more than a little insecure when it comes to women. Lately however those nagging fears seemed all too palpable. Heather seemed distant. I didn't need Sebby dredging up her past life. I wanted her to be happy in the present with me. It was tough enough constantly trying to win over her dad without a college diploma from UW (or anywhere else for that matter). I knew he had her ear. I knew all too well that he thought his little girl deserved better than average Joe, blue collar me. But I could only hope that would change as my business took off and I became successful. Maybe then he would consider me worthy of his daughter. More importantly, maybe then Heather would be truly proud to be married to me and not pass me off when she was around certain other people as her cross to bear for not making it big herself.

Chapter 3

Build It and She Will Come
Told by Peter

It only began to really bother me when I overheard Heather talking to some old college girlfriend one night on the phone when I came home late from the job site and she didn't know I was in our house.

"No I haven't seen him yet," she spoke into the receiver. He must be thirty-two or thirty-three now. . . . No, Peter said he wasn't married. I wonder what he's like now?" Heather purred excitedly. "Oh, I remember everything, Cindy, believe me. . . . Yeah you told me. . . . Oh yeah, S.E.K. was S.E. X. Y.!" Heather laughed devilishly into the phone. "SEKsy, I know. He soooooo was! . . . Yes I know how good he was. . . .You told me, that's how! You wouldn't shut up about it. . . . It, you know . . . IT! Don't you remember? Oh, I know you do, Cindy, you must! Unless you were lying to me back then!" Heather stopped and caught her breath."You said he was the best! . . . You said he was hung like a—" Her voice reached a fever pitch just as I entered the room.

"Hi, honey, I'm home!" I snorted out loudly. Heather's mouth dropped to the floor as I finally made my presence known. She was as white as a ghost, and for a woman with dark-olive skin, that says a lot. She obviously knew full well at that moment that I understood who she was talking about.

Needless to say there was an uneasy silence that night and for the next few days in our home. Heather's new personality just brought up too many past feelings of inadequacy in my own life that I thought had disappeared when I started dating and finally married her. I wanted to blame Heather. I wanted to blame Sebastian. But I loved my wife and thought Sebby seemed like a pretty great guy. Besides, he was my one and only client. I had to get past this, keep my cool, and keep him happy, but I also needed closure. So I decided to take a chance.

The week before, when I had met Sebby at the house site, he introduced me to his girlfriend, Heidi, all of twenty-five or twenty-six, I guessed. She hadn't ridden in with him but rather met us there at the end of some super long run. Short, blonde hair; Oakley blades; an athletic cropped top; short shorts; and Saucony running shoes that, of course, matched perfectly with the rest of her ensemble; Heidi looked like she had just step out of a fitness magazine ad—more likely, off the cover. Fit didn't begin to describe her body. Tan and ripped, abs like a turtle's shell, legs from the ground to God, and to top it off, piercing, cobalt-blue eyes.

When Heidi took off her sunglasses and introduced herself as she caught her breath, I in fact had to catch mine. Those eyes, I will never forget those blue eyes or the confidence that shot out from within them. Imagine a young Claudia Schiffer not only competing in the Ironman at Kona but in contention to win it, and you might get the picture. At that moment, I knew what women (including my wife) probably felt upon meeting Sebby. I was weak, disoriented, and mesmerized. They made an extremely beautiful couple.

At our next meeting, I commented to Sebby about Heidi, trying to change the subject from business into a more social context, and for once he didn't seem to need to be somewhere else. He almost seemed excited to talk about her. Heidi had been a cross-country, track, and swimming star in high school. She came from nothing, graduated salutatorian, and got a scholarship to Northwestern. Now with a newly minted MBA, she worked as a junior PR rep, traveling the country to ensure her agency's clients were content, while constantly drumming up new business.

Sebastian and Heidi met on an airplane while traveling to New York City nine months earlier. She was flying back to the main office after the last leg of another tour around the country, and he was heading out to film a guest spot on CNBC as Promise Wealth Management's star analyst. It was another feather in his hat, as well as good PR for his company, Heidi was certain of that. Maybe Promise was in need of her services, she wondered out loud. At that moment Sebby knew full well that he was in need of hers. She offered him her business card, adding "call me," and Sebastian gladly accepted. Was it for PR or more personal reasons? He had to find out.

Dinner in Manhattan soon led to layovers in Milwaukee while Heidi was on business or on her days off. Not long after, she moved up from Chicago to her aunt's house in Whitefish Bay on the near north side. Heidi could really live anywhere she wanted as long as there was an airport nearby and a T1 line available for work.

"Pete, I can't believe it finally happened!" Sebby later confided. "I'm hooked. . . maybe even in love. This must be love." He spoke like he was in shock, in a sort of start-and-stop conversation he was really having with himself. "Heidi is great! I think she might be the one! She's smart, funny, athletic, and sexy as hell. I mean, did you see her? You saw her, right?" he asked, as if I hadn't been there a week earlier and somehow missed the sweaty, tan Swedish supermodel on my job site. Yeah, like that sort of thing happens all the time. It was as if he needed my approval. I managed to agree as nonchalantly and as businesslike as possible even though Heidi had already burned a place in my brain the previous Tuesday.

"And the sex!" Sebby said, interrupting my daydream. "Uninhibited, athletic, catch-your-breath-and-go-again sex . . . you know?" he prodded. Unfortunately I didn't.

He just continued on in his blissful rant. "On the boat. In my truck. We even did it in front of a full-length window on the fortieth floor at a hotel in Manhattan so everybody and anybody could watch! Can you imagine that?" he asked.

I couldn't, but oh how I wished I could!

"I'm done!" he declared abruptly. "Done with all this dating stuff . . ." He paused briefly. "Tag and release . . .you know, Pete?" But again, I didn't. I'd only ever been with one woman. "I'm done!" he reiterated. "In fact . . . truth be told—and I don't think I have admitted this to anyone, let alone myself—she's the reason I'm building this house and moving out of the Third Ward. Well, Heidi and my new gig at New Millennium Capital Investments in Mequon. They offered to bring me in as a junior partner. I think Heidi needs to see that I'm ready to settle down if I'm going to get her to move in with me. Do you think she'll like the house?" he asked, finally beginning to come down off his Heidi high.

"Who wouldn't?" I chimed in, half bragging about my work and half admitting that maybe money could buy love. Then Sebby went back into his sales pitch, as if the merits of dating Heidi would be lost on any red-blooded male with a pulse.

"She travels a lot, you know, so it's like the best of both worlds. When she's around, we have so much fun together, and when she travels for work or to compete in her triathlons, I'm free to be me," he continued, his voice becoming more animated, like an adolescent describing some major crush. "It's like committing without full-time commitment, you know?" Sebastian declared. "It's going to be great!"

I realized at that moment that Sebastian was many things: charismatic, athletic, smart, wealthy, and stylish, but, above all, he was abrupt, outspoken, and honest to a fault. His mind never filtered what came out of his mouth. I had picked up on this more than once in our meetings. He never hesitated to speak his mind or share his ideas, even if it meant pushing other people's educated opinions to the floor. I kind of liked that about him. In some weird way I suppose he reminded me of my brother.

"I don't care if the architect says it won't look right this way. I like it this way!" Sebastian commanded. Or "I think this color (or this fixture) is the way to go, don't you, Pete?" he would ask, but only rhetorically, because he had invariably already made up his mind. I never had to second guess what he wanted, which made my job in some ways easier, but in other areas harder. Where was I supposed to get hand-hammered Austrian pewter door knobs? (Salzburg!)

Sebastian lacked tact, but he was my boss, my only client, and my number one priority. I knew this job, this guy with his contacts and clientele could lead to more business if I did it perfectly. I also knew as the summer of 2003 wore on, that my promise of a new home for Christmas was hopeful at best and more doubtful with each rain delay or contractor snafu.

I needed to be open and honest with Sebby about this matter, as he was looking to put his Third Ward condo on the market in early fall, and selfishly I still wanted to burst Heather's egocentric trip down memory lane, so she would look at me again and stop thinking of what might have been back in college. I figured it wouldn't hurt to see Heidi again, especially in broad daylight instead of occasionally at night in my dreams. Could I accomplish all of these things in one fell swoop? I had an idea, but I took a chance and invited them both over for dinner the next Saturday.

Heather was excited and nervous when I told her half of the news. "What should we make? We have to clean! Maybe we should just go out?" The ideas and questions flew out of her mouth in rapid succession as she brainstormed a myriad of scenarios for the evening, one of which I was sure ended in a three-way with her and Sebastian—as for me, well, I would probably be the wallflower as usual, but at least I would get to watch. *Is that still considered a*

Ménage à trois? I wondered. *You hopeless piece of shit, get it together.* My adolescent mind with its insecurity issues was in full control of my imagination now, and it was running way off kilter. I let her rant and ramble on and on about food, wine, beer, mixed drinks, appetizers, dessert, and the table setting until she settled on petite filets, grilled asparagus, a bottle of Malbec, and some raspberry cobbler and ice cream to keep it casual.

Heather was just about finished with the theme for that Saturday in her own mind when I decided to finally drop the bomb. We would need a table for FOUR and at least another bottle of wine. This wasn't a business meeting, this was purely social. I didn't mention my need to discuss and soften my scheduling problems with Sebby. She didn't need to know. I doubt she cared. But a fourth for dinner? She cared about that. Sebastian was bringing a date—Heidi, my ace in the hole. That was the rest of the story, the icing on the cake.

It occurred to me that Sebby was to me what I hoped (spitefully, I'll admit) Heidi might be to Heather. The measure of perfection she wished she was, the woman my wife could only dream of being. What would it be like to be that successful, to be that attractive and smart, to have any woman—or, conversely, man—she wanted (money no object), and freedom? I couldn't even imagine. Sebastian and Heidi were those rare specimens: perfect! Not only that, they had found each other. They were *the* perfect couple; at least I thought so, like the Bowies or Beckhams or Tom Brady and Gisele Bündchen, the focus of magazine covers and Hollywood news.

What woman wouldn't find a tall, athletic, suave, wealthy, French Polynesian man desirable? What man wouldn't obsess over five feet eight inches and 115 pounds of brains, beauty, and brawn? Self-made, self-confident, not cocky, just the embodiment of inner strength, outward calm, and quick-witted flirting all wrapped up in an unattainable package. Unattainable, that is, to almost anyone except a guy like Sebastian Everest Koh.

By seeing Heidi with Sebastian, I hoped Heather might realize that the crowd she used to run with in high school and college had indeed evolved, leaving some, like cream, to rise to the top, while others, like Heather, sank further down and just blended in. I wanted her to see that this was okay. That was, after all, how the world worked, in my opinion anyway.

I understood my place in the pecking order of things, so why couldn't my wife? In some weird, demented way, I wanted her to realize that she was as lucky to be with me as I was with her. I wanted Heather to come to the realization that some people were just out of her league. I felt that way about Heidi; could Heather accept that about Sebastian?

I have always held that people in successful relationships find their own level like water, that marriages without mutual admiration and respect, beyond love, seldom work out. I thought Heather and I were on the same level, although I doubted Heather felt the same. Out of spite, or maybe my recent desperation, I guess I just wanted Heather to get knocked down again, like when we met after she had dropped out of UW Madison. Maybe then she would love me again happily and not seem constantly saddened by the diminished expectations of her youth. I wanted "my" Heather back. The one I got to know *after* high school up until the last month or so. I didn't want to lose her to some faulty notion she had concocted that she could do better, but my insecurities were calling the shots.

Maybe (and I hated to admit this to myself) she was right. Maybe Heather could have done better. Maybe she deserved better. Maybe after three years of dating and five years of marriage, I was nothing more than a good friend, and not the love of her life. Maybe she *had* settled. I resolved to redouble my efforts and become the successful man she would long for. Now if I could just lose twenty pounds and grow four inches, Heather wouldn't be able to resist me.

Chapter 4

Drop It Like It's Hot
Told by Sebby

I told Heidi I would pick her up at five thirty for the drive up to Port Washington and dinner with Peter and Heather at six. I liked Peter more and more as my project commenced. He was an excellent carpenter and craftsman and had a good eye for the details that I would have missed if it wasn't for his expertise. I could see how passionate he was about his work and business. And he was a perfectionist, so I felt fortunate to have him on my team, so to speak, but I questioned whether a social outing was a good idea. I needed to keep things professional and on schedule; this was business—no emotions, no sincerity, no favors, no excuses, and no more gawking at my girlfriend. Jeez, I really didn't like him constantly checking out Heidi, although in some bizarre way it was sort of flattering, and honestly, she was so hot! I resigned myself to the fact that I better get used to other men staring at her and get over it otherwise it would drive me crazy. Not the worst burden to have by any means. I shouldn't be so lucky.

Early that Saturday morning, Heidi ran a 10K in a town just west of Milwaukee called Delafield and insisted I be there to cheer her on. Even though I was exhausted from all my hours as the new junior partner at New Millennium, I made it out of bed. My body protested and my mind was in full revolt, but I made it over to Starbucks, drank a "truce" with two extra shots of espresso, and found Heidi by seven a.m. I reminded her of our dinner plans and told her she could find me later at the marina working on my boat.

Needless to say, by the time three o'clock rolled around, I was truly exhausted and suffering not only from dehydration but sunburn as well. I was in no mood for pleasantries and small talk with Peter and his wife, who, after four months, I still hadn't met. But a promise was a promise, so after a quick shower and shave, Bermudas and a polo, I was off to pick up Heidi in my red 911 Porsche convertible. (Man, I loved that car! I should never have sold it. I won't make that mistake again.)

I drove up to her place at four o'clock. Seeing Heidi quickly raised my spirits as well as my blood pressure. She met me at her door in what can only be described as trouser shorts (I'm no fashion expert) rolled and cuffed high and tight; strappy, barely-there thong sandals; and a *very* loosely woven off-white cotton sweater—the light from the afternoon sun revealing just enough for me to notice that she wasn't wearing a bra.

"You're early," Heidi noted in a very flirty tone. "Would you like to come in?" she asked playfully as she tried to make eye contact with me, which wasn't working, because for obvious reasons, my eyes couldn't get above her neckline. "I think we have a little time before we have to leave," she added suggestively.

Heidi was always horny after a race. You would think she would be exhausted, but she was the Energizer Bunny. Unbelievably, I deflected her advances and managed to talk her into a beer on the sofa. *I really must be getting old,* I thought to myself, but for the first time, I didn't have the energy—or desire for that matter. I was content to just curl up on the couch with her and talk. I chalked it up to being in love and quickly fell asleep.

She must have dozed off too, but only for a bit, as she woke me up by pushing me off her and announcing that we better leave or we were going to be late.

"You can't go dressed like that!" I blurted out, still trying to come to. "At least put on a bra!"

"Oh, yeah, I forgot," she admitted, looking down at her sweater. "Those are for your eyes only! I guess you're either bored with me already or lying to me about your age!" she chided.

(Ouch! That one stung a bit!)

"I was hoping for a little—" Heidi paused. "Actually, I was hoping for a lot. I missed you this week!"

"Me too, baby," I offered apologetically. "But we have tonight and all day tomorrow. Let's make this dinner thing short and get to BED!"

The ride up Hwy 43 to Port Washington was beautiful, and I wished we had time to stop by the new house. I was ready to pop the question—no, not marriage, but rather my idea of cohabitating together. But it wasn't happening that night.

Heather and Peter met us at the door and immediately ushered us around the back of their home to a small fenced-in yard for drinks and assorted appetizers. I noticed to my dismay that Peter was already checking out Heidi, but even more oddly, I noticed Heather checking me out. Were they swingers or something? It just felt odd. Small talk about the house, the weather, and the Brewers led to grilling some steaks and more drinks.

By the time dinner was finally ready, I'd had a few too many and just wanted to go home. Heidi would have to drive. Unfortunately both of those options were out of the question. Heidi would not be getting behind the wheel of my Porsche anytime soon. The clutch couldn't take her abuse, and I needed to sober up before I could drive us home. We couldn't leave, thus the polite thing to do was eat.

At the table, Heather corralled me into a conversation that left me, to say the least, a little uncomfortable. "Peter tells me that you went to Madison for your bachelor's degree," she baited. "Were you in a frat there?"

"Sigma Chi," I offered.

"I think I remember you. Didn't you date Amy

Anderson her freshman year?"

"Yeah . . . wow, what a small world," I said while simultaneously pleading with my eyes to get Heather to stop with the ex questions before Heidi tuned into our conversation. Then for just a split second, I recounted the A years ('90 to '92): Amy, Ashley, Amanda, Aspen. *Okay, stop it,* I thought. But it was already too late.

"You two know each other from college?" Heidi chimed in.

"NO!" I said, now disgusted, embarrassed, and a little drunk.

"Did you go to Madison?" Heidi asked Heather.

"Yes," she replied confidently.

"I don't remember you," I said unapologetically. "Have we met before?"

***

Part Two: *told by Peter*

Strike One! Sebastian didn't remember my wife from college. Now I was tuned into their conversation and could tell this fact was only just beginning to sink in and bother Heather.

"What did you major in?" Sebby asked her, trying to gracefully change the subject from exes to anything but.

"I started pre-med and then switched to law!" Heather proclaimed, never thinking she might have to face a follow up, but Sebastian, as I already knew, was a pro at controlling the conversation.

"So what year did you graduate?" he prodded.

After what seemed like an eternity with Sebby trying to hold her gaze, Heather cracked and looked away, admitting sorely that she hadn't.

Strike two! This was going great. Better than I hoped,

but definitely not as planned. I had thought the mere presence of Heidi on the arm of "Sebastian the great" would be enough to convince Heather he was out of her league and always had been, but there was Sebastian himself telling her that she had never played in his league to begin with. He didn't even remember her. Heather was never really in that social circle in college after all, even if some of her sorority sisters made her feel like she was.

Okay, damage done, it was time to pick up the pieces. I had to swoop in and do my part to save her ego from the master assassin. After all, that's what I did best, other than construction. The shoulder to cry on, the good guy, the nice guy; she would fall back into me, I knew it.

Trying to stick up for Heather a little, I interjected, "She got an internship the summer before her senior year and did such a good job that they hired her on."

It was a small lie, but she was my wife. I loved her and didn't want to see her devastated any further. Heather a little hurt was good; wounded, okay; but now she was getting absolutely killed, and I had set this whole thing up.

Unfortunately, however, she wasn't done. Apparently the flight or fight reflex in my wife prompted the latter. "Didn't you date Leah Aspen for a while?" she asked Sebastian knowingly.

"She was my roommate until *she* dropped out."

I glared at her, trying to get her to stop.

"In fact, I think you waited for her a few times at my place early on before she basically moved in with you!" Her voice was becoming slightly agitated. "You really don't remember me?" she asked again incredulously.

Heidi was now listening very intently, and Sebastian was getting increasingly uncomfortable. I was more than a little nervous as to where this was all headed. When Heidi and Sebby both glanced uncomfortably away, I mouthed to Heather, *PLEASE STOP THIS*, but she continued on unabashedly.

"You know," Heather lowered her voice and paused for effect as if spreading some really juicy gossip, "I think Leah was pregnant when *she* dropped out of college." Again her emphasis was lost on everyone except me. "But she wouldn't admit it to me or anyone," Heather continued, looking for the upper hand in the conversation.

Sebastian and Heidi just stood there in stunned silence as my wife continued her rant, and my hopes of completing their new home began to crumble with each venomous sentence spewing from her mouth.

"I knew she would never get an abortion," she said, pausing again to let what she was insinuating sink in. "She was really religious. . . . Maybe she gave it up for adoption," Heather added checking Sebby's reaction. "She just disappeared. Her family was very protective of her, you know." At that, she got up from the table very nonchalantly before the ticking time bomb she had just programmed could explode.

She went inside the house under the auspice of plating the cobbler and ice cream for dessert but also to cool off and sober up. I knew that Sebastian not remembering her burned her up inside more than any snide comment I could ever invent. She had apparently also downed a few more gin and tonics before our get together than I had witnessed, partially explaining her irregular and offensive behavior. Perhaps she needed more liquid courage than I did to confront Sebastian, but whatever issues she had needed to stay strictly in the past as far as I was concerned. This was neither the time nor the place.

I followed her into the kitchen, furiously talking at her under my breath so Sebastian and Heidi wouldn't hear. "What are you doing? Are you crazy? What are you trying to do? Get me fired? Then what?" I paused to catch my breath. "How are we—I mean, you—going to smooth this over? . . . Forget it!" I demanded disgustedly. "Just talk to Heidi and leave Sebby alone!"

"His name is Sebastian, Peter!" she shot back inappropriately. "You think Heidi is HOT, don't you?" she asked jealously.

"Don't change the subject!" I nearly yelled before I could regain my composure.

This was going really badly, and I feared it would only get worse. We couldn't stay in the kitchen all night. We couldn't go back out there. This was an unmitigated disaster, and I still hadn't told Sebastian about the lagging schedule. No way was I going to bring that up now—talk about pouring gasoline on a fire. I could only imagine the conversation the two of them were having outside on the deck. I was sure that they had heard us and felt the tension between us.

Hell, Sebby had basically just been attacked. Maybe they would politely decline dessert and head back to Milwaukee. I could only hope. But for now, we had to go back out there.

By the grace of God, Heather somehow got it together, kept it light, and began to talk more with Heidi. I salvaged up every last ounce of courage I had left and changed the subject to anything but the conversation from the last few hours. It was getting late. I hoped I still had a job come Monday, but I wasn't sure I wanted to have a wife by then.

Sebastian and I ran out of small talk and sauntered back into the girls' conversation after it became clear he was ready to leave. "I love those shorts!" Heather admitted in a fresh, airy (fake) tone. "Where did you get them? Talbots? Boston? Banana?"

"Actually they were an old pair of pinstripe suit pants I wore at work." Heidi smiled, unashamed and as confident as ever. "I just couldn't bring myself to throw them away."

Wow! I thought to myself. *Beauty, brains, brawn, and thrift, Daddy never taught any of that to Heather.*

Finally Sebby proclaimed, "Baby we've got to go. I need to get some sleep." So after a few more pleasantries, they left to go back to their perfect world and left us to clean up our mess together—yet utterly alone—in devastating silence. Our house would remain that way for the next week.

Chapter 5

Keep the Blue Side Up
Told By Jon

I never want to relive 2002 and 2003 ever again. I remember at one point, one horrible day, walking my dog through a business office parking lot, crying openly, and talking to (as well as cursing at) God out loud. I was losing it big time. But life is a rollercoaster I guess. Sometimes you just have to let it all out and scream at the top of your lungs. Our struggles with infertility had brought Elise and me to the depths of despair. We needed to get off this ride and try something else.

***

Salmon are anadromous fish. Just ask my wife, she will tell you if you ask her. Elise is the smartest woman I know. A high school biology and chemistry teacher by trade, she knows more than she lets on, and she will tell you all about salmon. You see, they don't breed in or near the salt water in which they spend the vast majority of their lives. Instead, salmon travel tens, if not hundreds, of miles inland up freshwater rivers and streams to breed, spawn, and then die in the place where they were born.

Elise and I hoped we were anadromous. That was our theory anyway, so in early summer 2002, we packed up our old Isuzu Rodeo and moved back to Wisconsin, the place we were both born. We left Portland, Maine, the ocean, the salt water, and LL Bean. We had lived a few other places as well, but always near the ocean. Elise and I loved the ocean, but now we were back. Back to our birthplace, inland, near Lake Michigan, fresh water, loud Harleys, big bratwurst, Brewers baseball, Miller beer, and cheese, lots and lots of cheese, and I wasn't happy.

I had left Wisconsin in 1989, immediately after high school—and I do mean immediately. I enrolled for the summer semester at one of the universities I had been accepted at and subsequently chosen and started there less than two weeks after graduation. I just couldn't wait to get out of town and start the next chapter in my life.

In hindsight, though, I did miss out on a heck of a summer with all my friends back home, but I just had to start seeing what the rest of the world had to offer. I had been dreaming of far off places with oceans and mountains for a long time. Wisconsin had neither. I vowed right then and there at the age of eighteen to never come back, except for family visits. Little did I know I would meet and fall in love with a girl from Wisconsin.

I remember when I was little my minister telling our congregation once, "If you want to make God laugh, tell him *your* plans." Well, I guess the joke was on me. I hope He got a good chuckle over this.

Elise was twenty-eight at the time of our move and wasn't happy for different reasons. She wanted to have a child, and we weren't having much success in that department. But at that moment, she was still probably happier than me. She still had hope. Elise had never felt the need to escape Wisconsin as I did in my youth and thus didn't feel as if she was being trapped again.

I, on the other hand, felt like a wild animal experiencing my first days in captivity. I'm told animals have no concept of the future. They cannot garner any idea of ever being released. So when they are penned in, they either accept their immediate fate or go insane. This zoo wasn't where I wanted to be. I wanted to be in Casco Bay or on the Appalachian Trail, the Allagash River, or anywhere else but here, back in Wisconsin, away from our beloved ocean, trying desperately to have a child or at least get pregnant. Would I ever be released again into the wild, into the mountains, or back into the sea? Some cars I remembered used to have "Escape to Wisconsin" bumper stickers on them in the eighties. Now all I could think about was escaping *from* Wisconsin and trying not to go insane.

Anadromous—we hoped that was us. We just needed to surround ourselves with family, friends, and fresh water, and it would happen. That's what we told ourselves. But as 2002 became 2003 and specialist after specialist said it didn't look good, our salmon theory seemed to have been proven false.

***

Elise is the strongest, prettiest, and most honest person I know. That we are actually married—I mean, that I am actually married to her still astounds me. We met in, of all places, a movie theater lobby where she worked during college. She was wearing a black polyester tuxedo and selling tickets at the front counter. I don't remember the movie my friends and I were going to see that night, but I do remember distinctly (and will swear on the Bible if asked) that her eyes actually twinkled at mine as she asked for the money for my ticket. I couldn't even speak, let alone make correct change, as I stared back at her. I am sure I appeared to be a blithering idiot, but thankfully she doesn't even remember that night.

It wasn't until three months later, a few more movies, and a serendipitous bumping into each other that I finally got my courage up to ask her out. Unfortunately she was already seeing someone, but I didn't let that stop me. Her social calendar eventually opened up, as she was once again single, and after a few phone calls, we had our first date. This was miraculous, because she admitted later that on our first phone call she confused me with someone else, somebody she had no interest in dating. She in fact was waiting for me to call, but had my face and name mixed up with another guy. Whew! I am sure glad we got that straightened out.

Elise had a pet turtle that we took for "walks," an old red Horizon compact car that she drove happily, a penchant for TCBY yogurt, and apparently a soft spot for me. We had the same taste in music and food, a great love of the outdoors, and a connection that was not only magical but seemed to grow with each passing day. We just fit. I was smitten, and I think she was too.

Elise's most prominent personality trait is the steely determination she puts into everything she touches and aspires to. It is not unlike Kerry Ann Moss's character, Trinity, in *The Matrix* trilogy. She looks like her too—tall and thin with black hair, fair skin, and green eyes. She is a beautiful woman from Irish stock and fits the mold. I am a lucky man, and I know it.

The other side to Elise though is quite the opposite. Patient and caring, quick-witted yet loving, she is very endearing, if not a little anal at times. Courtney Cox's character, Monica, on *Friends* comes to mind, and I'm not the only one who sees this side of her. All I know is that her smile makes my day, and her soul is the beacon that guides me home.

***

You're not supposed to have to schedule your very life around some mysterious moment of ovulation—never quite sure if or when it is supposed to happen or that it actually did take place for that matter gets really frustrating. A couple shouldn't have to plan an agenda to make love. Shouldn't it just happen naturally between two people who care deeply for each other? You shouldn't have to inject your wife with big needles and gonzo expensive drugs. It is emotionally and financially draining. Money can't buy love, and it sure shouldn't be the deciding factor on who gets to have kids, yet there we were trading my new SAAB 9-5 SE station wagon (the perfect family/kid car if there ever was) in on some old ratty VW just to scrounge together more money for another attempt at in vitro fertilization, which would take about three months and cost about ten thousand dollars. Insurance didn't cover a lot of it, including many of the hormonal drugs, which ran an additional three thousand dollars easily for a three month trial alone.

We lived in a crappy apartment right (and I mean *right*) next to a major interstate. With the constant hum of traffic less than fifty yards away from our bedroom window, I couldn't sleep. I tried everything from Styrofoam in the sill to fans and white noise generators, but nothing worked.

I missed Maine terribly, but then again, I figured maybe it wasn't Maine that I really missed. Maybe I just missed the happiness Elise and I had experienced there. Since moving back to Wisconsin, everything seemed bleak and took more effort. Even our relationship was difficult now. I missed the carefree, easygoing days that Maine afforded us. I wanted to return to those times, even if we couldn't go back to that place.

Elise was a wreck. She had gotten to the point where she couldn't go to the local Target because it was so full of moms with their babies. She would break down and cry a lot, sometimes even in public. Shopping wasn't on our list of fun things to do anyway.

I was thirty-one years old and had left a beautiful home in the quiet countryside near the ocean, the islands, the lobsters, and lighthouses, and I was living in an apartment where I couldn't even see out half the windows because their seals had long since broken and become foggy and filled with mildew. Our heating and cooling bills were huge, and I was sick of listening to the ever-present roar of the interstate highway.

I was so tired, so fed up, and so devastated. As outrageous as it sounds, one day I just lost it and openly cursed at God while I was walking our dog. I yelled up at the sky and asked "why?" over and over again between bouts of crying and stopping to pick up bits of dog poop with blue pine-scented baggies. To this day, I wonder what the people in that office complex must have thought as they watched the crazy man walking his dog and shouting at the sky.

Elise had just completed her third in vitro attempt. You do the math. That's a lot of money down the drain. Needless to say it didn't work, but at least Elise didn't have to go through another D and C like after the last in vitro and subsequent miscarriage. In some way it was just easier to have it not work than to get our hopes up for a few weeks only to watch the blood test numbers plummet and know the inevitable outcome before it even happened. The price we had paid both emotionally and financially was too astronomical to comprehend. Nowhere near the ocean, no breeding going on, no spawning in our future, without any kids on the way, were we supposed to go back to sea or just grow old here and die where we were born?

Elise was miserable. I felt lost. I would do anything to make her happy, but I couldn't make this right. I couldn't change our fate. The doctors said we both had issues. Elise had ultralow hormonal levels, resulting in an extremely long and unpredictable menstrual cycle. They doubted many times whether she was ovulating at all. I, on the other hand, had a low sperm count. To make matters worse, the urologist told us that the small remainder of soldiers I did produce apparently weren't that good at swimming.

You know the old saying "a happy wife makes for a happy life"? Well, it's true. Not only was our life bad, it just seemed to keep getting worse. It was not supposed to go in that direction.

Elise and I were in a huge downward spiral. Needless to say, our marriage was strained by all this as well, so we started to look into adoption. Even if Elise couldn't experience pregnancy, we could still be parents. After all, we thought, nine months was a mere fraction of time and only one chapter of the many we would have with a child. But that served as little consolation for Elise. She felt as if she was defective in some way.

I felt as if we'd somehow been betrayed. I couldn't help but think that at any given moment some baby was being born to parents who didn't want it or worse. Somewhere out there a child was being born with fetal alcohol syndrome or addicted to cocaine, whose mom would give him or her up because the dad was nowhere to be found, and she has no visible means to support it. Maybe the baby was the product of some one night stand or whatever; it didn't matter. Unfortunately there are a million stories all over the world each year of unwanted children who aren't even given a fair shake from the start.

These thoughts should have comforted me, as that very child could one day become ours through the adoption process, but instead I kept asking myself selfish questions. Why did those couples get to have kids and not us? Why should we have to keep paying just to have a shot at getting pregnant? What did Elise and I ever do that was so wrong that we didn't deserve to be blessed? Why do people who don't want to have kids, let alone love them or care for them, routinely get knocked up after a few too many drinks or a night of reckless passion, yet we couldn't bring a baby who would be so loved into this world? It just didn't seem fair.

I knew a few old high school friends who now lived in the area, as did Elise, so we tried to reconnect with them, but having moved away for so long, they had already filled their respective circles. Our social calendar was empty. Elise made a few new friends at the high school where she was hired, but I didn't have anyone outside of her to confide in. She had her family close by. Mine was on the other side of the state.

Once I met Elise, I guess for a while at least, I never thought I really needed anybody else. She was, and still is, my best friend and confidant. I'm sort of an introvert. I think that a lot of pilots probably are. It's a personality trait that seems to fit well with the occupation as we spend a lot of time alone while traveling. It might be an overgeneralization, but many people probably fall into their respective professions not because they want that job but because in the end that career fits them. I could never be a teacher, like my wife. I frankly am just not that much of a people person, and I know I don't have the patience required. Elise wouldn't make a good pilot. It's just not in her makeup, but we are both good at what we do.

Anyway, when I got married, most of my single friends sort of left me at the altar. I think they might have feared I was contagious or something, since I was the first to get hitched. It's weird, when Elise announced our pending nuptials, all of her girlfriends were so happy and supportive. To this day they all still get together and hang out—married or single, it doesn't seem to matter. My friends, on the other hand, soon after started treating me like a pariah. One even went so far as to send me a condolence card. He wasn't mourning the loss of me to Elise. He literally said that I had died. My phone just stopped ringing. So for the first few years of marriage, I just sort of clung to my wife. That's great and all, but something was missing, and I couldn't put my finger on it for a long time. Elise and I went golfing, hiking, and skiing together and always had a good time, but every now and then I found myself wanting the banter—you know, the gentle ridicule and crude humor I used to share with my guys.

Then, out of nowhere, I met Sebastian. He understood me instantly, and we became fast friends. Those evenings at McKinley Marina, his car, his life, they were all welcome escapes, even briefly, from my own. He listened to my incessant investment questions and actually asked me stuff about airplanes and places where I flew. We actually talked. A lot of guys don't really talk. Sure, they sit around and watch the game together, cheering on their heroes and discussing the last play, but in my experience, it's a rare thing to find a guy intelligent and open enough to engage in a conversation outside the guy norms of sports, politics, sports, religion, sports, women, and sports. What else is there, right? How about life, hopes, dreams, and aspirations? How about business, travel, hobbies, good food, and great beer—*Oh, stop it! No other guy thinks that way . . . just you, pansy!*

Maybe it's just me, but I cringe when many of those earlier topics are broached, because it usually seems to end in an argument or silence. I hate conflict and I hate silence. I love—I mean, really love—a good intellectual, non-emotional, analytical debate or discussion. Intelligent conversation, information, inquisition, animated analogies, and what not—you know, the stuff on Bloomberg or NPR, Charlie Rose kind of talk, not the confrontational dialogue on the news channels most days and not, God forbid, the endless, pointless blather of sports commentators trying to one-up each other with their Monday morning quarterbacking on the sports channels.

Yeah, let's all sit around pontificating as to what we think or would have done last Saturday or Sunday if we were the coach or GM to win that all-important sixty-eighth game out of, I don't know, 160 ever-so-important games against division and non-conference rivals or whatever even though our star stud just injured his left oblique and pulled a groin muscle while partying with his entourage. Come on! We all know he shouldn't have bent over to pick up the rock that fell out of his earlobe (and would feed most of the homeless in America if it were sold!) when his velvet oversized top hat got caught in the sunroof of the stretch white Hummer limo he rented to go out clubbing the night before. He should have made one of them fetch it. After all, it was a must-win game!

But, wait, there's more. Next on Sports News 24/7/365: Four grown men will spend the hour not rehashing last weekend's events but instead prognosticating who will win not one, but every all-important, must-win game for the following weekend. Just in case your DVR is broken or you forgot to download the podcast, I'll let you in on a little secret: Do you want to know who's going to win the all-important, must-win game of the century, even though it's only midseason, and they haven't even had the all-star break yet? No, it's not the team who plays better on grass on even days under a full moon when the temperature is over seventy-five degrees and there is a Republican in the White House. Nor is it the team with pitchers with a combined ERA smaller than the square root of the opposing team's combined batting average multiplied by one hundred on odd days in even months when played on Astroturf indoors. Do you want to know who is going to win? It is simple. The team or athlete who scores the most points, finishes first, or crosses the finish line in the least amount of time wins. End of story.

They don't call it the boob tube for nothing. Many guys just can't seem to stop staring at it. Not one of those bloviating talking heads on TV is omnipotent. I get it that the game might be entertaining. Watching sports can be really fun. By all means watch the game—hell, watch two or three—but as for the other 150 hours in the week, turn off the so-called experts and enjoy life. Join a league, play catch, go fishing or golfing. Get outside. My God, the amount of hot air spewing from those stations is amazing. Do you know how I know that the atmospheric scientists studying climate change aren't into watching sports news? It's obvious. Turn to any one of those channels midweek, and the cause of global warming is right there in front of you. If they were fans, they would have figured it out by now.

I'd rather go sailing or golfing or skiing or hiking than be stuck inside on a beautiful day glued to the television, and so would Sebby. If there was one thing we agree on, it was this: In life there are two kinds of people: those that get out and do what they love and the spectators who prefer to watch it on television. Neither one of us wanted to be in the last camp.

***

Contrary to the downward spiral we were living, Sebby's trajectory always seemed to be heading up. It was fun living vicariously through him. Sebastian was busy with his job at New Millennium Capital Investments as their new junior partner and overall stud acquisition from Promise Wealth Management. He was building a new home near Mequon and dating some young, athletic woman named Heidi. I gave odds of 60/40 that she'd last the summer, although in retrospect, he did seem more serious about her than most of the women he told me about.

I met some of Sebby's new associates on a golf outing one day. To tell the truth, I was more than a little intimidated by most of them. They were all highly educated, extremely driven, and obviously doing quite nicely for themselves and their families—unlike me. All I had to do was look around at their new Mercedes and latest sets of thousand dollar Callaway or Ping clubs to understand that I didn't have "game," even if the Wilson K28s I had been using since I was fifteen hit the ball fairly straight. I guess at that moment I just realized how badly I was trailing "the Joneses," so to speak. I wasn't keeping up at all, and it bruised my ego a bit, but Sebby never made me feel anything like that. He had nice things but never dwelled on them. He was really down to earth.

We sailed *Slomocean* in the Queen's Cup Regatta across Lake Michigan and back. We talked, ate, and drank beer. I turned him onto Belgian white wheat beers; Blanche De Brussells is my favorite, but Hoegaarden is a close second. He counseled me on my 401k plan and took me out to his new house to show me the progress. It was quite the place—not size wise, but funky, minimal, and cool. It was mainly built out of concrete and Styrofoam but used posts and beams rather than two-by-four or two-by-six studs for some of the walls and all of the ceilings as well. The joinery was beautiful. The roof was made out of structural insulated panels (SIPS, as he called them) with a standing seam metal overlay that contained integrated solar panels on the south exposure. The inside was still very much a work in progress when we visited the worksite in early November to take a look around and eat some soup and sandwiches purchased to-go from a local restaurant.

"I won't be moving in anytime soon. It doesn't matter though; my condo hasn't sold anyway."

"How are things with Heidi?" I asked. "Is she going to move in with you or what?"

"Things are good, I guess," Seb said. "I haven't officially asked her yet, but I think she knows that it's coming. How is Elise? What's next for you two?"

"She wants to adopt." I quickly took a huge bite of my sandwich, trying to hide my apprehension.

"You down with that?" Sebby looked at me, trying to read my face.

"Yeah, I think so." I shrugged, still chewing on my lunch. "More and more every day."

But Sebastian could tell I wasn't okay with it. I wasn't a very good salesman. "Is it the whole biological thing or what?"

"No it's not that at all, Seb . . . I don't care if our child looks like us at all; I know Elise and I would love him or her either way. We just want to be parents."

"Well then what is it?" Sebby said between slurps of soup.

"I already feel like a failure in the man department, you know," I offered. "Elise really wanted to experience pregnancy and everything, but that's not even it anymore. It's this open-concept thing the adoption agency keeps trying to sell us on, where the birthparents can still be involved and have visitation rights and what not. It's freaking me out. We already have my side of the family and Elise's to worry about. Frankly I don't want some other family gumming up the works. I just want their kid. Is that selfish of me? I don't want to confuse the kid; I just want to be the parent and not have it want to go back to his or her biological parent if and when we have to enforce some rule or whatever. Worse yet, I don't want the biological parents changing their minds later on and interfering in our newly formed family. Elise and I couldn't handle that."

"Wow, I hadn't thought of that," Sebastian said. "I don't think that would happen." He was trying to cheer me up, I suppose, trying to assuage my fears, but it wasn't helping. That was the first time I had actually formed my fears concerning adoption into concrete terms, let alone said them out loud. I hadn't even broached this area of my psyche with Elise. I didn't know if I wanted to ruin it for her, because for the first time in a long time, she was actually optimistic about our prospects.

What I didn't realize was that by opening my mouth I had opened a wound within Sebby as well. He thought to himself for quite a while, considering our conversation, I guessed, only mumbling "huh," then silent again. I noticed that he looked rather dour now, as if something was weighing on his mind. Whatever it was, it was definitely the elephant in his future living room now.

"What is it, Seb?"

He wouldn't say, choosing instead to just sit there, cross-legged in the sawdust, slurping the last of his soup.

"What's up, man?" I asked again.

"I could be a father," he finally blurted out as if he was rather stunned by his own admission.

"What?" I said, startled. "Is Heidi pregnant? Wait . . . what about your vasectomy, man?

That's impossible."

"Ironic, huh?" He paused. "You trying everything you can to become a dad, and me trying to avoid it my entire life only to find out . . ." He didn't finish.

"What are you talking about Sebby?"

But he wouldn't say. He couldn't seem to find the words, until I decided to drag it out of him. Finally, after a lot of prodding, he opened up to me about the disastrous dinner date he and Heidi had with his contractor and wife. Then Sebastian laid out how he might be the dad of a ten-year-old kid. There were so many scenarios to consider. Was this lady lying just to get back at him for somehow wronging her back in college? Did he actually get Leah Aspen pregnant? Or was it somebody else's child—a boy from her home town on break, perhaps? Did she have an abortion? Did she give it up for adoption? Did she keep the baby? Was she married or single? Did her husband formally adopt the baby with her? Did Sebastian have any rights? Should he try and find her? What if she was married? Would she want him to know? Would she want him to find her and find out the truth? Did he owe child support? If given up for adoption, would the child come looking for him when he or she was older?

It was all too much for Sebby at this time. Too many questions and no easy answers. I wanted to console him, but I couldn't find the words. Apparently all this weighed on his relationship with Heidi as well. "Lately I'm sort of distant and confused, I guess. Not too fun to be around, I suppose. Maybe that's why I haven't gotten around to asking Heidi to move in with me. I need to figure this out for myself. I just don't know how."

After lunch he showed me around a bit more, trying to lift his own spirits, I figured, with the fact that this new toy, this home, would soon be his. But I don't know if it helped.

Chapter 6

Abstinence Makes the Heart Grow Fonder
Told By Peter

The house was silent for at least a week after our dinner party fiasco. Heather and I barely talked. I stayed busy on the job site, not even wanting to come home or be around her. I had met with Sebastian once since the party and apologized for Heather's actions.

He graciously responded, "No harm done! No apology is necessary." Sebby chalked it up to the booze. I wasn't fired from the project, and things were back on track, except that the lagging schedule was nowhere near on time for a Christmas move in, which I still couldn't admit to Sebby. I knew he had his heart set on a December completion, as well as selling his condo and asking Heidi to move in with him. I had to find a way to tell him the truth, hoping he had a little more pity and forgiveness left in his soul for me after our dinner disaster.

I don't know what finally brought Heather around. I damn sure know it wasn't me. I had hardly been home since the cookout. I wanted her to apologize to me on her own, because I wasn't going to ask her for an apology. She would have to come to that conclusion herself, or we were going to go down a very rocky path. But sure enough, a week or so later, there she was on the phone, sounding repentant and asking if I could come home early.

It was August 2003, a good hot, dry month, and I desperately needed to try and make up some ground on Sebby's schedule, so I really needed to stay on the job every moment I could, plus I was reluctant to forgive Heather, but I knew our marriage could stand a boost right about then, so I agreed. We hadn't been on the same page in months. We hadn't been intimate since I could remember.

She was all dolled up when she met me at the doorway from our garage. I, on the other hand, was a sweaty, stinky mess.

"I'm sorry, honey!" she immediately said with a really sugary tone of voice. "Please forgive me. I just got to thinking, and . . . well . . . I was wrong."

This is good, I thought to myself.

"I don't know what's gotten into me lately . . . I'm sorry," she reiterated. "Can you forgive me?"

And before I could get out more than a half-assed "sure," she was on me, kissing me like a soldier coming home from the war. I was stunned, thankful, impressed, and turned on as hell! We left a trail of clothes from the back door to the bedroom. Her silky blouse, my muddy boots, her lacy bra, my sweaty shirt, her lacy panties, and my old blue jeans ended up everywhere. I got her on our bed and gave her what she wanted, and to my astonishment, she wanted more, following me into the shower as I attempted to wash up. Shortly thereafter we ended up in our bed again. I couldn't remember the last time she was this passionate. I didn't know what had gotten into her, but I was sure glad it was me.

We didn't get downstairs to eat the great dinner she had prepared for us (which was now not only burnt, but cold) until after eight o'clock. But I didn't care. Heather loved me.

I thought back to what Sebby had once said about makeup sex. Now I actually knew what he was talking about, and it was awesome!

Feeling like a man again and walking with a confident spring in my step, I figured there was no time like the present to confront Sebastian with the scheduling issue.

But over the next three weeks, he was either unavailable or just too downright imposing as my boss for me to fess up and tell him the truth. I kept chickening out, but with Heather's encouragement, I finally got up the nerve. It was weird, as I thought about it, to hear her tell me, "Peter . . . he's just a man." I thought she considered him to be the end all, do all, most perfectly engineered male specimen of all time.

I found out full well after her apology why she had acted so stupidly the evening of our dinner. She told me about her college crush on him, even her bizarre desire more than ten years ago to be with him after her friend Leah had dropped out. It was an uncomfortable conversation and a strange revelation, but I guess Heather needed to get it off her chest, so I let her tell me everything.

The truth was, Heather wasn't really sure Leah had gotten pregnant, let alone by Sebastian. Leah was secretly still seeing her high school sweetheart on the weekends when she went back home to La Crosse. As for her dropping out of college, it could have been a baby or the simple fact that her parents didn't have a lot of money and could scant afford the tuition at Madison. It could also have been that her grades stunk from too much partying, and her parents finally said enough. It was a long time ago now. Either way, it was still a mystery, as was the fact that Heather still hadn't gotten her monthly visit from the menstrual fairy. She was on the pill. She hadn't missed any, she thought, but she did vaguely remember something that the doctor had told her about a side effect from the antibiotics she was taking. Could she be pregnant?

I was tasked with the "go get me some tampons, pads, and a pregnancy test" run at the local grocery store, just what every guy wants to do on a Sunday morning. I figured it was that or go to church and start praying, but would I be praying for or against a positive pregnancy test? I was just starting to consider all the ramifications.

As I drove back to our house with the shopping list complete, my mind was awash in what ifs: What if Heather was pregnant? Was that a good thing or a bad thing? How did I feel about this? What was I going to say? What if it was positive? What if she wasn't pregnant? Did she stop taking the pill? Was she trying to get pregnant? Did she jump my bones because she was truly sorry or because she was ovulating? She seemed to hate her job more lately . . . was this her way of having an excuse to quit and stay home?

I had so much shit going on in my head I could hardly keep my pickup on the road. I entered our house from the garage, where apparently this whole charade had started a few weeks earlier. She met me at the door again, grabbed the grocery bag from my hands, fished out the pregnancy test, and said bravely, "Well . . . there's no time like the present! I really have to pee."

Hell yeah there is! I thought. *I don't know if I'm ready to be a father yet.* My head was spinning. My heart was racing. Those five minutes felt like an eternity with my future hanging in the balance. I was just getting Steglin Homes, LLC up and running. I didn't have time for diapers, naps, binkies, and whatever else came along with parenthood. I didn't know the first thing about babies—or kids for that matter. I was, for the most part, still a child myself.

As I thought about all the possibilities at that moment, it occurred to me I could hardly take care of myself. *I'm not ready for this*, I admitted. Internally I prayed incessantly, *Come on blue . . . or green or whatever is negative!* I was acting like a gambler at a table in Vegas. I was in no mood for this. What could I give up? *I'll be a good husband, I promise. I'll do anything; just please don't make me a father yet!* I pleaded silently. *I don't have the tools for this! Let Heather have her period, and I'll go back to wearing condoms . . . anything . . . anything . . .*

As I collapsed into a ball on the floor sweating, Heather entered our bedroom. The smirk on her lips told me more than I ever needed to know. Our life was about to change forever. It was time for me to grow up.

***

I broached the scheduling issue with Sebby over lunch at Culver's the next week, my treat. I needed to soften the blow (and custard always helps with that), so I decided on a "good news, bad news" sort of approach, telling him *my* good news first before telling him *his* bad news. He took some time to consider something—I don't know what really, probably whether he was going to punch me or cuss me out or fire me on the spot or maybe all three. Thankfully instead he calmly tried to have me pin down a new move-in ready date. "Can I be in by Valentine's Day? You have to have it done by then, Pete! Come on, man, you're killing me here."

As much as I wanted to say, "Yes, sir," again, I now knew the problems and stress doing that had caused us both. Honesty was the best policy, and I was turning over a new leaf. I laid out the remaining elements of the schedule and discussed each in detail as we finished our lunch. It helped that much of what was left wasn't outside the house, because the cold weather was definitely on its way.

I think he appreciated my honesty and the openness with which I presented myself. I could tell he was miffed, but I was still in the game, throwing strikes. I told him that I couldn't guarantee Valentine's Day but that by Easter at the latest he would be in for sure. I tried to further persuade him that actually it was for the best, because we wouldn't be rushing or cutting corners.

"Nobody wants to buy a condo or move in the middle of a Wisconsin winter anyway," I added.

November along the lake offered up only a brief reprieve from the inevitable, and old man winter came in with a vengeance the week after Thanksgiving. I did all of

the painting and staining, as well as the installation of light
and bath fixtures. The tile, carpet, and hardwood floors
were left to the experts.

I wanted this house to be perfect, and that's pretty
much how it turned out. We didn't make Valentine's Day,
but by the end of February, it was ready. Sebby loved the
house and showed it to everyone he knew even before moving
an ounce of his stuff into it. Heidi called to congratulate
Heather and me on the news of our pregnancy and to gush
over the house. She couldn't wait to move in.

"It's a boy!" I exclaimed excitedly to her. Our OBGYN
had messed up the last ultrasound and revealed the sex of
the baby to us. I was ecstatic.

***

I had pulled it off. But the scary thing was that it
was almost spring and I didn't have any other jobs lined
up. I quickly went from being swamped to becoming a
couch potato with Heather, who was now in her nesting
stage. Fortunately though, Heidi, in gratitude to her aunt
for letting her stay at her house, sprang for some minor
cosmetic repairs and updates that her aunt had been
dreaming about since getting sucked into HGTV land.

I came highly recommended by both her and
Sebastian, and I was grateful for all of their PR. It was like
a giant billboard advertising my skills, and like moths to a
flame, it began to bring in new business.

With Heather now getting seriously huge and Steglin
Homes, LLC ramping up, I suggested she quit her job after
the baby came and work from home for us, taking calls,
mailing invoices, scheduling contractors, etc. so that I
would be free to do more hands-on construction, save a
little money, and grow the business. With her hormones in
overdrive and her back about to give out, Heather wasn't
too happy thinking of me as her new boss, but that wasn't

my intention at all. I knew she wanted to stay home when the baby came anyway. I figured I could use the help and was too cheap to pay anyone else to do it. I thought it would make her feel useful. I thought it would give her something to do to stay busy. Boy, was I stupid. The reality of what it would soon be like at the Steglin house hadn't even occurred to me at this point. I had no idea the full-time job our son had planned for Heather or me.

"We are a team, honey," I told her, trying to cheer her on. "We are in this together—partners and parents. Sounds pretty good, huh?"

She said she'd consider it, but now she had another project for me. Apparently we needed a nursery. This was right up my alley, so I was on it, off to Home Depot. I would make our little guy's room perfect.

I was really happy, and at the moment felt like I could handle anything. My business was up and running. My first house was a success. And my wife was proud of me. Everything was falling into place. *And* I loved the color blue. I wondered if I should change the name of our endeavor: "Steglin and Son Homes, LLC" had a nice ring to it. I said it over and over again on the way to the store.

Chapter 7

The Missionary Position
Told by Jon

By early 2004, Sebby's house was almost complete. He had come close to firing his contractor a few times, but he said he hadn't because he truly liked the guy. It had gone beyond business between them and turned into friendship. Besides, he told me, "The guy is expecting his first kid this spring. I just couldn't do that to him, even if he deserved it."

With his condo on the market and his home almost move-in ready, but his relationship with Heidi in a rocky patch, Seb suggested we take a ski trip out to Jackson Hole before it was overrun with spring breakers. Elise was busy teaching school and didn't have her spring break for another month. She said go, so away we went.

I grew up skiing in Wisconsin, the Upper Peninsula of Michigan, and the arrowhead region of northeastern Minnesota, loving it from when I first started at three or four years old. Jackson Hole is amazing, spectacular, and huge, but the thing about skiing in the Rockies, the Sierras, and the Wasatch Mountains is that once I skied them, everything else paled in comparison. It was kind of a blessing and a curse. I felt so lucky to have had those experiences: true double blues, blacks, big chutes, and deep powder—runs that go on and on. But then I came home and went to the local "bump" hill, and it just wasn't that fun anymore. So over the years I skied less locally and just hoped and prayed for a few days each winter out west.

I have skied Vail, Beaver Creek, A Basin, Alta, Snowbird, you name it. I've skied in Alaska, Canada, even Austria. They are all wonderful. I have skied the Birds of Prey, Born Free, The Big Burn, and more, but nothing, nowhere, except perhaps the Chamonix Valley (I don't know yet, but I hope to find out someday) is bigger and badder, steeper and deeper than Jackson Hole (Heli-skiing excluded). Corbet's Couliour made my knees knock just standing at the top, let alone dropping in. Truth be told, I haven't summoned the courage for that elevator shaft yet. The back country is amazing, and the tram is superfast. The weather and conditions can be so completely different from top to bottom, it will blow your mind. The snow can change from ice to corn to powder to crud in one run, depending on your elevation and the sun's rays. Just don't lose track of where you are for even a split second, because you could die up there so easily. No little yellow out-of-bounds rope or "cliffs ahead" sign is going to save you if you miss it in the fog or if it's buried in the snow.

Sebby and I lined up a couple cheap hotel rooms, bought some three-day passes online, and flew standby on my buddy passes. We landed at ten a.m. and were skiing by one, right in town on a small hill just to get warmed up. Snow King would be considered a big hill and great place in the Midwest, but in Wyoming it was just a bump, an afterthought for most tourists. It was a place for the local school kids and hearty-legs-and-lungs skiers to hike up and schuss down. I wished I could ascend like them. I used to be fit, but never like that. The elevation out West alone took a toll on us the first day or so, but it didn't matter. Sebby and I had a ball. Each day we pushed each other higher, faster, and farther until, by four p.m., we could barely walk. We followed up with the obligatory soak in the outdoor communal hot tub at the hotel and all the food and drinks we could stomach after our mountain workout, then we slept like bears. I could hear Seb snoring away in the room next door, but never for long before I too was out like a light.

Back home Elise got two good bits of news while I was away: A piece of investment property that had been bleeding us dry finally sold, and we had been accepted onto a waiting list for adoption by our agency, pending a check for three thousand dollars to secure our place in line. Once again the money went out as fast as it came in, but it didn't matter to Elise. She filled me in excitedly as soon as I hobbled into our apartment after my guy trip.

It was only a matter of time now before we had a child of our own—anadromous or not. We could be parents in four months, or it could take four years. We hoped for earlier, but we were constantly reassured by the agency that it was going to happen for us no matter what. For Elise in particular, it seemed like a giant weight had been lifted from her shoulders.

We celebrated Valentine's Day together that year, because for once I wasn't flying somewhere for work. After a great dinner downtown, we made it back to our apartment, where I surprised Elise with everything from chocolates to flowers. I had spent an hour or more a few days earlier cutting out hundreds of egg shapes from various shades of red and pink construction paper. Before we left for dinner that evening, I had excused myself from our car to run back inside for a moment and spread them up the stairs and all over our bedroom. I knew that real rose petals could stain our bedspread and sheets. But more importantly, I knew (as silly as this sounds) that these imposters would actually impress Elise more than the actual buds for that very reason. In simple terms, it meant that I knew her better than anyone else in the world, and she appreciated that, as well as the extra effort I put into my overture of love for her. I'm happy to report that it worked like a charm.

Sebby informed me that he and Heidi were moving into their new house in March and asked me to try and keep two dates in particular free. First, *Slomocean* was to be re-launched on the first of May with a slew of new sails, a fresh engine overhaul, and a new paint job. Could I help him out?

"Sure, it'll be fun," I told him. "If I can get the day off, I'll be there with bells on."

Secondly, Heidi and Sebby announced plans for a combination Cinco de Mayo and Syttende Mai "interdependence" day house warming party for May 12.

"Mark it on your calendars!" he demanded. "You WILL both be there!"

Apparently Heidi was Norwegian, I guessed, but as for the Cinco de Mayo party on the twelfth of May, that didn't make any sense. Sebby was French Polynesian, though he did love Mexican food. I guess they had to compromise and split the difference. Maybe this was a good sign. They were, after all, moving in together.

Elise and I spent her spring break just relaxing and hoping and praying and hoping and praying. You get the picture. We were finally in a good place (no, not that we had left our crappy apartment for better digs). We were in this together, and we could see the light at the end of tunnel, even if it was only a small, flickering candle.

On May 1, I helped Sebby get *Slomocean* back in the water. She looked great. We even took her out for a sort of rechristening sail late in the day, but May on Lake Michigan was still very cold.

I got the two days off over May 12 and 13, and we attended the housewarming party for Sebastian and Heidi. Their new home was spectacular. It looked as if no expense had been spared in its creation. We didn't know anyone there except Sebby and Heidi and were planning to make an early night of it when Seb stopped and got everybody's attention for an announcement.

"I had wanted to introduce you all to my builder, my buddy, my contractor, and my friend," he stated loudly. "But he was unable to attend our little soiree this evening! Apparently," Sebastian continued as he glanced again at his cell phone, "Peter is, at this very moment, a proud new father, and very tired! Owen, his new son, is nine pounds six ounces and twenty inches. He and his wife, Heather, are both healthy, happy, and resting." Sebby was beaming. "I have the text message right here to prove it." He lifted his Blackberry up for all to attest to.

Maybe it was the wine (although she hadn't had any) or just the moment, but I saw Elise saunter over to Sebastian and whisper something in his ear flirtatiously and secretively. Sebby, however, wasn't one to keep secrets, especially if they are good. I didn't know what Elise was telling him until I saw his reaction and hers as she glanced slyly back at me. She looked like the cat that ate the canary.

"You're what?" I saw him gasp, a smile extending all the way across his face. Heidi gave Elise a huge hug. "How?"

"When?" they asked in near unison.

"The old-fashioned way!" Elise laughed as I made my way over to them.

"I thought we were going to keep our little secret a little longer," I scolded.

"Really?" Sebby questioned Elise again, almost flabbergasted.

"No one knows us here except these two," Elise countered. "What could it hurt?"

"Well, congrats, dude!" Seb turned to hug me. Then unexpectedly he got everyone's attention again and asked them to raise their glasses for a toast. "To the missionar . . . ies!" he stuttered loudly, pausing as if he hadn't thought this toast thing through. Everyone stared at Elise and me. The room grew silent. Lord only knows what they were thinking. "And . . . all . . . they have done throughout . . . the world to bring children to deserving parents!" he finally finished after stopping and starting repeatedly. His voice reached a crescendo at the end as everyone else looked oddly in our direction and Seb wiped his brow in anguished relief after pulling something awkwardly out of nothing.

It was not his normal perfectly polished moment, but then again, it was an inside joke. The four of us laughed. "That wasn't for any of them anyway," Sebby said.

"Congratulations," Heidi chimed in. "I am so happy for you both! You're going to make great parents!"

Chapter 8

You Can't Always Get What You Want
Told by Jon

Elise glowed. She literally smiled every minute of every day. I've heard other women talk about being pregnant, the morning sickness, office visits, nausea, stretch marks, and what not. It didn't sound like fun to me, but Elise just beamed and never complained a bit, an ever-present dreamy look of hope and contentment emitting from her eyes. I fell in love with her all over again. We talked and shopped and decided not to find out the sex of the baby. After all, she commented, "There really aren't that many true surprises left in the world."

"You're right, honey," I said assuredly. "Whatever you want."

What we wanted right now was a house. We wanted to bring our little bundle of joy back to a home, not some crappy apartment. We wanted to have a room for him or her all fixed up and painted the way we wanted, not what our landlord required: white, beige, tan, or light grey. We wanted windows that didn't leak and a place for all the stuff we were now rapidly accumulating. Who knew you needed so much stuff for a baby? I sure didn't. But with it all scattered about our apartment, I quickly realized, as did Elise, that we needed to get on this. We desperately needed more space.

We spoke with Sebby and Heidi a little at their housewarming party about the merits of building versus buying. We talked to Sebastian about his builder, who he was eager to recommend even after the delays he had encountered. We came to the conclusion as we spoke to Sebby though that we probably couldn't afford his guy anyway. He wanted to call Pete for us, but as fate would have it, Peter was probably busy at the moment anyway with his own new little bundle of joy. (Seb had the text on his cell phone to prove it.)

Looking around at Sebastian and Heidi's new home, we quickly became enthralled with the idea of getting everything we wanted, where we wanted it. It was a huge selling point for building. The timing issue however was just as big a negative. Maybe we should just buy a house, we both thought. On the other hand, we had seen some builders advertising in the Ozaukee Press, a local newspaper. We decided to take a drive up around Port Washington, which was cheaper than in and around Mequon, and we immediately fell in love one blustery afternoon in late May with a country subdivision and one lot in particular with a sliver of a view of Lake Michigan. We met with the contractor developing the subdivision and dove right in—after all, time was of the essence.

Elise and I usually know what we want when we see it, but you know what they say: Always check the depth of the water before diving in or you can get seriously hurt. The contractor said all the right things and showed us all the options from home plans to kitchens, baths, shingles, siding, flooring, and more. I was like a kid in a candy store. We could have everything we wanted, where we wanted it, and even when we wanted it, which was by Thanksgiving, when Elise was due. I had heard this scheduling stuff before. Sebby's voice rang in my left ear while the contractor gave his best sales pitch in my right ear. I asked stupid questions: "Can we have a paved driveway?

Can we get that new fiber-cement siding? Can that plan be modified to include a three-car garage?"

Of course the answer was yes. I should have known better. You can get anything for a price, just look at

Sebastian's house. The trouble was, I didn't ask about costs above and beyond what the builder said was included. I was too giddy and stupid to think that far ahead. I just wanted to give Elise what Sebby had given Heidi. I wanted to make her as happy as she made me. I wanted it to be perfect, and that's what the contractor promised—*this* plan on time and on budget. He had a really large team, and they had built hundreds of homes in the area. What could go wrong?

We signed that very day on the dotted line and scrambled back to Mequon and all the banks to try and arrange a building loan as well as a mortgage.

I wanted to show Seb our house plans, ask him a myriad of questions, and get his opinion on what he would or wouldn't do if he had the chance to build again. Lately, however, he was always busy with something and seemed to be spending an inordinate amount of time at the marina on his boat, so Elise and I dug into magazines and books. We watched way too much HGTV and took long strolls through Home Depot, carpet stores, and tile shops.

She decided not to go back to teaching the following fall and turned in her resignation mid-summer. We both agreed that with my work schedule it would be hard to juggle two jobs and day care and everything else that entailed. We wanted to keep it simple. Frankly, we wanted what was going to be best for our child, at least in our opinion. Elise and I had worked and waited so long for this to happen, so we didn't want to miss out on anything.

I had been hoping to move up at the airline anyway; now I needed to try and recoup some of the income we would lose from Elise's former job. But it wasn't happening anytime soon. The airline industry as a whole was still reeling from the tragedy of September 11th as well as dealing with a SARS outbreak in Asia and skyrocketing fuel prices. Many of the carriers looked like they might go bankrupt—nobody was flying on their planes. All this meant the airlines were shrinking and wouldn't be adding routes or hiring any junior pilots below me for some time. I just prayed I would keep the job that I loved so dearly.

Those days were pretty dark indeed. I looked online at various job sites on my days off, but the only industries that were hiring at all were the medical fields and IT, neither of which I was qualified for. Truth be told, I wasn't qualified to do much of anything outside of aviation, even if I did hold a bachelor's degree and had graduated summa cum laude. My degree couldn't help me now. My parents' advice from years earlier now buzzed like a chainsaw in my head as I remembered them discouraging me from such a specialized field and suggested instead a broader degree in something like engineering or finance.

Oh well, there is always truck driving school! I thought to myself, referencing a favorite line from *Top Gun*, one of the favorite movies of my youth: "What's the number for that school again, Maverick? . . . I might need it!"

I spent my days off running around looking at, and sometimes picking out, things for the house: paint samples, carpet remnants, flooring samples, and fixtures. Elise and I agreed for the most part on everything for the house and the look we wanted. Trouble was, what we wanted now didn't dovetail with the floor plan and original exterior we so hastily requested and subsequently signed for.

"Could we make some changes?" I asked the builder at the site.

"What kinds of changes?" he wondered, probably thinking of minor stuff, but he ended up asking, "Oh no . . . now what?" by the time we had almost finished rambling on.

But the customer is always right, right? He agreed to a more formal meeting with Elise and me over lunch the next day. We had twenty-four hours to get our ducks in a row. We couldn't keep doing this or we would risk significant delays.

We met at a local luncheon place and mulled over the blueprints. As we guided him through the changes we wanted to make, he told us what was still structurally and aesthetically possible at this point in the project. We felt rushed, which is never a good thing when it comes to making important decisions, but at this point we had to press on—damn the consequences. Our apartment lease was up at the end of December 2004, and we could only renew our lease for six months or more at a time, which we didn't want to do. We asked him if Thanksgiving was still possible after all the changes. He did, after all, have a large crew and had built hundreds of houses in the area. How hard could it be?

"You're pushing your luck," he told us. "Thanksgiving's not going to happen. Are you absolutely positive you need to have ALL of these changes?" he asked us again, obviously more than a little frustrated with our new demands.

"Yes, absolutely!" we admitted sheepishly yet emphatically.

"We can have you in by the end of the year. How's that?" he asked. "I will guarantee it. You won't have to re-up on your lease. I understand your situation," he said soothingly.

We never talked about the cost. He knew we were anal. He knew Elise was pregnant, and he knew what he had promised; we made double sure of that. But did we know what we had just done to ourselves? Not at all.

Psychologists say the birth of a child, a death in your immediate family, moving into a new home, the loss of a job, and starting a new job are the five most stressful things a person can encounter. We were about to try to tackle three of them at the same time, and I prayed, *Please, God, don't let anyone I know die in the next six months.* Then I added, *Please, God, lower the price of jet fuel so I can keep my job* (as if He didn't have better things to do). I couldn't fathom having to start over again at another airline, none of which were presently hiring anyway. What else was I qualified to do? The reality of a single-income family weighed heavily on me now for the first time.

***

Sebastian's house had been chosen for the Greater Milwaukee Area Parade of Homes, a great honor to be sure, so Elise and I went to it, expecting to see him and meet his builder. We looked around his house again, but neither he nor Heidi were there. Everything about the house was absolutely perfect and well thought out. We tried to talk to his builder a few times to get some free advice on our project, but he was always in the middle of a conversation with some prospective client or realtor. Everyone seemed truly impressed. Who wouldn't be? When money is no object, you can get everything and anything your heart desires (a reality Elise and I were only now beginning to fully understand).

With a baby on the way, my career progression in a holding pattern, and the loss of Elise's paycheck, money was tight. We were cutting corners that we really didn't want to, but had to. Our house project budget was growing faster than our little peanut inside Elise's tummy. We wanted hardwood floors everywhere but settled for just the dining room. We wanted granite or soapstone or at least cement countertops but were forced to choose Formica instead. The three-car garage was quickly downsized to two. We wanted custom this and custom that, like we saw in all our magazines and on HGTV, but we had to order stock.

I'm not crying, don't get me wrong, Elise and I felt so lucky in many ways, but this was really starting to bum us out. We consoled our bruised egos and dwindling bank statement with what became our new mantra: We'll get back around to that someday. We'll do that the way we really want to someday. Someday we'll go back and change that.

You get the picture. We succumbed to the reality that we were building a cookie-cutter cape cod. It would never be as special or unique as Sebby's home or featured in some home show, but in the end what we realized was that it would be *our* cookie-cutter cape cod and a great place to raise a family.

We were both so happy. The last few years had been so depressing that it felt odd to actually feel "sunny" again. We loved our newfound gestational bliss, although we both still fretted about the very real possibility of a miscarriage. Elise's OBGYN was super happy for us, but she always cautioned us to this fact. We weren't out of the woods yet and wouldn't be for some time. Besides that though, everything was finally falling into place. How's that for optimism?

Then one day the phone rang, and I answered. It was the adoption agency. I was so happy watching Elise get bigger and busy with work and the house that I had forgotten about the agency, the waiting list, and our plans to adopt. I nearly fell over backward and dropped the receiver when the nice lady on the other end of the line gave me the news: They had a baby for us, a little girl. Elise would probably drive off the road or faint right then and there in some store if I told her the news over the phone. I couldn't take that chance, but I needed her to come home right away. This was way too important.

"Where are you?" I asked as soon as she answered my call.

"Up by Target," she responded. "Why? You sound like something's wrong."

"I need you to come home now," I said earnestly.

"Can it wait? I'm in the car and have two more errands to run."

"Just get home as quickly as you can," I said emphatically.

"What is it? What is wrong?"

"Nothing . . . Just come home as soon as you can. We need to talk." I hung up the phone so I wouldn't spill the beans.

Elise skipped out on her remaining errands and sped home. When she came in the door, she demanded, "What is the big deal, Jon? What is going on?"

"Honey . . ." I began, but I didn't know how to start. "You need to take a seat."

But she was already sitting. I hadn't noticed because I was so deep in my own thoughts. My head was spinning out of control. Should we adopt the little girl? Should we tell the agency that we were actually pregnant? (In hindsight, Elise and I probably should have done that a while back, I guess.) Would we be forced to pass on the adoption if they found out we were pregnant? Maybe we shouldn't tell them. What if we passed on the adoption to another deserving couple and Elise had a miscarriage again? Would we go back into the pool of prospective parents? Would we go back to the end of the line? What if the agency was so mad at us they kicked us off the list and out of the program?

All these thoughts and questions whirled around my brain as I simultaneously thought of how to break the news to Elise. My face must have been as animated as a comic as she studied me and tried to guess what was so important that she had to rush home. I had to stop thinking just to catch my breath. It was as if I had just run a race. (Man, I was out of shape.) I just stood there sweating, and I could barely breathe, but I managed to spit out, "The agency called. . . . A birth mother has selected us for her little girl. She's due in three months!"

Elise's eyes grew as big as saucers, as only then did she begin to share in the thoughts and questions I had been drowning in for the last twenty-five minutes. We just stared at each other in some kind of futile telepathic brainstorming session, but there were just too many things to ponder.

I wondered where adopting a child while building a house, along with having a child while moving into a new home after quitting a job and working your ass off landed on the old psychologist stress-o-meter thing-a-ma-jiggy. Did they make a stress meter that registered that high? I was pretty sure we were already off the chart. What more could anyone throw at us at this point? Yet as I finally got out of my own head and looked at Elise, she seemed oddly calm. She could tell I was buzzing, but she helped calm me down as well, like always.

"Let's talk about it," she began simply. "Let's talk this thing through. All we really need to figure out is what is right for us."

Elise made it sound so simple. She was so tranquil. I, on the other hand, was a wreck. We couldn't just play paper-scissor-rock or say "eeny meeny miny moe" on this one. We couldn't make a decision now and go back later and redo it like kitchen countertops or paint colors. This was a one time—and one time only—life-altering commitment.

We talked and talked and talked. What if we adopted her and had a baby as well? Two kids sounded perfect. Maybe Elise's pregnancy was in fact a one-in-a-million miracle that all the specialists in the world could never explain. What were the odds we would ever conceive again? On the other hand, she *had* gotten pregnant. Maybe we finally knew what we were doing. What if we passed on the adoption and Elise subsequently miscarried, then what? That was the worst-case scenario. Would we kick ourselves when we went back into the waiting pool at the agency, or would they drop us from the program entirely?

We discussed all these things, up one side and down the other. After trying to consider every conceivable angle, I started to calm down, but that doesn't mean Elise and I came together on an answer, or even agreed. Believe it or not, I was the one who still wanted to adopt. I was so scared of going through another miscarriage, of having to pick up the pieces and start over. I knew Elise would someday want more kids, so I clung to the notion that a bird in the hand was worth two in a bush. Elise was more confident in her body and our pregnancy than me. She also brought up the reality that it would be like having twins. "Two babies isn't twice as hard. It's an exponential thing. Do you think you're ready for that?" Elise asked me, trying to win a point or two. "I think we need to tell the agency we are pregnant and ask a few questions."

***

Sleep is something that normal people do. But our situation was anything but normal at that moment, so I couldn't sleep. Elise was even having trouble. Maybe she wasn't as calm, confident, and content with this decision as she let on. Then again, maybe it was her back or feet or our grapefruit-sized little peanut in her belly and its nocturnal exercise routines that were keeping her awake. We tossed and turned all night and called the agency in the morning. We talked with them for a long time, and it helped a lot. Unlike our experience signing the papers on the house, we didn't give the agency a definitive answer even as the same one took shape for both of us. Elise and I tended to be pretty quick, proactive, and definitive with our decisions, but this was the hardest decision we ever had to make.

We agreed to sleep on it (ironically) until I got back from my next trip. And as the conclusions we had struggled with began to sink in, I finally began to get some real sleep. This lack of sleep thing, I counseled myself, was just Mother Nature's way of preparing future daddies for the inevitable.

For the first time, I started to let myself truly believe in our pregnancy. Maybe Elise wouldn't lose the baby this time. I began to actually think of myself as a daddy. What could I offer up in terms of knowledge and ideas? What did I know about babies and diapers and ear infections and the like? What if it was a girl? How would I connect with her? What if it was a boy and he was very different from me? My head was spinning again. I needed more sleep. If Mother Nature was trying to whip me into shape, it wasn't working. I was already exhausted. If what I had heard about all the sleepless nights and early mornings was fact, I was nowhere near ready to be a dad. I craved rest, but my brain was on some weird adrenaline overdose and couldn't seem to stop working.

When I got back from my trip, it was obvious that Elise was comfortable with our decision, and to be honest, I was almost there too. We called the agency, passed on the adoption, and asked to stay on the waiting list, at least until we had our baby. We didn't want to have to start all over again if the worst happened. It was an extremely tough call to make and, in some ways, a decision that will haunt me for the rest of life. I wonder where that little girl is to this day. I hope she got great parents. I know I would have loved her even though we never got a chance to meet.

Chapter 9

You Can't Be Lucky and Good
Told by Sebastian

Living with Heidi was great. It was like we were married, only better, because we weren't. The house was wonderful. My condo in the Third Ward sold in April, and we finally got all of Heidi's stuff out of her aunt's place in Whitefish Bay just in time to unpack and get ready for our housewarming party. And *Slomocean* looked great now with her new red-and-blue paint job, so everything was in its place.

It all just seemed right. I felt lucky, and that's always a good thing. Heidi was traveling on and off for work and competing in various 5Ks, 10Ks, and triathlons. I was busy at New Millennium, which was now only a scant two miles away. In short, it was perfect—too perfect, even for me.

Looking back, it all started one day when I was at home and Heidi got the mail. She never looked through my stuff or opened anything that wasn't for her, and I returned that respect. She shouldn't have even questioned anything, but the return address on my bill seemed just too odd, I guess, not to ask.

"What is this letter from this cryogenics place about?" she asked. "Is this junk? Should I throw it away or what?" she continued louder, as I was in the bathroom.

"No, keep it," I said abruptly. "It's for me. I'll take care of it."

"Take care of what?" Heidi wanted to know. "Is it a bill?"

"Yeah."

"For what?" she asked again.

No big deal, I thought to myself as I sat on the toilet. *I'll just tell her.*

You know, some things never go quite as you plan, and in retrospect, maybe I should have handled it differently, but I didn't. I came out of the bathroom, sat on one of the stools at our kitchen island, and nonchalantly told Heidi about my vasectomy and all the sperm that I had frozen.

"This is my annual bill from the cryo lab." Open, honest . . . what every woman wants from her man, right? WRONG! Her comments and questions came at me so fast and furious I wasn't sure what she was really angry about.

"When did you get a vasectomy? Why did you get a vasectomy?" Her voice was getting louder and more agitated. "Why didn't you tell me this, like, A YEAR AGO? Were you ever going to tell me?"

"Sure I was, baby. It's no big deal. Really!" I pleaded with her.

"Don't *baby* me!"

"We can still have kids if and when—" I paused as those words slipped out of my mouth for the first time in my life, "we want them . . . honey," I continued weakly.

I really only hesitated for a moment, honest. After all, it was not only the first time I had ever spoken those words, it was, in that split second, the first time I had ever even considered wanting to be a parent. Did I really desire that lifetime commitment with another person—woman or child? I was either really in love or losing my mind.

I stated it matter of fact like, but apparently my hesitation and the uptick in my voice at the end of my grand declaration left it all hanging out in space as more of a question. Heidi was suddenly quiet, thinking and gathering up her emotions. She almost began again but stopped, silently staring at me, then the floor, and finally out our kitchen window.

"I froze a ton of the stuff for just *that* reason," I added politely, breaking the silence.

"You never told me! Why didn't you just tell me?"

"For just *this* reason," I said. I really didn't have an answer.

"What reason?"

"Look at you. . . . . You're acting a little crazy right now," I added softly.

"This isn't crazy!" she began anew. "Do you want to see crazy? Trust me, Sebastian, you DO NOT want to see my brand of crazy!" Heidi paused only briefly to gather herself. "Trust me!" she reiterated, as if victorious somehow. "I have been on the pill like forever. For a long time after we met, you used condoms." Heidi now looked confused. "What is up with you? Why wouldn't you just tell me?" she demanded again. "Didn't you think someday, if we got serious, I would find out? I want to have kids someday. I was beginning to think maybe we would get married someday. I want to make babies the old-fashioned way too!" Heidi said, referring to Jon and Elise. "I don't want some doctor sticking a turkey baster up there and shooting your guy stuff in me. . . . That's your job!" Heidi began to well up. "Conception should be beautiful, memorable, fun. That doesn't sound very fun. This ruins everything." She was sobbing now.

"No, it doesn't," I countered delicately. "It's no big deal . . . really."

"It *is* a big deal!" she replied, trying to choke back more tears. "It's about trust and honesty. I could have gone off the pill a year or more ago. Did you ever think of that? And you," she paused, "I get it when we first started dating, but why did you continue using condoms for so long? Did you think I was some sort of skank or had STDs or something? You knew I was on the pill. Or were you still seeing other girls when I was away on business?"

"No . . . No . . . No . . . . *No!*" I said emphatically. "Ever since I met you, there have been no other women, Heidi,

I swear." And it was the truth, but I could tell she was skeptical.

"I think you weren't monogamous until you stopped using them, that's what I think!" she decided. "Let's see . . . that was at least five or six months into it. Knowing what I think I do of your past and other asshole men like you, I bet that there were at least three or four other women." She was now acting more like the lead prosecutorial attorney in some defamation of character trial. "Does that sound about right to you?"

"No!" I said, as if I should have to testify in my own defense. I had done nothing wrong.

"There has never been another woman in my bed, or anywhere for that matter, since I met you. I swear. Honest! You have to believe me, Heidi. I love you soooo much!" I was looking for any crack in her new armor and trying to swing the jury that was obviously close to a decision in her mind somehow in my favor, but she wouldn't listen any longer. For the moment at least, she had made up her mind. I could only hope that her decision wasn't final.

Fortunately, or perhaps not, she was really busy with work and traveling. This gave us both the space we needed—for her, the time to sort through her emotions; for me, the time to forget that it ever happened, concentrate on work, and do a little sailing. The wind and the lake always helped clear my mind. I was asked to crew in the Chicago-Mac race on a big J/Boat named *Miss Ann Thropic* by my old boss at Promise. Peter wanted to present my house in some parade of homes, and Heidi would be away on work. So I agreed. Unfortunately it didn't seem to help.

Beyond this stupid sperm thing with Heidi, I couldn't seem to forget the conversation I had had with Heather. Jeez, it had been almost a year. Why couldn't I get over this? Was there some kid out there who looked like me?

Why was this nagging at me so much? Would he hate me? Did he even exist at all? If so, did he even know who his real father was? I mean, did he know he was adopted? And what if the *he* in the back of my mind was a *she*? I had enough girl problems; I couldn't handle anymore.

My work was beginning to suffer. I needed to clear my head, but since sailing on beautiful, windy, clear summer days didn't seem to help, I decided to go the other way—cloud it up, you know. I figured I'd peer into the fog and find the bottom of this or whatever else bubbled up out of the morass in my mind. Maybe I needed to run aground and get stuck instead of running away from my thoughts. In short, I needed to get a good drunk on, so I decided to call Jon. Boy scout that he was, I knew he would not only sit there and listen, he wouldn't drink himself down with me, and he would get me home safe. He was a good friend.

We went to a local bar and grill for no other reason than it was close. Although the food there was always good, I was intent on not wasting the space in my belly on anything but booze. I guess the old saying was true—she was driving me to drink, and Heidi really was. But that night, Jon was *actually* driving me to drink. I should have known better than to think it would help. He picked me up at seven p.m., and I don't remember making it home, but I awoke late the next morning sprawled out on top of my California king bed still in my clothes, reeking of smoke (neither Jon nor I smoke), with a foot-long sub sandwich, still in its bag, literally smooshed to pieces underneath my stomach and chest. I think it was turkey, bacon, and guac on whole wheat. My head was pounding, and I couldn't remember a thing, but obviously last night hadn't worked. I needed another solution.

All I understood at that moment as I willed my body up off the bed and into the bathroom for a glass of water and a long shower was how empty and silent the house felt. Seeing Heidi's stuff on the counter, her silk bathrobe hanging on a hook over the door, made me lose it. I crawled into the shower, turned on the water, sat down on the tile floor, and cried. I missed her so much. I needed her even more.

***

The next week, I did it up right and cleaned the house from top to bottom. Yep, I did it myself; I didn't even wait for our cleaning lady. She wouldn't be there until Friday, but Heidi was due back Thursday late afternoon. I made reservations at a great place downtown overlooking the lake, within walking distance of McKinley Marina. I figured maybe we could spend the night on the boat just like old times. I planned out everything and waited for Heidi to arrive. When she did, I told her of our dinner plans and the fun evening I had in store for us, but she seemed distant and preoccupied. I guess she still had a few reservations of her own.

After work on Friday, I came home for a quick shower and a change of clothes. She had worked out of our home office all day and was already gorgeous.

"I'm starving!" I declared excitedly. "Let's go get something to eat."

It was a perfect early August night, and Heidi looked as beautiful as ever sitting next to me in my convertible as we drove down Lake Shore Drive with the top down. Her spiky, blonde, pixie-cut hair was jutting out in every crazy direction from behind her wayfarer sunglasses. She had chosen a low-cut, loose-fitting linen blouse and a short denim skirt for the evening. Her long, tan legs were delicately crossed at the ankles as she sank deeper into the leather passenger seat of my Porsche. She was quiet, even more so than usual of late, and mostly stared straight ahead, commenting only occasionally on the beautiful houses along the street. I was admiring the view as well, but I didn't notice the houses. Besides driving, Heidi had my undivided attention.

The restaurant was awesome, and the conversation between us flowed a little better as the dinner and drinks continued. Somewhere in the middle of a shared piece of cheesecake, I suggested staying on the boat. I could tell she had preordained the notion that I had sex on the brain, as it had been awhile and, well, anytime we spent an evening on *Slomocean* that's usually what we ended up doing. In an effort to divert my all-too-obvious intentions, I suggested that neither of us was sober enough to drive and that we would just talk and snuggle on the boat before heading home if she didn't want to stay there. Finally, reluctantly, she agreed.

We walked slowly along the beach, talking in bits and spurts about anything and everything and yet nothing of substance. I told her some more about my week, and she recalled some more about hers. I told her about my evening with Jon, although I had to embellish a bit, because I still really didn't remember that much. I left out the details of the morning after and hoped she hadn't noticed any lingering smell of smoke in our house. (Heidi hated smokers.)

As we came up to my slip, I took her hand to both lead and help her in her high heels from the dock onto the boat. I confessed my love for her, bent down on one knee, and did what only weeks ago I had never thought possible.

"Will you marry me?" I asked simply and sweetly, abruptly and awkwardly. "You make me so happy," I told her softly. "We are perfect together. I'm sorry it took me so long to grow up and figure out what is really important, but I know now that you are the most important thing in my life! I love you."

I held her gaze as I looked longingly up at her, seeing that she was stunned by my proposal. It was just the reaction I had hoped for—shock and awe. I sensed she wanted to say something, but Heidi was way too reserved to just jump into my arms and shriek yes like some school girl upon being asked to the senior prom. I knew that about her. I loved that about her. I loved everything about Heidi.

It was perfect. The moonlight, the water, her eyes locked on mine. I smiled up at her, taking in everything. I knew I would remember this night forever. She slowly summoned her voice, and after what had seemed like an eternity (but in reality was a mere minute or less), Heidi said softly, simply, and sadly, "I can't. I'm sorry, Sebastian," and then there was silence.

I almost fell off the boat but saved my balance by continuing to hold onto her outstretched hand. (How awkward and pathetic is that?) Still gazing up at her beautiful blue eyes, I noticed a small tear slowly cascade down her cheek and fall into the lake.

I will remember that night, her eyes, and those words forever. It was not the response I expected.

Chapter 10

If You Can't be with the one You Love . . .
Like the One You're With
Told by Jon

Sebby called me up and wanted to go out. It was late July 2004, and he had just gotten back from the Chicago-Mac sailboat race, having crewed on some really rich guy's fifty-foot J/Boat. Apparently that was why he hadn't been around for the Greater Milwaukee Area Parade of Homes. I was anxious to hear all about the race and pick his brain over what was going on with our build, as well as drop some hot stock ideas I had fermenting in my brain for his perusal. I needed to make some real money really quickly, and I figured Sebby was just the man to help me do it. I also wanted to tell him all about the agency and the adoption and everything. I could really use a few beers and suggested a local pub and restaurant nearby. He asked if I would pick him up and sounded as if he really needed to talk as well.

I went to Sebby's at seven the next evening and, we headed immediately to the bar, which was only a few miles away. I started right in on him with questions about the race, the house, and work, but he seemed disinterested in any meaningful conversation. It was clear from the start this wasn't going to be a discussion but rather some bizarre counseling session once again for Sebastian, and Sebastian alone. I would feed him alcohol and get him to reveal his deepest, darkest, innermost feelings, then report back to him in the morning or the next week as to what those actually were—after he had sobered up, of course. So much for hot stocks and big yachts.

We did talk a little about the decision Elise and I had come to regarding the adoption, but that only seemed to dredge up his college paternity fears with Leah Aspen again.

"I can't believe you're still hung up on that, man!" I said, trying to cheer him up. "That was a long time ago. You used condoms back then, right? She was probably on the pill anyway."

"No, dude," he admitted. "She was really religious. I doubt it—I don't remember asking her." He stopped talking and ordered up another round.

"Well, you used a condom, so I am sure it didn't—"

Sebastian interrupted me mid-sentence, "Thing is, Jon . . . I've been racking my brain on and off for the past year. I can't remember, you know. Some nights, the parties at the Sigma house were crazy. What if there's a kid out there somewhere—"

Then I interrupted Sebby, "I'm sure you would have found out back then from her. If that was the case, you would have heard somehow. I'm sure it didn't happen that way, or Leah would have told you. Now, let's get some food."

"No food," Seb said, pounding his fist on the table abruptly and starting to talk like a caveman. "Only drink." He sounded stupid and a little crazy. "Food: waste of space. Need more booze," he announced as he flagged down our waitress.

Somewhere in the middle of our third round, Sebastian came out of his funk and changed the subject to Heidi. By now we were both feeling pretty good, and he started asking me crazy questions about what it was really like being married and committed and what not. He also asked me what it was like becoming a dad. I figured he was still getting used to the whole cohabitation thing with Heidi and just needed some reassurances that it was a good deal, but it soon became abundantly clear he was actually considering upping the ante. He told me about their big fight and her insecurities. He told me how much he loved her and how he didn't want to lose her, confiding in me how much he liked living with her and how it was the best decision he had ever made.

I needed to sober up a bit, so I switched to water. "You know what they say about whiskey, Seb?" I chided him.

"Yeah, I know, that it was invented so the Irish wouldn't rule the world," he replied exhaustedly.

"Well, yes, but I was thinking of another adage actually: Whiskey is like a woman's breasts: One is not enough, and three is too many!"

Sebby thought about my revelation for a bit before responding, "Too many, Jon? Man, you have lived a sheltered life. There is NO such thing as too many breasts, I can assure you!"

"I think maybe you should lay off the hard stuff and at least switch to beer," I told him admonishingly.

"Pussy!" he yelled at me across our table. "You're such a Boy Scout!"

"You're drunk!" I shot back sternly.

"That's the idea!" he countered, sitting up briefly from a slouched position in our booth. "I thought you were onboard?" He leaned in at me from across the booth.

"What are you talking about, Seb?" I asked incredulously. "I don't know where you're coming from. What has gotten into you?"

"PUSSY," he said again sullenly. "I thought you were my friend!"

By his fourth or fifth Seven and Seven, I figured that he had unloaded everything. Then Sebby dropped a bombshell. "I'm going to ask her to marry me, Jon," he said, beginning to slur his speech. "I have to, or I'm going to lose her."

"You have to . . . or you want to?" I asked, trying to clarify his intentions.

"I want to," he declared emphatically. "I really love

her. She's the one!"

"Are you sure?" I asked again. "This is a really big step, man. A life-changing decision; you just moved in together. This is going pretty fast."

"No, man, I love her . . . I'm sure," he admitted slowly. "It's going to be awesome!" He raised his empty glass in some form of awkward toast, then he proceeded to fill me in on his plan to pop the big question. I had to admit it sounded great. At that moment I wished I could ask Elise to marry me again, knowing I could do it better if only I could go back in time.

I guess the whiskey finally made it to the right side of his brain, and he turned ugly for a while. It was late now, the kitchen at the pub had long since closed, and the only thing open after eleven p.m. in sleepy suburban Mequon on a weeknight was a sub shop.

"I'm leaving," I announced.

"I'm hungry." He was now completely drunk. "Let's get some food, dude."

"Come on, man, I'm taking you home," I said, persuading him to get up. I needed to get some sleep.

***

Sebby didn't call the next weekend, even though I fully expected to hear his exuberant voice on the other end of the phone triumphantly announcing his impending marriage to the magnificent Heidi as she laughed in the background like a giddy little school girl. I figured they were so busy rolling around in bed or rocking the boat that they just didn't have time. After a few more days, however, I began to worry. Maybe Sebby was mad at me for some reason I wasn't aware of. Maybe I had said something to piss him off at the bar. I couldn't think of anything, though it had ended on a rough note when I had to corral him back into my car after he let loose some tirade about not enough guacamole on his sub sandwich. I will never forget the look in that poor high school boy's eyes as Sebby demanded another scoop of guac on his turkey bacon sub. "I'm going to have to charge you extra for that sir," the boy said politely.

"I don't give a fuck, JUNIOR!" Sebby declared loudly."More *green*, I want *more green*."

It was embarrassing, and he was drunk, so I took him home.

By now Elise was in full-on gestational mom-to-be bliss, and her tummy was starting to expand at an ever-rapid pace. She was in no mood to go out or do anything. I on the other hand was starting to go a little stir crazy even on my days off at home. I didn't need to do any more nesting. I needed to go out, so I tried to call Sebby and invite myself over for a celebratory beer.

He's always ready to cut out early from work or go out at a moment's notice, I thought to myself. But his phones were continually off or busy, so I decided to just drive over to his place and coerce him into going out when I got back from my next trip. Maybe he would share some good tidbits, not the details of how he proposed and how she responded (blah blah blah, I already knew how it was going to go down from our conversation at the pub). I wanted to hear about the after party. I wanted to know the rest of the story that evening, even though by now I had learned a thing or two about Sebby: The more serious he was with a woman, the less likely he was to spill the beans. Conversely the opposite was always true: If it was a simple fling, he would tell me everything, and I do mean everything. That, in a nutshell, was how I knew how serious Sebastian was about Heidi long before he told me he was going to ask her to marry him. With Heidi, Sebastian never said anything. He was obviously deeply in love.

I was not prepared for what I confronted. He came to the door in a dirty terry-cloth bathrobe. He hadn't shaved in days. Hell, he probably hadn't showered in days. He smelled of body odor and booze. His wavy hair was all tangled and matted down. His teeth were yellow, and his eyes were red—no, I take that back; his eyes were dead. I had never seen Sebby as devastated as this. Something was drastically wrong.

"She said no, okay?" Sebastian stated abruptly as he stepped back from the door. I hadn't even said hello yet. "Go away and leave me alone!" He sounded like some insolent child. "I really don't want to talk right now. I'll call you, man. You're a good friend checking in on me like this, but I'll be fine," he declared softly. "I'll call you sometime."

"You sure?" I asked half-heartedly, still shocked that Heidi had said no.

"Dude, I'm fine, okay?" He finally looked up from the ground to catch my look of concern and disbelief. Then he closed the door.

***

August flew by with house projects and office visits. September almost ended without a word from Sebby, but when Elise and I decided to invite him over for a fall cookout, he amazingly agreed. He confided in us the story of his proposal and her subsequent refusal. He told us how quiet the house was and how alone he felt. What Sebastian didn't tell us until we asked was that Heidi had already moved out.

"Even after she said no," he began, "I still thought we would live together. I figured it was just a rough patch, you know, a fight. I figured we'd get through it. But I wasn't the only one keeping secrets." Apparently Heidi had been offered a big promotion earlier in the summer but hadn't told Sebastian because it was a permanent position as an advertising and marketing director in New York City. If Heidi accepted the position, she would have to move. Maybe Sebastian's cryo bill and her insecurities about other women and trust were the final straw.

"So much for honesty and commitment," Sebby said snidely. "I am never going down that path again. No commitments . . . ever!" He was defiant, and for rest of the evening he was mostly silent, preferring instead to listen to Elise and I ramble on about everything in our lives. We felt bad for him.

Three weeks later we got an invite in the mail for a Halloween party at, of all places, Sebby's. Costumes mandatory, drinks on the house, bring your pjs, and leave your keys. We were stunned. This didn't sound like the man we had seen only weeks earlier crushed, devastated, and brokenhearted. This sounded like good old Sebastian Everest Koh.

Elise didn't want to go at first. She was getting really big and was tired all the time. I wanted to go, but she was in no mood to let me go alone. I rubbed my neck, as my collar felt a little tight. Maybe she would let go of the leash, if only for one night.

"I just don't want to go. Don't you want to stay home with me?" she asked.

I really didn't. I wanted to go to the party. There were bound to be lots of people there. It could be fun.

"I don't want to go, and I don't want you to go without me," Elise said sternly. "I bet Sebby invited every beautiful woman under thirty on the north shore."

That thought had occurred to me as well. *It doesn't matter where you get your appetite as long as you eat at home,* I told myself. I needed a distraction. We hadn't made love in three months, and I felt like I was going to burst. I was like a walking billboard for Viagra, except I was drug free—no ED here. Why wasn't Mother Nature preparing my body in some way for hibernation down there? After all, Elise was going through all kinds of changes.

"I am not going to do anything! Are you kidding, Elise?

I'll just go and be Sebastian's wing man," I said innocently enough.

"Jon . . . Sebastian of all people doesn't need a wing man," Elise countered. "You're just going to gawk at all those thin, pretty girls who hang on Sebby like stink on a skunk. They'll probably all be wearing naughty nurse costumes, "Baywatch" swimsuits, and little school girl skirts," Elise said disgustedly. (Admittedly, that thought had also occurred to me.) "You don't want to show up there with your fat wife," she said, deflated. "What would I even go as?" she asked. "It doesn't matter. You don't want me to go anyway. Just go!" She was trying her hand at reverse psychology momentarily. Then she stopped and added. "But don't you dare—"

"What?" I started to prod, but decided not to go there. "Honey, I want you to go. . . I want us to go!" I insisted. "You can go as a pumpkin," I said, trying to be sweet. "You can be my pumpkin." I poured on the sugar.

Somehow it worked. I got my way. We were going to the costume party—Elise as a pumpkin and me as a big spotted cow. I love that beer. I doubted anyone there would understand it as the reason for my costume selection, but who cares.

Three Saturday nights later, a girl in her mid-twenties greeted us at Sebby's door, and we entered the foyer. The house was all decked out for the occasion.

"I'm Taryn," she announced as she led us into the living room like we'd never been there before. "You can put your pjs," she paused, then added seductively, looking over her shoulder back at us, "if you brought any, that is, in any of the bedrooms and your keys in the bucket over there." She pointed toward the kitchen and a large orange Home Depot bucket.

"I'm familiar," I said nonchalantly, trying to be cool.

It was a frat party for adults. The house was awash

in alcohol, crazy costumes, loud conversations, and even louder music. Taryn was wearing a tight-fitting, black-and-white shirt over black leggings and high heels. She was very attractive, but who was noticing? My underused and underappreciated libido was killing me. Her shirt had an electrical wall outlet imprinted on both sides of it, and it hung down over her hips so the electrical receptacles, if that's what you would choose to call them (and I would), were in the anatomically correct positions both front and back (if you get my drift). Sebby saw us and came over wearing what could only be described as the giant head of an extension cord around his waist. It was awesome.

"You made it!" he proclaimed jubilantly as if we were the guests of honor or something. Sebastian tried to give Elise a hug, but between her big belly (well hidden inside her pumpkin costume) and the two large tinfoil prongs sticking out from his hips, it wasn't happening.

Elise looked at me, rolled her eyes disgustedly, and mouthed, "I told you so."

I rubbed my neck, and we left early.

Chapter 11

When it Rains it Pours
Told By Peter

Being chosen for Greater Milwaukee Area Parade of Homes the summer of 2004 was incredible. I couldn't believe my luck. Over a week's time, hundreds, if not thousands, of people took off their shoes, put on little paper booties, and admired Sebby's house and my handiwork. He was so gracious in letting me put it on display while he was away. I didn't know what to do or say to thank him and Heidi, but I couldn't ask for better PR than a house filled with fine furniture and an original style that somehow seamlessly blended Polynesian culture, Asian influences, Shaker minimalism, and modern architecture. Everybody seemed to like it. For one thing, it was original, not some cookie-cutter vinyl box. Heather was proud of me. Owen was proud of me. Heck, even Heather's dad gave me a pat on the back after having a look around. I must have gotten a hundred business cards from various contractors and realtors that week, and my phone started ringing off the hook.

Heather took on the roll of administrative assistant and bookkeeper that fall, soon filling my schedule with clients through the winter and into 2005. I even booked two more homes. I was so happy.

I sent Sebastian a bottle of Johnny Walker Blue; it was all I could think of to thank him. I tried to call him a few times, but he was never around or his phone was off. I didn't have Heidi's number, or I would have called her too, but I talked to her aunt, who told me things weren't good between Sebastian and Heidi and that Heidi was moving to New York. I was stunned but didn't tell Heather.

I spent the fall and winter on kitchen and bath remodels while also meeting with the two clients on their upcoming home projects. I wanted to handle everything professionally and perfectly. No more saying yes just to win their business. I was upfront and honest and laid out the process for them step by step, showing them all the expected costs line by line. They were both very appreciative and asked me repeatedly for my input on their projects.

As fun as it was guiding new clients toward their dreams, pushing a wall out here on blueprints or adding wainscoting there to give it that custom touch, the most fun by far was coming home to Heather and Owen, who was growing up so fast. He was already sitting up and trying to crawl as well as eating solid foods. Heather was a great mom and a huge help to me. Frankly I don't know how she did it all, juggling feedings and naps with phone calls, bills, cleaning the house, and running errands. She was busier than me, but she seemed really happy too.

I broke ground in early April 2005 on the first of my two new homes for that year and dove right in framing it up. Heather only insisted I stay home for an early breakfast and be back for supper every weeknight in order to see Owen. She prohibited me from working on Saturdays and Sundays, although occasionally it was a necessity to make up for the inevitable rain delay or whatever else didn't go as planned on the project. Things were going along great until we got some bad news: Heather's dad was diagnosed with cancer. He would probably need chemo, radiation, and surgery, and he would also need a lot of help. Unfortunately that job landed for the most part on Heather during the week, with me trying to help as much as I could on the weekends.

One afternoon, we got an invitation out of nowhere to see Sebastian off on some journey. Apparently he was going to sail his boat all the way to the Caribbean. But on the day of the bon voyage party and send off, Heather's father was scheduled for surgery. We couldn't attend and didn't feel much like partying anyway, as we were both pretty tired. And even though we weren't able to make it to the party, Sebby remembered Owen's birthday and sent him a card.

That summer after Heather's dad's surgery, we got more bad news. Apparently the doctors hadn't gotten all the cancer, and it spread. As they had predicted and we had feared, Heather's dad would need chemotherapy and radiation. It didn't sound good, but I soldiered on, framing the first house, doing much of it myself and soon becoming overwhelmed and behind schedule again. I was forced to outsource more of the framing, roofing, and sheathing (my favorite parts) than I had planned, but it got me back on track quickly.

By late summer 2005, the first house was nearly enclosed, and I turned over most of the inside work to other licensed professionals, plumbers, and electricians. I started on the second house and began the process all over again. I was loving it. On the home front, Heather's dad completed his second round of chemo and was very weak, but the doctors were optimistic, which was welcome news.

I got a postcard that fall in the mail with only a buxom woman's cleavage in a red string bikini top on the picture with the caption, "Wish You Were Here?" (instead of "Wish You Were Here!") It was postmarked from the Florida Keys, and on the back, Sebby had written, "Drinking big martinis and watching little bikinis!" I had a good chuckle over that, but Heather wasn't amused.

By the time the first snow fell in late November, the second house was nearly enclosed and the first house was finished—on schedule and under budget. *Damn, I'm good*, I congratulated myself. In celebration, I booked a sitter and took Heather out to a fancy place downtown. We stayed out late and stayed up late. It was our first night away from

Owen as well as our first night together in a long time.

"We need to do this more often," I insisted as I lay in bed with her afterward. She agreed, and we both fell asleep. It was awesome—so awesome. It was good—too good.

Heather had stopped taking the pill when she found out she was pregnant with Owen after the antibiotic oops, and she never went back on them again after he was born. Yep, you guessed right. The period fairy missed our house again that December. Santa found it though. He gave Owen every plastic hammer, saw, drill, and wrench he could carry. I gave Heather a set of diamond earrings. She gave me an envelope containing a new contract for another house. It hadn't been signed yet, but she said, "The couple loved what they saw so far. They can't wait to meet you after Christmas." They were away for two weeks over the holidays and only asked one thing: Could I start in early spring 2006? They wanted to lock me in before somebody else "got me," according to Heather. She was beaming. It was the best Christmas present I had ever gotten—not the contract, but her proud look. I loved her so much, and we made a great team. Steglin and Son Homes, LLC was on the map.

Chapter 12

There's an Old Kid in Town
Told by Sebby

Somewhere along the line I found the courage to get back out there again. It was the checkout line at the grocery store, to be exact. Taryn, a beautiful young brunette from Fox Point, spilled her container of cherry tomatoes on the ground in front of me, and I bent down to start picking them up. Turns out I picked her up as well, and before long, I was back in the saddle again. We dated for almost three months but never made a lasting connection. I think she knew I was on the rebound, and she may have thought I was too old for her. I don't really know.

I started going downtown again, but Milwaukee wasn't the same city in the winter and seemed to have changed since my time in the Third Ward. It wasn't that long ago, was it? Maybe I was the one who had changed. Perhaps I was getting old, but I tried to avoid those thoughts. I called Jon a few times, wondering if he wanted to go out downtown. But as the new proud papa of a bouncing baby girl named Bergen, he seemed more than happy to spend every waking moment with her and Elise when he wasn't flying all over the world. I called Peter, and it was much the same thing. He was always busy with work or playing with his son. I was on my own in more ways than one.

***

It didn't really hit me until one Sunday morning in February. I had met a girl downtown three weeks earlier and gone out with her a few times. Her name, ironically, was Summer. We were taking it slow, and I liked her. On Valentine's evening, we had a great dinner and ended up back at my place. The next morning as I lay there in a tangled mess of blankets, pillows, and clothing, I channel surfed over to VH1 Classic just for the music. I liked doing that on lazy Sunday mornings, and it had become somewhat of a routine.

Summer was in the bathroom in her bra and panties brushing her teeth and hair when, noticing the flickering of my television off the mirror, she asked me what I was watching.

"Sports," I said stupidly, knowing full well she could hear the music through the glass door.

"Who's playing?" she asked.

Is she kidding? I thought. *It's ten o'clock on a Sunday morning.* "It's a repeat of last night's Bucks-Pistons game," I blurted out. In reality it was a Fleetwood Mac retrospective of their best songs, and it sounded pretty good, but I couldn't bring myself to admit to her that I was somewhat addicted to VH1. That just seemed pathetic, so I just lay there staring at the ceiling as I listened.

"Do you always listen to music over sports on the TV?" Summer asked.

I didn't answer.

"Who's your favorite player?" She sauntered out of bathroom toward me.

The old Sebastian would have just shut up right then and there and gone back to doing what I did best, and by her body language, I could tell she was interested. That morning, however, and for no reason in particular, I just didn't care anymore. Summer was a great girl, and looking at her in the morning light, I'll admit for a split second I considered myself crazy, but I was no longer interested in casual sex.

"Stevie Nicks!" I said to see if she would laugh.

Summer was now sitting on the corner of the bed and looking at the TV as well." Who does he play for?" she asked naively. "The Bucks or the Pistons?"

"The Pistons," I said, flabbergasted that she didn't get the joke. She was watching the show along with me now and still had no clue.

"What ancient band is this?" she inquired snidely. "Why did you turn off the game?"

"The Bucks lost." I just wanted her to leave. She didn't know me at all. I don't follow sports, least of all the NBA. Anyway, Summer didn't even know who Stevie Nicks was. With age comes wisdom, and obviously she had neither. I guess beauty *is* only skin deep, but stupidity goes all the way to the bone.

Furthermore, it occurred to me, that's who was out there: Younger women who now seemed like girls to me and with whom I had nothing in common (hell, they probably considered me too old as well) or divorcees or cougars or ticking clocks, all who wanted a man in their lives for preordained reasons, none of which meshed with mine. Was I destined to become some older, more pathetic type of Sam Malone or Joey Tribiani character, routinely sitting at a bar similar to *Cheers* or hitting on women like in an episode of *Friends*? (*Hey . . . how you doin'?*) I needed to get a life.

I began getting up earlier in the morning and going to bed earlier at night. I started staying home on Friday and Saturday nights instead of going out drinking and chasing skirts. I tried looking at books I had bought years ago and meant to get around to someday. I even read a few. I renewed my gym membership and actually began using it regularly. Coffee became my new best friend, and the ellipticals at the gym became the test of my manhood. It was there that I finally decided what I really wanted to do next.

I called up Jon and met him for some morning caffeine in Mequon. It was early April 2005, and just over a year had passed since Heidi and I had moved in together. She was now living in Manhattan and sent me emails every now and then to check in.

"I'm going to quit Millennium," I told him.

He just about fell out of his chair. "You've lost it, Sebastian. Are you crazy? You have it all and you get paid a ton. Did you get a better offer? You're moving to New York, aren't you? Going to work on Wall Street and make the big bucks, huh? You're going to leave me and go chase after Heidi . . . try to win her back or something!"

I tried to reassure him but could hardly get a word in edgewise. It was actually kind of flattering. He really cared.

"Who am I supposed to go skiing with? How else am I going to get out on the water? I can't afford a boat! Geez!" Apparently he had already had too much coffee that morning, because he was literally buzzing.

"So that's what I am to you, huh? A recreational director? No, Jon, I'm not moving to New York, but I am leaving, for a little while anyway," I finally interrupted.

"Well . . . what are you going to do then?" he shot back, only then realizing what a complete ass he had just made of himself.

"A little sailing," I said, a sly grin that I couldn't hold back spreading across my face.

I told Jon of my plan to rent out my house to an old friend at Promise Wealth Management and head south, out of Lake Michigan, down the Illinois and Mississippi Rivers and gunk hole around the Florida Keys, Bahamas, Turks and Caicos, and the BVI. "Wherever the trade winds take me, dude." I laughed, putting on my best Jimmy Buffet impression. "I need a change in attitude, so I'm going to change my latitude."

I was happy, and after everything was laid out in front of him, I could tell Jon was happy for me as well.

It took a month for me to get all my stuff in order at the house and at New Millennium. Jon helped me get *Slomocean* back in the water at a guest slip in Port Washington's harbor, as I wouldn't need my slip at McKinley Marina anymore. We spent the first week in May testing all the equipment and provisioning her for the journey, as well as taking a few sunset cruises for old time sake.

Jon, Elise, and Bergen invited everyone from my old job as well as a few people they remembered me mentioning at parties from Promise, New Millenium, and around Mequon to an impromptu farewell breakfast at Harry's Diner in Port Washington. It was May 12, 2005, one year to the day since our Cinco de Mayo-Sytennde Mai interdependence day housewarming party. A lot had changed since then, and a twinge of doubt crept into my mind that morning as I prepared to sail south. I was actually a little melancholy as I considered this next chapter. I hoped I hadn't been too hasty and naïve in thinking this option was the perfect prescription for what was ailing me, but my mood turned on a dime when I saw everyone who came out for me.

I will never forget that send off. It made me feel happy and sad at the same time. I was so excited to leave, yet only then did it strike me what and who I was leaving behind. After breakfast, I handed Elise two cards. One was a thank-you card to her and Jon for the bon voyage party; the other was a belated birthday card I asked her to put in the mail for Owen Steglin, who was turning one. It wouldn't get there until at least tomorrow, but by then I would be well underway.

As I motored out of the inner harbor toward the breakwater and the lighthouse late that Saturday morning, there stood twenty or so people cheering me on. Besides my extended family far away in Tahiti, almost everyone I held near and dear to me was present—except for Heidi, who was somewhere in New York City, and Peter, who was at the hospital tending to Owen and Heather, as her dad was battling cancer. Jon was also nowhere to be found until I saw that he had walked all the way out to the lighthouse at the end of Port's breakwater to see me off, which was a really cool gesture. I almost didn't notice him as I was busy hoisting *Slomocean*'s main sail, but I heard him call out over the sound of the engine, "You're my best friend, Sebby! You big pussy! You'd better write!"

With a wave of his hand, he began the walk back toward the harbor, and I began my journey south, not knowing if I would ever come back.

Chapter 13

Home Sweet Home
Told by Jon

When Bergen was born in November of 2004, Elise and I were overjoyed. Eight pounds six ounces and twenty-two inches long, she had all ten fingers, ten toes, and a grip on my heart so strong I could barely go to work. Flying three- and four-day trips felt like an eternity, not only for me but Elise as well. Bergen wasn't eating and was up a lot at night with colic. Like most new parents, Elise was worried and exhausted. That dreamy look in her eyes during the pregnancy had become something more like quiet desperation. When I was gone for work, it was even worse. Elise confided in me that she felt like a single parent much of the time and didn't know how those who actually were did it. With me on flights all over the place and returning home jetlagged and Elise up at all hours with Bergen, we were pretty messed up. We slept whenever we could, at all hours of the day and night just to keep our heads above water and our sanity in check. Fortunately, her mom was simply the greatest, helping Elise when she most needed it. Watching them together, I could only hope that Bergen and Elise had that kind of relationship someday.

We were tired yet on top of the world, but I think Sebby at this point in time was hitting rock bottom. I wished I could have been there for him, but I was so busy and exhausted, I didn't want to go out. I don't think Elise wanted me hanging out with him either after the Halloween party and our encounter with young Taryn. She was pretty disgusted with Sebby and didn't feel the sympathy she had for him only months before. "Heidi must have seen it," she said one night after I declined again to go out with him over the phone. "She was right about him, you know. Sebastian is a playboy and always will be. And I thought he was such a good guy."

"He *is* a good guy," I countered while making dinner. "He didn't do anything wrong! He didn't cheat on her ever."

"Are you sure?" she asked.

"Sebby *is* a good guy," I reiterated. "He loved Heidi. Yeah, he got a vasectomy before he met her. Why should that be a death sentence?"

"Who gets a vasectomy at thirty-one anyway?" she asked skeptically. "That's just weird."

"A guy who was almost trapped by a psycho, gold-digging bitch, that's who," I protested.

What were we fighting about? I had told Sebby I couldn't go out. *Maybe I should have gone out*, I considered. If this was going to be our dinner discussion, I didn't want to have any part of it. I didn't want to fight.

"It was the honesty thing," Elise commented.

"Honesty is a two-way street, honey," I said, after reminding her of Heidi's job offer. "Don't judge someone until you walk a mile in their shoes." I was reminding myself of this as well. Things were going so well for us lately I didn't want to fall back into my bad habit of being quick to judge other people.

Christmas was approaching, and our landlord wanted us to re-sign for six months or move out. We didn't know what to do. The house still wasn't ready and wouldn't be for a while. I tried to get a month-to-month lease, insisting that no one wanted to move in the middle of a Wisconsin winter anyway. The landlord called my bluff and insisted he had a waiting list for the apartment because they were one of the only complexes in Mequon that allowed dogs.

I didn't know if he was lying, but we signed on another

dotted line. It was our fault. We decided on the changes we had to have no matter what for our new home. We were slow in picking out fixtures, tile, carpet, and colors. These were big decisions for us that sometimes required compromise. We were, in a sense, our own worst enemies.

I'm sure our contractor was as frustrated with us as we were with the construction schedule and progress, but in the end we didn't blame him. I just hoped we weren't still in our apartment six months from now. I thought I could see a light at the end of this tunnel, if only faintly.

It didn't matter though; Bergen was a blast. I was the proudest daddy of them all. And as the first grandchild on either side of our respective families, she was loved, adored, and spoiled rotten. To say she was the center of attention would be a vast understatement. Everybody doted on her morning, noon, and night and showered her with presents. With all the joy and excitement surrounding Bergen, Christmas 2004 was the best ever (even though Bergen slept through almost all of it).

I continued to dodge Sebby at Elise's request, and in early 2005, I got assigned to a larger aircraft at the airline. It meant almost a month away at the airline's training center, but it also meant more money once I was flying again on trips. Elise agreed to weather the storm, and we made it through to spring.

Once I got home again from my stint at school learning the new airplane, things got back to semi-normal. Elise had found a new inner strength and settled nicely into momhood. I noticed her mastery of all things baby my first week back. She was amazing.

Sebastian and I hadn't seen each other in quite some time, so I was excited when he called me up one evening and invited me to breakfast the following day. Elise was okay with this and actually encouraged me to go and catch up with him. But she was surprised when I came home and told her his bewildering news.

"Sebby's leaving. He's quitting his job and—"
"He's what?" Elise interrupted me. "Where's he going? Why?" It was as if she was conducting an interrogation.
"He's taking his sailboat on a trip to the Caribbean," I said.
"With some girl he met, I suppose," she countered.
"No. By himself, I'm pretty sure."
I was losing a friend, and I didn't have many of them to lose.

***

Working at an airline is different than almost any other job I can think of. Men and women living everywhere throughout the country, and even sometimes the world, commute into work. More often than not we are only in flight operations at our domicile for a few hours before flying our trip. When we arrive back at the base after three to seven days of hopscotching around the globe, we catch another flight and go home. I might not fly with the same captain for months or longer. I might not see another first officer I know very well for quite a while. We often fly alternate schedules, and if we do connect, it's usually on a trip when two flights overlap somewhere, but that is only a random occurrence at best. It's not like other industries where coworkers live nearby. Many of my pilot friends live over two thousand miles away. I can't just call them up for a round of golf, a burger, and a beer.

Sebby truly was one of my only local friends, and it was obvious I might not see him for months or longer, but what really bummed me out was the vague idea festering in my head that I might never see him again. Either way, I was going to miss him.

Elise and I put together a little send-off for him in Port Washington. A bunch of his friends and old coworkers showed up for breakfast, and I walked all the way out to the end of the breakwater to a small white lighthouse to watch him go. I didn't know what to say, but I yelled, "If you make Bitter End, Sebby, you'll be lucky!" The Bitter End was a great harbor resort in the British Virgin Islands. "You'd best turn right!" I bellowed, referencing his heading and his need to head toward Chicago. Yeah, I said "right" instead of "starboard." I'm a pilot, not a sailor, by trade. He probably couldn't hear me over the noise of *Slomocean*'s motor anyway. I gave a wave and walked back toward town. When I finally turned back to look, Sebastian was well underway.

Bergen, Elise, and I spent the last part of May and most of June moving into our new house. It was wonderful finally bringing our baby home. Sure it was a cookie-cutter cape cod, but it was ours (at least it would be after another 359 payments). It had two bedrooms and a bathroom upstairs with the remaining rooms on the main level. The siding was gray with white trim, and there was a different color in every room inside, including brick red and dusty sage. Bergen's room was painted a pale yellow. Our former landlord would have hated it—not a beige or white wall in the place.

We were ecstatic. Everything was where we wanted it for the first time in years, and best of all, it was quiet. We were miles away from the interstate.

When we finally got our mail delivered to Port Washington instead of Mequon, I was pleased to find a postcard from Sebastian, the first official piece of mail we ever received at our new address. There was some Mardi Gras scene from New Orleans, and he had written, "I'm heading out to sea to see what I can see!"

For a split second I felt a tug at my heart strings. Remembering the smell of the salty ocean, the sea breeze, and the gulls made me homesick for Maine, but then Elise brought Bergen over to me, and I remembered instantly where I was supposed to be. Home is where the heart is, and mine was right there in my arms.

Summer flew by and turned into fall with a myriad of home projects and play dates at every park within driving distance. Every summer, Port Washington hosts Pirate Fest, Fish Day, The Maritime Heritage Festival, and Music in the Park on Fridays and Saturdays in a band shell near the harbor. It is a great place to raise a family, and that was what we finally were.

Chapter 14

No Going Back
Told by Sebastian

Sailing down a river is like serving time in prison. Actually, I know it's probably not even close; I'm not that naïve, but to me it sure felt like it. I was so impatient to get to open water, to see blue water again, that I felt trapped. I was a prisoner biding his time, waiting to be released.

For a sailor used to wide, open, blue spaces, a lazy, brown, shallow river was a three-walled cell. Two of the walls were the opposing shorelines stretching on endlessly toward the horizon. The third wall was the back of the cell, forcing me to look in only one direction: forward. I needed to look back, but the flow of the river simply wouldn't allow it for anything more than a minute or two. The current pushed me in one direction only. I didn't like it. On a big lake or the ocean, I could work with the wind and even make my way against it by tacking across vast expanses of water at an angle, and although my forward progress would be slow, there was a freedom in choosing which direction I wanted to go, but now I didn't have that option.

I wanted to head southeast toward the Caribbean, my final destination (at least for now). The problem was, to get from Port Washington, Wisconsin, to the big blue, there were only two choices. I could head north up into Lake Huron and then south toward Lake Erie and east into Lake Ontario, followed by either the Erie Canal and the Hudson River or the Saint Lawrence Seaway toward the Atlantic, or I could choose the second option. I was heading southwest out of Chicago on the southern tip of

Lake Michigan along the Illinois River toward Saint Louis, Missouri, and the mighty Mississippi. Either choice would be a long, circuitous route and an arduous journey, but this lazy, brown river was sheer torture.

I was beginning to regret not following the water's natural path out through the lakes. Maybe Mother Nature did know best. I was already considering turning around, but I couldn't. There was no going back. I had quit what was a very lucrative job and probably burned a few bridges in the process. I had rented out my house for a year, sold my Porsche, put my old Land Rover in storage, given up my slip, and told everyone my plans. If I went back now, what would they think of me?

This river closed in around me incessantly, forcing me to turn when it wanted me to instead of when I wanted to, pushing me relentlessly southwest, seemingly farther from where I wanted to go. I couldn't just stop and float. The current always captured me in eddies and cajoled me toward the outer bank of every bend. It was a wicked brown snake, and I didn't like pandering to its whims. I couldn't even use the wind to my advantage most of the time. I sailed a little when I could, motored some, and drifted. I liked drifting the best. I was good at it. It occurred to me that I had been drifting for the better part of my adult life. Mostly though I just sat at the helm, deep in my own thoughts, a prisoner in a cell, staring forward, biding my time until I could turn south and finally make my way back to open water.

Unfortunately the mighty Mississippi wasn't much better than the Illinois River. Although wider, I couldn't sense its natural ebb and flow like the Illinois. I always had to stay alert for log jams and barge traffic. What I had thought would be a relaxing drift down ol' man river was proving to be anything but.

Other than a couple of days in Saint Louis, I pushed it pretty hard, not wanting to stop and rest for anything other than necessity until I made my way into the Gulf of Mexico. Besides, the one and only bar I stopped at along the river south of Saint Louis sort of freaked me out. The lady bartender there was, to quote an old saying, good from afar but far from good. When she finally made her way over to me out of the darkness at the other end of the tavern, everything changed. Her teeth—what was left of them, that is—were so screwed up, she could have eaten corn on the cob through a tennis racket. I'm not kidding. Apparently (and I'm only guessing at this) meth is really hard on a person's pearly whites. I vowed right then and there to stay on my boat and keep heading south.

It was a long sentence, but at some point, gravity and God must have figured I was penitent and had served my time. They let me off for good behavior June 28. I could smell the salt air, if only faintly, and was ready for the fun to finally begin. I dropped a postcard in the mail to Jon, restocked *Slomocean*, ate some great Cajun food, and headed southeast!

***

I had sailed across Lake Michigan many times while growing up in Chicago. My father had taken me from west to east and back again as well as south to north into Lake Huron on his sailboat, *Comfortably Rhumb*, a singular reference to rhumb line navigation, though I found out as I grew older and wiser that it was more likely an ode to Pink Floyd and my father's penchant for hard alcohol—rum and Cokes, to be exact, which he routinely drank at all hours of the day.

My father killed himself (and thankfully only himself) in a drunk-driving accident when I was sixteen. The authorities ruled it an accident, but I knew better. My father never failed at anything his entire life until his financial firm bet big on the wrong stocks and bonds that year. When the margin calls started coming, the bigger fish followed and began feasting on the smaller, weaker ones until it became a feeding frenzy. I guess he should have zigged instead of zagged. Apparently the world bet against him and went the other way. My father was blindsided and had no choice but to sell his company as well as his seat on the Chicago Mercantile Exchange to pay off the positions he held in the wrong stuff. It was either that or declare bankruptcy and suffer the indignity that came along with besmirching his own name.

To my father, his name was everything, his reputation and standing in the community priceless. I guess it all became just too much, a fatal blow. Maybe he figured he would never recover, so he finished the job himself. But I digress.

***

Lake Michigan is a "great lake" to be sure, some three hundred miles long, ninety miles wide, and in places over nine hundred feet deep. It is in fact an inland sea that can turn violent and deadly very quickly. My father taught me many things in life, the greatest of which was respect for big water.

My original plan as I headed out into the gulf was to make a beeline for the Florida Keys, but I remembered the lessons my dad and the lake had taught me. Chalk it up to divine guidance or just my conservative nature with anything except fast cars, fast women, hot stocks, and liquor, but I decided right then and there to hug the shoreline wherever I could, play it safe, and enjoy the ride. It was really a matter of shifting mental gears. I had pressed so hard to get south to salty blue water that I had to remind myself to slow down over and over again. *It's not the destination, but the journey*, I reminded myself over and over, and it soon began to sink in. The other thing I still hadn't gotten entirely used to was the solitude. I had sailed many times for days or even a week with a crew, but I had rarely sailed more than a day or two by myself. I am social by nature. I love tranquility but hate silence; there is a big difference between the two, at least in my mind.

Having no one to talk to forced me for the first time in forever to talk to myself, to listen to my head as well as my heart and attempt unraveling my own brain. It would prove to be a twisted, knotted, tangled up mess. I have always been able to read other people like an open book, but was I willing to begin this autobiography of self-discovery without reading the book jacket first? Was it a sexy romance novel, a psychological thriller, or a gruesome tragedy? I wasn't sure I wanted to find out.

As I headed east southeast along the panhandle of Florida, I thought a lot about my dad, my privileged, misspent youth as an only child, and my mother's insistence on parochial school. I wasn't the most religious person in the world, preferring instead to consider myself spiritual. Maybe that was a cop out. Shouldn't all of those years and all that money somehow have instilled in me the perfect moral compass? Maybe I was choosing not to follow what I knew to be true as a form of rebellion even now. Maybe I was just too stupid to listen and learn. I didn't know. My mind always retreated back to Leah Aspen and whether I had a kid out there somewhere. After my paternity scare with Courtney and my subsequent vasectomy, I thought I had put all those fears behind me. Now, some thirteen years since graduating from UW Madison, they were keeping me awake at night, and I couldn't get past them.

My father would have killed me had he still been alive and I brought this on him. He probably would have found Leah himself and taken her to the clinic. He wouldn't let anything stand in the way of the successes he had planned for his son. His expectations were as high for me as, well, Mount Everest. As the first man from his islands to summit it before I was born, he knew what it took to make it to the top, and he never let me forget it: "Only the best for my boy!" or "You have to pay attention to the details. Now do it again until you get it right!" I heard him tell me these things over and over again growing up. "You haven't earned it yet," he bellowed more than once as I invariably asked for something that I had to have growing up. I was spoiled rotten, but pushed hard.

On the other hand, I could hear my mother, Evonne, the faithful follower: "God sees everything," or "Remember, Sebastian, if she'll do it with you, she will do it with anyone, and she's probably already done it with everyone else!" Not the kind of ego boost you want to hear as a seventeen-year-old boy heading out the door on prom night. What was I? The bottom of the barrel when it came to dates? My mom had a peculiar way of reminding me of everything I had ever done wrong. Maybe that's why I routinely got in trouble for larger and larger crimes and greater sins in her eyes as I got older. Rebel, why not? I was never going to be forgiven for my past sins or screw ups anyway.

Evonne would have insisted I marry Leah and never ever even think of divorce or separation. An abortion would have been out of the question. Everything in her eyes was black or white. The color grey didn't exist. She didn't have a deep, abiding faith, even though she thought she did. Oh no, faith is a belief in something you can't prove. Evonne claimed to have official, yet undocumented proof, that her beliefs were facts; she just couldn't substantiate them. Her morals were an ironclad dogma, and she expected full well that everyone should see things the way she did. In her eyes, love had nothing to do with a successful marriage, only the number of years a couple stayed together. You take your vows, you keep your promises to God, and you never bring disgrace on your family. I couldn't win that battle either way. If I had gotten Leah pregnant, I had already brought disgrace on my mother. A ring on Leah's finger would have served as a mere Band-Aid for my mother's own mortal wound.

I figured Evonne was the reason for my rebellion and inability to commit to anyone, with the exception of Heidi, so I just blamed her. It was the easiest solution. After all, she left me, not the other way around. No . . . I'm not talking about Heidi. My mother moved back to Tahiti my freshman year of college at Madison. Apparently my choice of attending "the Berkeley of the Midwest!" and "the most liberal school east of the Mississippi" was the final straw after my father's death. I had chosen his liberal, free-spirited ways over her very conservative ideals, and that was a deal breaker in her mind, even between a mother and son.

Ironically she wasn't even Polynesian but was born in the south of France. Her parents immigrated to America shortly after she was born at the end of World War II. Evonne loved the island life, hated winter, and I guess felt no further reason to stay, not even for me, so she left and never returned. My father's life insurance policy would pay my way through Madison and subsequently my MBA at Northwestern. I remember her telling me before she left how fortunate it was for me that my father's death was ruled an accident and not a suicide.

Was I really supposed to feel lucky? He was, after all, dead, and then, at the age of eighteen, I was suddenly and unexpectedly on my own. I should have grown up right then and there, but I didn't. Even now, with seventeen more years under my belt, I didn't feel any older or wiser. I had to face my greatest fear, but to do that, I had to figure out what it was.

The good thing about sailing solo with no schedule or appointments to keep, no specific destination or agenda in mind, was time. I took a vow of technological silence. I turned off my Blackberry and shut down my email account.

I started to embrace time as a gift, the solitude onboard *Slomocean* a subtle sort of psychotherapy I so desperately needed. I tried to grow up, but it wasn't easy.

Sailing southeast along the western shoreline of Florida, I spent a day or two in Pensacola, Panama City, Clearwater, Sarasota, Fort Myers, and Naples respectively, but I never felt like staying any longer.

In Fort Myers, I met a wealthy divorcee one evening at a bar and grill next to the marina.

"What do you do here in town?" I asked her, hoping to strike up a small conversation.

"Oh, I work out and lay out," she offered, smiling slyly as she uncrossed and re-crossed her legs, twirled her hair with her fingers, and sipped what can only be described as a jumbo cosmopolitan. She was wearing a short tennis skirt and was really tan—incredibly tan, Florida tan, you know? "I like to lie around and watch the people and the birds."

"You're a birdwatcher, huh? That's your job?" I inquired incredulously.

"I'm divorced. I don't have to work anymore. I find that people are a lot like birds," she said, baiting me in.

"Really? Well, what kind of bird am I, then?" I asked her inquisitively.

"Hmmmmm . . ." She smirked and looked me over. "Maybe a woodpecker or woodcock . . . I'm not sure yet, but I'd like to find out!"

Man, what a pick-up line! This cougar is a real live wire! "Well, now you've got my attention," I told her. "I have to ask, then, what kind of bird are you?"

"Hmmm . . ." she said again, pausing to contemplate my question and add a little intrigue. "Honey, I like you," she began, smiling a wry smile, "so I'll tell you the truth." Her southern drawl became more and more apparent as she spoke. "I'm a double-breasted mattress thrasher!" she professed devilishly. "What you see is what you get, and what you get is *real good!*"

Holy cow! I thought. *I have never in my life met a tiger as upfront and forward as this!*

She was beyond confident (a huge turn on for me) and nothing if not honest, which was surprising since I found out later on that she had served on the state assembly in Georgia or somewhere, I think (our conversation jumped around quite a bit). Both educated and well to do, what was she doing hanging out in a marina bar anyway? Maybe she owned a boat here or something. I never found out.

Unfortunately for her, and maybe even for me, our evening together ended abruptly before it really got started. Her opinions were as out there as her desire to get some, and that proved to be the straw that broke the camel's back. We didn't see eye to eye on much of anything, and besides, I despise most politicians. I feel like I've been screwed by them enough already. I went back to my boat and agonized over that decision for the next few days.

***

I thought about Heidi more than I had in the last year. Our time together was etched in my brain, and I could still envision every last inch of her, still taste her lips and smell her scent (an odd mix of pool chlorine, baby powder, and Clinique Happy.) I wondered what she was doing. Hell, I wondered *who* she was doing. It was cruel punishment for something—but for what? I wasn't sure. I wished things had gone differently between us, but I still believed adamantly that I had done nothing wrong. I questioned whether I would find someone like her ever again, and I doubted it.

I was in a relationship again now anyway, I realized. I talked to *Slomocean*, and she spoke to me. We communicated in a language of creaks and groans, of gentle rubs and pats. We talked a lot on our journey south together. I began to measure speed in tenths of a knot instead of miles per hour.

I learned to estimate the depth of water beneath me not in feet, but by the ever changing shade of blue over which we traveled. And I started to figure out the temperature and predict the weather by studying the clouds overhead. Wind speed and direction, sail shape, and steering became more intuitive than I could have ever imagined. We were connected, man and boat, as if one entity.

I could never know a woman like this! I thought.

By the time we reached Key West, it was late fall back in Wisconsin, but you wouldn't have known it there. The bikinis were in full bloom—red, pink, and white (every color of the rainbow actually, but I preferred those colors the best). I sent off a few postcards and decided to stay for a while to enjoy the scenery before restocking and continuing on. I still didn't have any answers, but I think I finally had a bead on the right questions to ask, which was a good start.

It occurred to me one evening over fish tacos and margaritas that I had been celibate for six months. I thought that had to be some kind of record! But I wasn't bragging. I hadn't gone that long since my freshman year of college. I needed to get laid.

Chapter 15

Be Careful What You Wish For
Told by Peter

I built Sebby's house in 2003 and 2004, completed two homes in 2005, and ended up booking three for 2006. Steglin and Son Homes, LLC was doing great. By late spring '06, I knew I needed to hire some help, but it was hard to find because everybody was so busy. Clients fell out of the woodwork for remodels and fix ups, but I wanted to make a name for myself with new construction and started holding out for houses exclusively. (This decision would come back to bite me with a vengeance.)

Since everyone was so busy themselves, I decided to take on some young guns. I figured I could get them cheaper and mentor them along the way. That's how I had learned. I convinced myself it would be great, but hiring took time, and I was booked full.

Finally I found some future talent. Now all I had to do was train them, but teaching also took time, and mistakes cost money, so I had to hire even more hammers just to equal the output of some experienced yet more expensive old hands. I was beginning do less construction myself and more task management, but that was the price I had to pay to expand the business.

With money coming in, space tight at our house, another baby on the way, and the real possibility of elder care for Heather's sick dad, I figured it was high time for a bigger house as well. We could buy and fix up, but why not build and get what we wanted? After all, that's what I did for a living. We could use the new house to show off our best ideas and construction methods to prospective clients.

Heather was in full-on mom mode now with Owen in his terrible twos. With all the new help I had hired, she also bore the brunt of payroll, insurance, and everything else that came along with success. It didn't ever get any easier. She wasn't ready, willing, or able to commit to the thought of building or moving, scared we would end up with two mortgages. I sold her on the fact that we could do it cheaper with all our inside knowledge and sweat equity, and I told her how hot the real estate market was. Everything was moving fast. Everyone was moving up. We were moving up. She finally, begrudgingly, agreed.

We bought the last lot in a great area on the northeast side of Port Washington; it was the best of both worlds—close to schools and a grocery store yet nestled in some trees. I felt like I was in the country; Heather felt like she was in town. What a great place to raise a son and *daughter*. Yep, we had decided to just go ahead and find out. Steglin and Son Homes, LLC would remain so for the near future, although Steglin Homes, LLC was beginning to sound more equitable. I didn't want to play favorites. We were ecstatic, but who am I kidding? We were overwhelmed. The only saving grace was that it appeared as though Heather's father was in remission. His hair had come back, along with all the piss and vinegar that accompanied his former persona. I had to stop and count our blessings. It couldn't get any better—or busier.

***

Quality control is a bitch when time is of the essence. Fortunately most of the young guns I hired were quick learners, and the rain always fell on weekends that summer. The first house we framed was a nice little colonial with nothing unusual on the plan. It proved to be a great training ground for my new guys. We broke ground on the second house early summer 2006, a shake shingle cape with some post and beam elements. It became a sort of graduate school for the men I considered ready to promote.

Hiring guys was easy. It's all good news. I met with them and said something like, "If we can use you, we'll call." The ones I wanted to hire were called back the next day. The ones I didn't want, well, I just never called them back. I guess I'm not that good with bad news or conflict. I'm a hammer, not a manager. I didn't have those skill sets. Now, as I started moving men around and promoting those who excelled, I had to make decisions that sometimes weren't popular. At the height of summer and at our busiest time, I had to let a guy go for his repeated inability to show up for work, as well as a litany of other offenses. Like my father used to say to me just before he'd spank me, "This is going to be harder for me than it is for you. . ." WHACK!

I never understood it at the time but was now beginning to. I had the hardest time getting up the courage to fire this guy, but I knew if I didn't the others would soon walk all over me as well. It didn't help that he was a giant of a man, a full six inches and fifty pounds above my squat build. A construction job site is full of power saws and pneumatic nail guns that are at least as deadly as a pistol at close range. I didn't relish the thought of a gun fight, especially in front of the others. I needed to at least appear boss-like.

Somehow, someway, jacked up on caffeine and fed up to here, I confronted the NFL linebacker and sent him packing. I remember looking around the site wondering which of my men would side with me and which would help him if we came to blows. Fortunately that didn't happen. I learned a lot from the experience but hoped I would never have to do anything like that again. The rest of the summer went smoothly as I turned over much of the interior on the colonial to other contractors and concentrated more on the shingle cape and the tudor mansion on paper for the fall.

Heather was getting huge and having a hard time finding the energy for our little Tasmanian devil, Owen.

"Could you work a little less and give me some help, Peter?" she asked, both emotionally and physically drained. "I can't even bend over anymore, let alone pick him up. I have to pee constantly! Help!"

How could I refuse my very own desperate housewife? Truth was, I couldn't. I have always been a pleaser. The business would have to be run by phone, because I had to stay home.

Thankfully Heather was not only at the end of her rope but close to the end of her pregnancy as well. I don't know if the shingle cape or the tudor mansion would have ever gotten finished or even started if I'd had to continue my stint in daddy daycare. For that matter, I doubt I could have survived it. Building houses was easy compared to raising a two-and-a-half year old boy. Now try doing it while carrying a bowling ball around on your stomach. I don't know how Heather held out as long as she did. She was obviously more of a trooper than I ever gave her credit for.

Campbell was born healthy, happy, and huge on September 22. Owen was now a big brother. He was super excited at first, but like with most new toys and the growing realization he was no longer the center of attention, the luster soon faded, and the terrible twos returned. He wanted to be a Backyardigan for Halloween, while I was hoping for Handy Manny or Bob the Builder again. For Christmas he wanted paints, crayons, and a Dora the Explorer doll. I wanted to get him Lego Duplos. I felt like I was already losing my son, but I was too busy to try and change his mind and too exhausted to show him the joys of construction.

Was there any joy? Frankly, I didn't know anymore. My stress and headaches only seemed to grow in intensity the more I tried to grow the business. I needed a break. I needed a drink—no, what I really needed was a boys' night out.

Chapter 16

Old Dog New Trick
Told By Sebby

Key West that fall proved a bust. Maybe I had lost my mojo, too long out at sea or something. Everywhere I went, everything I tried didn't work. At one bar I was too old. At another I was obviously fishing for something they didn't offer. I was a square peg trying desperately to fit into a round ho—well, you get the picture.

It wasn't that there weren't opportunities, even if Key West in the fall was relatively quiet. I just couldn't seem to find what I was looking for. As I'd heard said: "The odds are good, but the goods are odd!" It was a valid description for the most southerly tip of the lower forty-eight. Every time I struck up a conversation with a potential friend for the evening, it all too soon went something like what happened my third or so night at the bars there. This tall, voluptuous, red-haired woman approached me when I was a little drunk and began, "I know what you're thinking: Does the carpet match the drapes?"

"Well, does it?" I asked her, half in the bag from too many Mai Tais and margaritas.

"Actually," *he* replied slyly in a new and deeper tone of voice. "I have a hardwood floor.

Are you into manscaping?"

"No . . . but I am more than flattered that you had the balls to ask. You're hot, dude."

"Thanks," he said. "I'm Vivian, but you can call me Vance."

"Cool, man, I'm Sebastian. Pull up a stool if you

want."

We struck up a hell of a conversation, and I learned a lot. Vance was from Kansas City and said that he felt like he didn't fit in there, so after cruising around for a few years, he found himself and found that he liked it here. "You have to have the courage to ask yourself the tough questions and then follow through and be true to you, ya know?" he said.

It was uncanny, like he was speaking directly to my soul. "I'm trying, man. I am trying," I said, but I didn't elaborate much further.

Other nights, it was less obvious but twice as awkward: "You're way hotter than my husband back in Kentucky!" (Doesn't anyone wear a ring anymore?)

I almost picked up a lady one night until the bartender informed me that she was in fact a hooker. "We secretly call her Our Lady of Negotiable Affection," he confided in me. "Apparently she's very religious, believe it or not. It's up to you. I just thought you should know."

"Thanks," I said, leaving him a big tip as I left while she was still in the bathroom.

More than once I was told, "I would love to introduce you to my kids!" or "You remind me of my dad." Ouch! Yuck! I wasn't that old, was I? Sometimes I didn't even get that far before having to politely excuse myself from the conversation.

"You know where I can get some dope?"

"I'll doing anything for a little buzz!"

"My aunt's a real cougar! She would love to—"

"So sorry, but I have to go!" I would interject. *Run away! Run away!* I screamed internally. A few times I got close, but invariably they wanted to go back to my place. There was no way I was taking anybody back to *Slomocean*. She desperately needed a cleaning. To be honest, she was more than a little ripe from the cruise south. Besides, we were already in a relationship. There was no way I was going to cheat ON her.

Looking back, I think it was just me. I could have sealed the deal a few times, but that wasn't who I was anymore. I didn't really want to wake up in some unfamiliar bed in God knows where with a dog licking my face and a woman who I couldn't name in the kitchen asking, "You want some coffee, baby? How do you take your eggs? Don't mind my dog. Lester's like that with every guy I bring home."

No way. After only a little more than a week in Key West, I restocked *Slomocean*—this time with better food, more drinks, a good array of fishing equipment, and a stack of girly magazines. It was time to venture out into the big blue.

We headed northeast up the east side of the Keys, stopping in Marathon, Islamorada, and Key Largo for a night each before heading to Miami and trying it on for fun. Unfortunately that was only more of the same. After three days in Miami, two days in Fort Lauderdale, and two more in West Palm Beach, I finally summoned the courage to head east toward Freeport.

The Bahamas were so amazingly beautiful, they defied description—azure-blue water, white sand beaches, I shouldn't even try. I sailed a meandering course resembling a poorly written backward *S*, hopping from one island to the next, hugging the shoreline and enjoying the view. I trolled lures off the stern or sometimes drifted over deep reefs catching a menagerie of different fish, many of which I didn't even recognize. I read a lot, and we stopped in Freeport, Nassau, and Georgetown, as well as practically every little harbor and cay along the way as we made our way very slowly southeast toward the Turks and Caicos. It was a great sail.

I thought more about what I was afraid of. *What am I going to do next? I can't do this forever. Or can I?* The thought of becoming a professional bum sort of sounded appealing at the moment.

I thought about my friends back in Wisconsin and my mom. I wondered how everybody was. I missed them, and I was beginning to get a little homesick. It was winter up north, already 2006, and I wondered what important events I had missed.

One night a beautiful full moon hung low over the eastern sky, coaxing me toward the Atlantic. A soft but steady breeze from the southwest heeled the boat over to port as we sailed southeast for Puerto Rico. *Slomocean* was making steady progress toward San Juan when out of nowhere I had some sort of catharsis. I wasn't sure about it but figured I was on the right track.

"What is the worst-case scenario?" I asked myself out loud. "What is your biggest fear?"

Slomocean listened intently for my answer. She was always so patient with me, but more questions kept popping into my head before I could respond. "What can you control? What is beyond your control? What are you going to do next? When are you going to stop running away? When are you going to visit you mom? When are you going to forgive her for leaving?"

But she left me just when I needed her most, I thought. *When am I going to stop blaming her for . . . She didn't make him commit suicide, Sebastian!* My mind was now in a battle with itself. *When am I going to grow up?*

"SHUT UP!" I screamed as loud as I could into the heavens. *Slomocean* creaked and groaned, apparently startled by my outburst. She righted herself and went off course downwind as I let go of the wheel. Her sail went slack momentarily before the wind captured it again on the opposite side. The boom almost hit me as it swung slowly across in a gentle jibe, as if *Slomocean* was trying to slap me, but I barely noticed, to be honest. I just ducked intuitively.

Stop it! I screamed internally while pausing to gather

my thoughts. *Answer the fucking question, Sebby! Figure this thing out . . . once and for all . . . NOW!*

My head prepared for a mutiny. My body prepared for a fight. I grabbed the rail, bracing myself for what seemed like an eternity, and stared up at the stars. For some reason, I wouldn't allow myself to sit. The sky was ink black to the west but emitted a more violet light to the east. In front of me I could barely make out the horizon as the sky and the stars wed perfectly with the ocean and a myriad of tiny sparkles on the water.

We drifted eastward, *Slomocean*'s sails now luffing in the wind, the Atlantic gently lapping at her hull. Long, low swells gently rolled past, rocking us like a mother comforting a sick child.

"Okay, so I'm thirty-eight or forty-one someday or whatever, and he knocks on my door. Maybe he is a she. What if she hates me?" I wondered out loud. "I'll work through it. It will be okay. It may never happen. It may never have happened. I can handle it. I WILL BE OKAY! I WILL GET THROUGH IT!"

I willed myself to believe. For a second I actually thought my sailboat was speaking to me. She was a good counselor; then again, maybe it was my dad. Somewhere up there, with an open connection to my soul, uninterrupted by technology, schedules, stresses, wants, needs, or desires, talking to me, and for the first time in a long time, I was ready to listen. We talked all night, with *Slomocean* as our intermediary, reminding me, nudging me, encouraging me to take it all in, to take this to heart.

The next morning as the sun broke the southeastern horizon, it lifted my spirits as well as a giant weight off my mind. I turned toward the light. I couldn't put it in words, but I was close to an answer. Even my boat was happy for me. She could tell by my lead we were coming about. She could hear in my voice a new calm. She noticed in my mannerisms a more gentle touch. She knew we were back on course.

***

I had been on the water or in sleepy little harbor towns for the better part of four months. *Slomocean* could use a rest, I figured, and I could use a real shower. On Puerto Rico's northeastern coast sits San Juan, a vibrant and busy city. The hustle and bustle of the pavement seemed oddly appealing the closer we got, and I found myself looking forward to once again experiencing an urban environment. We made port a day later.

I found a slip for her and a room for me, gathered up a bunch of dirty clothes, and made my way into the heart of town. It was as if a pilgrim stepping off the Mayflower landed in present day New York City. I forgot to look before I stepped into oncoming traffic and was nearly run over. I had trouble making change at a store. San Juan soon engulfed me, and I felt as if I would drown.

I quickly retreated to my hotel room to recover and turned on CNN, but I wasn't familiar with any of the lead stories. The world had changed. I was particularly interested in the markets. CNBC brought back a lot of fond memories and stirred in me a feeling I hadn't had in a long time. All too quickly I was once again addicted. (Besides, the girls on there were hot.) I called up a few old coworker friends back in Milwaukee, who reiterated that the markets were on a tear.

It's funny, in the peace and relative quiet of my comfortable hotel room, I found myself missing the action, but when I walked outside for lunch or dinner, I felt like a Quaker at Studio 54. The noise, my God, the noise was incredible—horns, sirens, cars, trucks, people. It seemed as if I would be crushed by the masses at a local McDonald's as everyone shoved and pushed to queue up to the counter for their Big Macs.

I remember quarter pounders tasting much better than this, I thought as I sat down to eat.

But these fries are amazing!

We spent a week in San Juan but soon decided it wasn't for us. *Slomocean* didn't like being tied up, and I didn't like being tied down. I missed the freedom of the ocean, the pace of a day not measured by a clock but rather the sun and stars. I missed being rocked to sleep. Frankly I could hardly get used to the lack of motion as I walked down the street, let alone in my hotel bed. Even with all the plush pillows and clean sheets, it still wasn't comfortable. I couldn't get a good night's rest the whole time we were there, so I made hasty plans to leave and bought provisions for the next leg of our journey.

***

A boat can spend a lifetime in the lakes. Fresh water isn't corrosive. Salt water, on the other hand, is a cancer for anything foreign. You have to constantly treat the symptoms or it only gets worse. In the end though, in many cases, it will get you no matter what you do. It's simply a matter of luck or, really, the opposite. I should have stayed in San Juan for some much-needed small repairs, but I didn't. I couldn't stand it there any longer. I missed small islands and private coves; small, sleepy harbor towns; and local bars.

We left Puerto Rico for the Virgin Islands and never looked back. It was none too soon. *Slomocean* didn't need any coaxing. The trades were howling, and she jumped at the chance. We made a great couple, and we even thought alike. I hauled her in close and tacked toward Tortola in the BVI. "The winds will ease up once we make the shelter of St. Thomas and some of the lesser islands in the U.S. chain," I assured her.

She didn't seem to mind, and she gave me all she

had. Surfing down swells while heeling well over on her rail, we made very slow forward progress. It was as if we couldn't get away from the big city fast enough, but once back on the water, *Slomocean* lived up to her name.

For some reason though, I was once again impatient. Our lack of headway bothered me, but I tried not to blame her. I urged her on and she signaled back confidently that all was well . . . until the moment it wasn't.

I was tied into *Slomocean* with two lifelines along two separate nylon straps that ran the length of her. She gallantly crested wave after wave as they in turn rolled over the now growing swells underneath that pushed on us like a bulldozer to the west and impeded our progress east. I noticed something wasn't right with her. She was trying to tell me something, but with the wind and waves, I couldn't make it out. Something didn't sound right. I watched from the helm, scanning every inch of her rigging and sails for the ominous sign my ears had already picked up on. She was singing off key. I could hear it, and I could feel it. Slomocean just wasn't acting like her old self. I needed to figure this out and fast.

The water around us was getting bigger. Too big for a great little sailboat and a stupid guy who was supposed to know better and respect big water. *We shouldn't have left San Juan,* I cursed at myself. *We should have waited for better weather. Damn it!* "Get it together, Seb," I said out loud, trying to calm myself down. *Figure this out NOW!* All of this and more spun around in my head like a tornado. *Should we turn back or continue? Where is the equal time point between islands?* I quizzed my GPS for answers.

Then I saw it coming at me out of the corner of my eye just before it hit. One of the port turnbuckles that kept tension on a shroud must have broken or come undone. The shroud (a large cable that helps support the mast) surrendered its job to the others and came flying at me like a bull whip, uncoiled and flung from the top of the mast, which was now being tossed about wickedly by the ever growing ocean around me and pitching *Slomocean*'s deck in some weird form of demonic possession. It was as if King Neptune himself had taken control of the boat and was going to beat me into submission for not paying him the proper respect.

The shroud made a loud cracking sound as it ripped into the fiberglass stowage bench cover next to me near the helm. It flailed about relentlessly like an angry serpent baring its fangs as it readied itself to take another bite out of the stern or perhaps my face (at that point I didn't know which). I lunged for it a few times while simultaneously trying to guide *Slomocean* over, up, and down the ever-growing sea, but the wind kept getting stronger, and the seas kept getting bigger. I desperately needed a second reef in the main sail to reduce its size to avoid capsizing, but now I had this shit to deal with as well.

I let the main sheet (a rope that controls the sail) almost all the way out to alleviate the way the sailboat was leaning over on its side, but the boom was still dragging in the water. The stout sailboat heeled over so far, her starboard rail was often submerged. I needed to furl the jib sail completely. I wanted to check the remaining stays and shrouds that supported the mast for security, but at that time, I didn't dare leave the helm. For a moment it occurred to me that I might lose the mast. I had to get a hold of that cable before it killed me.

Bobbing and weaving like a punch drunk boxer, I juggled the helm with one hand and the main sheet with the other, waiting and watching for just the right moment where I would either wrestle the bundle of wire into submission or suffer a knockout blow to my head. The combination of a wet pitching deck and blowing spray made this harder than facing Mike Tyson in the ring, but desperate times required desperate measures. Even more, they required action. I willed the confluence of the waves and wind to coincide with the motion of the boat, and at just the right moment, I let go of the rope in one hand, clung to the wheel with the other, and lunged for the cable, grabbing it as it whipped about my head.

"Fucking piece of shit!" I screamed at the shroud as I struggled with it for submission. The serpent cable bit into me with its long, needle-like fangs (the individual wires had broken and begun to unravel). "God damn it! . . . SHIT!" I yelled as blood poured onto my forearms from my fingers and the palm. Why hadn't I put on my sailing gloves? The shroud was all frayed and sharp as hell. Its individual wires unraveled farther as I tried to hold onto it and tie it off somehow. I had to let it go.

My hand hurt so bad, but as I continued to watch the snakelike cable flail about mercilessly, I knew it was only a matter of time before it would come back to bite me again. This was a fight I had to win no matter the pain or injury to myself, so when the wire whipped past my head a third or fourth time, I lunged for it again with my bloody palm. In a split second I realized I could barely hang on to it and decided to trade the pain and agony of my left hand for some anguish and suffering in my right, all the while hoping that farther up the cable it would smooth out. But I couldn't reach any higher without jumping up off the pitching deck, risking not only losing my balance but also my hold on the shroud if I fell down. Now both my hands were ripped and bleeding. Obviously that wasn't my best decision.

I grabbed for the wheel with my left hand again to steer *Slomocean* up a large swell as my right hand held agonizingly onto the shroud. It was not unlike gripping razor or barbed wire for support while trying to stand up on a carnival ride after being sprayed with cold water. When I couldn't stand it any longer, I switched the shroud back to my left hand, knowing full well the insufferable pain and damage that would ensue as I searched desperately for something to tie the shroud off with my right. The cable jerked and pulled, went slack, and jerked again, ripping the flesh from my fingers and cutting deeply into my palm, but I didn't let go. I lost track of how many times this happened. It was hellish.

The blood from my palms and fingers now covered my face as I traded hands with the devil wire again and again along with the need to wipe the salt spray from my eyes. The water on deck became a weird mix of cotton-candy pink and white foam. It was the most pain I have ever experienced. It was excruciating, the salt water only making it ten times worse.

Finally I got control of the shroud and tied it off. I reefed in the main and checked the mast and remaining rigging for security. It would hold. I managed to make it below for some rudimentary medical attention, but the prognosis wasn't good. My hands and palms were lacerated to shreds. I couldn't get them to stop bleeding, and I couldn't get myself to stop shaking. It hurt so bad, I was ready to faint, but I knew I couldn't let myself.

I doubted I could grip the wheel, let alone any ropes or lines. I didn't even know if I could make it back to land, but at that moment, I didn't have a choice. I bandaged up both hands into makeshift pompoms with gauze, old t-shirts, and socks and bound the white cloth with duct tape. Then I just stood there wobbling as I studied them, hoping I wouldn't see red. I wouldn't let myself sit down for the longest time, fearing I might pass out. Funny as it sounds (and opposite of what I would usually think), my instincts were right. That was what I needed to do to survive.

Agonizingly I made my way back outside and turned toward St. Thomas, using my legs and feet to steer and support myself at the helm. Fortunately the diesel engine in the boat's belly fired right up; it was music to my ears—the first and only bit of good news that day.

Now with the trade winds softening a bit and the waves subsiding in the lee of the islands, it should have gotten easier, but with the adrenaline finally leaving my body and brain, the realization of what had just happened began to sink in. I was scared. I couldn't stand the pain in my hands. The bandages on them were turning pink. I felt weak, and St. Thomas was still a long way off. With two reefs in the main, and a fully furled jib, it would take a while even with the boat's motor pushing us. I knew I couldn't raise the main again, not in my condition. Maybe I could let out the jib and limp into St Thomas. I had to try.

Thankfully *Slomocean* rescued me from my own stupidity and guided me safely to port. She had saved me. Some locals tied her off safely as I looked on dazed, delirious, and dehydrated. For the first time in a long time, I was thankful to be on land rather than at sea. The locals then graciously took me to the Charlotte Amalie Hospital. I needed a doctor.

Chapter 17

Here We Go Again on Our Own
Told By Jon

Something happens to women after the birth of a child. I know it should be obvious, and to some extent, it is, but the loss of my wife was so insidious, it took me by surprise. Elise loved being a mom, and I loved being a dad. I never thought anyone could capture my heart and hold it hostage more completely than my wife, but Bergen was a daddy's girl from the beginning. She had me wrapped around her little finger. I was smitten and loving every exhausting minute of fatherhood.

Maybe it was because I was so tired, I don't know. I was flying internationally now on a wide-body jet, logging long hours across multiple times zones. AM and PM had become mythological delineations for when other people slept or were awake, but not me. My jetlag carried over into our home life as well, and Elise and Bergen suffered the brunt of it. I was often up at night and sleeping during the day. Elise was on her own many days, even when I was home. She needed a break from momhood, and we needed to reconnect.

It had been months since we really talked, uninterrupted by life. It had been forever since we'd made love. We hadn't even christened our master bedroom, let alone any other spontaneous and interesting areas of our new home. I had lost my wife. She was now a full-time mom and seemingly had left the previous chapter in her life behind. I missed my wife, and I loved her even more now, if that was possible. Seeing her transform into a mother after the birth of Bergen was the most amazing metamorphosis. But once a cute, playful, and attentive caterpillar changes into a strong, beautiful, and amazing butterfly, it can never go back.

Fortunately for me and our marriage, Elise's mother had recently retired from her job as an insurance underwriter and was always asking to help. I had to do this up right. It had to be big. I had to have Elise all to myself again. No offense to Bergen, but I missed being the center of attention. I had to lure Elise away, even if only for a few days, so I decided to take her to France. Paris is for lovers, some say. I needed to find out if that was urban myth or actual truth. I was hoping for the latter.

The great thing about working for an airline is being able to take full advantage of just this kind of opportunity. I had flown to Paris probably a dozen or more times during the past few months and was getting fairly comfortable with the lay of the land, if not the language. I've never been very good with other languages. I'm sort of a bilingual illiterate, but I can get by in many places around the world.

I looked forward to showing Elise what I knew. It was great to see her excited again as we planned our getaway, and for reasons other than the "first this" or "first that" of Bergen's recent exploits. She was a great mom, but I wanted my wife on this trip.

Everyone talks about Paris in the spring, and it is great, but fall is wonderful there as well. All the local Parisian shop owners are back in their stores after August break, and the weather is usually warm and dry. The best part of seeing Paris in the fall is the lack of tourists. Sure there are some still there; they are ever present, but the huge throngs that inundate every museum, palace, and cathedral during the summer have left, and the crowds are now more manageable.

We arrived in the morning after an all-nighter in

coach across the Atlantic. I was hoping for a free upgrade to business class or even first, as we were traveling space available standby, but it wasn't in the cards because it was a very full flight. Actually we were just lucky to even get on, but we made it. Elise couldn't stop smiling. We were tired but excited.

We took the train into Paris from Charles De Gaulle Airport and unpacked at the crew hotel. As much as we both wanted to immediately go out exploring, our bodies were in full revolt from the flight over and the onboard movies. (Damn, Seabiscuit, you are just too awesome of a horse.) Now we had to sleep. It was a blissful rest—no baby monitor, no crying, no checking on Bergen just to check to see if everything was okay, just sweet dreams.

After our afternoon nap, we ventured out around Sydney Place, Peace Park, and the Eiffel Tower, which was awash in sparkling lights. But nothing beamed as brightly as Elise as we walked and talked and looked at each other. We even held hands. I felt like I was twenty-five again. I wanted to take her to this tiny bistro I had been shown by a former crew. It only sat twelve or sixteen people and was run by a gentleman chef named Phillipe and his wife. That was it—small, intimate, amazing food, and great wine. It would be perfect. I didn't know the name and would have butchered it if I did, but I thought I knew the location well enough.

As anyone who has wandered the back streets of Paris will tell you, it's easy to get lost, especially at night, and we found that to be true. Apparently I wasn't the tour guide I thought I was. Then it began to rain. We didn't have an umbrella, but Elise was wonderful. She didn't hold it against me. She just smiled reassuringly, saying, "I'm sure we can find any number of amazing places to eat. This is Paris after all. I'm in Paris! We're in Paris! Can you believe it?" She smiled at me. "Thanks for this. . . . I love you." I don't even think she noticed the rain.

Those were the words I needed to hear. There was the look in her eyes I had missed for so long. I needed to feel like more than just a breadwinner. I needed to feel wanted. I wanted to feel desired. After that moment I would tell you it didn't even matter what we did, but that would be at least a fib if not an outright lie. We found a great little French restaurant and enjoyed an exceptional three-course meal uninterrupted by life. Cocooned within our own conversation, we talked for two hours about everything (including Bergen, of course, as we both missed her so). We finished off a wonderful bottle of cabernet, then retired to our room, well rested for once. It was an amazing night. Elise had gone shopping before the trip back in the states, and I had been working out. I think both those things helped. Apparently Paris is for lovers after all.

In four days and four nights, we managed to see most of the big stuff. The Eiffel Tower was cool but paled by comparison to Notre Dame and Sacré-Couer. The Louvre and the Palace of Versailles were fun, as was the Champs-Élysées, but my favorite thing, as corny as it sounds, was just hanging out with Elise again, like we were dating, like when we were younger, with no mortgage, no schedule, no worries or cares, just the two of us in our own little world. We reconnected over lattes and chocolate croissants for breakfast. We snacked on cheese and baguettes for lunch. We invariably found a bistro that was unbelievably better than the one the night before for dinner, and then we retired to our room for dessert.

I think, looking back, Paris was more fun than our honeymoon in the Cayman Islands. By this time in our lives together, Elise and I were more than comfortable with each other, where we were in life, and where we were headed together. At the time of our wedding, we had faced a huge move from Wisconsin to Alaska for my job immediately following a week in the Caribbean. Our honeymoon should have been the most romantic vacation of our lives, but instead of letting loose and enjoying the island, we mostly just sat around discussing what we needed to remember and do the following week. Some honeymoon. In a nutshell that was Elise and me: responsible, proactive, and anal to a fault—the two least spontaneous souls on the planet, but we were perfect for each other, and in the end that's what mattered most.

All good things must come to an end, however, and soon enough we found ourselves in business class flying comfortably back to Chicago and Bergen and life. With eight and a half hours still to ourselves, though, we decided to take full advantage of our time together. (No, not the mile high club; it's nothing as salacious as that. Did you read the last paragraph? And come on, I didn't want to get fired from my job.) I don't know if our newfound intimacy had rekindled something inside Elise or her absence from Bergen left her wanting more, but the subject of trying again for another child came up somewhere over the British Isles early on in the flight and consumed us all the way back across the Atlantic, as well as our drive home.

"We don't know if Bergen was a one-in-a-million miracle," Elise began. "I think we should start trying again. I want Bergen to have a sibling . . . or two," she admitted, smiling. "I think it's important, and it might take a while!"

I mostly agreed with her. I was all in favor of trying and, if at first we didn't succeed, trying again and again. What worried me was going back to all the specialists and the artificial inseminations and, most of all, the in vitros. We didn't have the money now with our new house and all the bills that came along with it. To my surprise, though, Elise was in full agreement. We would do it the old-fashioned way or not all. If it happened, it did, and if it didn't, we had Bergen. Hallelujah!

**

We spent the rest of 2005 without technological assistance, so to speak, trying to get pregnant, until one day after the New Year I found a box of ovulation tests in our bathroom. Elise was upping the ante. I could go along with this, but no further. *We are not going down this path again*, I thought.

Soon after that, however, Elise sweetly suggested, "Maybe you should get tested again, just to see."

"I thought we agreed on this!"

"What could it hurt?" she replied. "It's no big deal!"

But it was a big deal to me. I was just starting to feel like a man again, confident and virile. I really didn't want my ego shattered again. I didn't want the blame. But I knew that Elise was nothing if not persistent. I even loved that about her, so I held her off as long as I could but reluctantly booked an appointment with Dr. Slocum for March.

***

Sitting in the doctor's office again brought back a lot of uncomfortable memories and feelings. It was like nothing had changed—except me. I was now just that much older. I knew what Elise and I had agreed on, but I also knew her determination to have more children. I knew the costs. I knew everything, and I wasn't happy. While I sat there thinking these things, my phone rang, and I answered it abruptly without even looking at the caller ID.

"WHAT?" I asked rudely, fully expecting to hear some sort of soothing sugary encouragement from Elise on the other end. But it wasn't her.

"Dude . . . Jon boy." It was Sebastian. "What's up with you?" He didn't even wait for my response. "I'm in a hospital in St. Thomas for a checkup!" Sebby yelled as if he had a bad connection on his end.

"Are you okay?" I asked, still shocked I was actually speaking to Seb after all this time.

"Yeah, I'm okay," he insisted. "I tore up my hands pretty bad on a shroud that broke and unraveled. I'll have to stay here for a while," he continued. "They're pretty bad. What's up with you? Where are you at?"

"You're never going to believe this, Sebby," I said, trying to build up a little suspense.

"Go ahead, try me, dude," Sebastian countered.

"I'm sitting in Dr. Slocum's office as we speak, waiting for the blue room," I admitted, although I was more than a little embarrassed.

"BOOM!" Sebby made some sort of loud noise on his end of the phone. "Dude, I just fell out of my chair! You're shittin' me! That is too funny," he said, laughing.

"Yeah, Elise and I are trying for another and not having much luck so—"

"Try some different positions for Christ's sake!" Sebby interrupted, still laughing.

"Yeah . . . well . . . I have to get my numbers checked," I said sheepishly. "How are you, old friend?" I asked, trying to change the subject.

"Good . . . really good. Except for my hands," he continued. "I met a girl. . . ."

Of course you did, you old dog, I thought as I smiled. *Probably two or three or five!*

"She's a doctor here at the hospital," Sebby continued. "She was born in the U.P." He was referring to the upper peninsula of Michigan just north of Wisconsin. "But she was raised in Washington State near Seattle. I think I'm going to ask her out—"

"Keep in touch, Sebby," I interrupted. "They're calling my name. Can you believe the magazines in the waiting room still haven't changed?"

"Fuck, you're kidding me, dude," Sebby said in disbelief. "Say hi to Candace for me in the blue room!" He laughed. "July Playboy '99."

"I gotta run, Seb. Thanks for the call!" As I hung up

my phone, I entered the blue room to do what I had to do. *Honestly, I don't think I can do this*, I thought to myself. Too many things were swimming in my head. I had severe doubts I could make anything swim in a cup. Now I was even thinking about Sebby and some hot doctor. *My old friend, the stud*, I thought. *Myself, the old dud.* This wasn't helping. It just made me feel worse, more inadequate, impotent, and less manly. I considered just leaving. I could come back another time. I'd just tell Elise I couldn't do it. *I should go get a nice coffee, a little pick-me-up for the morning, and go sit out by the lake. Or I could just go home.*

But I didn't. I sat there for what seemed like forever, lost in my own thoughts, thumbing through magazines, completely disinterested, alone, embarrassed, and confused. I felt hungry. I had a headache. Maybe I was suffering from low blood sugar or something. I hadn't eaten much of anything that day. *Maybe I just need a little pick me up*, I thought again. Then I found some: Candy, right where old Seb said she'd be.

Chapter 18

Goodbye, My Love
Told by Sebastian

As I sat in the emergency room waiting area for non-critical patients, I felt lucky to be alive. It had been a harrowing couple of days and a big test that I barely passed. My hands ached immeasurably, even after the pain meds the physician's assistant administered to me intravenously began to kick in. Dehydrated and exhausted, as well as delirious now from the drip, I couldn't see clearly. Was this an angel walking toward me or the hottest doctor I had ever seen?

"I'm Dr. Tilsen," she said as she began looking over my file. "You can call me Whitney," she added sweetly.

I think we just made a connection. She isn't wearing a ring, I noticed hopefully, the pain in my hands disappearing as rapidly as the smile on my still bloodied face spread.

I completely forgot that I looked like hell and probably smelled worse. I should have been delusional in thinking I could somehow turn on the old Sebastian charm. I was in love, or at least lust. I tried to turn it up a notch, maybe less. I don't know, I was pretty out of it.

"I'm Koh . . . Sebastian Koh," I added deliriously in my best "Bond . . . James Bond" impression.

"So it says here!" the doctor commented assuredly. "You look like hell," she added, deflating my ego just as it began to get pumped up ever so slightly. Aren't doctors and nurses supposed to have a good bedside manner? That seemed a little callous. "I hear you're lucky to be alive." She studied my makeshift bandages inquisitively.

"Yeah . . . I guess so," I admitted meekly, as only then did I begin to notice my overall appearance and odor.

"What happened?" she asked, though I think she was only making polite conversation as she began to unwrap the labyrinth of wet, pink cloth from my hands.

I wanted to tell her everything. I wanted to tell her how brave I was and how swiftly I had acted to overcome the myriad of obstacles that threatened my very existence. I wanted to expound on the weather and the sea and my boat. I wanted to brag and impress her. I wanted her desperately to look me in the eyes again as she had only briefly when she entered the room, but she just continued working on my bandages.

I just silently studied the top of her head as she sat on a stool in front of me unwrapping my hands. I didn't know what to say. I had no mojo whatsoever. My hands and fingers were ripped to shreds as if I had stuck them in a blender or something. White, pink, pale and pruney, they would need a bunch of stitches, but at least they had stopped bleeding.

Dr. Tilsen told me her intentions while delicately completing an exam on my scalped fingers. "You're going to need a lot of stitches, maybe even a small skin graft. You up for a little more pain?"

"Jeez, Doc," I began. "Can't you up the drip a bit or something?" I asked.

"Oh, you're a big boy," Dr. Tilsen said wryly. "You can take it." She glanced only briefly in my direction to show a sly smile on her lips, obviously not impressed by what she had been told by the nurses, who were informed by locals, who were enlisted by the dock hands that tied up *Slomocean* and got me in a car to the hospital. I know how stories have a way of changing the more times they are told, but I didn't have the energy to refute the discrepancies in her retelling as she plunged a small hook needle over and over again into my left palm.

If only she would look into my eyes, she would know the truth, I thought as I watched her. But Dr. Tilsen just continued talking and answering her own questions while sewing up my hands.

"Did you check the weather before you left San Juan?" she asked. "I would have checked the weather," she said defiantly before I could even answer. "Salt water is hard on boats, you know. You have to respect big water—"

"Look, lady!" I interrupted abruptly and chauvinistically. "I have a great respect for big water! I did check the weather!" (I hadn't.) "My boat was in good condition." (It wasn't.) "I know what I'm doing!"

"By the look of these," Dr. Tilsen said confidently, "you don't. I grew up sailing and have never been hurt or hurt anybody—"

"Yeah . . . well . . . I grew up sailing too," I interrupted again. "I've been sailing since I was a boy." I weakly tried to stick out my chest. I must have come off sounding like a child in an argument. It was a strange rebuttal. This wasn't going at all like I had hoped, and Dr. Tilsen just laughed a small sort of confident laugh—not an *ah ha* funny laugh, but the kind rather that puts you in your place, the kind of laugh that makes you feel small. I didn't want the hole I was in to get any deeper, so I quickly decided to keep quiet.

"Where did you learn to sail?" she asked sweetly after a few agonizing minutes of silence, apparently realizing that maybe she and her open opinion of me had probably crossed the line from professional to personal.

"Lake Michigan," I answered more calmly.

"I grew up in Washington State," she offered. "Near Puget Sound. My dad taught me how to sail."

"Mine too," I replied softly. "I've been out cruising for a year."

"Wow, I bet it was fun until this happened. Is your boat okay?"

What kind of woman asks about a boat like that? I

thought. *I like this one.*

For the next couple hours, we bantered back and forth about everything. We had a similar repertoire of stories to share. I stared at the top of her sandy blonde and brown hair and her white lab coat while she concentrated on my now swollen hands.

"You won't be doing any sailing anytime soon," Dr. Tilsen announced. "Do you have a place to stay in town, or are you going to fly home?"

"I hadn't gotten that far yet," I responded, hoping she might offer something, anything, but she didn't. "I'll probably just stay on *Slomocean* or—"

"Slow motion?" she asked inquisitively.

"Yeah, my boat. But spelled s-l-o-m-o-c-e-a-n," I replied.

She nodded a little. "I like it!"

"Or I'll just get a room and recuperate before continuing on," I added.

"You're not going home?"

"No . . . I still haven't found what I'm looking for," I admitted obtusely.

Finally she looked up at me, right into my eyes. I thought she might ask what that was or offer up some local insight into where I should stay. I thought she might at least say something like "Nice talking to you!" But she didn't. She just looked me straight in the eyes and said, "Well . . . we're done here. I'll write you up a few prescriptions. The PA will explain them, and the nurse will see you out. Good luck."

She wasn't impressed or interested. I thought in my delirious state that we had made a connection, but obviously we hadn't. I wondered if all my time at sea had really messed up my radar, made it rusty and what not, but it probably was the pain killers. What else could I do now except sleep, eat, pop antibiotics, and figure out what to do next?

After a few days, I began to think more clearly. I

wandered the streets of Charlotte Amalie, the capital and largest city in the Virgin Islands, and waited for my hands to begin healing and return to their normal size. I visited *Slomocean* to make sure she was okay and apologize for getting her into this mess and not taking care of her better. I found a boatyard and made arrangements for her repairs. I called my mom and told her what had happened, speaking in reverse chronological order. We talked for hours, and my phone bill was astronomical, but we hadn't really communicated like that in years. For once she really listened, even though I think it was probably the middle of night or something in Tahiti.

I couldn't live aboard my boat, since she was in for repairs, so I found a long-term rental. At my first few checkups, Dr. Tilsen told me my recovery might take some time. I think she was shocked that I hadn't just flown back to Wisconsin and put my boat up for sale, but I was beginning to look forward to my checkups and was always disappointed when another doctor looked me over. I wanted her to look me over. I desperately wanted to look her over from head to naked toe, but she always kept it professional. I couldn't get her to go out with me for dinner on a real date, but I finally convinced her to join me for coffee one morning on her day off.

Maybe she has a boyfriend, I considered. *Maybe she thinks I'm some kind of playboy. Maybe she doesn't think about me at all. She's probably in a serious relationship. She probably gets hit on all the time.*

I thought about her constantly; besides watching CNBC, there wasn't much else to do. I think she knew I was a short timer, a sailor in port looking for some easy action, and Dr. Tilsen was anything but casy. I had to convince her I had changed from the person I was a year earlier (the person she had never met) to the man I was at least attempting to become now.

After a month of checkups and small talk, we finally

met outside the hospital. It was splendid. I found out that Whitney was thirty-two and a UW alum as well, but for her that meant the University of Washington. She had taken two years off to make some money before starting med school, as her parents didn't have much, and was finishing her third year of a six-year residency commitment to the hospital in Charlotte Amalie that paid for the majority of her med school. Soon the elder resident would move on to greener pastures back in the states, and Whitney, the junior doctor, would step up and begin mentoring a fresh med school grad. For the next three years she would be the senior resident, as the two positions at the hospital always switched at the halfway mark. But at this time the resumé on her new understudy was still blank. She didn't know from where he or she was graduating or when they would be arriving. Whitney was an indentured servant but loved her work and the Virgin Islands.

Whitney was driven, but soft. She was beautiful but never made herself up. She had a crazy athletic fashion sense, but I could tell she didn't give a damn what other people thought, least of all me. I, on the other hand, was mesmerized. For most of the morning as we had our coffee, I just sat and listened, trying not to stare at her too long at any one time. I only asked an occasional follow-up question for clarification. She was guarded. I could tell she had already made up her mind about me and wasn't about to become my trophy, but yet she seemed to like talking with me, so there was hope.

I began to open up to her. "I don't know if I have it in me to go back out there again. I'm thinking I might have to sell *Slomocean*. I never thought about what I would do once I got here. To tell you the truth, I don't know if here is where this is supposed to end . . . whatever this is. This crazy adventure of self-discovery I am on. I just had to get out of Milwaukee. I don't think I have it in me to sail her all the way back home . . . you know? Is that weak of me?" I wanted her input. "But I don't think I can leave her . . . sell her, you know?" I asked again, seeking her permission to ease my conscience for what I had in reality already decided. This conversation and my feelings for both *Slomocean* and Whitney had me flustered. I couldn't form my thoughts into coherent sentences. Even as I spoke, I knew what a pathetic, indecisive idiot I sounded like. *Where was good ol' confident, decisive Sebby?*

"That's tough," she said frankly, looking into my eyes. "Life is full of tough choices." She spoke as if she knew what she was talking about. "I'm sure you'll figure it out one way or the other." It wasn't the warm, fuzzy answer I was hoping for, but then that was the Whitney I was just beginning to know.

I talked to the men at the boatyard and put out an ad on the internet. I felt like the owner of a beloved family dog faced with either expensive long-term critical care or the easy but cowardly option of simply putting Fido down. I couldn't bear the thought of selling *Slomocean*, but the alternative meant another six months or more under sail back to the Midwest. I was homesick and selfishly wanted a faster mode of transportation back to Wisconsin. Besides, watching CNBC and Bloomberg Television while recuperating had stirred in me an intense desire to get back in the game. If Whitney had given any hint of our coffee talks leading to something bigger, I probably would have considered staying, but she never did.

My hands slowly found there natural size and began healing. My visits to the hospital became less frequent, but our breakfast dates continued on steadily. Whitney was so easy to talk to. She made me laugh with how she always looked on the bright side of things, but conversely maintained a stoic and guarded persona. She was an enigma, an optimist and pessimist at the same time. Whitney seemed to like and want the finer things in life but always understood the value of a buck. She clearly knew what was important to her in life, and what was just fluff. I admired that about her.

I couldn't read her, but I'm sure in her eyes my motives seemed obvious, as I still hadn't perfected Sebastian 2.0 (the man I was trying to become.) I think it helped that I didn't push myself on her, respecting her boundaries and not inquiring as to what lurked on the other side of the walls she so carefully maintained.

Are we becoming friends? I had to ask myself. I didn't know. I had never been friends with a single woman before sleeping with her first. This was virgin territory for me. Whitney had me all befuddled and confused. I felt like a virgin myself. It was weird.

At the same time, I was struggling with the inevitable. I couldn't just stay here forever, and my hands had, for the most part, healed up. Should I fly home and just leave *Slomocean* in Saint Thomas? What if she didn't sell? What if she did sell? That almost seemed worse. What kind of asshole sells the love of his life to someone he doesn't even know? Would she ever forgive me? This was crazy. *It's only a boat*, I tried to remind myself repeatedly, but I couldn't lie that easily to myself anymore.

In the end, I found a serious buyer for her in Grenada. The problem was I had to sail *Slomocean* there for him to look over once she got back in the water. I had to get back on the horse that only two months before had so violently bucked me off, and I was scared.

I spent my last month on St. Thomas readying *Slomocean* for the journey south and preparing myself for what I had never feared before: big water. The truth was I could have gotten underway in just a few days, but I kept delaying, hoping against hope that something between Whitney and me would spark and light the fire I felt smoldering within me. She helped with my provisioning and proved to be more than an angel by agreeing to sail with me on her days off. We took *Slomocean* out a few times together under the auspice of testing her out, when in reality I was testing myself and my arthritic-like hands to see if they were ready.

It was great sailing with Whitney. I wasn't sure I wanted to leave, but my radar hadn't picked up on anything with her other than the status quo, so after three months, it was time to head south. We agreed to be infrequent pen pals.

When the time came, I knew what to expect from Whitney, and although disappointed, I finally read her perfectly. There wasn't any long good-bye or tearful, tender moment between us. She wouldn't even give me a hug, just a handshake and a simple, "Good luck! If you're ever back in St. Thomas, call me. Or if you want, you can write me sometime!" She helped untie the boat and gave me a final wave without even waiting to watch me get underway. I guess she had to get back to the hospital or something. I had hoped for more, but it wasn't in the cards.

***

Slomocean and I picked our way cautiously through the BVI toward the Netherlands Antilles and Antigua. Before long, I began to feel comfortable again with everything except my hands, which were still somewhat tender and stiff. I took it very slowly, hugging the shoreline wherever I could and diligently checking the weather before making any attempt at a longish passage between islands.

The southeastern Caribbean was sparse compared to the north. The islands were larger, more mountainous, and more densely populated than the numerous small, empty cays in the Bahamas and Turks and Caicos. This sail had a completely different feel than the winter before. For one thing, it was hot! I quickly became a bronze man; SPF 1000 wouldn't have kept my skin from broiling. I lived in running shorts and survived on water, tea, and any other form of liquid I could get my hands on.

With her repairs back in Charlotte Amalie, *Slomocean* felt like a new bride. She glistened and glowed under the ever-present sun. She sailed wonderfully, and I think maybe she forgave me for ignoring her care for so long. But did she know what I had in store for her? I tried not to think about it. I couldn't bring myself to tell her, but I had to.

As the summer of 2006 came to an end, we turned southwest from St. Lucia toward the Grenadines and, finally, Grenada. I cried more than once as we sailed alone together in a vast blue void of sea and sky. I tried to talk to her and explain why this had to be, but the words didn't come easily. I always felt like I was lying. As much as I tried to console *Slomocean*, I had a harder time consoling myself. I know it sounds crazy, but she meant the world to me, and yet I was giving her up.

Entering the harbor at St George's that September, it was all I could do not to turn her around and head north, but it was the height of hurricane season, so it wasn't an option anyway.

Another excuse, I thought to myself.

I gave her a hug and a kiss on her mast. I cleaned her out a little and said a long goodbye. Handing over her keys was one of the hardest things I've ever had to do in my life, but the new owner promised to take good care of her.

"You better!" I said adamantly with tears welling up in my eyes. "She's the best little sailboat in the whole world!" I could hardly spit out the words. "Goodbye, my love," I told her, softly touching her helm for the last time. "You're the best thing that ever happened to me! I owe you a lot. I owe you my life . . . . in more ways than one."

The buyer took two pictures of me standing next to her stern with an old Polaroid camera. A harbor sign in the background gave my location away. I asked that he not rename her (but I don't know if he ever did). I kept one picture for myself and mailed the other to Whitney. Not knowing what to say, I just wrote "Thank you!" on the back with a red Sharpie and made a small heart for the dot in the exclamation point.

I left Grenada with only the shirt on my back, a small stuff sack full of crappy clothes, a camera full of memories, and a check that I didn't know if I could even cash. I thought of catching a connecting flight out of San Juan to Chicago or New York but instead bought a ticket to Miami and on to the west coast. I had decided to go to Tahiti. It was high time I visited my mom.

Chapter 19

Swimming Upstream
Told By Jon

My numbers weren't good. That was the unfortunate news we got from Dr. Slocum. We had two options. We could just continue trying and praying and hoping and trying and praying and . . . well, you get the picture, or we consider a second varicocele surgery to see if my numbers improved.

As Elise and I discussed this in his office, I already knew what was next. The steely look of determination in her eyes, now mixed with more than a hint of desperation, told me everything I needed to know. There was only one option for us. Maybe Bergen was an inexplicable one-in-a-million miracle. Maybe we would never have another child. Maybe conception wasn't in the cards for us without further assistance. But we had to try.

Varicocele surgery is only minimally invasive. Basically a small incision is made somewhere in the body and a very small shunt is placed in a blood vessel upstream of the male's testes, which blocks the blood flow downstream and thus reduces the temperature ever so slightly in the area of sperm production in the hope that this helps produce a better end product. How's that for a generic clinical description of an awkward operation? This surgery, which Dr. Slocum scheduled for May 2006, would be my second. Apparently I was just too hot in the crotch.

I wasn't a wreck, but I wasn't myself anymore. I had regressed to a place only months before I swore I would never revisit. I wasn't lost, but I wasn't sure where I stood.

Elise and I had agreed to be happy with our little Bergen and continue trying the old-fashioned way. Was she now willing to do anything under the sun to conceive again? Was she ready to go back down that road? Thankfully not. We spoke openly and candidly about how far we were willing to take this. Elise drew a line in the sand after artificial insemination. It was far less costly and invasive than in vitro fertilization.

I was skeptical, but I agreed. I could only hope that we wouldn't cross that line again, even if we could somehow afford to, even if that was the only option we had left.

Our budget was tight with little house projects and various baby toys, clothes, and diapers eating incessantly into what had once been a small but comfortable financial cushion. Who knew a little angel could make that many "messies"? Not me! I was already working a ton, so I couldn't fly more trips even if I wanted to.

Elise was consumed with Bergen and told me that if it didn't work she could be happy with one child. I was more than happy. Bergen was amazing, but Elise truly wanted to have another child, and I knew that. I could read between the lines. We were both growing older. The clock was ticking, and at some point, time would run out. Unfortunately, by then, even the prospect of adoption would become more difficult, as most agencies and birth parents preferred to place babies with younger families. We both had siblings, and Elise routinely reminded me just how different we both would have turned out without that brother or sister in our lives. It was an important point.

Staying home all day, every day, day after day also made Elise recognize the importance of having other options. She had never completed her master's degree and figured now was a better time than any. When Bergen was old enough to go to school full time, if we weren't blessed with another child, Elise wanted to return to teaching. Apparently with this very thought, Elise concluded that our prospects were dim.

"I want to enroll for the fall semester," Elise told me. "I'll work around our schedule, then I'll be able to earn more when I go back to teaching with a master's degree." She was a great salesperson. I just hoped we could swing her tuition and the pending bills that came along with our quest for a sibling for Bergen. We would really have to pinch pennies.

We spent the summer of '06 blissfully bouncing around the area, taking in whatever was inexpensive or, better yet, free. Our parents and siblings visited often and spoiled Bergen rotten with attention. Now one and a half years old, playful, and precocious, her budding personality was beginning to show, and I couldn't believe how much more I loved her every day.

I started to realize how great it would be to have another child, and I could see the longing in Elise's eyes as she looked at her and then to me. Wanting to make her happy, I began the layaway program at Dr. Slocum's office. The second surgery had indeed improved my numbers and apparently their ability to swim as well. Now all we needed was another miracle. Once every week or so, I paid a visit to Candy and Patsy and Christy. Why do the girls' names in those magazines always seem to end in Y? Was there a link? As I realized this, I thought, *I'll do anything to keep my daughter off the pole or in print. Note to self: If we are lucky enough to have or adopt another child, don't name it any name that ends in Y. Anything to help keep my kid on the straight and narrow. Anything!*

I was losing my mind with worry, and we weren't even expecting. *The ends justify the means*, I told myself. *The only thing that matters is my family. A happy wife is a happy life. I have to do this, so stop thinking. STOP THINKING!*

It didn't help.

I was a shell of my former Parisian self. Elise noticed it as well. She understood my anxiety and tried to soothe my bruised ego as best she could, but she couldn't hide her newfound optimism. The good news, in her eyes, was that my numbers had improved dramatically since the surgery, even if my self-esteem was now at an all-time low. Apparently my temperature down there was linked to more than just production. It affected my mental state as well. You would think I would be happy and optimistic like my wife, but for me it was just the opposite.

"Maybe you should skip a week at the office, Jon," Elise suggested coyly, as intercourse while trying to stockpile your stuff is strictly forbidden. Her amorous offer wasn't lost on me for a moment, so we arranged for a sitter, made a reservation at a great place downtown, and forgot about trying to conceive—at least I did. I just wanted to feel normal again, like a man instead of a vending machine. I thought Elise did too, especially after shef ound a beautiful outfit and insisted I dress up for the occasion as well. She put on a great act.

It was a gorgeous evening. The food and our conversation flowed for three hours as we talked about everything—well, almost everything. We reconnected both mentally and, later, physically. It was a great night, a night to remember.

Apparently, though, she had an ulterior motive all along. Elise was ovulating, and for once I wasn't somewhere else in the world flying a jet. Elise admitted it to me the next morning. We never keep secrets, for very long anyway. I lay in bed feeling betrayed, but I tried to counsel myself that it was worth it, if for no other reason than not having to go to the blue room for another week or so. *Besides*, I thought, *if you don't use it . . . you lose it.* I missed my wife and should have felt some sort of post-coital bliss, but I couldn't easily forgive her trickery, not this time anyway.

Looking back, I guess I did suspect it, but I chose instead to believe that she wanted me for me and not just my stuff. It was another blow to my battered ego. My self-esteem was once again back below zero.

I simply withdrew, which I'm really good at it. I drifted off into my own world for most of the next few months and concentrated on me and myself alone. Out of spite more than anything I distanced myself from Elise and gave her the cold shoulder whenever I could. When I was away at work, I didn't even call to check in.

Let me tell you, spite is like a drug, at least with me. Once I started "using" it, I wanted and needed more. Crazy as it sounds, the more I withdrew, the more I wanted Elise to notice I was withdrawing, and if she didn't, I got even colder. I never once told her why I was doing this. I guess I thought it was rather obvious, but in hindsight it probably wasn't. I was being a jerk, and I knew it. Somehow I felt like she now had everything she desired and didn't want me around anymore. I theorized that I had served my useful purpose, and except for a paycheck and the slim possibility of further procreation, I wasn't needed. I wanted to feel appreciated and loved, but lately I felt washed up, tired, and, most of all, used, and I was sick of it.

When I was home, I didn't even give Bergen the attention she needed. I realize now *that* was the worst part of my behavior. She didn't deserve it. Then again, neither did Elise for that matter. I am not proud of it now, but at the time it felt somehow like an eye for eye, the old quid pro quo, you know? But that's no excuse.

I suppose I learned this tactic, the silent treatment, from my parents. I don't know, but I was taking it to a whole new level. I always knew when my parents were upset with me, but when they went silent, I knew I had really screwed up. It was as if they were saying, "Okay, if you're so smart, have it your way," or "You got yourself into this situation, you can get yourself out!"

With my silence and indifference, I was trying to tell my wife the same thing. Honesty is a two-way street. Love and respect have to be reciprocated, but it was a muddy message, I'll admit. Although Elise definitely noticed the sudden change in my behavior, she failed to put two and two together. And for now anyway, I wasn't very interested in helping her with the math.

***

Fall is a great season near the lake. The water, finally warmed by the summer sun, moderates the weather near the shore and produces marvelous days you can hardly imagine. The trees turn every shade of yellow, red, and orange, the wind dies down, and the days grow shorter, foreboding the future onset of winter.

I always seem to appreciate those beautiful fall days more than any others for the simple fact that I know they won't last forever. Sooner than any of us ever hope, winter always blows in from the north, ushering in darkness, snow, and a cold that even holiday cheer cannot overcome, at least for the long run. I love skiing and winter in general more than most, but even I, on those early fall days, feel a tinge of resentment that they too will soon end.

October that year brought a bounty I could not have predicted. The good news was that Sebby was heading home. The great news was that Elise was two months pregnant. She didn't want to jinx it, so she hadn't admitted it to herself, or told me, until she was absolutely positive. The surgery had been a success, and we had indeed done it the old-fashioned way. Even our doctors were shocked. Lightning never strikes the same place twice, some say, but we had proved all the specialists wrong again. Bergen was not only going to be Piglet for Halloween, she was going to be a big sister by the following summer.

We couldn't be happier as parents, even if at that point we were still at odds as husband and wife, but with her good news, I had to stop my act. I guess the thought of a new baby made me finally snap out of my funk and forgive Elise. Call it woman's intuition, but her plan had worked, and the ends justified the means. I dropped my grudge and begged Elise to forgive me. Thankfully, she did so happily, and we were back on track.

I thought that maybe, just maybe, we could finally put all this behind us. Did Elise want to go for three? Selfishly I hoped not and decided to just revel in the moment. After all, she was busy with grad school now. That would keep her busy until our new baby arrived.

We were blessed and we knew it. Thanksgiving brought more good news for our families: Elise's older brother was getting married, and my older sister was changing careers. Both of our parents were now fully retired and more than ready for another grandchild. It felt like everything was really coming together.

We wanted Bergen to get excited, to share in our joy, so we decided to find out the sex of our new little peanut and tell her. We were ecstatic to find out we were having a boy. That Christmas is one that will linger in my heart and mind as possibly the best ever. We were blessed with not only one little miracle, but the promise of another. It was magical.

Chapter 20

And the Walls Come Tumbling Down
Told by Peter

As busy as I was, the winter of '06 to '07 with the tudor mansion, I found time in my schedule somewhere to meet with prospective clients. I took on three more houses and decided to make ours my fourth. It would mean hiring more help, but I just couldn't say no. I decided that if we started our new house late in the fall it would be none too soon, as our present home was bursting at the seams with bouncy chairs and toys. I was as busy as I'd ever been. There wasn't time to go to a single Brewers game or even watch the news, and the news wasn't good. The only thing I knew was that oil was skyrocketing. It cost me over eighty dollars to fill up my new Ford pickup. I guess people were starting to get nervous around me, but I didn't see it, because business was still great. Maybe somebody saw it coming, but I didn't. The end was near.

***

Mequon and the north side of Milwaukee in general is fairly to extremely affluent and white collar. Doctors, business people, pharmaceutical sales reps, and the like frequent boutique "caffeine bars" and shop at bespoke clothing boutiques for both men and women. It is as close to a status address, like Park Avenue or Rodeo Drive, as you can probably find in Wisconsin.

Mequon is a suburb filled with ladies who lunch and men who golf at exclusive clubs while sending their kids to expensive private schools and universities. Mercedes, BMWs, and Land Rovers are more common than Fords or Buicks. Status is as important as keeping up with the Joneses. Job titles mean something there, even when they shouldn't. Maybe we can be friends. Then again, maybe we can't.

"What did you say you did?"

"Where did you get that tweed and leather riding jacket with the crest on the pocket?"

"I just have to know!"

"I have to have one!"

I've overheard every kind of conversation imaginable in grocery checkout lines and coffee shops there, and felt as a general contractor, successful or not, that somehow I just didn't fit in.

Everywhere you look there are beautifully decorated shops, yoga studios, health clubs, and, of course, financial advisors (there is at least one on every block). I could recognize some of the larger firms, even with my limited knowledge: Charles Schwab, Fidelity, Scott Trade, etc. It was the more discreet firms, though, that probably catered to the heavy hitters in the area, and there were a lot of them as well.

I figured that's what Sebby's old firm, New Millennium Capital Investments, was as I drove by it one day. You know, one of those places where a guy like me would walk in, even after I'd cleaned up, and not feel truly welcome. Yeah, their secretary would pleasantly greet me and ask if I had an appointment, then offer any type of coffee drink imaginable except actual black coffee, but they would know instantly, by my clothes or questions or whatever that I didn't have the bank roll to solicit advice from them, not yet anyway. Besides, I was wearing Carhartt pants and work boots, not a suit by Brook's Brothers. They would never take a blue-collar guy like me seriously. So socking it away for retirement and my children's education would have to wait. I was still growing my business.

I heard from Sebby and, to my astonishment, he was back to town after his long journey. I really wanted to go out with him, hear all his stories, and live vicariously through his sex life in the Caribbean. I wasn't getting any, and the forecast didn't look good for the next ninety days at least. I managed to pull myself away but ended up only making an enemy of Heather when she found out. I should have known better than to come home from a bar at two a.m. smelling of cigar smoke and whiskey and trying to pawn it off as a client meeting. It was a hell of a bender though. I liked having Sebby back.

After that, he started visiting the job site whenever he could. He seemed a little lost or bored or something. I wasn't sure; most of the time I was too busy to talk. He just sort of hung around listening to me on my phone or helping the guys when they needed an extra hand lifting or holding something. When I look back now, I should have just hired him. He was a big, fit, strapping guy and presently unemployed. What was I thinking?

It also occurred to me that Sebby *had* been hanging around, and we'd had beers a few nights after work. Shouldn't *he* have told me what was about to happen with the economy—not in his terminology, but in lingo I could understand? Maybe then I would have changed my business model and taken on scores of smaller projects instead of trying to slay elephants. But he didn't. Perhaps he didn't see it coming either.

Woulda coulda shoulda, but I didn't. By the time I was breaking ground on our dream house and finishing up the last of my other homes for 2007, CNBC and Bloomberg Television were apparently buzzing of an imminent collapse in the markets, but I didn't know, because I wasn't listening. I was too busy working away on a one-a-kind masterpiece for my wife and kids.

Some people say hindsight is 20/20, and I'm sure

that's true, but I couldn't see what was right in front of me, let alone happening on every financial advisor's computer across Mequon and America, or I would have done things differently. As they began to batten down their clients' portfolios and sell advice to do the same, I planned to include every option in our dream house I could possibly acquire. *It will help the business in the long run*, I told myself repeatedly. *This home is an extension of the business.* Antique nickel fixtures went extremely well with whitewashed Sitka spruce trim and espresso stained wideplank South American hardwood flooring. Everybody was doing granite. I thought soapstone countertops would add a lot to our kitchen, as would super high-end appliances. A see-through wood-fired oven would be great for pizza, and an authentic Japanese hibachi grill was way cooler than a traditional cooktop. In-floor radiant heat, motorized skylights, and a fully wired home audio system were all added, as was a nifty central vacuum system and carriage style garage doors.

I was acting like one of my recent clients instead of me. I hid a few of the bills from Heather. She had enough on her plate with the kids. But to make matters worse, her father's cancer had returned, and the prognosis didn't look good. The oncologist was recommending a much stronger regiment of chemotherapy this time if he was up for it, while cautioning us that even with everything he had to throw at the cancer, it might not be enough. So Heather started spending a lot more time with her dad, discussing options, hoping for the best, and preparing for the worst.

The downturn in the market didn't register on my radar until the first home that Steglin Homes, LLC booked for 2008 suddenly fell through. I had long since reached the point of no return on our house, but I was happily looking forward to another big year and the money that came with it. I had to begin paying on our dream.

Unfortunately the money never materialized. As fast

as the housing market had gone up, it began to cascade down. As the contagion spread through the markets in early spring '08, a mountain of money was lost in an avalanche of debt. In my little corner of the world, that meant everything had to be put on hold indefinitely. Every time my cell phone rang, I feared somebody was looking for money. Bills were coming due, and paychecks had to be paid for my construction crew, as well as the last of the 2007 construction loan I had taken out to grow the business. Our house was nowhere near completion and yet I had to continue pouring money I didn't have into it. The only home I would complete in 2008 was my own . . . or was it the bank's? I didn't want to think about it.

***

Heather is no dummy. Even with all the time she spent with the kids and her father, she knew the numbers. She had done the math, and it didn't look good. I hate conflict, and more than anything I hated being a disappointment to her. The look on her face every time we crossed paths in our tiny home could have stopped a charging rhino. I spent as much time as I could at the new house or with our kids at one of the local parks.

I cannot say she was happy for the help, because she wasn't. It only freed her up to take her father to more and more appointments at the hospital. They also began seeing a lawyer. I guessed at the time that it was for estate planning. He would be going into hospice care at some point in the near future and probably wanted Heather to be power of attorney or something like that. Maybe he needed a living will or wanted to leave end-of-life instructions. I didn't ask, but I should have. Little did I know, Heather was hatching a plan to keep her expected inheritance not only secret, but hers and hers alone. She had already written me off. Now she just had to get a lawyer to write me out of the will.

Looking back, I bet Heather wasn't really sad that her dad had died as much as she was mad that he had died before she was free of me. For her, that would have been so much better, but that isn't how it unfolded.

When Heather was home, I did try to talk to her a few times. I wanted to tell her that I knew I had made a mistake. I wanted to comfort her and say things like, "It will get better," or "We'll get through this," but she wasn't having any of it. She kept our tiff a secret from the kids and was always congenial around them, but inside she must have been a boiling cauldron of angst and disgust. I could sense it, so I just stayed away from her. Then I began spending more time at the bars and less at the new house. That wasn't good. Coming home smelling of beer and cigarette smoke is never good!

Finally it happened, and like the financial crisis around me, I honestly never saw it coming. Apparently Heather was having a meltdown herself. I don't know to this day what the final straw was, but she dropped the hammer on me late one Friday night.

"I want a divorce!" she yelled as I came in the house."I have HAD IT!"

"What? Honey . . . What?" I asked incredulously, still staggering from the blow. "What are you talking about? What did I do?"

"What did you do?" she asked rhetorically. "Are you fucking kidding me?" Heater glared at me across the kitchen counter. "Promises, promises . . ." my wife began incoherently. "Peter wants to be a big shot. 'The housing market is red hot,'" she added snidely. "'What could possibly go wrong?' You're so stupid!" She was now beginning to talk more quietly, as the kids were asleep, but her verbal jabs only increased in intensity.

"Heather . . . honey . . . where is this coming from?" I asked innocently.

She just stared at me blankly. "You really are an idiot! I should never have married you in the first place!"

"Baby—" I started.

"Don't baby me," she interrupted, taking control of the conversation. I couldn't get a word in edgewise. Around and around we went for the better part of three hours, a verbal sparring match for the ages. Jab, counter, jab, rebuff, jab, duck. I couldn't make her understand that it went much deeper than she knew.

I told her, "Just hold on a minute for Christ's sake, Heather. I was doing it for you . . . I was doing all this for us."

But she didn't want any excuses. The night finally ended badly, with me on the sofa and her in our room.

Are we getting divorced? I wondered fleetingly. I didn't think so. I hadn't agreed to anything, or had I? I couldn't remember. My head was spinning. I couldn't sleep. *What am I going to do? What about the kids?* I just lay there on couch in the living room staring at the ceiling until morning. Then I left for some coffee and the sunrise over the lake. I hoped it would help me clear my mind.

I stayed away from home the better part of the morning, only returning to grab some tools. Heather had taken the kids to go visit her dad, and I figured a little project at the new house might help. But being there only compounded my anxiety, so I called up Sebby to see if he wanted some lunch. By two o'clock I was crying in my beer.

I asked Sebby for some advice, but he didn't have much, just the typical feel good bullshit you tell a friend when they're screwed. I was hoping for more. I don't know if it was my bad company or what, but he seemed genuinely disinterested in my plight. Yeah, he nodded and listened, but he never asked any tough questions. I thought he might ply me with some great truth or knowledge he had learned on his sailing expedition. I needed a zen master to guide me through this. Truth was, I had idolized Sebastian since the first time we met, but that day at the bar he was just another average distant Joe. I could have been spilling my guts out to the poor bartender, trapped in my pathetic conversation by the very counter he kept, unable to get away, but I didn't. I just kept buying beer for myself and watching Sebby refill his iced tea over and over again while he listened half-heartedly to my autobiographical obituary. He wasn't even drinking.

"Man, why aren't you drinking? A friend is supposed to drink with his buddy."

"It's not even five o'clock, Peter," Sebby said.

"What's five o'clock got to do with anything? I thought you were my friend, Seb," I said pathetically.

"I am, Peter. I am taking you home."

"I can't go home," I said weakly.

"Then you can stay at my place."

By the end of summer, Heather and I had officially separated. She was living in the new house and I was in our old one. Fortunately, though, Owen and Campbell weren't old enough to understand the ramifications of our new situation. I wasn't sure I did, for that matter. I repeatedly asked Heather to go to marriage counseling, but she refused, so we put on our happy faces and threw our little girl a birthday party. From the outside I'm sure it looked picture perfect. The successful contractor and his beautiful wife and kids enjoying their new home and perfect life together, but it was nothing like that at all. I was miserable. I felt lost. I went home from the party to our old empty house and cried. I don't think I moved for days.

Chapter 21

Timing is Everything
Told By Sebastian

Traveling to Tahiti to visit my mother ended up being one of the best decisions I have ever made. We spent two weeks rekindling a faint, flickering flame into a roaring fire of a relationship.

Evonne had mellowed from what I remembered growing up or even experienced over the phone. She had softened her stance on many things that years earlier she saw as simply either right or wrong. Being in the islands around family and friends had broadened her mind to at least consider other possibilities and opened it to many unsolvable mysteries and ideals that were, to say the least, inconceivable in the past. Evonne had faith again in humanity and a renewed faith in God, but it was now hers alone. She didn't need to force it on anyone else to make it real. My mother was relaxed, attentive, even congenial and warm. Apparently life in the islands with my father's family was good for her soul.

We talked for hours at a time. She even agreed to come visit and see my new house in Milwaukee, but only in the summer. She had a good life and surrounded herself with many friends and relatives. It was great to see them, many of whom I had never actually met. Only then did I begin to understand why she always held "family" in such high regard. They were her safety net, her inner circle. I didn't have that growing up in Chicago, and neither did she. It occurred to me that maybe that was part of our problem back then, and I began to envy that part of her life now. I had friends back in Wisconsin and around Chicago, but it was nothing like what I witnessed during my visit with her those two weeks.

On the way home from Tahiti, I stopped in Honolulu and San Francisco each for a few days and sent off a bunch of postcards announcing my intentions to return home. It must have been confusing for anyone receiving a postcard that wasn't from the Caribbean. They probably thought I had made it around the southern tip of South America or transited the Panama Canal. How else could I have ended up in the Pacific? But *Slomocean* wasn't that fast.

I wondered what my old boat was doing at that very moment. I pictured her tied up neatly in her slip, bobbing gently on the waves in the late fall sun. I worried every time I got wind of a tropical storm or hurricane in the Atlantic heading west northwest toward her. In my mind, I walked on her deck and went below. I still knew every inch of her as vividly as when we lived together. I liked that. I wanted to keep it that way. I missed her desperately and still couldn't bring myself to cash the check. I felt somehow that if I cashed the check and took the money, then it was over, and she wouldn't be mine anymore. I still wasn't ready to give her up completely, even if in reality I already had.

When I finally made my way to O'Hare before connecting to Milwaukee, I walked through the terminal in Chicago hoping and searching like a child for a lost toy. I was looking for Jon—maybe he would be between flights or just starting or finishing a trip. How cool it would have been to just bump into him randomly after all this time.

I remember getting off the plane in Milwaukee and heading out to the parking lot to find my car. The cold, crisp October air caught me more than a little off guard; I didn't even have a coat. It was the first time I had been cold in a long time. It was if I had been in a time warp for eighteen months. I didn't have a car at the airport. I didn't even own a car, and my old Land Rover Defender was in storage.

As I rode home in a cab late that October afternoon, I marveled at Milwaukee. The Allen- Bradley Clock Tower, the big bridge, Miller Park, and Marquette University were still there. Maybe the world hadn't changed after all. But I had.

I walked into a clean, empty, quiet house that seemed only eerily familiar now. It sure didn't feel like home. I had no emails, no phone messages, no real mail, nothing. I was alone. I couldn't even go to the store. I didn't have a car, so I called up a local pizza place and ordered a large pie and a two-liter bottle of Coke, then I sat there in utter silence, trying to figure out what to do next. That was the ten-ton elephant in my living room. I had burned through a lot of money on my adventure and needed to start making some again. A myriad of thoughts ran through my mind, but I wasn't going to jump into anything quickly. First I had to get acclimated. I turned on my old stereo softly for company and drifted off on the sofa until morning.

When I woke up the next morning, I thought, *First things first, cash that check, buy a car, and join a health club. Jeez, man, you need get back in shape.*

I found a used Volvo XC-70 and began provisioning my home for my new life. It took days to get back to normal. Mail, cable, phone service, and internet. I was busy again and had to pace myself. It was weird being back, and I couldn't get used to the cold. I guess I had become thin-skinned while away.

I went to the mall to restock my closet and ran into Elise, who nearly hit the floor. "Sebastian . . . how are you?" she asked, beaming as she leaned in to give me a hug. I started in, wanting to tell her some interesting snippets of everything that had happened, but I was immediately cut off. "You're never going to believe it, but I'm pregnant!" she announced.

"Well, congratulations!" I told her and gave her another hug. I wanted to find a place to sit and talk. I wanted to find out everything. I wanted to tell her some of my stories, but she had to run.

***

It is easy to forget the constraints of time when you have the luxury to avoid it. Back in the real world, everybody had a schedule to keep, errands to run, rushing around like busy little bees. I hadn't fully readjusted to that fact yet. I really didn't have anything I *had* to do, so I called up Jon and Peter and a couple of other old chums until I found one who was free. It was difficult reconnecting.

I started hanging out with Peter more. He was doing really well, and I admired the man he had become. He was no longer the consummate "yes boy" from years back; he instead had become a good businessman, an astute manager, and a patient mentor. He ran his crews like a well-oiled machine, the houses he built were beautiful, and he had really made a name for himself. He was even gracious enough to thank me over and over again for giving him his start.

Peter called his own shots and had grown his business successfully from the ground up. One day it occurred to me that perhaps I could do the same. Maybe I didn't have to work for somebody else. Maybe I could get back in the game and not be subject to the constraints I felt I might no longer tolerate.

***

By late fall of '07, things were different; there was a change in the air, and it had nothing to do with the impending onset of winter. I began having to babysit Peter, who was a sinking ship, if only slowly sinking. His life and business were unraveling all around him, but I didn't know what to say. I was scared he was going to ask me to loan him some money or something. Truth was, I didn't have it to loan even if I wanted to. I was in my own economic storm, grasping at ideas and trying to figure out which course of action to take that would not only prove safe, but successful. I wasn't a very good friend, but I did let him crash at my place for a while that winter. I liked the company.

I hatched a plan for my future and called it Summit Financial. *Never Stop Until You Reach the Summit* became my slogan. *How high do you want to climb?* became the question. I didn't have an office but instead worked the phone from my house. With the markets in an ever-steepening downward spiral, you would think it was a terrible time to talk about investing, but to my astonishment, the opposite was true. I knew a lot of people from my days at Promise and Millennium. I knew a lot of people on the north shore. I fell back on the oldest card in the deck and began cold calling them and asking them to switch advisors. My reputation, I'm happy to say, from my time at Promise proved especially invaluable. People still recalled my correct intuition in 1999 when I called the tech bubble crash of 2000 and became *the* star analyst of the moment. Many of those I called were already in cash or had lost a bunch and were ready to consider switching to cash for protection in the near term, as well as ditching their current money guru. Such is the way of financial advisors; you are either a hero or zero, and nobody calls it correctly forever.

"What have you done for me lately?" was always the unspoken question asked across the table. Big wigs, heiresses, and trust fund teenagers, now in their thirties and forties, couldn't fathom having to actually work for a living and were all running scared, more than happy to bet their money on a fresh horse and put their trust in an old kid who was sort of new again in town.

The best thing was, as I slowly began picking off clients in the spring of '08, the market only worsened. I know, you're thinking: How could that be a good thing? The reasons are threefold. First, the worse the market became, the more scared individual investors became and thus the more eager and receptive they became to my sales pitch of safety, security, and long-term success. Secondly, people talk. The more people who signed on with Summit Financial, the more people began to tell their friends and family. Everybody wants to be the smartest person in the room, how better to appear that way than to convince those around you that you have the solution to their problem? After a while, I didn't even have to use cold calling. My phone just kept ringing. Thirdly (and this is the best part), as the market tanked in 2008, I was sitting on an ever-growing hoard of cash. Even though I wasn't producing any real return of any kind, my clients were just happy not to be losing their shirts. They had very low expectations, which were easy to meet. The truth was, because many of them were already in cash when they switched over to me, they wouldn't have lost any further capital. They just needed to feel proactive. They needed to do something to save themselves, and I happily provided a new outlet for their anxiety.

By fall 2008, the realization that my business was now growing enthralled me. This was going to be fun. I was sitting on a mountain of cash just waiting and watching blissfully as the market tumbled. I had to play my cards right. I spent hours researching and analyzing, planning for an eventual move into the markets. For now though I was content to weather the storm from the safety of the harbor. I guess I had gleaned a thing or two on my voyage of discovery. But one thing was clear: I needed a real office to hang my shingle on. It was time to put a public face on my business persona.

Chapter 22

The Toughest Job You'll Ever Love
Told by Jon

Remember those ads that used to be on television way back in the glorious eighties with a photo montage streaming across the screen of a refugee camp and peasants? A team was digging a well for fresh, clean water or building a new school. It looked hot and remote. Everybody was sweating, but everyone was smiling. Then after twenty seconds of soft, endearing music and five seconds of silence, the man or woman in the center of the screen turned and looked directly into the camera. Through the miracle of television, it was as if they were peering directly into your soul. Finally, after a virtual eternity, everything around the volunteer faded away into the background, and he or she would proudly say, "Peace Corps . . . the toughest job you'll ever love." Deadpan, poignant, and serious, it was a great ad. Trouble was, THEY WERE LYING! The Peace Corps has got nothing on parenthood; trust me. A friend of mine went to Tanzania for three years to teach math, a noble endeavor to be sure, but he still found time to email and update his Facebook page. Elise and I didn't have time to update our clocks after daylight savings time let alone flit about in any cyber social circles.

***

Ben Foster was born May 12, 2007. Bergen was now a proud big sister. Elise and I were ecstatic. Nine pounds ten ounces, our little brute proved how different he was right off the bat by eating like there was no tomorrow. It's weird how two kids from the same gene pool can be so different. Mother Nature has her own ideas, I guess.

Everybody, including Sebastian, stopped by the hospital to take a peek and say congratulations. He offered up a half-hearted "good luck" to Elise and me. I think he looked more overwhelmed at that moment than me, as he was probably taking a moment to walk in my new shoes.

Elise and I were overjoyed, but we too were soon overwhelmed. We consoled ourselves with the idea that although we could no longer tag team Bergen, at least we could play one-on-one defense with her and baby Ben. I couldn't imagine having to play zone defense with three or more kids. Come to think of it, I hate sports analogies. I just don't know how single parents or large families do it. The thought of a vasectomy was already on my mind. We had one of each; there was no other possibility. I wanted this chapter in our lives to end. I didn't relish the thought of any more kids. Although, ironically, it did seem like we were finally getting the hang of this conception thing.

I wanted to go under the knife, but Elise wasn't so sure. "That seems so final," she said.

"Are we that old already?"

"I know I am!" I declared. This time I was bound and determined to get my way, even it meant not having her permission, but I didn't tell her that. Between my flights and Elise's stints as a quasi-single parent, we had nothing to worry about as far as a third child was concerned anyway. We chose celibacy and sleep every single time over intimacy. It wasn't even close. Nighttime feedings and a busy little Bergen made for chaotic days and sleepless nights. It occurred to me that having kids might just be the best contraceptive ever invented—well, for Elise and me anyway. There were no pills to take, nothing to buy, just a mutual look from her pillow toward mine of *Are you serious? You must be joking. Not tonight, honey.*

As for the vasectomy, we would have to agree to disagree for a while. That didn't stop me from bringing up the topic of getting snipped with Sebby one afternoon over lunch. "How bad does it hurt really?" I asked. "I've heard a lot of stories. I hate to ask, but . . . does stuff still come out?"

"Dude! You are totally spoiling my Caesar salad over here!I asked for the dressing on the
side," he said, laughing. "Calm down. It's no big deal."

"But . . ." I interjected.

"But what?" he replied. "Jeez, man, I swear, you've had more stuff done to your junk than any other man on the planet! Have a drink, Jon. . . . Chill out."

It was good to have Sebastian back. We had only made it out together a few times, but we had already fallen back into the truthful banter only good friends share. He was once again a sounding board for me, and I was a great listener for the copious quantity of stories he shared with me from his voyage of discovery to the south.

I told him about my ongoing bout with abstinence, hoping he would regale me with all the wondrous escapades he had compiled on *Slomocean* as well as on land. Instead he just laughed. "I haven't gotten ANY since before I left for the Caribbean."

"You're joking," I said, simultaneously deflated and flabbergasted.

"No, dude, two years and counting."

"You're kidding?" I was still in disbelief.

"No, seriously, I haven't been with a woman since Summer, 2005."

"But wait," I countered. "Summer of 2005 you were already on your boat heading south."

"No, I mean *Summer*," Sebby laughed, "the girl. . . . Didn't I ever tell you my story about
Stevie Nicks?"

Now I was only more confused.

"The thing is, it's not so bad," he continued.

"What?" I thought of our phone call."But you told me you met a girl . . . in St. Thomas, I think," I said.

"Yeah, but we never DID anything," he recounted.

"Not up to your standards, huh?" I asked, trying to egg Sebastian on.

"No, actually . . . way above. We still write and occasionally even talk on the phone. I see things a lot more clearly now."

I finally convinced Elise we were done having kids, although it was more likely the sleep deprivation from her master's thesis that finally brought her around. I was going back to Dr. Slocum . . . again!

"Say hi to Candy for me," Sebby chided over the phone one day as he laughed.

"Oh, I will," I responded.

After a few weeks and a few flights, Sebastian invited me out golfing for the last round of the season. We got stuck behind an extremely slow foursome and thus had ample time to talk. He told me about his plans for Summit Financial, which sounded pretty cool. I could tell he was excited about his new venture. Once again I found myself a bit envious of him. It sounded pretty good being your own boss.

Sebby mentioned his builder and friend Peter Steglin and suggested I meet him. He apparently had kids the same age as mine. "We should all go out sometime, Jon. I can't believe you two have never met." Seb also told me that he was still writing and calling back and forth with Whitney.

"Phone sex?" I asked eagerly and inappropriately.

"No . . . but I think we're getting close," Sebby admitted wryly. "Actually, she invited me to visit her while she attends some medical conference in Washington D.C. for a few days. Do you think I should go?"

"Heck yeah!" I said.

"Then again, I don't want to blow this," he admitted.

"Yeah, you just want her to blow that!" I interjected stupidly, pointing at his pants. That wasn't like me at all. *I must be losing it again,* I thought to myself.

"Jon . . . I'm shocked!" Sebby remarked loudly. "Where is the proper little Boy Scout I met so many years ago in Dr. Slocum's office?"

"Corrupted by Candy," I replied coolly. "I've developed a sweet tooth for sex, but I'm presently on a diet. It's tough."

Sebby laughed.

"Actually, I think I'm hypoglysexic," I said.

"You mean hypoglycemic?"

"No, hypoglysexic," I stated, matter of fact like. "When I haven't . . . in a long time, I start to go a little crazy."

"I think you need to see the good doctor about that, man," Sebby said, stirring the pot a bit.

"No, what I need to do is see if the old plumbing still works."

"You mean you haven't . . . since the surgery?" Sebastian asked.

"No, but I think we're getting close."

Sebby smiled and looked at me. The foursome in front of us finally made it off the green 190 yards away, and I found my club of choice. "Your honor, your honor," he said, "it's time to make the donuts. You're number one for the deck, Maverick. Call the ball. Be the ball . . . be the ball . . . be the ball! NOOOONNAAAAAN!" I sliced that five iron so far into the woods I didn't even see where it landed.

"Where'd it go, Seb?" I asked incredulously.

"Right in the old lumber yard, man, right in the old lumber yard!" He couldn't stop laughing.

Chapter 23

When There's a Will, There's a Way
Told By Sebby

I ran into Heather one day while out exploring my options for new office space and told her how sorry I was about her father's cancer returning, then gave her a small hug. I knew how ravaged Peter was by their separation, but she seemed more than fine.

"What have you been up to?" she asked politely. "What are you doing with yourself?"

I figured she would know, that Peter would have told her, but apparently they weren't talking at all. I filled her in on my need for a new office and my budding business. She seemed impressed and interested. She confided in me that she was expecting a large inheritance, as her father was now in hospice care. Heather told me she didn't know the first thing about money and needed to plan for her future as well as the future of her kids after the divorce.

"Peter is such a deadbeat!" she told me off the cuff.

Doesn't she think I'll tell him all this? I thought as I listened to her. *This is awkward. This is uncomfortable. This is more than a little weird. Why does being around this woman always freak me out?*

"Divorce" I asked incredulously."I know you two are separated, but you can work through it." I tried to sound upbeat.

"That's never going to happen," she stated emphatically.

While she was telling me all of this, I wondered if she thought I was bound by some advisor-client privilege thing like with patients, doctors, and attorneys, and was she seriously considering me as an advisor, or was she just talking to talk? I didn't want to find out, so after a few further comments and pleasantries, we parted company.

I wondered if I should tell Peter that I ran into her, and I wondered if I should tell him she was hell bent on divorce. Then again, I thought, maybe he already knew, so I decided to keep it to myself and not get in the middle of their business. After all, I had my own business to attend to, and I didn't want to have to babysit Peter anymore.

But it was too late. In a rapid succession of events, his future unfolded abruptly. The good news for Peter was that their old house finally sold. The bad news was Heather had officially filed for divorce. The ramifications of this meant Peter needed a place to stay until June 1, when he could rent an apartment he found in Port Washington for cheap. It looked like I had a roommate again, for the next few months anyway.

Fortunately I wasn't home much during the day to wallow with him in his agony and sorrow. I gave Peter a job as the contractor for the build out on Summit Financial's new digs. I knew the look I wanted and knew Peter was the man for the job. Besides, he could use the business and the distraction. Other than that, I wasn't much of a friend, I know, but there were bigger fish to fry.

As 2008 rolled into 2009, I accumulated more capital than I ever imagined, but one fact became abundantly clear. I was now the head of an investment firm with no investments.

What would my clients think? I began to ask myself. *Am I a banker or a broker?* I had to jump in at some point.

So with construction going on all around me and with the accompanying dust on my computer screens and noise from Peter's nailers and saws, I began putting my clients' money where my mind was. The first few weeks were brutal as the market continued to dive faster than an otter on an oyster. I kept buying as it sank, but I was beginning to get a little scared. After all, I didn't want my new clients retreating to their old haunts.

Fortunately my indicators proved accurate, and the market began to recover in mid-March. In fact, it did more than recover. Stocks ricocheted off their lows and went on marching upward for the rest of 2009. Summit Financial was now a player, and I became somewhat of an instant local celebrity. It was awesome.

Peter moved into his new apartment the first week of June. Three weeks later, I received a phone call from Heather, who told me her dad had passed away a few months back. I extended my condolences to her, but she didn't seem to be in mourning. What she wanted to talk about was money.

"I would really like to meet with you sometime," she began earnestly. "I have to figure out a solid plan for my inheritance. Could we meet?"

I didn't know if I wanted her as a client. It didn't feel right knowing Peter and all, but I decided that it wouldn't hurt to talk. Maybe I could guide her intelligently to another advisor.

Owen and Campbell are Peter's kids too, I reminded myself. If I could help out Heather, in some vicarious way I was helping out Peter.

"The trouble is," Heather began innocently, "I have the kids all week. Could we possibly meet at your house on Saturday? Peter has the kids for the Fourth of July weekend. They're going to the zoo."

To this day, I don't know why I said yes, but I did, and before I knew it, Saturday morning arrived. My doorbell rang promptly at nine a.m. Still half in the bag from the night before with some old friends from Promise, and not finished with my shower, I didn't remember I had an appointment until I opened the door.

Heather stood in the doorway as a light summer

breeze drifted inside, carrying her scent toward me. I instantly started to get aroused. *Stop it!* I told myself, willing my groin into submission. It chose not to listen. She was wearing a slim-fitting, khaki pencil skirt, brown high heels, and a fitted, white blouse that wasn't buttoned appropriately for business. A small leather satchel purse was tucked neatly and discreetly under her right arm.

I, on the other hand, was wearing red nylon sailing shorts and nothing else, not even underwear. In my rush to answer the door from the shower, I had just thrown on whatever I could find. This was not the most professional way to start a meeting or woo a prospective client, I know. In reality, I wasn't planning to sell her on Summit Financial's services at all. I just wanted to help—honest.

I invited her in and quickly excused myself, apologizing for my inappropriate appearance. Heather just smiled wryly and said, "No apology necessary." I found a pair of jeans and an old, but clean, button-down linen shirt and rushed back to the living room barefooted while still trying to finish getting dressed. I figured I didn't have time for a suit. Besides, she had already seen me like that, so this was an improvement. Heather had already made herself comfortable on my leather sectional when I finally made my second appearance. We sat next to each other on the sofa, but not too close.

I usually have a standard spiel with new clients, but I forgot all about it, as I was constantly distracted by her long burgundy fingernails delicately caressing the leather on my couch. She kept crossing and uncrossing her tan legs as if she couldn't get comfortable. She had olive skin like mine, I noticed. *Stop it!* I scolded myself again, giving my privates a second warning.

"Where are my manners—" I began. We both stood up facing each other as we spoke at the same time

"Could I use your . . . bathroom?" Her hand was outstretched as if she was trying to point across the room.

The aisle formed by the coffee table and the sectional negated any form of alternative passageway, and in an awkward instant, we bumped into each other. Her outstretched hand, once pointing toward the bathroom, now rested squarely on my linen shirt right where I had neglected to finish buttoning it.

Heather's long index finger slowly and reflexively slid across the hair on my chest until it came to a stop on the last button I had secured before stopping in my rush to change attire. Her thumb was already there waiting, wanting. She looked up at me seductively with her big brown eyes, and I began to melt. Heather's intentions were suddenly crystal clear.

Stop it please! I willed myself internally as she nudged up against me, still holding my gaze with her hypnotic eyes.

What I couldn't admit to myself or her was already painfully obvious. She felt it as much as me. I was an aching, throbbing mass of a man, and she had all the power in the now silent room. She looked at me for approval, and while I don't think it was implicit, it was definitely implied. I hope there's a difference.

Heather lowered her gaze and began painstakingly unbuttoning the last of the buttons on my shirt. She stopped at my waist and reversed course, this time letting her fingers splay across my lower stomach as she slowly yet repeatedly moved them along the various contours of my abs. I was rigid. My mind was in a battle with my body, and my body was winning, hands down.

"Where does this go?" she asked provocatively as both her thumbs and her eyes followed
the path of hair from my navel southward into my jeans.

All I could manage was a faint, "Heather . . ."

She took that as a yes and began unbuttoning my jeans. I finally regained an ounce of composure and reached for her hands before she could undo my fly. I still wasn't wearing any underwear, and I knew the force that lived behind that zipper.

She looked up at me again, holding my eyes in hers, and then placed her hands on herself. She watched to see if my eyes would follow. She didn't have to ask. Slowly but confidently she began to unbutton her own blouse, revealing a lacy underwire bra and the top half of her voluptuous body. I hadn't been with a woman for over three years. I know that's no excuse, especially with your friend's wife, but I couldn't stop staring.

My eyes were already halfway down her torso, and without removing her eyes from mine, she found the two large brown buttons on the belt of her skirt and expertly unfastened them with two fingers, just as she had my shirt and hers. Then I watched motionless as she ever so slowly undid the back zipper. Her skirt fell flawlessly to the floor, encircling her ankles and brown high heels. She had glossy, dark-red toenails that matched her fingers. I hadn't noticed them before, but everything else was now practically in plain sight. I could see her nipples protruding through the lacey cups of her low-cut bra. I could sense a smallish patch of black hair behind the intricate floral mesh of her white string panty. I would have never guessed the body she possessed. Peter was a lucky man. My mind drifted momentarily as she watched me look her over.

She's married! I screamed at myself.

They're separated, my body countered.

Peter is your friend, YOU IDIOT!

They are getting divorced! my zipper replied.

You can't do this! my brain responded.

I want her! my lower half rebutted as it strained to be free.

It was an agonizing few seconds. In the meantime, Heather had moved in closer again, her scent only enticing me more, her fingers once again looking for somewhere to go. This time, when Heather reached for my jeans, I let her, and in an instant revealed myself to her completely. Her eyes, which were now as big as saucers, told me what she couldn't say with her mouth. (She was too busy trying to close it.) I watched her as she looked me over, and knew what I had to do.

Heather seductively reached for me and motioned intimately what she wanted. She intuitively moved into me as if I would finally take her right then and there or at least lead her into my bedroom. But I had a better idea. I pressed into her and reached around her back, slowly massaging her cocoa butter skin the entire length of her spine until I reached her shoulders. She wanted to kiss me, but I stopped her. We held each other closely, but awkwardly, in a weird sort of embrace. Then I slowly turned her around. At first I think she might have been startled, as her mind apparently raced too far ahead in what she imagined.

Come on, I thought, noticing her reluctance. *That's not what I had in mind. Guys like foreplay too. I'm not looking for a quickie. I'm not looking to get any,* I vowed.

Then she noticed what I had in mind. Beyond the floor to ceiling windows in my living room and past the teak patio deck outside was my hot tub. It was the perfect cure for a hangover and the best way I had found to relax on a Saturday or Sunday since returning from sailing. It turned on automatically every morning and was enticingly bubbly and steamy. Heather liked the idea immediately and forgot where she thought we were headed.

This Saturday morning, my Jacuzzi turned on at precisely nine a.m., about the same time I was being turned on by the curvaceous brunette with brown eyes who was now looking up at me over her shoulder as she undid the clasp on the back of her bra only to let it fall away mercilessly.

Heather led me by the hand as I walked behind her toward the deck and then stopped. She paused and then delicately caressed the lacey, silk string panty off her hips and bent over slowly, fully, to place it on the floor rather than let it fall. I was directly behind her, and the view was decadent. While still there, she paused again and glanced up at me over her left shoulder but never made it high enough to make eye contact.

We continued toward my hot tub. Then, for no reason, she stopped a second time and reached behind her back as I bumped into her.

"Still there?" she asked, although I don't think she was talking to me. Heather found what she was searching for without glancing backward, and like two train cars coupling, she held me firmly in her hands for a few seconds.

"MMMMM good!" she said confidently. "I thought I'd lost you for a second." But again I was pretty sure she wasn't talking to me. Then she reached for my hands and lead me into the Jacuzzi.

"I want you!" she said possessively. "I've always wanted you, Sebastian," she added as we descended into the froth and steam.

"I have some champagne and strawberries in the fridge," I told her. She hesitated, not wanting to break the spell she had over me, but I stared back at her, and reluctantly she agreed.

"I love foreplay," I said, trying to sound as manly as possible. "But I can't wait for the main course."

Revenge is a dish best served cold, I thought as I slowly climbed out of the water, glistening wet, toned, and firm. I wanted her to get a good, long look at me. I didn't want to break the spell I had over her either. As I slowly walked back toward the house, I paused only briefly to glance backward to see if she was still watching, and to my delight, she was.

Cruel as it sounds, this was the best part. As I got dressed (underwear and all this time), I kept looking out the window to see what she was doing. She was getting impatient, that was obvious. I'm sure she was thinking, *How long does it take to pop the cork and get some strawberries?* She was definitely hungry, but not for food.

I gathered up all of her clothes as well as her purse, found some paper, and wrote her a note. I put every piece of her clothing in my car, left the note I had written on her windshield, placed the purse on her front seat, and took the batteries out of her garage door opener. Then I simply started my car and drove off. I had to go and find a trash bin somewhere for her ensemble.

It was glorious. I don't think she even heard me drive off over the noise of the Jacuzzi. I was giddy. After a little while, I parked across the street from her house. It was like I was on a stake out. This was better than sex. It took her a while, but she finally showed up. Watching her hesitate when she tried to use her garage door opener and then scream when she realized it wouldn't work didn't even compare to the scene that ensued as she ran to the front door and fumbled with her keys while trying to hold an open black umbrella sideways between her thighs.

I had seen the walk of shame a few times back at UW Madison, but this was so much better. As I hunched down in the front seat of my car, trying not to bust a gut laughing, I began to speculate as to how long it took her to finally give up and leave. I pondered what Heather must have thought when she finally realized I wasn't there or if it occurred to her in hindsight that it was me in control of the situation all along. I also wondered if I remembered to lock all the doors or if she had just destroyed my place. Maybe that was why it took her so long to finally come home.

Then, for the first time, I thought about Peter. I wasn't about to lose a friend over a woman like Heather. I once knew a guy in college whose friend dated his ex-girlfriend after they had broken it off for a while. I asked the ex-boyfriend, "Would you ever do that to me?"

He told me, "I would never lose a good friend over a girl . . . but he has."

I remember that like it was yesterday. That's just rule number one in the guy handbook, but what was I going to tell Peter? I wondered if I should just keep it to myself. But this was just so juicy!

My head was spinning as I drove up my now empty driveway. My eyes immediately locked on a small piece of crumpled up paper. It was my note to Heather.

Heather,

My mother always told me, "If she'll do it with you, she will do it with anyone!"
I can't do business with you. Not like this anyway.
You'll have to find somebody else for money advice or whatever else it is you're looking for. Peter is my friend.
He is a good man. I doubt you can do better.
I know I can't!

Sebastian

Chapter 24

Do Ask, Do Tell
Told By Jon

It was just one of those extremely long, bad days that started in the early the morning with the typical kid stuff and only got worse. Everything was stressing me out, and I had to go fly a ball buster of a trip from Chicago to Sao Paulo, Brazil, that evening. I tried to get a nap in at some point in the afternoon before driving to O'Hare, but with kids, noise, daylight, and a huge to-do list, the deck was stacked against me from the start.

I was tired by the time I got to work. (I know that sounds really bad for a pilot, but on long flights, the airlines are actually required to staff the airplane with an additional pilot or two to provide rest and fatigue relief.) Departure time for the red eye to Sao Paulo was after nine p.m. It was a ten-hour flight down, so it was a true all-nighter and really hurt the body and brain.

Thunderstorms and high-frequency communication requirements as well as many national airspace boundaries and language barriers made for a busy flight. By the time I got to the hotel in Brazil, it was nine a.m. back home. Besides a brief doze in the crew rest seat when we weren't getting bounced by turbulence on the flight south, I had been up for twenty-six hours and was exhausted. Everything was bothering me. *Why do people wear sunglasses indoors?* I asked myself at the airport in the Brazil. *It's not even bright in here. . . . Ummmm, helloooo, you're able bodied, it's called a walkway for a reason. WALK!*

So after being up the better part of twenty-six hours,

traveling four thousand miles, and drinking almost that many cups of coffee, I hit the bed in Sao Paulo for a well-needed rest. Man, I tell you, when I'm that tired, I can really sleep—Rip-Van-Winkle-like sleep. I was in a coma.

Sometimes on trips, when I wake up to go to the bathroom or to get a drink of water, I completely forget where I am and walk into walls and everything. That day in Brazil was no exception. I was *out* when my cell phone rang. In my comatose state, I missed the call, but then it rang again. *Oh shit*, I thought to myself, because Elise never called me abroad unless it was an emergency. *What's up at home? Car accident on the way to school? Sharp knife? Pointed scissors? What happened?* I answered the phone without even checking the caller ID.

"I almost slept with my best friend's wife!" came the opening salvo from Sebby on the other end.

"Elise?" I asked, half of me still thinking somehow she was on the other end of the phone, and half asking Sebby whether he meant MY wife. After all, I was his best friend, wasn't I?

"No, stupid . . . Heather," Sebby responded.

"Who's Heather?" I asked as I finally came to.

"Peter's wife," Sebby said.

"I thought I was your best friend."

"What are you talking about?" Sebby asked. "Dude, you're missing the point. Where are you? We need to talk. I need your advice big time."

"Who's your best friend, Sebastian?"

"You are stupid." Sebby was exasperated. "Meet me for lunch. We have to talk."

"Ahhhh, Seb man, that's gonna be a little difficult. I'm in Sao Paulo."

"Where?"

"Brazil. I won't be home and copacetic for two or three days."

"We'll talk now," Sebastian insisted.

"No way, man," I replied. "If this isn't an emergency, I'm going back to bed."

"This IS a fucking emergency, Jon," Sebby said. "Should I tell Peter?" He began to calm down. "I really got her good!" His tone was changing from nervousness to outright laughter.

"Wait a second . . . I'm confused," I replied. "I thought you said you ALMOST slept with her?"

"Yeah."

"Dude, this is costing me a fortune!" I told him. "Can't this wait til I get home?"

"Um . . . yeah, I suppose," Sebby agreed reluctantly.

"You work on your story, and I'll sleep on it."

"Some best friend you are," Sebastian remarked.

"I thought that was Peter." I chuckled and hung up the phone.

After a couple of days back home, Sebby and I finally met at a Mexican restaurant in Port Washington for lunch. He insisted we sit way back in a corner booth. It didn't take much prodding before we were in the thick of it, every sordid detail. He described what she was wearing and what he wasn't. He told me how his lower half kept disobeying his brain. He told me how embarrassed he was at his erection but how in the end it worked to his advantage. He really did get her good. I guess she deserved it for some reason. I didn't ask about that. It was something with Heidi back in the day and her leaving for New York. Obviously Sebastian had a score to settle, but I didn't care about those details, just the steamy stuff between Heather and the stud.

I swear Sebby is the luckiest guy in the world. First of all, he had more than his fair share of beautiful women, but now he had to go and fulfill every other average guy's second fantasy as well. Call it spite or revenge, but I can't think of a better dream date than to turn the table on a former Miss Popularity, homecoming/prom queen, sorority b!&ch. Every guy who was ever "just a friend" in high school or college wants to be desired desperately but then turn the screws on a woman like that just to show her how it feels and take her down a notch or two. Now Sebby of all men got to do that as well. It wasn't fair. It just wasn't fair. Man, it sounded hot, but then again, it sounded so cold. It was beautiful. I was on the edge of my seat the entire time.

"Where did you get the idea to take the batteries from her garage door opener?" I asked.

"A guy at Promise did it once," he said, beaming. "Can you imagine, after all that, coming home to a locked house, naked, and having to go to your front door instead of being able to sneak in through the garage . . . in town, with all your neighbors around, on a Saturday morning! Poetry, man, sheer poetry! I even got a picture to prove it! The problem is Peter. I don't know if I should tell him." He was suddenly serious. "It's freakin' me out."

"You have to tell him, Sebastian."

"Really?" Sebastian asked sheepishly.

"Of course, man. I would want to know. I mean, you don't have to give any of the gruesome details, but he needs to know. He's going to find out sooner or—"

"Who's going to tell him? Heather?" Seb interrupted. "She won't tell a soul."

"Speak now or forever hold your peace," I said. "He deserves to hear it from you. Hell, he might even find it funny."

"Would you?" Sebby inquired.

"Heck no!" I shot back. "But if Elise wanted to divorce me for no good reason I might!"

Chapter 25

Speak Now, Awful Heather Held Your Piece
Told By Sebby

How do you tell your friend you almost slept with his wife? How would I tell Peter that I saw his wife naked? How would I tell him that I was the one who got her that way? What kind of a low-life bastard friend was I anyway? I considered all these things as I tried to get to sleep each night.

***

I remember one time flying home on a red-eye flight with Heidi and another couple from Vancouver to Chicago after a few days of skiing at Whistler. Some snafu in the airline's reservation system led to us all being separated, with me way up in front of the airplane and Heidi and my friend Beau subsequently being seated together at the last minute in the back, unbeknownst to me as I slept the entire way home. After the flight to Chicago, as I waited at the gate for Heidi to go to the restroom, Beau confided in me jokingly, "I really enjoyed 'sleeping' with your girlfriend last night!"

This was so much worse. Too many questions swirled around in my head, too much guilt. I couldn't go back and change what had happened or how I had handled it. I would just have to tell Peter and hope he didn't ask any details. That could be devastating.

In the meantime, I had another problem. I wondered whether I should tell Whitney what had transpired. Did I owe her that much honesty? We had become very close over the past few years via phone, email, and some impromptu visits at a couple of medical conferences she wanted to attend, but we never discussed any significant others—or flings for that matter. *But this wasn't a fling,* I had to keep reminding myself. *NOTHING HAPPENED with Heather! I should be proud of myself for handling it so well.*

It was probably a moot point anyway. After what had almost become a regular weekly date night type phone call with Whitney, recently our conversations had almost entirely ended, and rather suddenly too. Maybe she met someone or I had said something that didn't sit well with her. Whatever the reason for our conversations ending, I was beginning to really miss them.

***

One day I finally got the courage to call up Peter and ask him out on a man date for burgers and beers. This wasn't going to be easy.

"Heather wants a divorce," Peter began before the waitress even brought us each a pint.

"I know," I said stupidly before my brain took control of my mouth.

"You know?" Peter asked, surprised.

"Yeah, I ran into her a month or so ago. She wanted my advice for all the money she's inheriting from her dad."

"Why didn't you tell me—Wait! What money?" Peter asked incredulously. "I didn't know about any inheritance. Heather told me her father burned through almost all of his money on his cancer treatment and—"

"Peter, man," I interrupted, "Heather is trying to pull one over on you with this divorce thing. You need to get yourself a good attorney who understands estate planning as well as—"

"But I don't want to get a divorce, Sebastian. . . . I

love Heather," he said quietly.

"Peter, I need to tell you something, and this isn't going to be easy."

Over the next few rounds and some greasy appetizers, I tried to educate Peter on his own wife, at least my impression of her anyway, and my theory on what she was trying to accomplish. I still hadn't brought up our encounter, but I managed to get him fired up enough about the money that I figured he may finally see her for who I thought she was. It was now or never. I told Peter as generically as I could what had transpired, leaving out every delicate detail that would somehow incriminate me. I told him how his wife had always wanted me back in college and reminded him of our awkward dinner all those years ago at their house. I basically suggested to him that she had tried to seduce me.

He sat there in stunned silence. I didn't know whether to continue or let him recover and begin his cross examination, either option was obviously fraught with peril. I ordered us up another round and hoped that today he would be a mellow drunk. Then again, maybe he was getting ready to blow. For the longest time, he was utterly silent, a glazed look on his bewildered face, as the reality of how quickly Heather could switch gears and look at other men only then began to dawn on him. He didn't even blink, and I was really getting uncomfortable. *Yeah, great, Seb, think about yourself, you ass!* I thought. *You did this to him. You have to make it right.*

"I know a great bunch of attorneys over at Dewey, Cheatum, & Howe," I said, trying to make a stupid joke, but it went right over Peter's head.

I started talking again just to break the agonizing silence, and eventually I corralled the conversation, as well as Peter's brain, back toward the issues of his looming divorce and Heather's inheritance. I did know a couple of really good attorneys and suggested them to Peter. I prodded and pumped up his bruised and battered ego as best I could. After all, he had done nothing wrong. I reminded him about the whole better or worse part of their vows and how she wasn't keeping up with her end of the deal, let alone her lack of honesty regarding the money. I was good at talking about the money. In fact, I was relentless. Like a boxing coach in his fighter's corner, I had his ear and intended to keep it that way.

"You have to fight this thing, Peter. You have to make Heather pay. You didn't do anything wrong!" I told him. "Nobody saw this economy collapsing like it did. It's not your fault."

After a good ten minutes, he slowly regained his shaky composure. I could tell he wanted to ask me about that Saturday, but he was struggling with how to phrase the questions. I braced myself for the inevitable and made an oath to myself to be honest and accept everything that went along with it. Peter finally found his voice. "Heather is beautiful, isn't she?" he asked.

How the hell was I supposed to answer that question? I hesitated and Peter continued, "I always knew she was too good for me."

"What?" I interrupted. "You are too good for her," I proclaimed defiantly. "You're confusing her looks with her acts, Peter. You have to get your head on straight. You deserve better."

"No, my kids deserve better!" Peter shot back. Apparently he still had a spine. "No matter what happens now, they're going to lose."

I felt terrible. Peter looked like he had been punched in the stomach. He slouched down on his side of the booth and just looked at his beer. I didn't know what else to say. I couldn't make it better.

Chapter 26

My Any Me is My Friend,
But My Enemy is My Friend Too
Told by Peter

It took me a long time after the bombs going off around me stopped exploding to figure out who I now was. I had considered myself a dutiful husband and father, a successful businessman, and subsequently a failure. Where should my loyalties lie? With my kids, obviously, but what did that mean? Did fighting my spouse in divorce proceedings make me a better or worse dad? Would standing up to Heather and prolonging the inevitable bring me justice or just a huge stack of attorney bills that I couldn't afford?

Maybe I should just roll over and die, I thought to myself. *Anything I win in a settlement will be given to my lawyer anyway. Maybe we could get counseling? Maybe we could save this thing for the sake of the kids. I really am pathetic, weak, and a sucker! I have to fight for our kids! I better fight for myself. I better figure out who I am. Suck it up, move on, and don't look back! No emotions . . . None.*

I called up Sebby and asked him to help me. I needed professional guidance and thought he might know someone, as I vaguely remembered him mentioning something to that affect, but my mind had been spinning that day.

In the meantime, I needed to find more work. My phone wasn't exactly ringing off the hook. Fortunately, Home Depot was hiring and I fit their mold pretty well. I hoped that, even though the pay was minimal, my position there might open up some contacts for contracting with customers.

Sebby wanted to go out, but apparently he had an ulterior motive in mind: He needed a wing man. It was still a little weird between us after the incident with Heather, but I hoped that a night out might alleviate some of the awkwardness. I didn't hold what had happened against him and had even begun to see the humor in his actions. I had finally started to man up to the notion that divorce was not the end of world. The thing that ended up helping me was the decision I ultimately made to fight her and her devious, petty, greedy ways. Surely good would triumph over evil.

Sebby took me out to some thirty-something club/bar in downtown Milwaukee. While he scanned the room for possible targets for his libido, I tried desperately to get his full attention and advice, but it wasn't working. He was in a foul mood, admitting only that he figured whatever he had going on with a doctor in St. Thomas was probably over, although he didn't know why.

"You ought to be happy," Sebby said as he looked around the room. "You've never been with anyone other than Heather?" he asked again, confirming what he had learned from an earlier conversation during the car ride into Milwaukee. "One word, Peter," Sebby paused for effect. "I have one word that will motivate you. Now listen and listen good," he commanded, although he still never looked in my direction, choosing instead to continue scanning the club for women. "Uninhibited!"

"What are you talking about, Seb?" I asked.

"Dude," Sebby began, "do you read *Cosmo* or *Women's Health*, *Marie Claire* or *Glamour Magazine*?" He didn't even wait for me to answer. "No, Peter, *you don't*. Men don't read *Cosmo* or *Women's Health* or whatever unless it's the last thing available in the bathroom. We do however see the cover of those magazines on the rack as we wait patiently in line at the grocery store. Am I right? You've seen those magazine covers."

"Where are you going with this, Seb?" By now I was more than a little bewildered.

"I'm glad you asked, Pete," Sebby responded confidently. "You know those magazines? Invariably in bold print somewhere on the cover is some snippet alluding to an article inside entitled something like 'Ten New Positions to Try with Your Man!' or 'Awaken His Inner Animal. Don't be Afraid to Talk Dirty. Here's How!' or 'Blow His Body and His Mind Tonight!' You get the picture. You've seen the covers, right?"

"Yeah, so?" I said.

"So has every man in America as they wait to buy milk, bread, and eggs. The same guys also see their wives and girlfriends reading those magazines, romance novels, or watching Lifetime Television, and *Sex in the City*. Did Heather read any of those magazines?"Again, he didn't wait for my answer. "Yeah, I know she did. But did she ever try anything like what's in them on you?"

(Silence on my part.)

"Well?" Sebastian finally waited for my response but apparently grew impatient with my hesitation to answer and went on without it. "Had your sex life with Heather become routine or, worse yet, stale and boring? Come on, man, be honest with me. Did it sometimes even seem like charity?"

I was shocked. It was bad enough he had already seen Heather naked. Now he wanted to know about our sex life.

"Believe me, I've been there!" he admitted. "What's so frustrating is the obvious disconnect. You see them reading the magazine. You know the article is in there. Hell, you even sneaked a peek at the article yourself in the bathroom, right? Then you waited and waited for the article to play out . . . for Heather to take the bull by the horns and ride you until you bucked her off or simply died from exhaustion."

Sebastian continued on his inspirational rant, sparing

only a moment to catch his breath and collect his errant thoughts. He didn't want my input, just my attention. He had transformed into some kind of sexual Svengali and was proudly giving me his innermost appraisal of why most relationships fail. I guess I asked for it, although when, I wasn't sure.

"But that rarely, if ever, happened. Why?" he asked, although by this point I was sure he already knew the answer."What is in all those steamy romance novels, if not tips and techniques to try out? If they enjoy reading about it so much that it sells books and magazines, wouldn't you figure women would like it even more in reality? Go figure. Men give love to get sex, and women give sex to get love, Pete. I think the problem is, after a woman gets her man, she knows she is loved. She's got the ring to prove it. So the honeymoon is over, dude. After that, it's just a vicious downward spiral to divorce. Those small packages from Victoria's Secret stop coming in the mail. The man begins to feel neglected and unloved. He stops working out or bringing home flowers for his lady and is often unwilling to be romantic and loving in return. The woman then doesn't feel loved and therefore withdraws from any physical intimacy on her part, and the man then retreats even further into his job or sports or whatever because he doesn't feel desired. It's a circle, man, a vicious one, you know?" Sebby asked me again. "I equate sex with love, I'll admit it!" he said. "I bet you do too! I know what you wanted for Christmas, New Year's, and Valentine's Day every year you were married! You wanted Heather." He looked at me knowingly. "But there was a caveat!"

"Where are you going with this?" I finally asked.

"You wanted Heather to focus on you instead of the chocolates and flowers or jewelry and whatever you gave her so that you could in turn focus on her. Not too much to ask for a present, huh?" Sebby asked. "The more you give, the more you receive." He was on an unrelenting rant. "I think a lot of women in relationships forget this. Why do you think I've never gotten married?"

Then Sebastian finally paused and took a breath. He once again started scanning the club and taking it all in like a hunter scanning the horizon in front of him for prey. "What you see before you here are ticking clocks, divorcees, and cougars. Many of them have learned this lesson the hard way," he stated anew. "They've all loved and lost. These women now read those articles, take them to heart, and put them to use. They will do anything to get their man and keep him happy.

AND I DO MEAN ANYTHING," he reiterated loudly over the now blaring music. "You know all those things you've thought or read that Heather probably never did, or only occasionally, or refused to completely? Well . . . they know," Sebastian said, pointing around the room. "THEY KNOW!" he said more loudly over the music. "And they're not afraid anymore. They are more afraid of ending up alone than letting go and trying new things. Uninhibited, Peter . . .They are uninhibited, my friend."

"Or they just married the wrong guy, Sebastian," I offered weakly. "Some guys are jerks, and these women not only found the courage to leave them, but they are here trying to give it another go. That takes guts," I said a little more strongly.

"What are you talking about, Pete? I'm just trying to psych you up, not bring you down.

Geez, man, you don't have to get all uppity on me."

"I'm just saying they all have stories too. Maybe their guy just wouldn't man up and commit or whatever but—"

Sebby interrupted abruptly, now annoyed with where this conversation was headed.

"Hey, man I resemble that remark," he said and walked away from me.

The truth was, I had only recently ever entertained

the notion of being with anybody other than Heather. I was still pretty confused about my motives. On one hand, it was obvious that someone new might be fun, even exciting, but with that came a lot of performance anxiety. After all, I thought, these experienced women also expected me to be the same, and I wasn't—far from it in fact. Nobody wants to go on stage after a star performs. What would they think of me after the likes of a stud like Sebby or some younger man who wasn't twenty-five pounds overweight? My ego wasn't ready for rejection that evening, let alone the morning after.

Another strange emotion urging me into the fray however was sheer spite. It was odd, but somehow I thought sleeping with another woman would be a good form of revenge, even if Heather never found out. That is an odd admission, but honestly I felt more giddy about the revenge part than the sex. I must have needed a shrink.

Somewhere in the middle of all these thoughts, Sebby came back with a pint and placed it on the table in front of me (a sort of peace offering, I suppose, but only noticed later). Then he excused himself to go to the bathroom. I don't really know how long he was gone. I was too lost in thought. Then, just as I began to get out of my own head, I watched a woman as she stood up and started walking clumsily toward me. I looked over my shoulder to see who she was approaching, but to my astonishment, nobody was behind me. I felt eerily alone and totally unprepared.

"I'm barren," she said loudly over the music with a strange look on her face. I think she was more than a little tipsy.

"Hi, Karen, I'm Peter," I stuttered back nervously.

"No . . . I'm barren!" she announced more loudly and sullenly, the smell of cigarettes and scotch wafting around her like a very bad version of the perfume section at a nice department store. She was obviously drunk.

"What?" I asked. I couldn't hear her clearly over the music.

"My husband divorced me because I couldn't have any kids," she began, her speech slurred. "My friends dragged me out here tonight and pushed me onto your friend Sebastian. Apparently they think I need to get some. He passed me off onto you, soooo here I am," she said depressingly. "My name is Melanie."

Wow! I thought. *And I thought I had low self-esteem.*

We tried to make uncomfortable conversation over the music and frequent stares from her group and Sebby as they cajoled us from across the room, but it wasn't happening at all. If this was what the singles scene in Milwaukee was like, I was going to have to focus harder on work and my divorce.

Finally, mercifully, Sebastian gave up, and we headed back to his place to crash. The next morning, Sebastian gave me the card of an attorney friend he said owed him a favor and told me to call him on Monday. He also finally finished telling me about Whitney and how, for the past month or so, their online relationship had dried up. He sounded like he really missed her.

Over coffee he repeated some of his favorite stories from his sailing adventure, and even though I'd heard many of them before, I let him embellish. I had nowhere else to go. Heather had the kids that weekend for some reason and wasn't about to share them with me out of the goodness of her heart. We had drawn our respective battle lines, and unfortunately Owen and Campbell were now caught in the crossfire.

Two weeks later, Sebastian's attorney friend Paul agreed to meet and educate me on what was to come. He would charge a flat fee after the fact or a percentage of the proceedings, whichever was greater. This surprised me, as I thought I would have to pay up front. Paul told me I had a case, so I hired him. I really just wanted someone to be on my side. I needed somebody to empathize with my view of how everything had gone down.

Apparently I had a few things going in my favor. For one thing, Heather was already living in the new house. I was in a crummy apartment. Second, my only visible income at the moment was a near minimum wage job at Home Depot. Third, I was apparently a messy computer user and never emptied my trash bin or old email folders. And fourth, Heather's signature was on every invoice, contract, or check we ever signed at Steglin Homes, LLC.

My old computer files and emails would prove especially valuable, Paul assured me, as they not only showed my intent to seek counseling but also that I was given no information regarding Heather's inheritance. Her emails on my computer, on the other hand, painted a very different picture indeed, including meetings with an estate attorney before and immediately after her father's death. The data also forecast the intentions she presented to some of her friends before she changed email accounts and passwords. But best of all, when it came to the business, which she told me over and over I had ruined, her signature was on each and every document, some of which were in error monetarily. They proved not only complicit consent (whatever that meant) but that her mistakes were a part of our misappropriation of funds.

I really only wanted what was best for Owen and Campbell, but with this apparent evidence in my favor, I was emboldened to proceed and fight her in court, if I had to. This was not only a divorce, Paul informed me, but the dissolution of a partnership and business.

I have heard so many times of these divorce cases where the husband does or (in some cases) doesn't do anything wrong and ends up losing half of everything to his ex (and, yes, ladies, that second man does exist!) I took it upon myself to stand for every man, any man, who didn't do anything wrong—didn't cheat, didn't lie, didn't get drunk, high, or violent—and still had to give up half of everything to the ex-wife who did do one, some, or all of those things. Right or wrong, I created a persona for myself in my head who was some sort of superhero, and I ran with it. I got caught up in the fight, with Paul and Sebastian urging me on from the sidelines. For the first time in a long time, I could look at myself in the mirror and not shrink back into my shell. I even began to walk upright again, shoulders back, rather than slouched over and dragging my feet. I strode around Home Depot with a spring in my step and looked people in the eye.

"I'm Peter Steglin," I told them from behind my orange apron. "How can I help you?"

Chapter 27

A Picture is Worth a Thousand Words
Told by Sebastian

A month or more had gone by since I last spoke to Whitney on the phone. A few emails and texts trickled in, but it wasn't the same. I resigned myself to trying the Milwaukee dating scene again and invited Peter to tag along. It wasn't like I really wanted to go out, it just seemed better than staying in and sulking. But as soon as we walked into the club, I knew it wasn't good. Looking around a room at other thirty and forty year olds only made me more aware of my own fleeting youth, as well as more than a little self-conscious—or, to be honest, more like self-loathing.

I can't believe I used to find this so fun, I thought to myself.

After a long, pathetic weekend of burgers, beers, and busts (I'm not referring to breasts, but striking out, although I wasn't trying very hard, if at all, to be honest). I headed back to work. At least business was still good.

The first matter of business on Monday mornings was to check my email and snail mail, write back to any clients, and check in with the markets. But I couldn't get anything done, because one envelope in my pile of mail in particular had me transfixed, and I sat frozen in my seat for a long time, just staring at it, unable to move, think, or even fathom its contents.

For some reason, even though Whitney and I had conversed only over the phone and through emails and texts, I knew it was from her. My eyes immediately fixated on the St. Thomas postage mark, even as I failed to recognize her handwriting. I shuttered at what lay inside. Apparently we had to "talk," and this was the only way she could bring herself to end whatever we had.

I fell back into the chair at my desk, unable to put the letter down, let alone open it. I couldn't bring myself to look at emails or turn on CNBC or anything. I had broken up with more than one girl with a poorly written note in junior high and high school. Perhaps this was karma for some of my past sins. I willed myself to find the letter opener; for a moment, I thought about stabbing myself with it instead. The ensuing pain wouldn't be nearly as bad as what was to come.

Inside the envelope I found a neatly folded single page of paper, and I could tell from the blank side of the page that only a few words were on the opposing side, along with some sort of picture.

This was either way worse or much better than I originally thought. I flipped it over. At the top of the page was the picture of me standing next to *Slomocean* in Grenada. Photoshopped into the picture next to me was a picture of Whitney, smiling brightly and holding a cup of coffee. Below the picture she had written:

> Meet me for coffee Tuesday, Sailor!
> Alterra Coffee, Bayshore Mall
> 9 a.m.
> We have to talk.

Holy crap! Whitney was in Milwaukee!

I wanted to call her or email or text her, anything, but nothing worked. She wouldn't answer. I couldn't stand it. I couldn't wait until tomorrow, even though I knew it couldn't be good. I thought about driving around Milwaukee and every street in the surrounding area in the vain hope of finding her, but I collapsed again in my own thoughts. I was a wreck the rest of the day. My clientele would have to wait.

I bet she's getting married, I told myself, thinking she met some guy a year or so ago and slowly got serious. She just couldn't tell me, so she suspended our texts and chats, but now she needed closure. Yep, I was sure I was doomed.

I left the office early and went to the gym, thinking if I ran my ass off maybe that would relieve the stress ball that was gestating in my stomach. But that didn't help either, so I went home. A couple of shots helped my body finally mellow out, but my brain was now cloudier than ever. I couldn't even eat.

Should I bring her flowers? I wondered. *What should I wear? How should I greet her after all this time? What is her fiancé's name? I wonder what he does? I bet he's younger!* My mind wouldn't let up. Morning took forever to arrive, and I needed a coffee just to get ready to go have coffee. I looked like shit and felt even worse. This wasn't going to be good.

I drove down to Bayshore, a local mall area on the north side of Milwaukee, earlier than I intended to and circled around Alterra Coffee a dozen times or more until I found the perfect spot to scope out the place. I hoped to spot Whitney walking in. Somehow I figured by even catching a glance of her beforehand, I could avoid the stupid, surprised, awkward look on my face and moment that followed. The long, silent pause thing was my worst nightmare as I envisioned myself waiting for her to drop the axe on my exposed neck.

I sat in my car for a long time (twenty minutes or more) waiting and watching for Whitney to walk into Alterra. It was now already a little after nine, so I decided to walk in, find a seat, and wait for her there, thinking she was running late. But as I snuck in, I locked eyes with her immediately. Whitney was already inside.

"Sebastian Everest Koh!" she said, sort of snickering loudly. "Why *ever* did you circle the place and sit in your car for so long before coming in? I was beginning to think you were going to chicken out!" Whitney smiled at me as she stood up from her seat.

Damn, she looks good! I thought. I couldn't speak. I just wanted to hear the sound of her voice again. I walked forward and gave her a big hug. Inappropriate or not, I wanted to hold her for as long as I could, and my hug continued for too long.

"What is up, Sebby?" she asked, sounding now more like a friend instead of the sensual and strong, yet vulnerable, woman I so desperately wanted her to be. I still couldn't speak. I just looked at her and offered awkwardly for us to sit by motioning to move her chair for her, even though it was already away from the table. Whitney looked at me and smiled a mischievous smile. I remembered her allure and the walls she'd built up to protect herself, but at this moment, I didn't care. I just wanted to soak in her aura and drown in her presence. I knew she had something to tell me, but I hadn't really tuned in yet. I wanted this moment to linger forever.

"Are you going to speak?" Whitney asked. "Or is there something I'm missing? Maybe I shouldn't have come!" she blurted out, exasperated by my silence and puzzled by the strange look on my face. I was still mesmerized at the fact that she was in the same room as me.

"I . . . I missed you so much," I finally managed to stammer. "I miss our talks, Whitney. Just tell me the bad news and—"

"What bad news?" she interrupted.

"What's his name?" I asked bravely.

"Who?"

"The guy you met and are marrying or whatever?"

"What are you talking about, Sebby? Have you lost your marbles since we spoke last?"

"Why have you been so distant then lately?"

"I've been really busy packing up and getting ready to move to—We need to talk,

Sebastian." She stopped and began again with a weird tone of voice. "But I'm afraid to start."

"You're killing me here, Whitney!" I told her. "This isn't going how I expected."

"Well, how did you expect it to go?" Whitney asked, smiling crookedly.

"Well . . ." She really had me flustered. "One of two ways, I guess."

"Shoot," she offered. "I promise I won't bite." Her eyes looked flirtatiously into mine. I could tell she had something really big to tell me, but her body language and genuine warmth began to assuage my fears a bit.

"First . . . I figured you were going to tell me you were getting married and couldn't continue talking with me anymore," I said.

Whitney laughed. "And second?"

"Well, I'm not really sure," I said sheepishly. "Maybe you won a free trip to Wisconsin or something and just wanted to surprise me, but that wouldn't explain . . ."

"Explain what?" Whitney asked.

"Why you've been so distant the last month or two," I told her, obviously frustrated.

"My parents sold their home in Seattle and moved back to St. Paul, Minnesota, to take care of my mom's mother," she told me. "They'll probably end up staying there after she dies. She's not doing too well."

I listened intently to Whitney, but I had no idea where this was going.

"I finished my residency at the end of summer and have been entertaining several offers. One is here in Milwaukee," she finally admitted, as if it could somehow be a question or an issue.

I smiled a big smile. I think the color finally came back to my cheeks, and I began to breathe again. I sat back in my chair and just kept on staring at her. "Please continue," I said hopefully.

"Here's the thing, Sebby," Whitney started. "All those times you offered and wanted to visit me in St. Thomas . . . I really wanted you to, but . . ."

"But what?" I asked, still lost as to where this conversation was headed.

"I need to come completely clean with you and take my chances or . . ."

"Or what?" I asked, more than a little intrigued.

"Or I will regret it for the rest of my life," she said unapologetically. "Damn the consequences! But I need the truth."

"What is it, Whitney? Just tell me please!"

"Well," she paused again, trying to formulate her thoughts. It was obviously something she had rehearsed, but the words just wouldn't come out. "I think it's obvious I like you," she began again with starts and stops. "And I think you like me too . . . otherwise . . . Maybe I better stop right here. Are you seeing anyone, Sebby?"

"No!" I replied, not wanting to impede the progress we were making.

"Okay, so I said it."

"Said what?" I asked, just to make sure.

"I really like you, Sebastian. I have since we met in the hospital, but . . ."

"But?" I waited impatiently.

"I have a job offer in Portland, Oregon; Stillwater, Minnesota; and here . . ."

"And?"

"I want to take the job here if we have a chance, but," she hesitated. "First of all—and I know it's a lot to ask—but do you think we have a chance?"

"Yes, yes, yes!" I told her enthusiastically.

"Okay, well, you need to . . ." The tone of her voice changed.

"This is great—" I blurted out, not even realizing her reluctance to say whatever it was she was trying to tell me.

"Hear the truth," Whitney interjected sheepishly. "I haven't lied to you, Sebby, but I haven't told you the whole truth either," she admitted.

"What are you trying to say, Whitney? What is it?"

"I wanted to tell you in D.C., Sebastian, at the conference, honest, but I was falling for you, and I just couldn't. And that weekend in Miami," Whitney paused, "you were such a gentleman, even when I wasn't a lady. I tried to tell you so many times over the phone, but something always stopped me. I thought you might stop calling or writing, I guess. Your letters and email and calls really helped me get through my final couple years in Charlotte Amalie. Without you, I felt pretty alone. I . . . I . . . ." she stuttered.

"What, Whitney?" I asked impatiently. "You can tell me anything."

"I have a little girl, Sebby," she finally admitted in a scared but proud way. "And she is wonderful!" Whitney began to cry.

"It's okay," I said, trying to comfort her, but she immediately read more into what I said than what I meant.

"It is?" she asked as she looked back up at me from the table with her big, teary, green eyes.

Only then did I realize what she was really asking. I really liked Whitney and was so excited to see her again, but this was a BIG question. I needed to give her an honest answer, and at that very moment, I wasn't sure my emotions were in synch with my brain. I sort of froze up for a second, and she immediately caught on. "It's not okay, is it?"

"I didn't say that!" I said, trying to quickly regain my composure.

"I need to know, Sebby, before I take this job whether you're serious enough to get serious. I know it's kind of sudden—"

"Kind of," I interrupted. "But in a good way."

"Really?" she asked, smiling shyly again as she wiped the last tear from her cheek.

"Yeah . . . Really!" I reiterated. "I'm really glad to see you, Whitney." I reached under the table with both of my hands to hold hers.

For the longest time we just sat like that, silent, looking at each other, studying every little nuance and expression and not saying a single word. It was fun, and it didn't feel awkward at all. Then we really began to talk, and it was just like old times.

Whitney told me all about Abigail (or "Abbey" as she called her). She told me how she had gotten pregnant toward the end of her first year of residency in St. Thomas. The senior resident at that time, who came from a long, prestigious line of doctors in Massachusetts, was the baby's father. She confided in me the pressure she felt by him and herself at the time to have an abortion, but she just couldn't bring herself to do it.

Whitney talked about how devastated she was when he admitted he didn't love her and didn't want a child— or anything, for that matter—coming between him and his supposed destiny in private practice outside Boston. Residency was hard enough without being pregnant, let alone as a new mom, but as it was the senior resident's kid, he cut her some slack, and she agreed to raise Abbey on her own. That was why she didn't want to get involved with me in St. Thomas. That was why I wasn't allowed to visit. Whitney had kept her distance and her secret—reluctantly, she admitted—to save her residency and avoid further complicating her already complicated life in Charlotte Amalie.

As I listened to her tell her story, I saw that she was an amazingly strong woman. I was glued to my chair as she talked. It was like we were in our own little bubble, oblivious to any and all around us.

Abbey was now almost five and needed to start school. Whitney wanted to settle in somewhere and find a place for them both but admitted that the thought of bumping into me, if I rejected the notion of a serious try at commitment, scared the hell out her. If that was the case, she wanted to know sooner rather than later and take one of her other offers.

Since we were spilling all our beans, I decided to put myself out on a limb as well. I told her about my paternity scare a few years back, as well as the ongoing fears I kept sequestered in the back of my mind about the possible child I may have fathered in college. "How's that for honesty?" I asked Whitney. "Are you sure you want to get serious with a jerk like me?"

"You're not a jerk," Whitney said calmly. "You're just scared. It's okay. You don't have to give me an answer today. I need you to be completely honest with yourself before you're honest with me. I'm in town for a few more days with Abbey, showing her the possibilities. Would you like to meet her?"

"Yeah," I admitted nervously.

I had a lot of thinking to do. Whitney not only understood, but I think she appreciated the effort I was putting into making an open and honest decision. We agreed to meet at the zoo when it opened the next day.

That night as I lay in bed staring at the ceiling, I felt apprehensive yet amazingly calm. As I struggled with my pillows, trying to make myself comfortable, my cell phone began to vibrate. It was a text from Whitney that read: "Are you OK? Are we still on for tomorrow? The weather looks great. Abbey can't wait! Thinking of you. W. T."

I smiled and read it over and over again. Then I wrote back: "I'm thinking about everything you said. . . . I'm thinking about us. I'll see you both tomorrow. SEK"

I rolled over, turned out the light by my bed, and, believe it or not, slept great.

Chapter 28

If the Shoe Fits
Told by Jon

I hadn't seen Sebby since just after the episode with Heather, and then suddenly there he was, walking in front of me at the Milwaukee Zoo with a gorgeous woman and cute little girl about Bergen's age. I didn't know whether to avoid them to maintain their anonymity or go over and expect introductions, but it was already too late.

"Hey, there's Sebastian!" Elise said loudly enough that everyone within earshot could hear. "Who's that he's with?" she asked me more quietly as he spun around to see us looking in his direction.

"Elise! Jon!" Sebastian said joyfully as he approached us. "How have you been?" he asked. He seemed to be glowing, and he had a strange bounce and confidence in his step, as if he was ten years younger. "Whitney, this is Jon Foster, my good friend who I've talked about so many times," Sebby said. "And, Jon, this is Whitney, the one I told you about from St. Thomas."

"You didn't tell me Sebastian was seeing anyone, honey," Elise said incredulously and awkwardly right in front of Whitney. She was obviously taken back a bit, as we didn't keep any secrets.

"I didn't know she was in town," I shot back. "But I'm sure I told you about her."

"I'm sure you didn't. She is beautiful," Elise whispered, though I knew they could probably still hear us.

"She's a doctor," I whispered back.

Elise was correct. Sebby had told me about Whitney,

and I thought I had adequately described her to Elise at some point, but I wasn't prepared for another Heidi. No man should be as lucky with women as Sebastian. I suppose I shouldn't have been surprised, but come on. It's like he belonged to some super-secret ultra-exclusive online dating group where only Ivy League, PhD-candidate, runway fashion model, star athlete females are allowed to join. Seb had a "type" he was attracted to, and Whitney fit the bill perfectly. She reminded me of Lindsey Vonn, the US Olympic skier and World Cup champion from Minnesota—more than impressive.

"Sebastian has told me so much about you," Whitney said as she looked up at me and bent down next to a cute little girl I assumed was hers. "It's nice to finally meet you. . . . This is Abbey, my little girl," Whitney said, beaming as she picked her up. "Abbey, Mr. Foster is a pilot. He flies big airplanes way up in the sky all over the world."

"When I grow up, I want to be a pilot too," Abbey admitted energetically.

"Well, you can't do both," I told her.

Abbey looked puzzled, and Whitney did too at first until Sebby began to laugh. He was one of the few people who really got my sense of humor.

"You can either grow up, or become a pilot," I explained further, "but you can't do both.

Just look at me." I chuckled, but Abbey still wasn't so sure.

"What are your kids' names?" Whitney asked Elise.

"Well, this little guy is Ben," Elise said proudly as she pointed to our stroller.

"And this is our daughter, Bergen," I interrupted. "She is almost five."

"Abbey is almost five too," Whitney informed Bergen.

"Do you like elephants, Bergen?" Abbey asked Bergen shyly.

"Uh huh," Bergen replied quietly.

"Well, that's where we are headed next," Sebastian proclaimed. "Do you want to tag along?"

"If we aren't intruding," Elise and I said almost in unison.

We spent the rest of the afternoon wandering around the zoo, chasing the kids, and soaking up the last real weekend of the summer. I didn't get a chance to talk to Sebby much, and when we did talk, we kept it pretty light. But he kept giving me looks when Whitney wasn't watching, obviously asking for my approval, which wasn't hard to give.

Whitney talked with Elise and played effortlessly with both Bergen and Ben. Abbey and Bergen took to each other like only kids can. By the end of the day, it was as if they were best friends, each begging all of us to get pizza or come over to the other's house. But Sebby and Whitney needed some privacy, and Elise and I needed to get home. I had just gotten in from a flight that morning and needed desperately to rest, so against a huge backdrop of tears and protests, we took leave of each other and started back toward Port Washington.

"How long have they been seeing each other?" Elise asked me inquisitively. "Are they serious?"

"To be honest," I told her, "I didn't know she was anything more than a sort of pen pal- phone sex buddy—"

"What's a phone six buddy?" Bergen interrupted from the back seat of our car.

"Daddy misspoke," Elise told her as she glared at me from the passenger seat.

"It's a person who is number six on the speed dial of your phone," I said.

"What's speed dial?" Bergen asked.

"I'll have to show you sometime when we get home, honey," I told her. "I have to drive now." I smiled as I looked at Elise out of the corner of my eye.

"When can I see Abbey again?" Bergen asked.

"I don't know, honey."And that was the honest-to-gosh truth. My mind was still reeling after running into Sebastian and Whitney. He had never told me that she had a kid. The old Sebby I knew never would have entertained the idea of dating someone with a child. Yet he seemed so amazingly happy and calm, almost glowing, as if somehow Abbey was his own. It was odd. They seemed so in synch—not just Sebastian and Whitney but, surprisingly, the three of them. They looked like a family.

"We'll have to call and see," Elise added reassuringly while looking quizzically at me.

"Yeah . . . we'll definitely have to call and see," I reiterated.

***

I flew a couple trips over the following weeks and helped get Bergen settled into her new routine at preschool. Fortunately it only took a few days before she began to like all the activity and interaction with other kids. After that, it wasn't hard persuading her to go.

I called up Sebby to see if he wanted to go out one night for some Tex Mex or something, but he surprised me by asking if Elise and I would be interested in a couples date instead. Whitney didn't know anyone except him, as she hadn't started her new job yet, and she had been super busy getting Abbey settled into preschool as well as moving both of them into a townhouse she had rented in Mequon. She wanted to get the lay of the land from another woman and really enjoyed her brief encounter with Elise at the zoo.

I asked Elise if she was interested in a couples' night out, and she was on board with the plan, so she found a babysitter for the following Friday. It was a date. Sebastian and Whitney dropped Abbey off at our house to play with Bergen and then drove us all to a cool restaurant in an old mill next to the river in Cedarburg, a quaint enclave between Port Washington and Mequon. We had a great time as Whitney regaled us with the story of her first meeting with Sebby and subsequently the time they spent together on St. Thomas. She was lovely, smart, witty, and very down to earth. Elise took to her instantly, and soon they were like little school girls at the corner of our table sharing secrets and laughing while Sebby and I checked in during lulls in our own conversation.

It's always interesting to get another person's take on someone you think you know, but what is really intriguing is when it differs so vastly from your own experience. Was the Sebastian I knew really the same person I experienced that evening with Elise and Whitney, or was he just putting on an act?

Maybe that's who he really is, I thought, feeling a bit confused. *Maybe he just acts differently around me. Or maybe he's a changed man.*

I couldn't put a finger on it, but Elise noticed it too and commented to me after our date about how real he seemed and how in sync they were together. She really liked Whitney, but she was admittedly leery of investing too much into a new friendship with her based on Sebby's history.

I told her, "Regardless of what happens between them, you can be friends with her, you know. Besides, Abbey and Bergen have really hit it off."

"Yeah, but if they break up, it could get weird for all of us"

"I don't know, honey. I think this one's got legs!"

"You noticed those, did you, Jon?" she asked jokingly.

"Yes, as a matter of fact, I did, but that wasn't my point," I responded with a laugh. "I think he really likes her. "

"So do I!" Elise agreed happily. "So do I."

Chapter 29

The Art of War
Told by Peter

I think Heather just expected me to be the lap dog that she had groomed for so long. She wanted me to roll over and scamper back to my pathetic little apartment with my tail between my legs, but I wasn't having it. Everything I had ever done since my early twenties—both successfully and in failure—was for her and our kids. I had made mistakes, I'll admit, but they were all well intentioned. I was through beating myself up over them and over her. She had obviously moved on. It was high time I did the same.

I spent most of my time working at Home Depot or doing the occasional odd job for cash on the side when I wasn't spending time with Owen and Campbell. Fortunately they seemed to like my little place in town. We could walk to almost everything, so I kept it simple. Walks by the harbor led to play time at Fish Park or the Possibility Playground nearby. We fed the ducks and went to the library. I took them to a local coffee shop on Main Street. They loved the treats, and I loved watching them grow up. It was happening so fast. I made a promise every night as I prayed to do everything in my power to not let our divorce affect them, but I knew it would. It already had. How could it not? Owen was especially full of questions: "When are you coming back to the house, Dad? When can we all go out like we used to? Do you still love Mom? Are you mad at her? Are we going to live with you here in this place or at home?"

I tried to answer his questions as openly and honestly as I could, but more than once I had a hard time finding the right words. I tried not to cry in front of them, but sometimes our new reality just hit me like a ton of bricks. It bothered me that they considered the big new house their home and not my little apartment. I couldn't blame them, but it still hurt. I had built that place with my own two hands, yet I never got to spend one single night in it with them, so they didn't associate me with the house at all. I was already a separate entity.

When I wasn't working or with the kids, I spent my time following Paul's instructions to gather tax returns, credit card receipts, phone records, and any emails or text messages I could get my hands on. Heather didn't know I had hired an attorney, but she would soon find out. I even asked her to consider marriage counseling again, this time at Paul's request. She declined.

When Heather finally got wind of my attorney through her own, she was shocked. "What money do you have to pay an attorney?" she texted me. "This is going to cost you a fortune."

I wanted to write back and tell her that it was going to cost *her* a fortune, but I understood, at Paul's instruction, that from here on out anything said could be used against me or Heather in the proceedings. The plan was to stay cool and delay, delay, delay until she imploded or at least caved, giving us more ammo. This was war, and only the first salvo at that.

Every time she declined counseling, I asked again. Every time she wanted to meet, I was busy working or Paul couldn't make it. Every time we were scheduled for some preliminary hearing or whatever, it was more of the same. Fortunately, since Paul and I weren't doing much more than an occasional phone call (no texts or emails between us were allowed), he promised me I wasn't ringing up any kind of tab above or beyond what we had already agreed to. I don't know how Heather was doing it on her end. We just kept hitting the ball back into her court and letting her lawyer decide what to try next.

When we couldn't delay the proceedings any longer, we finally agreed to a first meeting. I hadn't seen her much in the past few months other than to pick up or drop off the kids, but Heather looked tired. Paul and I were ushered into a room by some secretary or assistant and seated in large, plush leather seats next to a huge mahogany table adjacent to her attorney's palatial office to discuss some kind of deal while the rest of his staff readied papers and fetched us both drinks.

"She must be paying this guy a fortune each hour," Paul told me.

I had already agreed with my attorney to let him negotiate, as he understood my terms fully. It would be better to let him become the enemy, Paul confided in me, and for me to remain aloof.

I guess it's always customary for ladies to go first, and thus her attorney presented Heather's ideas for a settlement, none of which I found acceptable. But I did what I was told and just sat there, staring not at Heather but at her attorney while he read all the legalese he could muster. When I wasn't looking at him, I studied the table or looked at Paul, who took copious quantities of meticulous notes, often forcing the opposing lawyer to pause or reiterate what had just been said, so he could catch up.

"Why don't you just record all this?" Heather's attorney queried more than once, apparently exasperated by the slow progress we were making.

"No, that's okay. I like to get it all down on paper," Paul replied simply and repeatedly.

Paul asked meticulous questions and seemed to require copies of everything Heather's attorney had in his possession, which further delayed the proceedings as we waited for his staff to Xerox them before we could continue. Paul found inconsistencies in the opposing presentation and burrowed his way under her attorney's skin like a tick. It was tense between the two of them, but then, just like that, Paul found common ground, complimented his rival on something or inquired about sports or fishing or politics, and off they went on some tangent discussion while Heather fidgeted impatiently in her seat.

I only glanced at her occasionally, and then only for a split second when she wasn't looking. It was Paul's idea to only take meetings on days when Heather had the kids so that I didn't miss out on any time with them. But it slowly became apparent to me after my third hour in my plush leather seat (which I had now studied from armrest to armrest and back again a hundred times) that Paul had other ulterior motives as well. He was not only playing Heather's lawyer like a cheap fiddle with his awe shucks banter and contrasting stinging dissection of every piece of legal minutia his opponent presented, he was delaying the proceedings minute by minute with his note taking and constant requests for copies or clarifications on purpose. He was tireless. Yeah, I was paying him a percentage if we won, but my wife was paying her hired gun, as well as her babysitter, by the hour.

Once I finally figured out what was going on, the meeting took on a new life. It was as if I could now hear the narrator in the background and the heckles from an imaginary crowd opposite my own. I began to smile a little as I listened in.

Heather definitely noticed the change in my personality, even if it was ever so slight. I think that only annoyed her more.

Finally, after four hours, I prepared myself for what I thought would become the climax to Paul's performance. I figured it was time to get down to brass tacks and begin some sort of actual negotiating, but as I looked on, Paul simply gathered up his things, said a few polite comments, and motioned for us to leave.

After all that, we just took their offer and left. Heather

didn't know where I stood or anything. As much as I was impressed by his tactics in the boardroom, I must admit I was a little miffed that we didn't at least put our cards down on the table as if to say, "Oh yeah? Well, take that! Yeah, I see your three of a kind, and I'm going to raise anyway!"

On the short ride back to my place, I shared with Paul my confusion and disgust at how we had just left without negotiating anything.

"All in good time," he counseled me reassuringly. "All in good time." He sounded like some sort of ancient philosopher.

It was obvious he was not only confident in how the proceedings had gone, but he was enjoying the chess match between him and his colleague. "I went to a small state college in bum fuck nowhere," Paul told me as he dropped me off at my apartment. "He went to some private east coast university, I can tell. This is going to be fun! I'll call you next week. Remember," he warned me, "if Heather calls you, only answer after your answering machine picks up, and let it keep recording everything. Got it?"

I nodded.

"Good job today, Peter. Talk to you soon," he called as he drove off.

Chapter 30

Worth the Wait
Told By Sebastian

I have never had erectile dysfunction or performance anxiety in my entire life, but as Whitney settled into her new job, townhouse, and life with Abbey in Mequon, I started to have some anxiety anyway. Here was this beautiful, vivacious woman who was interested in a rapidly middle aging man who hadn't been in the saddle for a long time. I worried about the saying: If you don't use it, you lose it. Well, I had used it myself, but that probably didn't count. What if it wasn't like riding a bike? What if I didn't measure up to her expectations?

We were growing really close really fast. I had told her about my vasectomy and the copious quantity of stuff I had frozen and placed in layaway early on after we met for coffee the first time. To my astonishment, it didn't freak her out at all.

I slowly began spending small snippets of time with Abbey and found her to be every bit as amazing as Whitney told me she was over and over again. Whitney was a really great mom and a more amazing woman than I ever even imagined back in St. Thomas. Almost immediately, her walls came down, my fears of commitment began to evaporate, and our desire for intimacy grew.

"You know, Sebby," Whitney said one day over lunch at the hospital, "most girls have a three- or five-date plan in mind when they meet a guy. Nobody wants to be considered easy. I have a three-year minimum waiting period, so I'm anything but. You're the first guy to ever make it," she said flirtatiously.

"Make it?" I asked intently. "Where?" I urged, though I knew what she meant.

"I think you should talk to Jon and Elise." Whitney caressed my leg under the table. Damn, she looked sexy in scrubs. "I think Abbey wants to have a sleepover with Bergen. I think she's ready. I know I am!"

"For what!" I asked playfully as I began to play with the fingers of her outstretched hand. This was way better than phone sex.

"A sleepover, Sebastian. . . . What do you think? I went shopping at Victoria's Secret!"

She didn't have to say any more. My mind was already racing ahead as I tried to find the speed dial on my cell phone for Jon's number. Unfortunately he wasn't available, so I tried their home in desperation. Elise answered. She could always read me, and I know I sounded desperate. I didn't want to waste another weekend waiting, so I abruptly handed the phone to Whitney to make pleasantries, small talk, and the necessary arrangements. She handled it like a pro.

I think women have some sort of sixth sense about this stuff. If I would have asked Elise for this kind of favor, it would have come out all wrong, but the mere fact that Whitney suggested the sleepover with all the implied ulterior motives that came along with it only seemed to motivate Elise more to make it happen. I was not only enthralled but quite turned on as I watched Whitney negotiate the scheduling. She was talking to Elise, but looking at me, flirting under the table, smiling devilishly and mouthing various words from her conversation. Her eyebrows danced up and down. Apparently her mind was wandering a little as well.

The next Friday night, we dropped Abbey off at the Fosters' and headed south past Mequon toward downtown Milwaukee for dinner at a fancy place on the lake. But just before we passed our exit, Whitney informed me she had forgotten her purse. I wasn't mad, but I just wanted everything to go perfectly, and I didn't want to miss our reservation. I was obviously impatient but agreed without hesitation to go back for it and made the off ramp just in time.

I figured Whitney would just run in quickly and grab her purse, and we would head out again, but I was wrong. For some unknown reason, after she ran into her apartment, she came back out and asked me to come inside. She said it would only take a minute. I was worried there was some kind of problem with Abbey—not for her sake but, selfishly, for my own.

I got out of my car and went into her place, but she was nowhere to be found.

"I'm in here, Sebastian," Whitney called out from her bedroom. "Could you help me find my purse?"

I entered her bedroom and found her standing in front of her new bed. She wasn't looking for her purse but instead was facing me and unzipping her little black dress as I came in.

"We can eat later," she said coyly. "Do you want to try out my new bed?" She let her dress fall off her shoulders and gather around her ankles.

"Victoria's Secret?" I asked as I undid my tie and the top button of my shirt, trying desperately to catch my breath.

"Do you like?" Whitney asked as she glanced down at her lacey attire. "I've never bought lingerie before. . . . I didn't know what to get."

She looked so innocent, so vulnerable, so beautiful. It was more than any man could ask for. I think at that moment, the last of Whitney's walls came down. She gave herself to me slowly, fully, and unabashedly. We didn't have sex. We made love effortlessly, an intimate and comfortable love. We savored, explored, and tasted each other for hours.

We talked and laughed. We tickled and nuzzled, nibbled and kissed. It was wonderful—no, better than that; it was perfect.

I would say she made me feel young again, but it wasn't that at all. For the first time since maybe forever, I wasn't performing or jumping relentlessly from one position to the next in an effort to impress. This was interaction, give and take, want and desire, contact and recognition, gratitude and relaxation. We fit together perfectly. I didn't want it to end.

Somewhere around ten or eleven, I awoke from a snooze to an empty bed. Hearing Whitney in the kitchen, I threw on my boxers and wandered out into the light to investigate. She was making an omelet. "You hungry?" she asked after smiling warmly in my direction.

"Yeah!" I admitted, patting my stomach. "I think I worked up a little appetite."

"Me too," Whitney said. "I'm sorry I forgot my purse. I really want to check out that restaurant sometime." I watched her stir the eggs and smiled. I didn't know whether she had really forgotten her purse or was just making a little joke, but I was too smitten to care. "Are you okay, Sebastian?" she asked, noticing my reluctance to enter her kitchen.

I just stood there in the entrance from her hallway admiring her aura. Tousled hair, no make-up, and bare feet, all wrapped in a ratty, old, white bathrobe, she was more beautiful than any woman I had ever known. In fact, at that moment, I realized that Whitney was the only woman I had probably truly ever known. The years of emails and hours of phone conversations we shared had given us a foundation that our newfound intimacy only built on.

I walked over to her and hugged her from behind, nuzzling her shoulders and kissing her neck. She began to forget about the eggs as my hands found their way to the terrycloth tie that held her bathrobe together and loosened it, giving me more access to her neck.

"Sebastian," Whitney cooed.

"I love you, Whitney," I whispered in her ear. "I have for a long time. "

"I know," she said seriously. But then seductively she added, "I can tell," as she reached around behind me, urging my hips closer with both her hands. Apparently my erection had already announced its intentions for round three. Whitney managed to remove my boxers as I worked on her neck from behind. Then she turned around and looked up at me. She found my hands and led them inside her bathrobe before it too fell on the floor. We stood there, naked, in the dim light of her kitchen looking at each other for what felt like minutes. Then Whitney looked straight into my eyes with every bit of seriousness and honesty her soul could muster and said, "I love you too, Sebastian. I have for a long time. I hope I was worth the wait."

"I hope I was worth the wait!" I told her, surprised at her words.

"I haven't been with a man since Abbey's father," she told me.

"I haven't been with any women since before I left to go sailing," I said.

"And your vasectomy, huh," Whitney noted, looking down where my boxers had been. "Well, we don't need Viagra or condoms, that's for sure. You make me so happy!" she told me as I took her in my arms and lifted her up onto the counter.

"Shut up and kiss me," I commanded as we met each other halfway.

"You don't have to ask twice!" Whitney whispered in my ear. We began to find a new rhythm together. Then Whitney suddenly interrupted our progress. "Hey, back in St. Thomas," she asked abruptly as she tried to catch her breath and counter my advances, "did you ever find whatever it was you were looking for?"

"Whitney," I said exasperatedly. "I . . . I . . ." I stammered, trying to catch my breath as well. The motion between us stopped. I looked straight into her beautiful green eyes, paused, and said, "I found you, Whitney. I think I was meant to—Maybe you found me, I don't know. But I'm not letting you go . . . ever!"

I gathered her up in my arms again and carried her back into the bedroom. The omelets would have to wait until morning.

Chapter 31

Reawakening?
Told by Jon

Many people are baby people, but I am not one of them. Some people love toddlers and everything that happens in the years from one to three, but I am not one of them either. Through conversations with many other pilots I work with (most of whom are older than me), I have formulated a theory, and here it is: There is a small window of time with kids—from around five to twelve—where everything is as good as it gets. So far, my relationship with Bergen was proving this right. I only hoped I could survive long enough for Ben to make it to this period of nirvana.

Here is the math, as far as I can figure it. You start by taking the age difference between your oldest and youngest children and add five years. Then subtract that number from the number thirteen. Then you pray that the answer isn't a zero or, worse yet, a negative number. Let's say you have two children ages six and three; their age difference is three. Add five and you get eight. Now subtract that answer from thirteen. The final answer is five. But what is five, you ask? It is your window of nirvana. What is the window of nirvana? It is that brief moment in time when your oldest child has not yet reached puberty and your youngest has achieved some modicum of self-sufficiency. In this example, you have five years.

Let's say you have three kids ages nine, five, and one. You basically got pregnant every four years on November fourth because you didn't like watching the election returns or something like that. Well, I hate to break it to you, but you're screwed (just kidding!) Actually, you have three choices. First: Suck it up and bide your time for twenty-five years. (I'll explain this math later!) Second: Try and change and become a person who loves conflict. Personally I hate conflict. Or third: Choose to go with the flow.

The age difference between nine and one is eight. Eight plus five is in fact thirteen. Thirteen minus thirteen is zero. So by the time the youngest child in this example is five, the oldest is already thirteen and entering puberty, with all the angst and arguments and everything that comes along with it. By the time that happens, you and your significant other are in it until your youngest emerges from the dark side of the moon at seventeen or eighteen—twenty-five years from the time you change your first diaper on your oldest child until your youngest is, in a word, an "adult." It could be worse if your answer is a negative number, but I'll let you work out that nightmare scenario equation for yourselves.

I say this facetiously, but I choose to use seventeen as the gateway to adulthood in this equation because, believe it or not, I'm an optimist. Kids are always at least one. Nobody is ever zero. During the first year or so, we all talk in terms of months. That math gets too complicated, and nobody likes decimal points or fractions, so I choose to keep it simple: 1+17= "adult."

If you don't have that window of nirvana in the midst of the two storms (i.e., early childhood and adolescence), my heart goes out to you, but then again, I'm not a baby/toddler kind of guy. Maybe I'll handle my kids' sexual awakening and the sullen rebellion of puberty better than what my coworkers have counseled me to expect. I can only hope.

In the meantime I didn't want Bergen to get any older, but I needed Ben to hurry it up a bit. I wanted them both at that perfect age. I wanted them to still want me, to want us as parents, to still look to us for the majority of their advice, and to still have some control over their choices. I knew it was a fleeting moment in the grand scheme of time, but I secretly hoped that when we finally got there, it would last forever.

***

It's really odd how two kids from the same gene pool and raised by the same two parents can be so elementally different. In some ways it is really cool to see their individual personalities develop. On the other hand, the nurture versus nature debate becomes a moot argument.

Right off the bat, Bergen was into dolls and fairies, princesses and pink. Elise is a bit of a tomboy, so we sure as heck didn't influence Bergen in that way. And by the time Ben was two, he was digging in the dirt, banging trucks together, and kicking a ball around. I'm not a gear head or a jock. Was he really my kid? (I had a roommate in college for a few years who graduated and chased odd flying jobs all over the country to build up his logbook and resume before he finally settled in Florida and went to work for another airline. We lost track of each other for a few years but then reconnected on Facebook. Turns out he had married a lady named Elise Olsen, the same as me. What are the odds? Anyway, ever since then, the running joke between us has been that when I am on a trip, Elise heads south, and when he is on a flight, she flies north. So was Ben mine? Of course. But the fake rumors being posted on Facebook at that point were just too funny to not play along.)

Anyway, to further differentiate our kids, we only had to sit back and watch. At the slightest spill or slip, Bergen would ball her eyes out as if she had broken her leg. (Oh, the drama.) Ben could fall down the stairs or crash into something full speed and literally ricochet off it, collapse into a heap on the ground, then check himself over from head to toe as he stood back up and declare defiantly, "I'm okay!!!" Ben was proud of his invincibility.

Bergen, on the other hand, was proud of her artistic endeavors. I routinely found lots of love letters and notes she had drawn for me secretly packed in my suitcase on trips abroad that always made me smile, and I saved a bunch of them.

Bergen was at that perfect age. She was mostly self-sufficient as far as getting dressed, eating, and using the bathroom, yet she still needed Elise and me and was always eager to share. Ben by contrast was not only needy but defiant. He continually pushed the envelope, where Bergen had succumbed to the boundaries and rules we established. We needed to try something different with him, but we were unsure how to proceed.

"Pick your battles," Elise reminded me when I got too frustrated or exhausted (or both). "It's just a stage. This too will pass."

I wanted to believe her, but the light at the end of tunnel with him at this age and stage seemed too dim to offer any hope for a brighter future. Elise was better at this stuff than me, but with my work schedule, we were continually in a state of flux. When I was away, she worked tirelessly on her own . When I was home, we often struggled with the structure she had created, as I wasn't consulted or hadn't agreed to it for that matter. I began to feel like a paycheck rather than a parent, a security blanket instead of spouse. In short, I felt like an outsider in my own home.

***

I love the fact that Elise is such a strong, independent woman. I think that was one of the first things that attracted me to her. When I asked her out the first time, she was already seeing someone, but she told me, "Check back!" as if she knew the relationship wasn't going much further, and she wouldn't mind having a backup just in case. She was confident and witty and more beautiful than I ever imagined I deserved. I loved her so much, but when she took control over everything in our house and daily life (which she had to due to my job), it left a sour taste in my mouth, as I'm a bit of a control freak. Then again, she is too.

Over the past few years, Elise and I had lost something and couldn't seem to find it. We were too busy just trying to keep our heads above water. We had become full-time parents and deadbeat partners, neglecting each other and ourselves. Elise was now the queen of yoga pants, t-shirts, and tennis shoes. Some days she didn't even find time to shower. She hadn't gone shopping or dressed up in ages. I had gained ten pounds and lost track of the number of projects around the house I had started and failed to finish, let alone those I hadn't begun. We reassured ourselves continually that it was for the sake of the kids. There were, after all, only so many hours in the day. "Me" time and "us" time would have to wait for a lull in the weather.

Somewhere before Ben's fourth birthday, the storm began to subside. The light at the end of the first tunnel became brighter, and our house regained some semblance of calm. It was almost perfect. Bergen and Ben actually began to play with each other and share things without the constant need for Elise and me to break them up. We finally got to take off our striped shirts and put down our whistles. Now if only we could forget to be parents for a little while and become friends and lovers again, it really would be heaven.

We did get sitters, and Elise's mom still babysat for us on the occasional date night, but all too often we used that time to run errands or do whatever seemed essential at the moment. Elise and I could never seem to put anything off, except each other. At least we were similar in that regard and in our freaky need to keep everything clean and organized, or we would have driven each other crazy.

We were a great team, but how that translated into true connectedness was sometimes lost on me.

Elise joined a book club around this time, and I started to pick up old hobbies again that I had put off for years. It might have been the first sign of a mid-life crisis, but I went out and bought an amp and electric guitar. I had played a lot on an acoustic over the years and always wanted one.

Heck, it's cheaper than an old Porsche, I thought.

It was refreshing just doing something spur of the moment for once, even though I still barely got a chance to play. When I did, it soothed me and opened up my mind to the notion of a new chapter emerging in my life, one not restricted by afternoon naps and feedings, continual supervision, refereeing, and anxiety. Elise was reawakening as well, but, unfortunately, separately from me.

An opportunity arose for her to take a long-term substitute teaching position at her old school for a friend out on maternity leave. She jumped at the chance. It would be a juggling act with my schedule, Bergen's, and Ben's lack thereof, but I could tell she needed to get out of the house, and I was happy for her. "Our" time together would just have to be put off until later yet again.

Elise worked like a dog between the new gig at her old school and her desire to still volunteer for everything at Bergen's school. I worked like a dog between flying and trying to keep the house up the way we liked it while simultaneously watching Ben. It was really hard, but it gave me a greater appreciation for everything Elise did while I was away flying hither and yon. Whenever there was a gap in our scheduling efforts, Elise's mom filled in. Thank God she was retired and willing to help us out, or I don't know what we would have done.

Our life became a sort of two-step dance at this point—two steps forward and two steps back. Every time an opportunity came up for a golf outing or an hour to rock the house with my axe (guitar), something more pressing always came up.

With Elise, it was unfortunately the same. Her girls' nights out—or "the book club," as she and her friends called it—were more often than not replaced with planning, prepping, and grading for next week's classes. Why did we always seem to bite off more than we could chew?

Finally, through some miracle alignment in the heavens, we got to go out on a double date with Sebby and Whitney. I could only hope that Whitney would somehow empathize with us a little, as Abbey had only recently entered into that perfect age as well. But I was reticent to complain too much for fear of scaring Sebby off on the whole relationship thing. They seemed to be getting quite serious, and Elise liked Whitney to boot!

It had been a while since we had gone out, so we made the most of it. As most double dates go, though, the men and women ended up talking separately most of the evening, with the car ride home being the place where Elise and I caught each other up on the flip side of our respective conversations.

It was a good evening, but it could have been a great night. I should have just pulled the car over and parked. We should have talked to each other about us, our thoughts, fears, anxiety, and what not. I should have just stopped right in the driveway and kissed her heatedly and repeatedly to break the impasse between us, but there wasn't a segue the entire ride home for any of those things. Other than the fill-in-the blanks conversation about Whitney and Seb, there was only silence between us, and it was deafening. We were now, like always, exhausted, and we both knew the inevitable. Tomorrow was another busy day. The sun and our beautiful children would rise sooner than we hoped. Elise and I looked at each other longingly as if to say I love you, but we didn't even mouth the words. We would be reawakening in six hours. "Our" time would have to wait again until the winds died down, the rain ended, the clouds parted, the sun came out, and we began our time in nirvana.

Chapter 32

Noemocean
Told By Sebastian

I rarely seek out advice, because I seldom take it to heart. I do occasionally ask for it but prefer wholeheartedly to make my own way and live with my mistakes—or at least bury them so far in the recesses of my psyche that they only rarely make an appearance. I hadn't done a lot of self-examination since Whitney came back into my life. I hadn't needed to because I was so content. Business at Summit Financial was good. Everything with Whitney and Abbey was good. But I found myself struggling with what to do next.

Since high school, I had discovered that I always did my best when I had some grandiose plan in mind, a big project or goal to achieve. I liked pushing myself. I liked new things. I guess that's why in my late twenties and early thirties I had put all my efforts into the pursuit of women. When any one mountain got too difficult, I simply abandoned that expedition and picked a different mountain to climb. Not the best analogy, I know, but it seems to fit perfectly with my upbringing and my father's history before me. I simply know this part of my personality came from him. It occurred to me that the only really good advice I had ever gotten since my father's death came from two places: *Slomocean* and my mother.

As I couldn't get my old boat on the phone for a heart to heart, and she in point of fact never knew my father, I decided late one evening to call my mom. I would talk; Evonne would listen. She would offer up some advice, and

I could take it or leave it. It sounded good.

Little did I know—or remember—that she was the master. I was but putty in her hands. Before we finished talking, she had invited herself to visit for the holidays so she could meet Whitney and Abbey herself!

I shouldn't have been so nervous. It was just that I had never taken a girlfriend to meet my parents before my dad had died and my mom moved back to Tahiti. Wasn't this the same? Then again, maybe not. I wasn't taking Whitney halfway around the world to meet her. She was just coming for a visit, and they would meet. I would make it brief.

When I thought about what was really worrying me, it was this: Yeah, I had never taken a girl to meet my parents ever, but I had been asked and invited to meet some parents of my exes. In my book, all too often after I met with the parents, the next chapter was the dreaded break up. I'll admit, I was a lot younger then and not looking for anything serious, but meeting the parents always seemed like a test to me on many levels. I liked testing myself, but I hated being tested. First of all, it meant whoever I was dating wanted to take our relationship to a much higher level. But did I want our relationship to go to another level? Second, it usually meant they were asking others to not only scrutinize me, but their feelings about me as well. They were in some weird way asking other people to tell them what they themselves should intuitively and inherently already know by that point: Am I seeing this guy correctly? Is he or isn't he as great as I think he is? Are we compatible? Do we match up well? Yadda, yadda, yadda, blah, blah, blah, etc.

Okay I'm a guy. I get it. I fit the stereotype. I don't like to talk about my feelings. I don't like to open up, and I don't want to seek out advice on any of it—well, most of the time anyway. What I really feared was that by introducing Whitney to my mother, she might feel the same way. After all, her parents lived a scant six hours away by car and had even visited her and Abbey in their new place, and she hadn't asked me to meet them yet. Right now we were on the same page in the same chapter of a great book together. Everything was going so perfectly between us. I just didn't want her to think we weren't on the same page. I didn't want to push Whitney into anything she wasn't ready for. I desperately didn't want any walls to come between us. I didn't want to lose Whitney. I didn't want her to break up with me.

What I needed was a few days away from everyone and the office. What I really craved was some wind, blue sky, and water—lots of water—but it was fall in Wisconsin. Most, if not all, of the marinas on Lake Michigan close by October 31, and all boats have to be hauled out by then before the harbors begin to freeze up.

I should have just booked a flight to the Virgin Islands or Florida Keys for a week and gone sailing there, but what would I tell Whitney? I wasn't going to lie to her. She could read between the lines. She knew I did my best thinking on a boat. If I left for a week to go sailing by myself, she would probably begin to worry and start preparing for the worst. But what I was thinking about was far from that; in fact, it was quite the opposite, but I couldn't tell her that either.

Instead, I began lying to salespeople. Yeah, I'm not proud. I desperately needed to go sailing, but I had lost touch with all my former sailing friends at McKinley Marina in Milwaukee, so I couldn't borrow a boat. To make matters worse, there was literally no place to rent a decent large sailboat anywhere on the lake without buying into some fractional timeshare type of arrangement or taking classes and on-the-water training. I just wanted a quick fix. It was like I was some kind of drug addict looking everywhere and willing to do anything to get off land.

So I lied. I began calling boat brokers and salespeople up and down the inland coast, posing as a party interested in making a steal on a boat before winter. I had heard from many of my former dockmates that this was a good tactic and could yield remarkable results, as the price and inconvenience of storing a large sailboat over the winter was considerable.

I drove everywhere from one hundred miles north to eighty miles south following up on leads and phone calls, looking at boats, and asking if I could take it out for a day or two, even if I didn't go far. I asked every single one of them if I could stay on the boat overnight—sail it around during the day, tie it up for the evening, and go out on it again. I knew this wasn't done. I knew I was asking for a lot, but I fell off the wagon looking at all those boats, and I needed my fix now worse than ever. Never take an alcoholic to a bar or liquor store. Never take an addict to a pharmacy or a rave. And never, never take a sailor to a harbor full of boats for sale.   Finally, after talking and hunting and looking, I met an independent owner in Racine, a city south of Milwaukee on the lake, who was as desperate to sell as I was to sail. I gave him some numbers of people I used to sail with as well as the storage yard and mechanic where I had wintered *Slomocean* for many years. I told him I wanted to come down to look at his boat and asked him to call all the numbers to verify my sailing credentials. Fortunately he recognized a few of them and agreed.

I lied about being a serious buyer, but I was up front about my intentions, informing him that I would need to try his boat on, so to speak. I needed to live on it for a day or two to really get the feel of it and sail it more than once. We talked on the phone for the better part of an evening and again the next after he had called around. I regaled him with stories of my trip south to Grenada.

After that, he didn't know I wasn't a serious buyer, but he did know I was a serious sailor. We agreed to meet the following Friday and to possibly let me sleep on his boat that night. Although skeptical, he knew my story checked out and vaguely understood my fictional intentions of living aboard for extended periods of time again, hence my strange desire to camp out in his boat. I brought my sleeping bag and another bag full of gear. It was so exciting buying new stuff again that I could hardly work that week.

I told Whitney the basics, but not the real reason for my wicked plan to go sailing. She thought I was crazy. "No man is going to let you take his boat out by yourself," she insisted.

"He said we would go for a morning sail together Saturday and—"

"He's trying to sell you his boat, Sebastian," Whitney interrupted. "He will say or do anything to get you down there. He can probably hear the desperation in your voice and thinks it is eagerness to buy his boat or something."

"Do I sound desperate?" I asked her.

"You sound delusional, Sebby!" Whitney fired back. "Good luck. . . . Have fun! Call me when you get back Saturday."

"I'm not coming back until Sunday night, I told you," I reiterated.

"Yeah, that's what you think!" she replied, laughing.

I met the owner, Perry, after work but before dinner on Friday night, bringing along all my stuff, including a cooler of food that I intended to cook and eat on his boat. He did sort of look at me like I was crazy, but I immediately began selling myself and proving my knowledge as he gave me the grand tour.

Perry was in his fifties and had owned the boat with his father until he passed away last winter. Now with winter approaching again and the necessities of storage and the payments he still owed on *Wind Warrior*, he was forced to sell. We bonded over our fathers' and our own shared love of sailing. I told him how hard it was for me to sell *Slomocean*.

Wind Warrior was a Jeanneau Sun Odyssey 43 DS, a big sailboat by most standards and incredibly well kept and equipped. Its sails, rigging, and lines were all in excellent condition, as was the diesel engine and immaculate interior. It was obvious that Perry and his father and family had taken excellent care of it. As he showed me around and made sure I knew where everything was, I began to get more than a tinge of guilt in the pit of my stomach. I didn't like lying to him, but I couldn't back out now.

After about an hour and a half, Perry excused himself to go home for a late supper. I could tell he felt apprehensive about leaving me alone on his boat. I couldn't blame him; we had only just met.

The weather looked brisk but clear for the morning, so we made quick plans to take *Wind Warrior* out and put her through her paces. I couldn't wait. In the meantime, I settled into its spacious interior and prepared myself some food, wanting to pretend that I was somehow back onboard my old boat, but the devil is in the details, and as I looked around *Wind Warrior,* I just couldn't. This boat was better than I ever thought in my wildest imagination.

The next morning, bright and early, Perry appeared at the dock dressed and excited to go with two large coffees and some muffins.

I've found over the years that sailors tend to fall into two categories: There are those who like to be in command and those who have no problem following orders. Usually, if not always, if two commanders are on the same boat, they tend to butt heads. Most captain types have a particular way they want things done. With Perry and me, though (thankfully), this wasn't the case. We seemed very in synch from the time we left the dock until we came back at noon. He was gracious in letting me try whatever I wanted. We took turns at the helm and hoisted—or at least unfurled—every sail in his inventory. We motored a little and even tried out the storm chute he had purchased but never used.

By the time we made it back to the dock, I can honestly say I had found a brother, at least as far as sailing goes. Beyond that, I didn't know much about Perry, but he seemed pretty cool. I promised him I would be careful with his boat, but I just wanted to try it single handed for a while, that I would be back in and tied up by dusk. I gave him the keys to my Land Rover for some kind of insurance. I asked him if it was still okay that I stay on his boat that night and told him I might need one more sail tomorrow, depending on how it felt today.

In lieu of a marine survey, I offered him five hundred dollars for his time and mine on the boat. He took it gladly, but he was still reticent to watch me head out of the harbor again. *It must be weird seeing someone else take your boat out*, I thought as I headed back east out of the harbor. I'm glad I never had to witness that with *Slomocean*. It might have killed me. Every time I looked back at the docks, Perry was still standing there. I vowed to stay close.

I felt sick. The pit in my stomach from the night before had metastasized into an ulcer in my stomach. My imaginary migraine was now a tumor in my head. They both grew in intensity and size that entire afternoon. What was I doing stealing some guy's boat for a joy ride and lying to him to his face?

The truth was, I loved the boat. The truth was, I loved Whitney. I already knew that. What I needed to figure out was if that meant we were supposed to get married or just keep on keeping on. I wondered briefly what she thought, but my mind kept scolding me for being such an asshole to Perry. I decided rather suddenly to shift gears and make good on the lies I had told him. I called him up and told him to come back to his boat after dinner Saturday night.

Wind Warrior was a big sailboat, more boat than I needed, but not more than I wanted or could handle. It was clear Perry still loved it and didn't really want to sell it. Maybe there was some middle ground. I tied it up, made a quick jaunt over to a nearby store in Racine, and planned my sales pitch.

Perry met me back on *Wind Warrior* around seven, and I offered up some wheat beers. "Let's talk turkey," I suggested. Perry was asking $198,000 for the sailboat, which was the mid-market price for such a nice yacht. I had done my homework, even though I really wasn't initially interested in purchasing anything. The last couple of weeks, and the last twenty-four hours in particular, had gotten me so pumped up that my mind was racing. What began as a snowball rolling downhill soon became an avalanche of discussion. Perry quickly dropped his asking price to $185,000 and then to $175,000, the low end of the price range for this particular make and model. He obviously needed to get out from under the bills that were about to stack up and the monthly payments that were slowly eating his lunch, but he seemed like such a decent and honest guy. I couldn't steal his boat even if I had the money.

Amazingly, what we formed was a sort of partnership right there on the spot. He seemed happy, and I was ecstatic. I would buy half of the boat now for $75,000 and cover all the expenses for haul out, derigging, and storage. Then over the next five years, I would buy the remaining fifty percent from Perry for $15,000 a year for a total of $150,000.

In the meantime, we agreed that the following summer we would split time on the boat equally. Thereafter he would give up ten percent of his time on the boat annually for the next five years until it was completely mine. After that he would retain the rights to eighteen days of usage each summer until I sold it or the end of 2019, whichever came first. Perry would schedule around my convenience and take the boat in blocks of at least six days or longer so he could sail it back down to Racine or up to Door County. Over a few more beers, we hammered out the remaining details of our budding partnership, and I agreed to call up my friend Paul to have him draft an official contract.

There was only one sticking point. I lusted after the boat. I loved the hull. I adored its colors inside and out, but I hated the name. I have never associated sailing with violence, so the name *Wind Warrior* didn't work for me at all. I know a lot of sailors are superstitious about renaming boats, but I wasn't one of them. Hell, if I adopted a fourteen-year old mutt from the pound, I would rename him or her without hesitation. Fortunately Perry didn't contest this, as *Wind Warrior* was the name given the boat from the previous owners. Perry's family never changed it at his dad's request, but Perry wasn't superstitious, so we immediately started brainstorming. Somehow we got off on a tangent, and I began sharing with Perry my philosophies regarding investments and the markets. When I mentioned something about no emotions, it sort of clicked. He loved sailing but wasn't tied to the boat. I liked the boat but hadn't formed any sort of connection with it either. This was a business partnership. We weren't friends. Perry had liked the name *Slomocean* from my old S2, and emotion could be spelled the same way. So *Noemocean* kind of struck us both, and in an instant, we formed a gentlemen's agreement with the shake of our hands.

By the time Perry finally left to drive home, it was almost midnight, and I was beat. I had bought a boat and couldn't believe it! That night, I slept on *Noemocean* guilt free and overjoyed. It was the most fun I had had with my clothes on in years.

Chapter 33

So Nice to Finally Meet You
Told by Sebastian

When I didn't call or come home to my place that Saturday night, Whitney was a little shocked. She had left me three messages teasing and chiding me for the scam I was pulling on Perry. But when I didn't call her back Sunday night, she apparently became concerned. I had turned off my cell phone while out sailing to think about her and our future and then somehow ended up in negotiations to buy a sailboat. In all the chaos, debauchery, and confusion, I didn't turn it on again until Monday morning. There were four messages from her and some texts as well, each one growing more agitated and elongated. She sounded exceedingly worried and mad. As I sat back in my comfy chair behind the desk at my office listening to them, she came charging in, fresh from dropping off Abbey at school.

"What the hell, Sebastian!" she yelled before she even sat down. I had never heard her say anything like that before. I was stunned. "I've been worried sick about you! You said you'd call Saturday night—"

"No," I interrupted, smiling coolly. "YOU said I would call Saturday night, remember?"

"I can't believe you are smiling after lying to that poor guy just to use his boat," Whitney scolded. "I thought I knew you better than this!"

"Turns out I didn't have to lie to him," I snapped back confidently.

"What are you talking about? He just let you stay on his boat for the weekend?"

"No . . . he agreed to let me stay on MY boat for the weekend," I said. "I bought a boat! Can you believe it?"

"You bought a sailboat?" Whitney asked in disbelief.

"Well, sort of. I'll fill you in on it over lunch or dinner. When can we meet?"

We agreed on a late lunch that afternoon. I was so excited. I couldn't wait to tell her all the details. So, later, over lunch at the hospital cafeteria, I told her about the deal I had struck with Perry. In the middle of my giddy narrative, though, I mistakenly spilled the beans on my mother's looming visit. I couldn't wait to show everyone the boat, and by everyone, I meant and mentioned my mother.

"Can I meet her?" Whitney asked excitedly."You've talked so much about her. Evonne sounds very interesting."

"Do you actually want to?" I asked her incredulously.

"Sure. I'll introduce Abbey to her."

"Really?" I asked her again, just to be sure.

"What is it, Sebby?"

"I just . . . I just didn't . . . expect . . ." I stuttered.

"Didn't expect what?"

"I've never met your parents," I stated sheepishly. "Did you ever want me to, or . . . I mean—" I stammered.

"To be honest, I've wanted you to meet them for a while, but . . ." Whitney sighed.

"But?" I wondered.

"But I didn't want to scare you off if we weren't on the same page! Are we on the same page?" Whitney asked abruptly.

"Yeah. I mean yes," I admitted, laughing at the coincidence. "We even use the same analogies."

"What are you talking about, Sebastian?"

"Never mind," I said. "That's why I struggled with telling you about her coming to visit. I do want you to meet my mom, Whitney. She will love you."

"And I want you to finally meet my folks too. Is that okay?"

"Yeah . . . maybe they could all meet!" I mentioned off the cuff.

Whitney was more than happy. I was more than a little relieved. "Do you have any pictures of the boat?" she asked as her pager went off. I started to hand her my phone, but she was already turning toward the hallway. "Call me tonight!" she said over her shoulder. "AND I MEAN IT!" she added loudly, laughing as she pointed an accusing finger jokingly in my direction as she hurried away. "I want to see those pictures!"

A few days later, I invited Paul out to my place to draft a contract for Perry and me to sign and seal the deal on the boat. He told me he was having fun helping Peter with the divorce proceedings, and I explained to him again the dire financial straits his client was in. For whatever reason, though, we got off on a tangent as well and ended up discussing my house. Paul apparently really liked it and always had and, out of nowhere, offered to buy it.

"Sounds to me like you're settling down," he said confidently, as I had told him about Abbey and Whitney earlier in our conversation. "I never thought I'd see the day. If you ever decide to build or buy or move or whatever, I want first dibs on this place."

"Dibs . . . Dude, what are we? Twelve?" I asked him. "What are you talking about, Paul?"

"I really like this place, Sebby. You might need something bigger or different some day. All I'm saying is don't put in on the market before talking to me first, okay?"

Jeez, I had just bought a boat. Now I need a bigger house! "Yeah, okay . . . whatever," I assured him.

***

November flew by with work and some alone time as Whitney and Abbey went to Minneapolis for Thanksgiving, and everyone else went to visit their families as well. Hell,

Peter didn't even want to hang out with me. I wondered why everybody loved hanging out with their families so much. They actually looked forward to visiting them, while I was dreading my mother's upcoming visit and counting down the days—not until she arrived, but rather until she would fly back to Tahiti again. I know that sounds terrible. I really did love my mom and enjoy talking to her, even spending some time with her. I just didn't want her critiquing my life or the way I chose to live it. I liked my privacy and my anonymity. I liked being able to pick who I show parts of myself to, or what I show them for that matter. I had always felt that way. It was a way of compartmentalizing my life that put firewalls in place so that my various acquaintances didn't mix. It was just easier. With my mom coming, I worried she expected an all-access pass into the very core of my existence, including my relationship with Whitney. I needed barriers. I wanted boundaries for my own mental health and emotional wellbeing.

Many people say guests are like fish; they begin to stink after three days. As I drove to O'Hare to pick up my mom, I considered this and did the math. She would be staying at my house for two weeks. That meant, by my calculations, eleven days of sheer torture. At least when I was on my trip to the South Pacific a couple of years back, I could borrow the car and go snorkeling for a day or whatever just to get out of the house. What would we possibly talk about for that long? How could I keep my mother entertained? What would she do all day when I was at work? I didn't have an answer for any of these things, and yet there she was walking toward me at baggage claim, a huge smile on her tired face, her arms already outstretched for a hug. I vowed in an instant to do my best and make it work. She was, after all, my mom.

We weren't ten minutes into the drive back up to Milwaukee when she said, "So tell me more about Whitney.

Is she the same woman you met back in St. Thomas and told me about then?"

"First things first, Mom!" I almost interrupted. "Did you bring a coat? It's winter, Mom. You didn't bring a coat! Well, we'll have to stop somewhere and buy you a coat." I didn't wait for any further response as I tried to control the conversation, but she would have none of it. She was the master.

"What kind of doctor is she, Sebby? How old is Abbey? That's her daughter, right?"

Mom didn't miss a beat. "When do I get to meet them?" And on and on it went all the way back to Wisconsin. *Only thirteen more days to go,* I counseled myself, but it didn't help.

With my mother now residing at my place, I quickly began to feel like a teenager with no place to go. I needed privacy; *Whiney and I* needed privacy. Her parents would be coming to stay for a week and then Abbey would be out of school for ten days, so Whitney and I had to find new and creative ways to sneak in a quickie at my office or her house during the school day or on our lunch breaks during the week leading up to their visit. We both knew after that it would be a long dry spell until after the New Year. It was fun while it lasted, sort of covert and sneaky, bringing a little spice and intrigue into our relationship, even if only for a week, and it made me fall in love with her even more. Unfortunately I also understood that our daytime dalliances were only a very pleasant distraction from the inevitable. It was, after all, long since time for introductions.

Whitney's parents drove over the following Saturday. They had just put Abbey's great grandmother in a nursing home and were very sad about that, but Whitney assured me they were excited to finally meet the Kohs. We decided to just have everyone over to my place at the same time to avoid more awkward moments than necessary. Whitney and I both thought one festive evening was way better than two separate meetings where I met hers and she met mine.

I informed my mother that any talk of religion, politics, or marriage was strictly forbidden, and Whitney did the same with hers. We had gone shopping together over our lunch break on Friday and self-catered an evening of simple salads, cheese, fruits, breads, and desserts. Who knew you had to throw a party to introduce yourself to the other's parents? We didn't, but we did it anyway.

We were trying too hard, and it was obvious. We were nervous, but Abbey soon became the adorable center of attention, and somehow we all ended up talking and drinking wine in the kitchen for most of the evening. It went well. Apparently envy and admiration make for good conversation. Whitney's parents were enamored with Evonne's travels around Europe, her family ancestry in the South of France, and her life in the islands. They had always longed to travel to far off places but never found the time or the means to do so. My mother, on the other hand, was taken with their strong and balanced relationship and the love they shared. They had a great marriage, and Evonne was obviously a little envious, as well as a little lonely. I felt for her as I listened in on their conversation. I think she longed for someone like that in her life. It had been two decades since my father passed away. I'm sure her life since then was nothing like she had originally imagined it would be.

Looking back, I struggle to remember any kind of symbiotic relationship between my father and mother, at least not the type I would require to stay in it for the long haul. Maybe my memory was clouded by youth. I wasn't really paying much attention to anything or anybody but myself back then—or for most of my twenties and early thirties for that matter. Listening to my mom talk to Whitney's parents about my father and their life together in Chicago revealed to me a lot more than I ever imagined. She loved him dearly and apparently didn't see or feel the conflict of interests that seemed to pull me in two directions at once as I struggled to please them both and question what kind of marriage they had to endure.

I guess sometimes opposites do attract, but it didn't work that way with me. Whitney and I were cut from the same cloth. We even finished each other's sentences. I realized that evening that every relationship had its merits, and to critique someone else's from the outside looking in is a foolish endeavor at best. What works for others probably won't work for you. My parents' marriage and the fear of God it put into me as I imagined being stuck in a struggle like that for eternity apparently wasn't like that at all for my mother. Whitney's parents had a wonderful relationship and an unsinkable bond that I could only hope to somehow to equal with their daughter.

Chapter 34

Patently Offensive
Told by Peter

I thought everything was going well fairly well with divorce proceedings. It was actually pretty interesting watching Paul work when I could forget for a minute every now and then that this was my life he was working on, my kids' new reality, and my financial future. I had an untarnished opinion of Paul and his supposed charity on my behalf until Sebby decided he needed a drinking buddy one night.

"Sure, I'll get another round," I told him after our third or fourth as I dug into my pocket wondering if I had enough money for the cab fare home. *I'll have to use a card.*

"Paul is pretty good for not being a real attorney, don't you—" Sebby began.

"What do you mean not a real attorney!" I blurted out from across the booth.

"Okay . . . He's an attorney . . . I guess," Seb said laughingly. "But he's NOT a divorce lawyer," he admitted happily, as if he had just pulled one over on me.

"You're drunk, Sebastian, and you recommended him. You'd better—"

"Better what? Relax! Paul is the best!"

"The best what?" I demanded.

"The best dude around," Sebby stammered. "He's a patent attorney actually, but he does SEC compliance for Promise for a living. He's got a great eye for detail and is a stickler on the minutiae that everyone else seems to miss. Best of all, he's a brilliant chess player, a former debate team captain, and a sheer genius when it comes to playing intricate pranks and mind games on people. Paul was the guy who helped me finish off Heather actually," Sebby said.

"What are you talking about?" I asked.

"The batteries man . . . when I took the batteries out of her garage door opener. That was Paul's idea!"

"No shit!" I said, pondering what he told me of that day again. I even smiled a little.

"And now he's sitting across the table from her, helping you," Seb added. "He hates to lose! You're in good hands!"

"Yeah, hands that get five percent of anything I get in the negotiations," I reminded him.

"We'll see about that," Sebby told me. "I'll talk to Paul again. . . . He owes me a favor."

I tried to get Sebastian to fill me in on what the favor was or how he figured I could repay Paul, but after another beer, it was Whitney, Whitney, Whitney, with a little of Abbey thrown in for good measure. I should have known that for all his good intentions, somehow, someway the conversation always reverted back to him. He was a good friend but a terrible counselor.

"If you had to do it all over again now, would you marry someone?" he asked me.

"If I loved her . . . probably . . . not . . . No," I told him. "But I've been married, and it burnt me badly. If I didn't love her, then no way in hell!"

"That's the same answer, Peter, you—"

"No, I meant, if I loved her, I would at least consider it, but . . ." I started.

"But what?"

"But I've been married and don't think I will again— for the kids' sake," I told him. "You don't have any scars or baggage. It's different for you. Do you love Whitney?" I asked bluntly.

"Yeah, I think I do . . . but the thought of marriage

and an instant family trips me up," he replied honestly. "How did you know?"

"I didn't really, especially as I look back now. It just seemed like the next logical step in our relationship at the time."

"No lightning bolt or hot moment of passion?" Sebby asked.

"Nope. "

"That doesn't sound right," Sebby pondered aloud.

"Maybe it wasn't right. After all, look where I'm headed," I noted.

"You're going to be fine, Peter. You're kids are going to be fine!"

I don't know if it was the time out of my apartment, the beers, or Sebby, but I felt a little better. The next time I talked to Paul, I confronted him abruptly about forgetting to fill me in on his actual job title and training, but he reassured me I had nothing to lose. Wisconsin, after all, was a no fault state. If nothing else, Heather and I would split everything fifty-fifty, and since I was living in an apartment and working for near minimum wage at Home Depot, I really didn't have anything to lose, except the kids, but he promised me that wouldn't happen. We would play the game as long as we could, and he would get me the best settlement possible. Then (and he didn't say this, but I reminded myself anyway) he would get five thousand dollars from me or take five percent of my settlement, whichever was greater. I really didn't have a choice. How else could I pay him? It was five percent of something or zero percent of everything without a court date, and I didn't want a public hearing. I couldn't represent myself, especially against a shark like the one Heather had hired. He would eat my lunch and then devour me.

Another month went by before Paul and I sat again at the big table in Heather's attorney's mahogany office mansion. After Paul finally presented our side, only then did Heather's motives for dragging this out become clear. She wanted full custody and as much cash as she could get. She wasn't interested in Paul's initial offer in the least. I thought what we offered seemed fair. Paul assured me that if a settlement wasn't reached, the courts would grant something similar, but Heather wouldn't entertain the notion of anything close to half. I think even if her high-powered, high-priced suit had advised her of the facts, she wouldn't hear it. She was deaf to anything except the sweet sound of revenge (for what, I'm not sure) that rang in her ears like tinnitus. Maybe she thought I put Sebby up to their encounter, I don't know. I knew she blamed me for the failure of the business, but I wasn't the only builder going practically bankrupt. Everybody in construction was really hurting.

What was clear was her desire to keep all the money she inherited, even though we were still very much married at the time of her father's death. On top of that, she was demanding alimony and child support far exceeding the income I made at the top of the housing boom, let alone what I presently earned wearing an orange apron at Home Depot.

Sometimes being a failure and underemployed has its advantages, I thought as I smiled silently across the table at her. She glared back at me, the veins in her neck coursing with venom and spite. *I think at our next meeting I'll invite Sebastian along just to sit in and watch the proceedings. I wonder how Heather would like that!*

Paul presented my side professionally and unemotionally. Heather's attorney tried to negotiate from her baseline offer of everything, but Paul quickly squashed any advances with a flurry of papers showing texts, emails, and transcripts we had recovered. It was obvious from their respective glances at each other that Paul's evidence painted a very different picture than what Heather had probably portrayed to her attorney in their initial meetings.

He offered that we both take some time away from each other to cool off. I didn't mind, and Paul seemed pleased.

Another month went by with nothing, but then came a new plea to meet with them again as well as an independent mediator. Paul took it upon himself to delay, question, and refuse every so- called independent mediator on various grounds, most of which were frivolous but hinged on the notion that anyone they suggested would somehow be more beholden to their side. In reality, it was just a way for Paul to up the ante and the price tag Heather would have to shell out in the end to pay for her well-dressed hired gun. After the evidence we presented to him, I would guess he began to see Heather in a new light and didn't mind the delay tactics we routinely deployed. He was, after all, a man—married or not, it didn't matter—and being paid handsomely to boot. I was sure he could envision himself in my shoes and didn't like the fit or smell of them, let alone the woman who had picked them out for me—his belligerent, insolent client, and my soon-to-be ex-wife. I hear in attorney circles that billable hours are everything. Well, Paul and I were handing him them by the shovel full.

Finally, when we could delay no longer, we met again with them and a mediator we chose. It was more of the same. I was looking for fifty percent of everything. Heather simply wanted everything and more. We would have to go to court or settle with binding arbitration.

I am sure Heather's attorney advised her that court was not in her best interest. Paul advised me that it was, however, in mine. The problem was that a court date would drag this thing out even more. I really wanted to get this behind me and at least know where I stood. It was a risk, but I just wanted it over. So we agreed to arbitrate.

Our combined assets, which consisted mostly of the equity in the big new house and Heather's inheritance, totaled around a million dollars. The arbitrator valued the house at just over $650,000 dollars, the face value on our property tax assessment, and original appraisal. Although I knew with the dip in the real estate market it was really only worth about $500,000 or so now, maybe a little more. We still owed around $400,000 on the mortgage after the sale of our first home. Since Heather and the kids were already in the new house, she got it which meant the equity in it was hers. That basically left the cash value of our assets on the table, 99 percent of which was formerly her father's.

The difference between the arbitrator's mistaken estimate of our homes value, and what we owed ($250,000 on paper) went to Heather, the remaining $750,000 was split, with $300,000 going to me and $450,000 going to Heather, the difference amounted to the alimony I owed. At first the numbers had me fuming mad. Curiously though Heather was furious too. I was mad because it appeared as if she had gotten $700,000 to my $300,000. Heather was angry because her father's inheritance had somehow now become her alimony, and she hated that idea. I found out after the fact that her attorney advised her it could have been worse and in fact it was.

First Paul calmed me down by pointing out to me that the new house was in reality only worth around $500,000, which I already knew, but failed to appreciate. This meant that in reality our combined total assets were really around $850,000 instead of just over one million. Heather had in fact been awarded $250,000 against that total in today's market dollars, which left $600,000 on the table.

Then Paul told me the good news and the bad news. The bad news was that she would get my truck, which was worth a lot more than our car. The good news was that Paul had proven to the arbitrator over and over again my desire for counseling to save our marriage. In contrast he showed with emails, texts and graphic phone transcripts her absolute refusals to my earnest requests. In that light the arbitrator further agreed to award my attorney's fees against her settlement.

In the end, after zero attorney fees, but before taxes, I came out of the trenches with $300,000, the kids on the weekends and Wednesdays, and not a penny owed in alimony. On paper it looked like Heather walked away with $550,000, but in reality, it was only $400,000, because of what our (her) home was really worth. Beyond that, she still owed her attorney what I can only imagine was a small fortune. Paul estimated it to be somewhere between $20,000 and $30,000, along with Paul's fees of $15,000, which the arbitrator forced Heather to pay for failing to try counseling first, which probably left her with around $360,000 or so before taxes.

Paul also pointed out that while I was renting and living very, very cheaply, Heather now was solely responsible for the remaining note on the house. She couldn't pay it off with her settlement, especially after she paid the taxes and attorney fees first. And with no visible income for the moment, making monthly mortgage payments meant digging further into her lump sum inheritance/alimony windfall, if you could call it that. In short it was now *her* mortgage. By the time Heather sold the house and paid a realtor, she would be lucky to have $75,000 cash, but then she'd be homeless. I didn't want our kids to be homeless. Sooner than later she would have to make some very hard choices, and she would have no one to blame but herself. I was no longer her scapegoat or cross to bear or whatever, but I still felt horrible. What had we just done?

"Maybe your kids will end up living with you after all," Paul offered. "No matter what, you'll have a front-row seat," he said energetically. "Let me know what happens, man. You won, Peter! You won!"

"I owe you one, Paul . . . but nobody won today . . . nobody," I reminded him soberly. He seemed a little taken aback by my sour rebuttal. "Thanks, Paul. Thanks for everything."

"It was fun, Peter. Keep in touch," he replied

considerately before he drove away.

Fun? I thought to myself. *He really doesn't get it.* This wasn't a game or some debate; this was four people's lives!

I saw Heather and her attorney leave the office As I sat in what was now "her" truck at the far end of an adjacent parking lot and just watched her. She was obviously shaken. It was the first time I had viewed her as anything but my enemy in over a year. It was the first time I had thought about her feelings in all this or our history together and the eternal connection we shared with our kids in even longer. I was mad at myself for how caught up I got in the fight. I felt sad knowing it was finally really over between us, and I was worried about our kids. In many ways, I still loved her and felt sorry for her. After all, she was the mother to my children and a huge part of my life. I was sad it had ended this way. We had both let Owen and Campbell down, but I hoped that in time we could attend events together and at least be friends.

For now, I was certain that ball was in her court. My priority was to somehow help my kids recover, for them not to be scarred for life, for them each to find love some day and take the plunge. I wanted to kiss Owen's fiancé on the cheek in the future and welcome her into our broken, but healed family at a rehearsal dinner. I looked forward to walking Campbell down the aisle and giving her away to the luckiest guy on the planet. Even now after everything that had happened, when I envisioned those thoughts in my mind's eye, I saw Heather there, sitting next to me at some fancy restaurant with a bunch of bridesmaids and groomsmen. I could picture her in the front pew of our church, wearing a fabulous dress and watching Campbell appear on my arm as I courageously guided her toward the love of her life and gave my little girl away. As I slouched down in the truck, my mind wandered over our history together. Most of it was pretty good. Those memories would have to hold me a while longer.

Chapter 35

Don't I Know You?
Told by Jon

Sebastian had mentioned a few times over the years that I should meet and get to know Peter Steglin. It was strange how up until that day on the playground we had never been introduced. I had heard his name and even sought him out a few times, and now he was right there living in Port Washington. We had probably crossed paths a hundred times and didn't even know it.

Now as I sought out the advice from a professional at Home Depot, I was forced not only to prove how stupid I was when it came to home repairs but make small talk with a guy I had only recently met, which wasn't a strong point for me.

"Have you seen Sebby lately?" I asked, although it was less than a week since we all talked on the playground.

"Nah. Did you see his new sailboat?" Peter asked.

"Yeah, holy cow, it's a yacht!" I responded excitedly.

"That Sebby," he said under his breath. "He must be the luckiest son of a bitch in the whole world, I think."

"You think?" I replied sarcastically. "He *is* the luckiest guy in the world. . . . I know it!"

And just like that we bonded over, of all things, another guy. It was as if we already had a history, even though we'd only just met. Peter and I knew many of the same stories but from slightly different perspectives. He had heard my name bantered about for many years, as I had his, and we both commented how strange it was that we'd never officially met.

"I bet you know about Sebastian and my ex-wife?" he asked bluntly but with a smirk.

I didn't know how to answer, but the awkward pause in our conversation spoke volumes.

"Yeah," I admitted.

"It's okay," he told me as he chuckled. "Sebby really got her good!"

"He has all the luck," I replied, hoping to change the subject.

"Yeah," Pete responded.

"How are you doing?" I asked.

"Better," he said hopefully. "I've been concentrating on my kids. . . . That helps a lot. I don't get out much other than that."

"We'll have to get a beer sometime," I told him. "Share some Sebby stories. You can fill in all the blanks I haven't heard."

"Sounds good. Call me if you need some help fixing your drywall."

"Thanks, Pete," I said, turning to walk away. "See you on the playground."

***

From there on, our friendship was pretty easy. Whenever I wasn't flying a trip somewhere, I was home for a few days at a time. I mostly flew over the weekends and was often the one picking up or dropping off Bergen at school on Wednesdays, so it became a sort of regular thing, and it was fun too. Peter told me "Sebby stories" that I had never heard before, for the obvious reason that they sometimes weren't the most flattering to Sebastian. I knew a lot about his trip to the Caribbean because we seemed to always end up talking boats. Elise and Whitney, as well as Abbey and Bergen, had become good friends, so I filled in the gaps for Peter on Whitney.

"Did Sebby ever tell you how he joined the mile-high club in college on a bet?" Peter asked me one day on the playground bench.

"No, do tell," I responded enthusiastically.

"He bet his frat boy buddies that he would not only get laid on spring break, but he would join the mile-high club too. A bunch of sororities and fraternities from UW Madison were heading out to Jackson Hole that year to go skiing. Sebastian bet his friends a hundred dollars that he could convince his new girlfriend at the time to do anything. Their only caveat was that it had to take place off the ground. In a hotel bed or closet or wherever didn't count even if they were above six thousand feet. Since they were all taking charter buses out to Wyoming, and not flying, they eagerly took the bet. There should have been no way for Sebby to make it happen, but he did it. Actually *they* did it—he and his girlfriend—in a gondola between runs. Even more amazing, she admitted it to her friends, so he had proof! He never told you about that?"

"No . . . and we even skied out there together one time. He must have forgotten," I replied, puzzled. "He's had more than his share of moments like that. After a while they probably all blend together."

"I'd give my left nut for one moment half as good as that," Pete admitted, and I wholeheartedly agreed.

***

More often than not, Peter and I struck up a conversation on the playground while Ben and Campbell played on the swings or slides, and we waited for Bergen and Owen to emerge from school.

"You ever notice how all the moms bond over parenting and stuff?" Peter asked me abruptly one day. "I mean, just look at them over there," he said motioning to the parking lot near the playground at school where a group of five or six moms were deep in loud conversation, comparing notes and laughing about this and that.

"I guess so," I responded.

"It just not the same with guys, I guess."

"Yeah, I know," I said. "I've tried numerous times to join in on the conversation, whatever it was, before or after school, but somehow the fun always ends about the time I show up. Like it's all some big secret that they share or like I'm a pariah or something. Hey, I would like to go for coffee after drop off and plan a play date for my kids too, you know, but alas I am a guy only attempting to be a mom at that point. I am not invited. I guess that's just the way it is, huh?"

"Yep," Peter agreed. "It's like when my kids are with me and something happens, and I'm trying everything to help and comfort and be there for them, yet all they want at that moment is Mommy. We can't ever be that, no matter how hard we try."

"But I'll let you in on a little secret, Pete, in case Heather never tells you. When Owen and Campbell are with her, sometimes they just want their daddy too."

"You think so?" Pete responded, smiling at this new revelation.

"I know so, man. Elise tells me all the time. You're a good dad, I know it."

"Thanks, Jon," he said and paused. "You know, it would be fun to get our kids together, but with Bergen and Owen, it's getting to be that boy-girl thing, you know? Owen only wants to play with other boys, and I suspect it's the same with Bergen?"

"Yeah, I guess that starts in first or second grade and continues on forever, doesn't it?" I agreed, adding, "Maybe it's true. Maybe men and women can never truly be friends like they are with one another?"

We both nodded and soon fell back into more familiar and easy subjects of conversation. It wasn't like we didn't try to talk about other things, but the Sebby stuff just came easier. Peter loved baseball and the Brewers. I found watching sports to be sort of an enigma, like enjoying watching fishing rather than actually going fishing, but I didn't tell him that. I loved talking about far-off places. But, other than Florida, Peter hadn't been anywhere. What we did share, besides our friendship with Sebby, was a deep love for our kids, a frustration with our finances and investing in particular, an interest in business in general, and houses and construction. Peter was an expert, but for me it was more intrigue and admiration. I loved talking to him about homes and everything that went inside them. He didn't seem to mind. In fact, I think he was a little flattered.

One morning, over a cup of coffee in Port Washington, I shared with him my frustrations over our home and the headaches Elise and I had building it. "If only I had hired you, Pete. Trouble was, I couldn't afford you . . . at least that's what I thought."

"I was super busy and choosy then," he said politely. "But you could afford me now. I'm not always at Home Depot. I do some small projects on the side, and I'd be happy to work with you on something if you want . . . no charge."

"I'd have to pay you," I offered earnestly.

But Pete was casual and cool. "Buy me a burger and a beer sometime. Like I told you, I don't get out much."

He was a good guy. I liked him and felt bad for him. I couldn't imagine walking a mile in the shoes he had been in over the past two years.

Sebastian and I played an early round of golf one day, and I told him about meeting up with Pete. "How come you never told me about the gondola and the mile-high club when we were skiing out at Jackson Hole? Or ever, for that matter—"

"What?" Sebby asked dimly. Apparently his mind was elsewhere.

"The bet, your girlfriend. Seb, what's up?"

"Did Peter tell you that? You two have been talking about me behind my back." Sebby wasn't his usual jovial self. "Leah Aspen was the girl," Sebby paused. "Leah was the one I might have gotten pregnant in college. She dropped out after that semester. I buried that thought as deep as I could a long time ago, Jon. I don't want to talk about it. Now or ever again! Things are too good now. Don't ever mention that subject again, understand?"

"Does Whitney know?" I asked without thinking.

"Jeez, Jon! Yes, drop it, will you?" he scolded me. "I have a lot on my mind. I need your help."

"Peter needs our help, Sebby," I responded, still not tuning into Sebby's urgency.

"With what now? I gave him a job building my office. I let him crash at my place. I even found him a good lawyer."

"He needs work. . . . He needs to get out," I told him

"Yeah, I guess I've been pretty preoccupied lately with Whitney, Abbey, my boat, and work," he admitted.

"I think we should bring him on the Mac race," I said bluntly, as if it was somehow my place to invite him, which I knew it wasn't.

"Really?" Sebby asked, half shocked. "I don't know if he even likes to sail. He's been out a couple times but . . . I don't want him getting sick or ruining it for me and Whitney or you for that matter."

"Whitney's going?" I asked.

"Yeah, if we can get find a sitter, sort of . . ." his voice trailed off. "I need your help, Jon," he began anew. "This is serious."

For the rest of the round, he talked, and I listened, which was how it typically worked between us. This time, however, there was a lot to take in, a lot to consider and remember. Once again, I became Sebby's sidekick, his partner in crime. It was the least I could do.

Chapter 36

Learning the Lingo
Told by Peter

Besides a long car trip or two as a boy, my honeymoon with Heather, and a trip to Disney World with our kids, I'd never been anywhere or done anything truly exciting. I never joined the Boy Scouts or went hiking in the hills for more than an afternoon. I tried hunting a few times. Shooting guns was fun, but hunting didn't take with me. It occurred to me one night that I had never really gone on an actual adventure. Now, as I was about to, I felt increasingly nervous, but not enough to bow out and stay home.

The sailboat race between Chicago and Mackinac Island was a pretty big deal in the sailing community, Sebastian informed me. Every July, more than three hundred boats carrying more than three thousand sailors travel more than three hundred miles from start to finish, in anywhere from roughly twenty-four to seventy-two hours. The year 2011 would be the 103rd year for the event.

Although storms occasionally caused some disruption, no one had ever gotten seriously hurt or killed in the history of the race. I wasn't surprised at this and must have seemed nonchalant in my appraisal; after all, it was just sailing. I always figure speed kills; sharp things and explosives kill, you know? But sailing? Come on, it's like nothing, right? Except for hypothermia and ropes and lines and shrouds and sharks and whatever, Seb corrected me.

"Come on, Seb, there aren't any sharks in Lake Michigan," I shot back.

"Okay, but this is serious stuff, Peter."

"Okay, Seb. Okay, whatever."

"No, Peter, trust me."

"I'll take your word, man. I trust you."

"You'd better," Sebastian reprimanded me.

This year, 361 boats entered the race, with 355 actually starting on either Friday, July 15 or Saturday, July 16. The race/regatta actually began on two different days with what is known as the cruising fleet starting just off Chicago's Navy Pier on Friday afternoon and the true racing fleet beginning their quest for glory on Saturday morning. The sailboats then proceed north northeast, choosing their own course, until turning more easterly and entering Lake Huron by funneling under the Mackinac Bridge, the narrowest part of the course, and coasting the final stretch into Mackinac Island, home of the famous Grand Hotel.

"You ready for some fun?" Sebby asked me as I boarded his boat."This is going to be AWESOME!" He sounded like some teenage surfer dude.

To be honest, I was surprised Sebby invited me along. I wasn't sure I even wanted to go, but I wasn't doing anything else, and Heather agreed to take the kids (at least we were on speaking terms again), so what the hell. Sebastian invited Jon and Whitney as well as a guy named Perry and his son Steve. Apparently Perry was somehow the co-owner of the boat. I didn't ask any questions; they both seemed cool.

Elise offered, and Abbey happily agreed to, an extended sleepover with Bergen. Then she was going to drive herself and the three kids all the way up to the ferry for Mackinac Island and watch us finish sometime the following Sunday or Monday.

My part of the bargain was to drive Jon's minivan back to Port Washington following the race and give the two couples and their kids the chance of a lifetime to bring *Noemocean* back home over the following week or more. As for Perry and his son, Sebby mentioned something about their family meeting them on the island, but I didn't know any of the details.

The six of us left Port super early on Thursday morning, July 14, and headed south toward Chicago. Sebastian and Perry's boat was spectacular. In short order, however, I learned that this wasn't going to be some pleasure cruise. These guys—and Whitney, for that matter—were serious sailors. They buzzed about on and below deck like beavers trying to repair a hole in a dam. I just stood there offering to help but feeling like I was already in the way.

When we finally got underway, Seb called our first impromptu meeting to discuss how this was all going to play out. Sebby and I would be a crew within the crew, as he had the most experience, and I had the least. Whitney and Jon, both more than somewhat familiar with wind, weather, sailing, and what not, would pair up, and Perry and Steve would round out the batting order. We were to be three separate teams within a larger crew, taking turns between steering the boat and trimming the sails, cooking and doing radio/navigational duties, or resting. We would work four-hour shifts at each and then rotate.

The first thing I had to learn was everything. Sebastian quickly put me at the helm and showed me how to steer the boat as well as find the apparent wind. Perry and his son meanwhile gave Whitney and Jon a crash course on the galley and all the electronics below. I was glad I didn't have to go below yet, as I felt a little queasy, but Sebby assured me it would pass or he would medicate me.

After that, I began to learn the lingo so that when Seb wanted or needed something done, I could understand what he was talking about. Ropes on a boat could be called lines or sheets or halyards, depending on their purpose. Port meant left, and starboard meant right. The bow was the front part of a ship, and the stern was the rear. The mainsail was the big one on the mast. The jib, or genoa, unfurled like a big triangle from the bow and fell to either side of the mainsail. A spinnaker was like a giant triangular parachute that pulled a sailboat along while looking like an inflated airbag. A storm chute was a round parachute-like device with holes in it; sailors actually threw it in the water when all else failed or all hell broke loose to keep the boat facing into the wind and not capsizing. (There. I think that about does it. Did I pass the test?)

After about three hours, I began to recognize the skyline of Milwaukee as it came into view. I was having difficulty adjusting to the slow pace of this voyage. I couldn't believe they somehow all found *this* fun and baseball so boring—well, except Steve; he liked baseball. I secretly wanted to be on his team—I mean crew. Whatever.

After four hours, we rotated to our next assignments. Sebby could tell I was still feeling queasy, so instead of heading below to educate me some more, he suggested we just get comfortable and relax for a while. I had been up since early morning, and to my surprise, the motion of *Noemocean* rocked me right to sleep; I dozed for over an hour.

When I awoke, I felt hungry, which Sebastian reminded me was a good sign. "We'll make a sailor out of you yet, old man!" he proclaimed.

We ate subsandwiches and continued heading south. Perry and Steve taught us and insisted on safety at all times. The person at the helm and the assistant on deck were to always have a small but incredibly loud air horn attached to their PFDs or harnesses. (A PFD is a life vest, and a harness is like the straps on a backpack, which we wore over our shoulders and around our waists at all times at night or in foul weather.) A large nylon strap ran the full length of the sailboat directly down the middle and over the top of the entry door that led below. At night or in bad conditions, the first priority when coming above onto the deck was to tether to this strap and attach it to your harness.

Perry informed us of the dangers of hypothermia and the risk of falling overboard if we failed to strap in. The odds of finding a person in any large body of water, let alone Lake Michigan at night, apparently weren't the best. She almost always claims her dead. I was taken aback by his bluntness. This really was some serious shit.

As we continued slowly south toward Chicago, Sebastian surprised us all by loudly blowing his air horn from the helm and throwing a round white life ring without a rope behind the boat.

"Man overboard!" he yelled loudly. Everybody jumped, practicing not only keeping track of the life ring as it drifted off in our wake, but the rapid succession of steps necessary to bring the sailboat around to rescue the ring or person. It was actually intense and kind of fun.

After that, things slowed down a bit onboard *Noemocean*, and Sebby broke out some tunes, blasting every nautical, blue-water, warm-weather, ocean-oriented theme song he could find on his iPod. Whether it was Christopher Cross or Gordon Lightfoot, Jimmy Buffet or Dave Matthews, Sebby demanded that we all join in and sing along at the top of our lungs. He called it team building.

Finally, after a few more hours, I thought I was ready to try heading below to learn what I needed about the radios, GPS, radar, and galley. Boy, was I wrong. It wasn't even that rough outside, but within ten minutes, I couldn't concentrate on anything except my urge to vomit and Sebby's insistence that I only do that on (or preferably over) the rail on deck. It was embarrassing, and it only made me more nervous for the race, as I could see the shoreline the whole way south. How would I feel when we were out in the middle of lake with no land in sight?

"Maybe I'll just get off in Chicago, Seb," I offered. "I don't want you having to babysit me. I could take a bus or the train back to Milwaukee."

Sebastian tried to reassure me again and offered me

some Dramamine, which, it turns out, I should have taken sooner. That stuff was wonderful. I could only hope that he had a million pills on board, because I figured I was going to need them.

"Better living through chemistry, aye, Peter?" Jon chided me. "It'll get better."

Twelve hours after leaving Port Washington, the Chicago skyline came into view as we tacked back toward shore. On land, the Mac race festivities were already in full swing. There were sailboats and sailors everywhere. It was like the Super Bowl. Funny how you can grow up in an area all your life and never even realize everything going on around you. That this was an annual event and I had never even heard of it before Sebastian inviting me was bewildering.

We finally found the mooring ball Seb had arranged for the boat and tied up *Noemocean* for the evening. Then some guys in two skiffs came alongside, picked us all up, and took us to shore for the short taxi ride to a restaurant right on the river called Baccino's in the heart of downtown Chicago just off Michigan Avenue. Sebby announced triumphantly that he was starting a new tradition, and all the pizza, wine, and beer we could drink was on him. It was amazing.

That night as I lay on one half of the settee bench that wrapped around the dining table on the sailboat, I already felt as if I had been on an adventure, but this was only the beginning.

Chapter 37

White Water
Told by Sebastian

Friday the fifteenth of July 2011 was born sunny and bright. I was already awake by the time the sun broke the northeastern horizon, casting a beautiful array of orange and yellow light across the still black waters of Lake Michigan and the couple hundred boats waiting patiently to begin the race. The big day had finally arrived, and I couldn't wait to get underway. Slowly but surely everyone onboard stirred awake to the smell of fresh hot coffee and Pillsbury cinnamon rolls, compliments of my amazing first mate, Whitney. Apparently, though, no one was hungry after gorging on the best Chicago-style stuffed spinach pizza on God's green earth the night before.

"They'll keep," Whitney announced to everyone, unoffended.

I spent the better part of the morning organizing various things onboard and making some phone calls to keep myself busy and pass the time a little faster. Everybody else did the same. Jon and Whitney found out from Elise that all was well with their brood, as did Peter. Perry and Steve got picked up by a little harbor taxi skiff and headed back into the city for some last-minute items. Everything was proceeding as planned.

Everyone made it back to the boat by one o'clock for our final preparations to untie and get underway. I knew this was supposed to be a race, but I wasn't in it for the race, looking at it instead as a sort of pilgrimage and a way of remembering my father. I think Perry felt the same way.

I offered that he and Steve take us out for the start, and they jumped at the chance. For a bit, while it was hectic, Whitney and I worked well together hoisting the main and getting everything put away. Jon assisted wherever he could, and Peter kept lookout for the myriad of sailboats jockeying to and fro for the start. It was often as if we were playing chicken with the other sailboats, and I didn't like it, but we finally got off without a hitch.

Perry and I routinely discussed with Whitney and Jon whether we should head straight north and then turn out across the lake or make an immediate jog to the right and take the shortest route possible, heading northeasterly toward the eastern shoreline of Lake Michigan and following the herd. I was torn. Part of what drew me to sailing was the solitude; part of what I liked about regattas and races was the camaraderie. Everyone agreed we didn't want or need to be in the thick of it all the way north, especially at night. It could be hard to keep track of other sailboats on dark nights as they changed course and snuck up on us, so we opted for more space. The consensus was to take our chances with the winds farther north in the lake and follow a course plotted directly from Navy Pier to Washington Island on the tip of Wisconsin's Door County.

With the wind out of the south, it was soon apparent that *Noemocean*'s big red spinnaker might be the best ticket for a magic carpet ride to the north. So with the help of everyone on board, we hoisted it up and out and then sat back to enjoy the day.

It was windy, but clear, and the lake was actually pretty flat, so we made steady progress to the north and had little or no work to do. But, unfortunately, we weren't alone. The vast majority of the fleet was cruising west of the rhumb line as well. (In simplest terms, the rhumb line is an imaginary dividing line running north and south the length of the lake, dividing it in half.) This was the opposite of what happened most years when many boats sail off to the eastern side of the Lake Michigan, choosing to run the shortest possible distance up the eastern shoreline from just after the start all the way to the finish.

The water was awash in light and bright spinnaker sails dotting the horizon like sun catchers on a blue window. We kept a close watch. It wasn't like we had anything else to do. Trimming and steering were easy. Nobody wanted to eat. The only thing I was worried about at that moment was the progress being made on my plans for our arrival.

Saturday flowed by effortlessly, and we all fell into the slow and steady rhythm of life onboard, talking and singing, sleeping and reading. Our trusty big red spinnaker continued to push us along effortlessly. The only problem looming on the horizon was some approaching storms from the northwest, which the National Weather Service began forecasting for Sunday evening in the northern end of the lake, right where everybody was heading. I suppose we should have continued straight toward Washington Island, but as the winds shifted more southwesterly on Sunday, we took full advantage. We needed to proceed more northeasterly as well, so we made plans to skirt just to the north of Beaver Island. Fortunately the thunderstorms they were forecasting were scattered and disorganized.

At first it didn't look like it would be very bad. Whitney, Perry, and I formed a decision committee. Jon became the go-to guy for advice on weather, as he routinely looked at this kind of stuff as a pilot. "I'll give you my best advice, Sebby. But it's way different down here cruising along at eight miles an hour than it is at thirty-seven thousand feet doing eight miles a minute. We go around the big ones, man . . . every single time," Jon warned me.

Perry, Whitney, and I decided to press on. We would make Beaver Island before night fall Sunday. After that it wasn't too far to anywhere, as the Great Lake funneled into a narrow corridor between the Upper Peninsula and lower two thirds of Michigan.

Around ten p.m. Sunday evening, the National Weather Service issued a special marine warning out of their facilities in Green Bay, Wisconsin.

[Winds forecast in excess of 50 knots /
High Waves / Dangerous Lightning]
[Possible Hail / Boaters Should Seek
Safe Harbor Immediately]

Unfortunately we hadn't made it to Beaver Island yet, or we could have just ducked in there. I suppose we should have turned back for Washington Island hours earlier or headed more easterly toward a few of the lesser islands south and west of Beaver, but we didn't. They were too far away now. We would never make it anywhere close to either of them in time. We were out in the open, exposed, and it was getting dark—I mean really dark. To the northwest, we couldn't even see the stars. A black wall was building off to our left, and everyone was getting nervous.

An hour or more earlier, after receiving the latest weather updates for the storm, we had dropped the spinnaker in preparation, which slowed our progress toward the northeast. Now I wasn't even sure that would be sufficient. We needed to batten down the hatches and prepare to ride this thing out. We left out just a bit on the forward jib and put two reefs into the mainsail, decreasing its size by over half. Perry readied the storm chute at the bow in case we needed it, and I told everyone to get everything stowed.

"Put on your storm gear and your PFDs and stay below or tie in with your harnesses if you want to be out on deck. It's going to get rough," I told them.

Two distinctly separate weather systems with three widely scattered areas of smaller thunderstorm cells merged in the span of an hour and came marching across the lake at thirty knots like an army hell bent on destruction. The

National Weather Service was now reporting the tops of the thunderstorms in the area at over fifty-five thousand feet. (For perspective, a big thunderstorm usually grows only into the high thirties or occasionally as high as forty-five thousand feet in the mid-latitudes of the northern hemisphere. Big cells rarely have the energy to push through an area in the earth's atmosphere known as the tropopause.) This was no ordinary storm, and these were no ordinary cells. They had combined to form super cells as we floated like a tiny bobber in the middle of the northernmost end of Lake Michigan directly in their path.

Perry, Peter, and I opted to stay on deck. Whitney, Jon, and Steve decided to stay below to man the radio and the radar. I think Peter was scared (I'll admit I was more than a little concerned) and thought he might puke, Dramamine and all. It was really quite thoughtful of him considering we were all in for a ride. I felt ready, but in retrospect, nothing could have prepared us for what happened next.

In the span of a minute or two, the wind whipped up from fifteen knots to over forty. To make matters worse, it changed direction so suddenly from the southwest to the northwest we didn't have time to turn into the wind, so we got slammed broadside. Perry went into emergency mode. For a moment, it appeared we might point downwind, which would have proved incredibly dangerous. In the meantime, we heeled over so quickly and violently that I lost my balance and slammed my head into the starboard side rail. By the time I realized what had happened, Peter was holding onto my arm and helping me back up. He got my attention and then glared at me as if to say, *You dumb shit! You almost went overboard! You should follow your own advice!*

I looked down at his hands in disbelief as he tethered *my* harness to the lifeline running forward. *How could I have been so stupid?* I wondered. Peter had probably saved my life, but there was no time for reflection or gratitude.

Perry was yelling for me to take the helm. It was just before midnight Sunday, July 17, and the storm was already upon us.

Perry screamed above the torrent for Peter to help him douse the mainsail as I struggled with the wheel, trying to get *Noemocean* to come about into the wind. The spray coming off the ever-growing waves stung my eyes as I attempted to peer forward into the night and simultaneously assist them at the rear of the boom. Rain dumped out of the ink-black sky like a monsoon but didn't hit the ground, instead choosing to fly horizontally across the water and pulverize everything it came in contact with. Sheet lightning lit up the night in brilliant flashes all around us but luckily missed our mast.

Between the roar of the wind, the booming thunder, the lightning, and the driving rain, it looked like a scene on the news using the grainy night footage from the beginning raids in the first gulf war. Shock and awe—I felt both. Adrenaline was coursing through my veins. A myriad of thoughts, concerns, and memories flooded my mind. The water all around us was now white.

From out of nowhere, Whitney appeared from below, tethering herself onto the strap running the length of the boat with her harness before coming up on deck. She was now standing barely four feet in front of me and yelling at the top of her lungs, but I could hardly hear her over the wind. It was something about the radio, like it was pretty bad. Steve was freaking out below, and Jon was manning the nav station like a bull rider trying to make it eight seconds without getting thrown off his seat, but this beast would buck much longer than that.

Peter clung to the backstay with both hands for support and dear life as Whitney, without anybody directing her, fought her way up to the bow against the howling wind and wicked rain to help deploy the storm chute. I managed to get the engine started. I wanted Peter to furl the remainder of the jib, but I worried he might do it wrong and send us back broadside to the wind and capsize us or knock Whitney or Perry off the bow into the water with the sail, so I yelled for him to steer so I could do it myself.

"ARE YOU FUCKING KIDDING ME, SEBBY!" he yelled."I DON"T KNOW WHAT TO DO!"

"JUST TAKE THE WHEEL AND DON'T LET IT DROP OFF TO STARBOARD!" I commanded. "DON'T LET IT COME RIGHT!"

"I'LL TRY!" Peter yelled as he braced himself and took the helm.

We all hung on with one hand and worked with the other. Peter kept us pointed into the wind. Perry and Whitney deployed the storm chute off the bow, then they made their way carefully back aft. I furled the jib over their heads and went below briefly to check the radar. I was completely drenched, as was the small stairway leading down into the interior of the sailboat. In my rush to get below and close the door behind me, I slipped and hit my head again. I sat up, more than a little dazed, and looked at the computer screen. The line of weather was over two hundred miles long, covering the northern two thirds of the lake like a green, yellow, and red tie-dyed blanket. Fortunately, as Jon pointed out while clinging to his seat with a death grip, it was moving widthwise across us, not lengthwise.

"I've seen my share of shitty weather over the years, but nothing like this! Next time I'm taking a jet!" he said, half serious.

Noemocean began to pull against the line off her bow and slide backward as the storm chute bit into the foaming sea. Waves raced past her hull in rapid succession like Indy cars on an oval track. Perry let off on the wheel as the boat headed up into the wind by itself, and Whitney made her way back below. I met her on the steps as I was heading back out.

"YOU'RE BLEEDING, SEBBY!" she yelled as she entered the cabin, blocking my exit and forcing me to retreat. "What happened?" she asked when she made it below. "Are you okay?"

"I'm fine." I showed her my hands. "They're not even bleeding or swollen," I said, making a stupid joke.

Whitney wasn't laughing. She insisted I stay below while she checked my face and scalp for the source of the blood. By the time she found it, things began to simmer down, and she saw that the cut was only minor.

What had seemed like an eternity was probably only twenty minutes or so, but it put the fear of God in each and every one of us. I don't care what anyone says. Nothing makes you feel more small and insignificant than a bout with Mother Nature.

In all, more than thirty boats withdrew from the race. Later we would learn that peak gusts were clocked at over sixty knots in a few places with sustained winds in some areas topping thirty knots for more than twenty minutes. Many boats also reported hail and incurred serious damage.

The real tragedy however was only now unfolding, as farther off to the east a boat had capsized, killing two crewmembers who had gotten trapped below and drowned.

Other boats, including a Coast Guard cutter, and a helicopter rushed to its aid, but they were all too late. The 103rd Mac race would go down in infamy for the ferocity of the storm that night and the casualties that ensued.

Dawn that Monday morning was surreal. The only thing that comes close in my mind was the way I felt when I finally made the harbor at Charlotte Amalie, although that time I only had myself to worry about. This was different. The safety(or lack thereof) of my crew based on the decisions we made the night before could have reverberated through so many more lives than our own, including Abbey, Bergen, Owen, Campbell, and Ben. I don't think anybody onboard blamed me for the position we had just gotten out of, but I blamed myself. It was a sobering thought, and we were all glad to be alive.

By the time we made Mackinac Island, it was late Monday morning. I had big plans in store for our arrival, but after what had just happened, it wasn't feeling like I imagined it would. Even then, I was more certain than ever that it was the right thing to do.

Jon whispered, "Is it still on?"

It had to be. Regardless of what had just happened, there were too many pieces to this puzzle already in place to give up on it now just because we had lost one in the trip not going as smoothly as planned. I could only hope it would somehow all end up okay.

Chapter 38

Say Anything
Told By Jon

As we approached the finish line and the harbor on Mackinac Island, I needed to be sure Sebby still intended to put his plan into motion. He assured me he did.

I sent off a text to Elise and inquired as to her position. We were getting close, but I couldn't see her or the kids yet. As we entered the harbor, I heard them before I found them with my eyes. It was awesome. Abbey, Bergen, and Ben were cheering for us at the top of their lungs, welcoming us into the docks like some kind of heroes. The voice of her daughter wasn't lost on Whitney either as she scurried quickly toward the bow to verify her perceptions. She was overwhelmed with joy at the surprise at the end of our adventure, but it wasn't over yet.

Elise was waving and yelling. The kids were waving and yelling. Then Whitney's parents appeared from behind them, almost unnoticed after the initial shock of hearing her daughter's voice. Next to them, Sebby's mother stood waving solemnly. He had flown them all in to Traverse City, Michigan, and they had driven up together. Something was definitely up.

They ran down to meet us where we docked *Noemocean* and began to tie her off. All of the sudden, there was a loud splash. Seb had missed the dock in his haste to get off the boat to hug Abbey and his mom. He fell into Lake Huron, and his PFD automatically inflated. Everyone laughed, including Whitney, while he floated there embarrassingly until the joke was finally over and the laughter subsided.

Then he got serious. Dressed in red nylon sailing shorts, a crappy old Patagonia t-shirt, and crappier still Sperry topsiders, Sebby, soaking wet in his bright-yellow life jacket, had a strange look on his face.

"Are you going to get out anytime soon?" Whitney asked incredulously."What's wrong?"

Sebastian just continued floating. He was acting weird, and Whitney noticed it too.

"Are you okay, Sebastian?" Perry asked, oblivious to what was about to happen. "I think that bump to your head might be worse than we thought."

Sebby returned his focus toward Whitney. "I've fallen for you," he finally said emphatically. "I . . . I think I fell for you the moment we met. I love you more than you know . . . and if last night proves anything, it's that I never want to lose you. Will you marry me and make me the luckiest guy in the world?"

By now, everyone in the whole marina had gathered around the dock and adjacent pier. Whitney stared at Sebby in utter disbelief as he pulled a small blue box out of a pocket in his life vest, ever so careful not to drop it in the water. The ring had been in his PFD the entire trip. He was beginning to shake. Maybe it was the water. Maybe it his nerves. Maybe it was the waning adrenaline coursing through his veins and the lack of sleep that now appeared to be delirium, but Sebastian was unlike I had ever seen him. He was trembling and speechless, helpless and vulnerable, yet in a subtle way, hopeful and unashamed. It was a priceless moment in time.

Whitney didn't say anything. Nobody said anything. She just walked to the back of the boat and stopped. It was obvious she was beginning to well up as she paused and looked at Elise. Then she turned and looked at her parents and locked eyes with Abbey as if trying to read her daughter's mind, but the expression on Abbey's cute face gave away her answer before she could even say it out loud.

With a second big splash, Whitney jumped in the water and surfaced next to Sebby. "Yes! Yes! Yes!" she answered loudly.

Everyone cheered as the couple floated in their life vests together. We all took pictures, then we unloaded the boat and were taken by horse-drawn carriage (as there aren't any motorized vehicles on Mackinaw Island) to the Grand Hotel. The rooms Sebby had reserved were amazing. The hotel itself was amazing. It was as if we had gone back in time to another era. We showered and agreed to regroup at six for drinks and an impromptu engagement dinner to celebrate the newly engaged couple.

As we walked back out toward the huge front veranda at the hotel a few hours later, Peter stopped me and asked, "Wasn't he already the luckiest guy in the world? How does he do it?"

"There's always more out there, Pete. You just have to look for it," I said. "And when you find it, go after it."

"Maybe some of his luck will rub off on us," Peter replied. "You think?"

"I think it already has, man," I told him. "I think it already has."

Chapter 39

Sunshine on My Shoulders
Told By Peter

The drive home in Jon and Elise's minivan after the regatta was a turning point in my life. Fortunately there wasn't much traffic in the Upper Peninsula of Michigan, or I might have gotten in an accident. My mind was on anything and everything except the road. I drifted over the center line or onto the shoulder more than once, only to be jolted into attention by the spray of rocks and gravel on the underbelly of my ride.

I had never experienced anything like what had just occurred over the past seventy-two hours. I felt really alive for the first time in a long time, and that made me feel almost joyous. At the same time, I felt sad because I hadn't seen my kids in almost a week. It was the longest I had ever gone without being around them since they were born. I was a little envious of Sebby, Whitney, Jon, and Elise as they continued on in their adventure sailing somewhere now southwestward, slowly retracing their way back to Port Washington.

What could I possibly give my kids that even comes close to something like that? I wondered as I wandered down the road toward Escanaba. *How can I repair the damage Heather and I have inflicted on them?*

Somewhere along the way, after a short stop for gas and a pasty, I stopped focusing on my own pity and began to think in terms of plenty. I had a lot, and I could start over. *It's never too late to begin again.* I told myself; after all, I still had my tools. My head would be my office, my abilities could once again become my advertising, and my heart and hands would once again provide not only for me, but for my children as well. I still had a passion for construction and a knack for business. I wouldn't make the same mistakes again. Maybe what doesn't kill you *does* make you stronger, and that goes for divorce as well.

I thought a lot about Heather. She would always be a large part of my life, even if it was different now than how I imagined it would be, and for that, I was grateful. I still loved her and found it comforting somehow that we were eternally linked by the creation of our kids. I knew she would meet someone sooner than later, as she was still a social butterfly and had a way about her that invited men to love her. I on the other hand wasn't so sure I would meet someone ever again. Right now, I wasn't looking anyway. Sebby wouldn't be dragging me out to more bars to meet women. Actually, old Seb wouldn't probably be going out much anymore anyway. I knew the road he was headed down, and it was wonderful. That honeymoon period in a relationship and that time with a new child is a priceless treasure trove of memories.

I hoped Jon might still want to hang out from time to time. He was a really interesting guy, even if he couldn't talk sports to save his life. I worried that without those two guys around I really would be all alone—except for my kids, of course, but sometimes you just need a friend.

As I came south through Green Bay, I decided to take a detour and headed up into Door County until I came to Whitefish Dunes State Park. I wandered down to the beach, plopped down in the sand, and stared out into the water for a long time.

It was somewhere out there that I was tested, I figured, remembering the storm and my anxiety over that moment and everything else that was swirling around in my life. Did I pass the test? I wondered.

I realized that I knew exactly where I was, and oddly

enough, I felt incredibly at ease without a care in the world.

I peered out into the lake again in the vain hope that I would somehow catch a glimpse of *Noemocean* coming down the shoreline toward me so that I could wave to my friends, even though I knew that was impossible. But what astounded me at that very moment was a new idea germinating in my brain that now anything was possible. I had somehow put a bookend on the previous chapter in my life and was about to begin a new one. I couldn't stop it from happening, even if I wanted to. I was just along for the ride. I guess what many say is true: It's the journey, not the destination, that is really the best part, so enjoy the ride.

I got back in the minivan and headed southwest along the lakeshore through Algoma, Kewanee, Manitowoc, Sheboygan, and finally home to Port Washington. And you know what? I did enjoy the ride. From that day on I have enjoyed almost every day of my life—rain or shine, hell or high water. Time is a gift. Kids are a treasure, and we are all blessed. The trick is to realize just how lucky you are.

Chapter 40

$$1 + 1 = 3$$
Told by Sebastian

Whitney and I were married in October 2011 in a tiny Norwegian Lutheran church on Washington Island, in Door County, Wisconsin. I was almost forty-one years old, but I felt like I was twenty-five. All of our friends and family were in attendance. I didn't have a best man, because I couldn't bring myself to choose. Whitney didn't have a maid of honor, to keep things even, but she made Elise her attending. The only person besides the two of us and a minister from Port Washington at the front of the church near the altar was Abigail, who served not only as the flower girl, but the ring bearer as well. She was glowing and giddy and so adorable.

I think it was in that very moment that I began to think of her as my own daughter. So when it came time to answer the proverbial big question, I not only looked lovingly at Whitney, but I paused and looked at Abbey as well before I said, "I do." It was the easiest question I have ever had to answer, and neither of them seemed to mind my hesitation.

The following spring, Whitney and I decided to build something a little more appropriate for a family and a lot less "bachelor-like," as she put it. We sold my house immediately to Paul with the understanding he couldn't move in until Peter finished our new home. I owed him, because he had probably saved my life, *and* he was a great craftsman. Paul subsequently hired Peter to make some changes to my old place, and before long, Peter was back in the construction business again.

Our new home wasn't showy or original, but it was comfortable and safe. Abigail loved her new bedroom and picked out every pink thing she could find to decorate it. Whitney and I felt so lucky. The only bad news came when Whitney's grandmother died the following summer. It was difficult, but not unexpected, as she was ninety-seven years old.

"If we can make it that long, then we're not even halfway done yet," I told Whitney.

"Always save the best half for last," she said, smiling back at me.

Heather got remarried to some lawyer and sold the house Peter had built. The kids call him Kyle, but they always call Peter "Dad," which in the end is what really matters. Perry continued sailing *Noemocean*, but his son, Steve, never went out with him again.

Jon started writing while on his layovers abroad. I guess it must get boring going to London or Hong Kong again and again. We should all be so lucky. He says he's working on a book, like it's some kind of big secret, because he won't show it to anyone.

We taught the kids to ski at a little bump hill one weekend nearby the next winter while Elise and Whitney took a quick girls trip to St. Thomas to check out some of Whitney's favorite beaches, drink some Cruzan Rum, and escape winter in Wisconsin. We were all in that window of nirvana Jon had talked about, and it was truly wonderful.

The neatest thing, though, was the following year when I formally adopted Abigail. I loved her so much. My mother flew in once again from Tahiti, and Abbey's grandparents attended when we signed the papers. It was a party, and we were now officially a family.

***

Jon, Peter, and I continue to hang out, though not as

often as we used to. We are all so busy with life. Whitney introduced Peter to a nurse she became friends with at the hospital, and they hit it off. Yeah, everything was as good as it gets until one day . . .

One day, there was a knock at our door . . .

CPSIA information can be obtained at www.ICGtesting.com
Printed in the USA
LVOW131406100613

337765LV00001B/1/P